SOPHIA

broadview editions
series editor: L.W. Conolly

SOPHIA

Charlotte Lennox

edited by Norbert Schürer

broadview editions

Library and Archives Canada Cataloguing in Publication

Lennox, Charlotte, ca. 1729-1804
  Sophia / Charlotte Lennox ; edited by Norbert Schürer.

(Broadview editions)
First published in serial form between Mar. 1760 and Feb. 1761 under title: The history of Harriot and Sophia. Published as a novel in 1762 under title: Sophia.

Includes bibliographical references.
ISBN 978-1-55111-641-9

  I. Schürer, Norbert. II. Title. III. Series.

PR3541.L27S66 2008   823'.6   C2007-905812-4

Broadview Editions

The Broadview Editions series represents the ever-changing canon of literature in English by bringing together texts long regarded as classics with valuable lesser-known works.

Advisory editor for this volume: Jennie Rubio

Broadview Press is an independent, international publishing house, incorporated in 1985. Broadview believes in shared ownership, both with its employees and with the general public; since the year 2000 Broadview shares have traded publicly on the Toronto Venture Exchange under the symbol BDP.

We welcome comments and suggestions regarding any aspect of our publications— please feel free to contact us at the addresses below or at broadview@broadview-press.com.

North America
Post Office Box 1243, Peterborough, Ontario, Canada K9J 7H5
2215 Kenmore Avenue, Buffalo, NY, USA 14207
Tel: (705) 743-8990; Fax: (705) 743-8353;
email: customerservice@broadviewpress.com

UK, Ireland, and continental Europe
NBN International, Estover Road, Plymouth PL6 7PY UK
Tel: 44 (0) 1752 202300 Fax: 44 (0) 1752 202330
email: enquiries@nbninternational.com

Australia and New Zealand
UNIREPS, University of New South Wales
Sydney, NSW, 2052 Australia
Tel: 61 2 9664 0999; Fax: 61 2 9664 5420
email: info.press@unsw.edu.au

www.broadviewpress.com

This book is printed on paper containing 100% post-consumer fibre.

Typesetting and assembly: True to Type Inc., Claremont, Canada.

PRINTED IN CANADA

Contents

Acknowledgements

I first began to enjoy Charlotte Lennox's writing, and to work on *Sophia*, in the course of my dissertation; I would like to thank my advisor, Dr. Jennifer Thorn, for her unflagging support over the past decade. Once this edition began taking shape, I benefited from both the suggestions and advice of the kind folks at Broadview, particularly Julia Gaunce. I could not have completed the textual work on *Sophia* without the assistance of various well-informed and helpful librarians at the British Library and at the Huntington Library. Part of my work was supported at my home institution, California State University, Long Beach, with a grant for release time from the Scholarly and Creative Activities Committee. Most of all, I would like to thank my friend and colleague Dr. Susan Carlile for her constant encouragement and scholarly support during the preparation of this edition..

Introduction

Charlotte Lennox was arguably the most important female writer in Britain around the middle of the eighteenth century. Of her better-known contemporaries, Eliza Haywood (1693–1756) was still writing, but Haywood's most influential books had been written several decades earlier; Sarah Fielding (1710–68) was publishing novels and criticism, but was overshadowed by her brother Henry; and Sarah Scott (1720–95) had not yet composed her more successful novels, which would be published in the 1760s. Lennox stands out from these and other contemporaries in two ways.

First, her work is notable for its portrayal (and at times its critique) of women's lives in eighteenth-century English society. *Sophia*, a novel written within both the moral fiction and the sentimental novel conventions, investigates some of the options available to women through the story of two sisters who are thrown into difficult circumstances and make very different choices in life. At first glance, the authorial voice seems to approve only of the decisions made by Sophia, the more "proper" sister; however, there is a subtext in the novel, indirectly creating space for an understanding of Harriot, the older sister.

As a writer, Lennox also explored the spectrum of professional possibilities for career authors, especially women. She was one of the first women writers to use the literary conventions of moral fiction and the sentimental novel to explore such issues as rank and money and concerns with female literary authority. *Sophia*'s original publication format was also innovative: it was one of the first novels written by a major author in the eighteenth century (of either sex) specifically for publication in a periodical—Lennox's own *The Lady's Museum* (1760–61, here it was titled "The History of Harriot and Sophia"; it was later republished in the form we know it today as *Sophia*). In addition, the novel breaks new ground in its material production with the two illustrations included in its initial release in her journal. By experimenting with these publication formats (and others), Lennox sought a more secure living as a woman writer and proved to be an adept, flexible, and fast-moving author. Given that the literary scene was almost entirely dominated by male writers, however, it was no surprise that Lennox faced many challenges.

The Literary Marketplace in Mid-Eighteenth-Century England

In 1740s and 50s Britain, two writers of prose fiction in England, in particular, towered above all others: Samuel Richardson and Henry Fielding. Richardson (1689–1761), a printer by trade, revolutionized conceptions of literature with his epistolary novel *Pamela* (1740), which spawned countless continuations and refutations, critical commentaries, operas, paintings, even waxworks and hand fans. *Pamela* tells the story of the eponymous virtuous servant, who is pursued by her master, "Mr. B—." Mr. B— initially tries to seduce Pamela by any means possible, including kidnapping and threatened rape, but by the end of the novel he is reformed and the two marry. While some contemporaries admired the novel's psychological insight and social critique, others saw it as a threat to the established order (a maid aspiring to marrying her master) and objected to what they considered prurient scenes (including attempted rapes and cross-dressing). In the preface to *Pamela*, Richardson himself mentions two goals for his novel: he wants "to Divert and Entertain, and at the same time to Instruct, and Improve the Minds of the YOUTH of both Sexes" (3). He later adds that instruction is more important than entertainment, and that "diverting" writing should primarily serve the purpose of moral improvement. His ultimate goal, he claims, is "to inculcate Religion and Morality in so easy and agreeable a manner, as shall render them equally delightful and profitable to the younger Class of Readers" (3).

Henry Fielding (1707–54), who started his career as a successful dramatist and later became a magistrate, responded to *Pamela* first with the spoof *Shamela* and then with his own first novel, *Joseph Andrews* (both 1741). *Shamela* parodies *Pamela* for its perceived naïvete about social interaction, while *Joseph Andrews* offers a "biography" of Pamela's "brother" Joseph, who has a very different idea of virtue than his sister. In the tradition of Don Quixote, the penniless and hapless stable-boy Joseph wanders around the English countryside, surviving a series of adventures that ultimately end with his marriage. In the preface to *Joseph Andrews*, Fielding calls his work a "comic romance" (25): it treats characters from the lower social classes (in contrast to "serious romance") and imitates the "real" world (unlike the burlesque, which made little attempt at realism). The first chapter places the novel in the tradition of biography that "affords [...] excellent use and instruction, finely calculated to sow the seeds of virtue in youth" (39). In his *Covent-Garden Journal* a few years later, Fielding elaborates on the connection between writing and morality: "Diversion is a secondary Consideration, and designed only to make that agreeable, which is at the same Time useful, to such noble Purposes as Health and Wisdom" (74). In other words, like Richardson, he insists that his primary objective for writing is education.

Between them, Fielding and Richardson staked out various important stylistic, generic, and authorial positions in prose fiction of the middle of the eighteenth century: while Richardson wrote epistolary fiction from a first-person point of view and concentrated on the travails of a small number of exemplary characters, Fielding presented frequently comical tales of less-than-perfect individuals from the perspective of an intrusive and sometimes unreliable third-person narrator. These positions were exemplified in these authors' next two works: Richardson's monumental *Clarissa* (1748–49) and Fielding's equally colossal *Tom Jones* (1749). By the end of the decade, however, contemporary literary critics argued that there were as many similarities between these two authors as there were differences, and their combined aesthetics were accepted as the "correct" way to write novels (Michie 37–92). Fielding and Richardson had already negotiated some of their differences in letters and prefaces, and now other writers continued the discussion.[1] The anonymous novel *History of Charlotte Summers* (1750),[2] for instance, not only refers to Fielding and Richardson in the same breath, but even calls them "brothers": "there are two Authors now living in this Metropolis, who have found out the Art, and both brother Biographers, the one of *Tom Jones*, and the other of *Clarissa*" (1:220). This author sees the similarities between the two writers—both tell stories as biographies, and both focus on emotions—and ignores the differences between the refined Clarissa and the rollicking Tom Jones. In this author's argument, the aesthetics of the

---

1 See William Park, "Richardson and Fielding," *PMLA* 81.5 (October 1966): 381–88.

2 About three quarters of novels between 1750 and 1800 were published anonymously (Raven, "Anonymous Novel," 162–63), so the anonymity of this source does not make the sentiments expressed any less reliable or representative. As a matter of fact, *The History of Charlotte Summers* was published in three editions in Britain and twice in French translations in the eighteenth century, attesting to a certain degree of popularity.

two writers converge in a style of writing close to what would later be called the sentimental novel. Similarly, the equally anonymous *Adventures of a Valet* (1752) criticizes novels in general for being products of diseased imaginations, but specifically exempts Fielding and Richardson: "It will not look like Adulation to except the Authors of *Tom Jones* and *Clarissa* from this general Censure" (I.iv). In their discussions of Richardson and Fielding, both of these critics depict the goal of literature as consisting of moral instruction combined with more light-hearted entertainment; and both stress the former, instruction, over the latter. For instance, the author of the *Adventures of a Valet* writes that "[i]f the real History of Life thus mis-spent may be the Means of saving others, [...] he shall [...] think his Pains in writing well paid" (I.viii).

Arguing that the novel's goal was moral instruction rather than entertainment was part of a time-honored tradition of literary criticism. The claim has a long and illustrious history, going back to the injunction of the Roman poet Horace (65–68 BCE) in his *Ars Poetica* (The Art of Poetry) that literature (in two different Latin phrases with similar meanings) should *prodesse et delectare*, "have use and provide enjoyment," and that it should be *dulce et utile*, "sweet and useful." The *Ars Poetica* was first translated into English by Queen Elizabeth I (1533–1603), and subsequently neo-classical English writers like John Dryden (1631–1700) revalued Horace's injunction to stress learning over pleasure. According to these critics, entertainment was clearly subordinated to instruction as the main function of literature, though the former could serve as a useful tool—a spoonful of amusement to sweeten the medicine of instruction.

Both Richardson and Fielding described their writing in these terms, as did another important literary figure of the time, Samuel Johnson (1709–84). He was the author of *The Rambler* (1750–52), a literary periodical, and later the authoritative *Dictionary of the English Language* (1755). In the fourth issue of the *Rambler*, Johnson wrote about the newly popular genre of "the novel," claiming that these books should "serve as lectures to conduct, and introductions into life" (Johnson, *Rambler* I.21): novels "may perhaps be made of greater use than the solemnities of professed moralists, and convey the knowledge of vice and virtue with more efficacy than axioms and definitions" (ibid. I.21n.).[1] For

---

1 For many other similar comments, see the material in the collections of Barnett and Williams.

Johnson, novels were better at teaching morality than books of philosophy.

Of course, to "instruct and please" was at least partly rhetoric; authors still had to negotiate their work within the reality of the literary marketplace (too much overt moral instruction was unlikely to sell as well as a more entertaining story). And there were other issues. For one thing, there was little agreement on what constituted moral teaching—Fielding overtly claimed that his works provided such lessons, but his critics strongly disagreed, calling his novels loose and immoral. There was an ongoing discussion about whether readers would be confused by "mixed" characters, i.e., those who were neither entirely good nor thoroughly evil.[1] There was also little agreement over whether readers could best be taught by appealing to their rational faculties or to their emotions. Another issue was related to the very claim of creating a didactic, improving work: in fact, many (if not most) authors were consciously creating works of art, independent of an improving effect on the reader. Richardson and Fielding, as well as most of their contemporaries, paid close attention to aesthetic composition in their writing; balancing artistic form with didactic function was not always easy. Nevertheless, the concern about the improving potential of fiction by these writers cannot be entirely dismissed.

Another important point is that both Richardson and Fielding were determined to distinguish themselves from the preceding generation of female novelists—Aphra Behn (1640–89), Delariviere Manley (c.1670–1724), and Eliza Haywood. These three writers, known together as the "fair triumvirate of wit," produced prose narratives usually categorized as "amatory fiction" starting in the 1680s; Haywood was still writing by the 1740s and 50s. Many of these commercially successful texts treated the lives and sexual adventures of women in a format not unlike today's romance novel.[2] However, many critics (including Fielding and Richardson) described these narratives as being dangerously immoral. It is not clear if they genuinely saw a significant difference between the earlier amatory fiction and their own supposedly more realistic novels, or if they were simply trying to situate their own writing as something entirely new. As early as the

---

1 This is the main topic of *Rambler* #4.
2 See Toni Bowers, "Sex, Lies, and Invisibility: Amatory Fiction from the Restoration to Mid-Century," *The Columbia History of the Novel*, ed. John Richetti (New York: Columbia UP, 1994), 50–72.

1720s, some male writers' hatred of their predecessors was epitomized in Alexander Pope's caricature of Haywood as the prize in a (literal) pissing contest in his *Dunciad* (Pope 741n., II 157–90). In the following decades she and the other two writers functioned "as negative precedents in the formation of the 'new' domestic novel of sentiment of the mid- to late eighteenth century" (Ballaster 198).

Fielding and Richardson dominated the field of imaginative prose literature around 1750, whether in terms of covering the spectrum of available styles between them or as a double-headed monolith: with a combined eleven editions each of their various novels by 1750,[1] their output far exceeded other novelists of the preceding decade. This dominance lasted well into the 1750s— their final large works of fiction were Fielding's *Amelia* (1751) and Richardson's *Sir Charles Grandison* (1754). Authors aspiring to the literary marketplace in the 1750s needed to situate themselves in relation to Richardson and Fielding. By 1760, the sentimental novel dominated, with Charlotte Lennox as the most important woman writer developing it.

Charlotte Lennox

When Charlotte Lennox (see Figure 1) became a key figure in the literary marketplace in 1752 with her most successful novel, *The Female Quixote*, she was a little over twenty years old. Lennox's early life had been remarkable: with her family she had traveled across continents and then, with a sudden change in fortune, was left to find her own way in London. Lennox was probably born as Charlotte Ramsay in 1729 or 1730 in Gibraltar, the daughter of an officer who traveled throughout the Empire to take up his posts with the British army (Carlile 392). Very little is known about her mother, though one source claims she was connected to Jonathan Swift (1667–1745), the author of *Gulliver's Travels*. According to this memoir of Lennox, printed while she was still alive, her father "commanded a company at the siege of Gibraltar in the year 1731" (see Appendix B1). Following the Gibraltar posting and a brief stint back in Great Britain, the Ramsay family moved to America around 1739, where her father was stationed in New York, Albany, or Schenectady (the military records are unclear). Lennox's last novel, *Euphemia* (1790), is set around this time in the New York colony and probably records experiences she remembered from her time in America.

---

1 Raven, *British Fiction* 15.

Figure 1:   Charlotte Lennox (engraving by Francesco Bartolozzi, 1793, after a now lost portrait by Sir Joshua Reynolds, 1761). First published in *Shakespeare Illustrated* (London: Sylvester and Edward Harding, 1793).

Around 1745, Charlotte's father died, and she was sent back to England to a relative "earnestly requesting to have the care of Miss Charlotte, then about fourteen" (see Appendix B1). Unfortunately, that unidentified relative died before Lennox arrived, so she was thrown onto her own devices—and just as unfortunately, nothing is known about this period in her life. Like the heroine of her first novel, *The Life of Harriot Stuart* (1750), who also travels from America to England, Lennox may already have had literary aspirations. At any rate, she subsequently made two important moves to establish herself as a writer. The first was to obtain the patronage of Lady Cecilia Isabella Finch (First Lady of the Bedchamber to their Royal Highnesses, the Princesses) and of Mary, Countess of Rockingham (Isabella's sister and mother of Charles Watson Wentworth, second Marquess of Rockingham and Prime Minister of England, 1765–66 and 1782). Few eighteenth-century authors made a successful living from writing alone—even Fielding and Richardson had other jobs—and one means of supplementing a writer's income was to find rich patrons for financial support through hand-outs or regularly paid positions. Both Finch and Rockingham had sufficient wealth and connections to help protect Lennox's reputation as a woman and to establish her as a writer. It was likely with their assistance that she published her first literary work, *Poems on Several Occasions* (1747), signed Charlotte Ramsay, and dedicated to Finch.

On 6 October 1747, around the time her first volume was published, Charlotte married Alexander Lennox. While the marriage may have been a love match, there may also have been other motives: as Lennox's only biographer Miriam Rossiter Small remarks, Charlotte's new husband "was an employee of William Strahan, the London printer" (7). Through Alexander, Charlotte was probably introduced to literary figures such as Samuel Johnson, then an up-and-coming author and critic. With this more informal male patronage, Lennox made further inroads as an author, and in November 1750 she published her first novel, *The Life of Harriot Stuart.* According to an anecdote (reported by Johnson's biographer Sir John Hawkins), Johnson, Lennox and her husband, and a group of about twenty friends celebrated the release of *Harriot Stuart* at an all-night party held in Devil Tavern (Hawkins 285n.). With the help of her female patrons and her male literary friends, Lennox had triumphantly entered the literary establishment.

Lennox published her second and most successful novel, *The Female Quixote*, in 1752. In addition to her acquaintance with

Samuel Johnson, she had also become friends with Samuel Richardson. As letters between the three in 1751 and 1752 show, both men assisted Lennox in finishing her novel and providing publishing advice. After working with two different booksellers[1] for her first two books, Lennox moved to Andrew Millar. Millar was one of the most prominent publishers of fiction in the eighteenth century—he had printed Fielding's novels, among others. With the support of Johnson and Richardson, Lennox convinced Millar to move the publication of her novel to a more advantageous time of the literary season. Both authors also seem to have read drafts of *The Female Quixote*. While the theory that Johnson wrote a pivotal chapter in the novel is now mostly discredited (Schürer 195), Lennox still imitated the styles of her mentors and referred to them admiringly in her text. Following its publication, the novel was given positive reviews by Fielding, in his *The Covent Garden Journal*, and by Johnson in the *Gentleman's Magazine*.[2]

At the same time, *The Female Quixote* is usually read by modern critics (at least in part) as an allegory of the limitations that women in general, and authors in particular, faced in eighteenth-century British society. It also raises issues about writing and authorship. At this time, women were considered to be inferior to men in many ways, and their sphere of activity was mostly restricted to the domestic realm.[3] By law, married women could not own property—including the copyright to any written material—which made it difficult to forge a career out of writing. Those women who did write and publish novels, like the "fair triumvirate" of Behn, Manley, and Haywood, risked severe censure. For some critics, female authorship was even akin to prostitution (Gallagher 1–48). Johnson, Fielding, and Richardson supported Lennox, but her publisher Millar and the anonymous readers he used to assess Lennox's manuscript criticized it, especially for a passage depicting a sexually active woman. In other words, these

---

1 "Bookseller" was the eighteenth-century catch-all term for publisher, printer, editor, wholesaler, distributor, and bookstore, sometimes all in one person or shop.

2 See Brian Hanley, "Henry Fielding, Samuel Johnson, Samuel Richardson, and the Reception of Charlotte Lennox's *The Female Quixote* in the Popular Press," *American Notes and Queries* 13.3 (Summer 2000): 27–32.

3 See Vivien Jones, ed., *Women and Literature in Britain 1700–1800* (Cambridge: Cambridge UP, 2000).

men linked her with Behn, Manley, and Haywood (in terms of immorality) rather than with her male supporters. This tension is clear throughout *The Female Quixote*, a picaresque novel in the form of a popular biographical tale of a young woman. Lennox's novel is a rewriting of Cervantes' *Don Quixote* (1605–15) from a female perspective: like the eponymous hero in Cervantes, Arabella in *The Female Quixote* knows the outside world only through books, namely seventeenth-century French romances. Since women have an exalted status in these romances, Arabella believes she should have the same standing. Accordingly, she constantly misreads people and events around her: she thinks her gardener is a disguised prince, she mistakes a "fallen" woman for a lady, and she is disappointed that her fiancé does not die of love before declaring his intentions to her. The book ends with her "reformation" and marriage, so Lennox may have thought she was on safe moral ground rather than continuing the legacy of Behn, Manley, or Haywood. However, before her marriage, Arabella behaves in a scandalous manner—unthinkable for any respectable early-eighteenth-century woman. These aspects of the novel challenged assumptions about "appropriate" female behavior, and no doubt incited the criticism from Millar and his readers.

As *The Female Quixote* questioned accepted gender roles, Lennox's next work, *Shakespear* [sic] *Illustrated* (1753–54)—the first book-length study of that author by a woman—flew in the face of received critical opinion by attacking Shakespeare's plays for their lack of unity and poetic justice. It is hardly surprising that Lennox's work met with immediate disapproval—the actor and dramatist David Garrick, for instance, accused Lennox of being more interested in demolishing than in celebrating Shakespeare, and of writing with insufficient gravity and seriousness (Isles 41). In the following years, Lennox did not have much more success, publishing a pastoral play that was never produced, *Philander* (1757), and a moderately successful novel, *Henrietta* (1758). In the absence of significant commercial success with her literary work, she was forced to earn money from the thankless labor of translating memoirs from French.[1] *The Memoirs of Maximilian de Bethune, Duke of Sully* (1755), *The Memoirs of the Countess of Berci* (1756), *The Memoirs for the History of Madame de Maintenon* (1757), and *The Greek Theatre of Father Brumoy*

---

1 See Susan Staves, *A Literary History of Women's Writing in Britain, 1660-1789* (Cambridge: Cambridge UP, 2006).

(1759)—all translations from French—were well-received, but they did not provide a release for Lennox's considerable imaginative energy. While she had been well-known briefly following the publication of *Harriot Stuart* and *The Female Quixote*, Lennox now found herself out of the limelight; she was in need of a new plan.

For the rest of her lengthy literary career—Lennox died in 1804, probably in her mid-70s, in abject poverty—she incessantly experimented with various ideas and projects to recover her status. In particular, she had her play *The Sister* produced at Covent-Garden Theatre in February 1769 (drama was usually more profitable than novel writing), approached ever more influential patrons (including even the Queen), attempted subscription publication (which at least assured a certain financial reward for each book), tried to compile an edition of her collected works in 1775 (a format that was in its infancy at the time), and appealed to the Royal Literary Fund (a newly founded charity for indigent authors). In this sense, Lennox was a consummate career author who, in Betty Schellenberg's formulation, "displayed a broad and growing range of authorial skills [that were] recognized by her contemporaries as beyond the merely mechanical" (102) and who "practice[d] both by choice and by necessity a more professionalized model of the writer, one that is more prescient of the future of authorship" (97). Her entrepreneurial practices show her to be flexible in her approach, quick to exploit opportunities such as the changes in copyright after 1774,[1] and willing to adapt her writing to ever new literary and material circumstances.

In 1760, after a decade of hectic activity composing novels and compiling translations in the wake of Richardson and Fielding, Lennox undertook the publication of a monthly periodical, *The Lady's Museum*, as another one of her professional projects.[2] In

---

1 See Mark Rose, *Authors and Owners: The Invention of Copyright* (Cambridge, MA: Harvard UP, 1993).

2 Kathryn Shevelow argues that stylistic evidence and programmatic similarities suggest that a letter signed "Mrs. Stanhope" in *The Lady's Magazine* of October 1759 was actually by Lennox and functioned as a kind of advertisement for *The Lady's Museum*. The author advocates female education, but only within the limits of a specific female sphere. (See "'C— L—' to 'Mrs. Stanhope': A Preview of Charlotte Lennox's *The Lady's Museum*," *Tulsa Studies in Women's Literature* 1.1 [Spring 1982]: 83–86.)

the middle of the eighteenth century, periodical publication could be relatively lucrative, at least more so than novel writing. Thomas Keymer writes that such journals, especially when they included fiction, were "a way round the adverse market conditions affecting novels at the time" (*Sterne* 129). The centerpiece of *The Lady's Museum* was a long piece of prose in monthly installments, employing various features of the sentimental novel, titled "The History of Harriot and Sophia" (Lennox later republished this as the separate novel *Sophia*, and this is how we know it today).[1] As well as being the centerpiece of Lennox's entrepreneurial periodical *The Lady's Museum*, *Sophia* was positioned as a sentimental novel, with didactic overtones, to a new market—distinguishing it from the earlier amatory fiction of Haywood and Behn, and even to an extent from her own *Female Quixote*.

Sophia as a Sentimental Novel

Novels claiming the goal of moral improvement for their readers dominated the British literary marketplace in the 1740s and 50s. This moral education often took the generic form of the *bildungsroman*, a novel in which the protagonist goes through a moral, spiritual, or practical education and develops into a different person during the course of the novel. Novels as diverse as Richardson's *Pamela*, Lennox's own *Female Quixote*, and Frances Burney's *Evelina* (1778) have been categorized as part of this sub-genre.[2] But the 1750s and 60s also saw the evolution of a different sub-genre, the sentimental novel, which reached its apex in the late 1760s. Key novels include Sarah Fielding's *David Simple* (1744–53), Frances Sheridan's *Memoirs of Miss Sidney Bidulph* (1761), Laurence Sterne's *A Sentimental Journey* (1768), and Henry Mackenzie's *The Man of Feeling* (1771). Lennox's *Sophia* is poised between these two conventions and reflects the tension between the two.

As the name implies, the sentimental novel is fundamentally concerned with human emotions and was partially a reaction to the philosophy of the so-called "age of reason." Philosophers

---

1 I refer to the serial publication as "The History of Harriot and Sophia" and to the book simply as *Sophia*.

2 On the *bildungsroman*, see Richard Barney, *Plots of Enlightenment: Education and the Novel in Eighteenth-Century England* (Stanford: Stanford UP, 1999) and Lorna Ellis, *Appearing to Diminish: Female Development and the British Bildungsroman, 1750–1850* (Lewisburg: Bucknell UP, 1999).

including the Earl of Shaftesbury, David Hume, and Adam Smith (see Appendix E) explored the idea that humans have an innate sense of sympathy for one another, known as "sensibility." In most cases, sensibility was not described as a quality that could be acquired or developed, but was rather depicted as unteachable and unlearnable; some individuals possessed sensibility, and others did not. At the same time, there were contradictions: on the one hand, philosophers and novelists appealed to an exclusive community of readers who already "possessed" sensibility; on the other, they promised (or at least suggested) that other readers might be able to join that community. By portraying this sensibility in fictional characters, novelists hoped to evoke in their readers—at least those with the "right" innate capabilities—feelings of sympathy. As Patricia Meyer Spacks writes about *David Simple*, "'[g]ood' characters within sentimental fiction feel a great deal; good readers will enjoy [...] comparable feelings" (134).[1]

The characters in sentimental novels are controlled primarily by their emotions, with little recourse to their rational faculties. The protagonist of *The Sentimental Journey*, for instance, is a parson who meets with many men and women in his travels through France and Italy. Each encounter is narrated not as an intellectual exchange, but in terms of sympathetic recognition. In Sterne's novel, as in those of Sarah Fielding and Frances Sheridan, humans can communicate better through nonverbal (and therefore unteachable) means than through language. In touches, glances, sighs, and tears (tactile, visual, audible, and somatic cues), typical sentimental characters come closer together than in conversation (Mullan 238–42).

Another important feature of the sentimental novel is (usually undeserved) suffering—experienced by the characters, witnessed sympathetically by the readers, and indicating virtue in both. The suffering is frequently inflicted by the villain and endured by the hero. In *Memoirs of Miss Sidney Bidulph* (1761), for instance, the

---

1 · Some critics argue that Richardson's *Pamela* is already a sentimental novel and that the novels of the 1760s and 70s were already almost parodies of the genre. In fact, instead of describing sentimentalism as a particular sub-genre of the novel, some critics speak of a "continuous repertoire in emotional representation" (Manning 82). Richardson was certainly interested in emotions, but his depiction of sentiment was different: he considered it "a statement of opinion or truth, which, though colored at times by feeling, stems primarily from reason or faith" (Keymer 583).

heroine's chosen suitor apparently turns out to be a seducer, so she marries a man who actually carries on an affair and banishes her; after Sidney and her true lover finally marry, he almost immediately dies. But the suffering can also simply be the result of the protagonist's highly developed sensibility in a world full of misery and pain. The protagonist's pain in *The Man of Feeling* (1771) is a case in point: he is so delicate that he is unable to reveal his affection for the heroine and ultimately dies of an excess of emotion. And here lies an important difference between the sentimental novel and the *bildungsroman*: the sentimental hero is "[a]ffected yet not changed [by his experiences], he may become sadder, but he cannot grow" (Starr 190). In the words of another critic, "[o]ne way of seeing 'the man of feeling' is as the Novel's alternative [...] to the picaresque transgressor of Fielding and Smollett" (Mullan 243). The protagonist of *The Man of Feeling* occasionally attempts to translate his sympathy into social action, but ultimately there seems to be little room for political change. Keymer argues that sentimental novels are driven by "a fundamental social conservatism" ("Sentimental Fiction," 591). Various philanthropic social reform movements—trying to change the treatment of "fallen" women, prisoners, and orphans, as well as addressing the horrors of the slave trade—were inspired by sentimentalism, but they all tended "to leave the existing social hierarchy intact or stronger than ever" (Starr 193). The suggestion of a common emotional network among social classes posed a potential challenge to eighteenth-century British society; however, ultimately sentimentalism functioned "as a kind of social cement that holds individuals together in a moralized and emotionalized public sphere" (Manning 83). The impossibility of a life of sensibility in the real world was expressed figuratively in the death of many sentimental heroes.[1]

In *Sophia* Lennox uses the same conventions of moral fiction as Fielding and Richardson, and she employs characteristics

---

1   For the twenty-first-century reader, sentimental novels often approach absurdity—the delicate feelings and emotional responses of the characters are simply unbelievable and easily ridiculed. Indeed, many of today's critics argue that Sterne already anticipated such reactions (Keymer 597, Mullan 239), and certainly later in the eighteenth century some writers—even Mackenzie himself—criticized or parodied sentimentalism (see Appendix E) as the genre fell into disrepute. Nevertheless, given that this kind of sensibility was seen as a human reality, most comedy in the genre was probably unintentional.

typical for sentimental fiction. At the same time, she pushes against the boundaries of both sets of conventions. On one level, Lennox situates her novel in the tradition of (Henry) Fielding and Richardson by presenting a morally pure and virtuous heroine who can serve as a model for teaching her readers correct behavior. But Sophia can also be read as a typically sentimental heroine, such as those created by (Sarah) Fielding and Frances Sheridan: she does not learn any lessons or change during the course of the novel, but possesses "correct" morality from the start. At the same time, however, Lennox's novel is not fully didactic in its acknowledgement of the more promiscuous sister as enjoying a greater range of freedom and of pleasure. Lennox employs the conservative moral and sentimental discourse of these two dominant literary genres, but she also plays them against each other, considering—however briefly—an alternative to the limited options faced by women who have to support themselves.

For one thing, *Sophia* differs from (Sarah) Fielding's and Sheridan's novels in its presentation of a female heroine rather than a man of feeling. Thus, Lennox's novel falls into what Janet Todd (analyzing the entire history of the sentimental novel from about 1760 to 1800) sees as the sub-genre of sentimental novels about (and by) the "woman of feeling" (110–28) such as Sheridan's protagonist in *Sidney Bidulph* or Frances Brooke's heroine in *The History of Lady Julia Mandeville* (1763). The presence of a female protagonist implies that men and women can both be sentimental heroes, equally able to possess sensibility and sympathy (by contrast, the majority of later protagonists in sentimental novels are male, and women are relegated to supporting roles).[1] Still, the novel about "women of feeling" in general and *Sophia* in particular are fundamentally conservative: no woman is envisioned permanently outside of marriage (even Harriot is married off to a wig-maker turned officer). According to Eve Tavor Bannet, *Sophia* is a conservative "Matriarchal novel" (83), where the heroine "teaches and governs others; they rarely teach or govern her. [She] mentors, reforms, and corrects those whom age, rank, care, or circumstance have placed *in loco parentis*" (83). Bannet points out that the management of the Darnley household is given over to Sophia at the very beginning of the novel, and

---

1 Here, it is important to remember that Lennox was writing ten years *before* Sterne and Mackenzie; so rather than responding to a set of conventions she was participating in their creation.

"[w]hile her mother's folly is exposed, Sophia's judgment and conduct are repeatedly marked as 'right' [...] by the outcome of events" (85). This puts the novel and its heroine in a curious historical position: the text is didactic (at least in terms of most of the minor characters), but not a *bildungsroman* (since Sophia does not appreciably change). At the same time, Bannet's claim that Sophia "mentors, reforms, and corrects" those around her is true only to the extent that their situations improve—there is no sign of real reform in Mrs. Darnley or Harriot.

Indeed, various critics have acknowledged an ideological problem in the sentimental novel with regard to gender (Starr 194–97, Todd 110–11). On the one hand, men of feeling—who take on what would have been considered female traits at the time, such as showing emotion or feeling sympathy—are constructed in opposition to dominant society. Women of feeling, like Sophia, merely embrace those qualities they are already supposed to have, thereby reinforcing the social order. In this sense, *Sophia* is definitely a conservative novel—its heroine embodies the role society prescribes to her, and her actions and beliefs are in many ways endorsed. This conservative message is undermined, however, by subtle negotiations: the doubling of the sentimental heroine; the novel's portrayal of the dangers of the "economics of status" in its depiction of rank, class, and money; and the concern with reading and authorship. While contentious ideas are ultimately contained within the didactic formulation of the sentimental novel, Lennox still raises some unexpected alternative possibilities.

Like many eighteenth-century novels, *Sophia* opens with a brief history introducing the main characters, providing their biographical background, and bringing the reader to the point where the story starts. Harriot and Sophia are two sisters, daughters of incompetent parents: their father is unable to manage his money, and their beautiful mother pursues a life of luxury. Like her mother, Harriot is beautiful, while Sophia is less overtly attractive but more intelligent and traditionally respectable. In Harriot and Sophia, Lennox contrasts typical qualities of "bad" and "good" children. Also, the family constellation emphasizes the nexus of rank, money, and beauty. The girls' mother is criticized, not for seeking a life of leisure, but for the discrepancy between her desires and her income: she has "a taste for luxury and expence, without the means of gratifying it" (53). She wants to live like an aristocrat, but that station is inappropriate. Harriot sees a slightly different connection between beauty and status:

A. Walker del. et sculp.

Figure 2: "Saying this, she flung out of the room, leaving her mother divided between grief and anger, and Mr. Herbert motionless with astonishment" (74). © British Library Board. All Rights Reserved (C.175.n.15).

she "was taught to consider herself as a fine lady, whose beauty could not fail to make her fortune" (55). While it remains unclear if Harriot is already profligate, it is evident that she wants to be rich and believes she will easily find a fortune through a husband, given her beauty.

Sophia is scorned by her mother: "Sophia she [the mother] affected to despise, because she [Sophia] wanted [...] those personal attractions, which in her [the mother's] opinion constituted the whole of female perfection" (53—"wanted" here means "lacked"). Mrs Darnley's judgement lacks wisdom and insight: "Mere common judges, however, allowed her person to be agreeable; people of discernment and taste pronounced her something more" (53). "Common judges" can only see a person's outward appearance; "people of discernment and taste" possess a moral sensibility that cannot be learned, but is innate.

There is a clear opposition between the two main female characters delineated in the opening of the book. This doubling distinguishes the novel both from Richardsonian moral literature and from sentimental fiction. Certainly, Sophia is a moral paradigm, but not because she learns morality—she embodies it from the start. She has the innate sensibility of a sentimental heroine, but eventually parlays this ability into an emotionally satisfying (and financially advantageous) marriage. Furthermore, in contrast to most contemporaneous fiction that only names the virtuous heroine in the title, Lennox names both sisters in the title of the periodical publication, leaving the reader guessing—at least for a moment—who the moral paradigm is supposed to be.

Much fiction of the 1740s and 50s, including *Pamela* and *Clarissa*, was concerned with a male villain and a female victim/heroine. But there is no clear villain in *Sophia*; rather, there is a reformable male[1] and two sisters. Michael Cohen dismisses the

---

1 For Mary Anne Schofield, Charles is actually the most interesting character in the novel: she argues that the plot "revolves around Sir Charles's romantic disguises" (141). In this interpretation, the novel "presents a black-and-white picture of the eighteenth-century world and its inhabitants: those who masquerade and those who do not" (142), and Charles is the only character who manages to move from one camp to the other. In addition, Schofield sees him as an early "man of feeling" and the novel as "another *Pamela*: reformed rake and innocent, impoverished heroine" (141). Schofield's analysis draws attention to another tension in the novel: Charles is a character who would be more at home in the didactic fiction of Fielding and Richardson (he reforms, like Mr. B— in *Pamela*, so he is not really a man of feeling); the women at the novel's

sisters: "Lennox's sisters have only limited interest for readers because they do not have any dimension beyond their antithesis, and they are incapable of affecting each other" (99). For Bannet, however, the moral evaluation of the two sisters remains important: "In *Sophia* the [...] triumph of the lady of superior sense and virtue over the coquette is played out by juxtaposing the fate of two sisters" (91). The two sisters make very different choices in parallel situations, demonstrating the superiority of Sophia's behavior and her assessment of the sister's position and opportunities in the world of eighteenth-century England. However, the novel may not be so black and white. Patricia Meyer Spacks argues that "the plot allows [Harriot] much greater freedom than her virtuous sister enjoys" (141). Harriot acts impulsively (one such action is visualized in the first illustration; see Figure 2), receives sexual and material attention, and thus "finds much more opportunity for action and expression than does her virtuous sister" (142). Within the limits of eighteenth-century moral fiction, Harriot is openly condemned; but by stepping beyond that limited framework, she can realize herself more than Sophia. While we cannot safely speculate too much about Lennox's motives, it does seem that the path of respectability followed by Sophia greatly limits her personal freedom as compared to Harriot. Lennox may have been trying to background Harriot's subversive role when she changed the title from "The History of Harriot and Sophia" to *Sophia*.

As the figure of the sentimental heroine is complicated in *Sophia* through her doubling, the conservative status of the sentimental novel is challenged through an explicit concern with rank, class, and money. Traditionally, the genre does not advocate social change, but affirms the social and economic order, promoting "an untroubled acceptance of things as they are" (Richetti 261). However, *Sophia* includes an analysis of the effects of poverty that goes beyond what is depicted in most sentimental novels. At the very beginning, the Darnley family finds itself in grave circumstances as a result of Mr. Darnley's inability to manage money:

> The death of Mr. Darnley threw this little family into a
> deplorable state of indigence, which was felt the more

---

center, on the other hand, belong to the sentimental novel genre where their moral value is established from the start. The world of "The History of Harriot and Sophia" may seem black and white, but the presence of Charles actually introduces some grey.

severely, as they had hitherto lived in an affluence of all things, and the debts which an expence so ill proportioned to their income had obliged Mr. Darnley to contract, left the unhappy widow and her children without any resource. The plate, furniture, and every thing valuable were seized by the creditors. Mrs. Darnley and her daughters retired to a private lodging, where the first days were passed in a weak despondence on the part of the mother, in passionate repinings on that of the eldest daughter, and by Sophia in decent sorrow and pious resignation. (56)

In contrast to many eighteenth-century writers, Lennox here lays bare the workings of the economy of status. Mr. Darnley wanted to project an image of affluence, but in order to do so he had to borrow extensively—which he was able to do because of his status as a member of the upper middle class. Following his death, his creditors (who in most novels of the period do not appear in person) deprive the remaining family of their material possessions. While many eighteenth-century novels have little to say about finances, the text here specifies what items are "seized by the creditors": with plate and furniture gone, the family has nothing (and no collateral for new loans). The Darnleys now must rent their accommodation, a notable decline in status. The blame for the family's situation is on Mr. Darnley; the three women are largely innocent victims of the economy of status. Furthermore, the problem here is the discrepancy between money and class: the Darnleys behave like members of the gentry, but they can only afford to live like members of the lower middle class. While that situation did occur in other sentimental novels and didactic fiction, it was rarely discussed in as much explicit detail. For instance, Fielding's Joseph Andrews is poor, but that does not seem to have a major effect on how he lives his life; similarly, Smollett's Peregrine Pickle in the 1751 novel of the same title spends time in a debtor's prison, but that place is "bursting with rowdy incidents and crowded with irrepressible organic life" (Richetti 169) rather than a scene of suffering or sorrow.

In the rest of *Sophia*, there is ongoing conflict between the mother's and Harriot's desire for social status and the financial reality of the Darnley family. Sophia looks for a workable solution—an eminently middle-class and common-sense response, rather than a sentimental submission to suffering. For an unmarried woman in eighteenth-century England, there were few options; but one respectable choice that Sophia is willing to try is to become an aristocrat's companion. However, Mrs. Darnley is opposed, for this would outwardly demonstrate the family's decline in social importance. While Mrs. Darnley simply closes her eyes to her financial straits, Harriot looks for a husband as a solution (the solution offered in many novels of the 1740s and 1750s) and ultimately resorts to a less reputable way of securing income: becoming the kept mistress of a gentleman. Even towards the end of the novel, Mrs. Darnley has difficulty deciding between accepting a more opulent lifestyle with Harriot, supported immorally (in eighteenth-century terms), and Sophia, in financially more restricted but morally irreproachable circumstances. Once again, the novel's sympathies seem to lie with Sophia, so the novel appears to promote a "realistic" view of the middle class and caution its readers to stay within their financial means. At the same time, however, the novel criticizes the "reality" that women cannot make a living on their own. The novel's section on the hypocritical "benefactress" Mrs. Howard exposes the dependence of aristocrats' companions, the one position Sophia is able to find. The novel overtly exhorts the middle class to live within their economic means (in the convention of didactic fiction) and stick to their social rank (in the convention of the sentimental novel). But there are also hints that a system providing so few choices for women to support themselves is fundamentally flawed.

A similar critique is implied in the presentation of reading and authorship throughout *Sophia*. Particularly in the first volume, books play a key role. Like the authorial persona of *The Lady's Museum*, "The Trifler," Sophia receives no formal education (see below, "A Note on Female Property and Education," 46), but Mr. Herbert, the old gentleman, indirectly educates her "by constantly supplying her with such books as were best calculated to improve her morals and understanding" (55). He later suggests a retreat to the country, telling Sophia that in the clergyman's house, "you will find books enough [...] to employ those hours which you devote to reading" (90). Here we see the rhetoric of the "right" kind of reading (didactic fiction) potentially improving the morality of its reader. Within this same rhetoric, *Sophia* also distinguishes this improving reading from other, more dangerous kinds. For example, Charles gives Sophia very different sorts of books as part of his seduction: "he brought her all the new books and pamphlets that were published which were worth her reading" (66). This reading material is "new" rather than classical, and it is contrasted to the morally uplifting books provided by Mr. Herbert. There is a rather sinister feel to Charles' "artful management" (66), but Sophia wisely refuses to read his novels. Reading can be corrupting or improving, depending both on the material and the guidance with which it is given. Harriot only refers to books when she misquotes a contemporary French philosopher to accuse her sister of pride—when the quote in fact confirms Sophia's virtue (see 96). Once again, reading is not just a transparent agent of moral improvement, but rather holds the possibility of misinterpretation and misappropriation. This recalls the depiction of reading and writing in Richardson's *Pamela*; in *Sophia*, however, the female protagonist is not in the physical power of the male, and also the correspondence takes the form of letters rather than a journal.

The second volume changes its focus from reading as consumption to writing as production, from reading books to writing letters. At the very end of the novel, Sophia's new status as Sir Charles' wife is confirmed by "writings" (197), namely the signed marriage contract. Many novels, like Richardson's *Pamela* and *Clarissa*, were epistolary fiction (i.e., claiming to be collections of letters), so in the many references to writing letters Lennox was following in a particular recognizable tradition, specifically that of Richardson.[1] As Pamela and Clarissa in the eponymous novels gain authority through their authorship, Sophia transforms her seducer/suitor Charles through her writing: "Several compositions of her own now fell into his hands: he read them with eagerness, and, charmed with this discovery of those treasures of wit, which she with modest diffidence so carefully concealed, he felt his admiration and tenderness for her encrease every moment" (151). Yet while *Pamela* and *Clarissa* were fictions composed by a male author with a secure career as a printer, *Sophia* was announced from the beginning as the production of a woman, giving the main character a different resonance. At least on one level—and readers would have been aware of this—Pamela was the female fantasy of a male author, while Sophia was the invention of an actual woman and thus written from a significantly more authentic subject position. Writing for a living must have

---

1   On epistolary fiction, see Joe Bray, *The Epistolary Novel: Representations of Consciousness* (London and New York: Routledge, 2003), Elizabeth Cook, *Epistolary Bodies: Gender and Genre in the Eighteenth-Century Republic of Letters* (Stanford: Stanford UP, 1996), and Robert Day, *Told in Letters: Epistolary Fiction Before Richardson* (Ann Arbor: U of Michigan P, 1966).

been an important issue for Lennox as she was composing "The History of Harriot and Sophia" (later republishing it as *Sophia*) for *The Lady's Museum*—and trying to make a career of her own authorship. As readers knew from the title page, this novel was not an instance of "narrative transvestism,"[1] but the genuine production of a female author in the same limited position as her heroine. As Sophia succeeds in the marriage market because of the transformation her writing brings about, Lennox was trying to make a career in the literary market by publishing a periodical. For that reason, it is imperative finally to look at the material context of the publication of "The History of Harriot and Sophia" in *The Lady's Museum*. As Jennie Batchelor writes, "we should read the narrative in its original context to unlock its full range of meaning" (93).

The Lady's Museum

The weekly (or monthly) periodical was a new form that evolved toward the end of the seventeenth century. In 1690, John Dunton started *The Athenian Mercury*,[2] a weekly page or "half sheet" that "dealt with philosophical, ethical, metaphysical, and scientific ideas" (Adburgham 26). The form immediately became a commercial success, and Dunton was widely imitated. From the very beginning, these journals included prose literature and poetry, and they also frequently featured correspondence columns. Periodicals specifically for women originated almost simultaneously: Dunton himself dedicated regular issues of *The Athenian Mercury* to questions from women, and in 1693 he founded *The Ladies' Mercury* as a journal of its own. According to Dunton's memoirs, women contributed to both of his publications (Adburgham 27), but it was not long before women started writing their own periodicals. For instance, Richard Steele's famous *Tatler* had barely begun publication—the first issue came out on 12 April 1709—when it was answered by *The Female Tatler* on 8 July. This journal was written by Delariviere Manley, the famous author of *The New Atalantis* (1709) and member of the "fair triumvirate of wit." Similarly, Steele and Joseph Addison's *The Spectator* (1711–12) was still popular enough three decades later to find a response in

---

1 See Madeleine Kahn, *Narrative Transvestism: Rhetoric and Gender in the Eighteenth-Century English Novel* (Ithaca: Cornell UP, 1991).
2 The first issue was actually titled *The Athenian Gazette, or Casuistical Mercury.*

Eliza Haywood's *The Female Spectator* (1744–46). Earlier, Haywood had written extensively for and edited the journals *The Tea Table* (1726) and *The Parrot* (1728). The content of women's periodicals resembled that of journals aimed at men, except that there was a stronger emphasis on topics like education (Italia 178) and more literary material.

With its interest in education and the inclusion of prose fiction and poetry, Lennox's *The Lady's Museum* is fairly typical. The first issue was released on 1 March 1760 from the booksellers John Newbery and John Coote (Newbery had already published various other journals). Like most periodicals, *The Lady's Museum* came out in individual but consecutively paginated issues that owners could later bind into volumes. *The Lady's Museum* was sold in eleven monthly issues, with the last appearing (because of an interruption in December) on 1 February 1761 (Isles 327). These were bound into two volumes with consecutive page numbers, with six issues in the first and five in the second. For the bound version, Newbery and Coote provided two title pages, a frontispiece, and a table of contents that functioned as an index. Like all eleven issues, the first one was 80 pages long and contained a variety of articles. The four largest items in the first issue of *The Lady's Museum*—which also included a brief introduction, a song, and some anonymous poetry—are the beginning of "The History of the Duchess of Beaufort" (32 pages) by the Duke of Sully, the first installment of "The History of Harriot and Sophia" (28 pages), Pierre Joseph Boudier de Villemert's "Of the Studies Proper for Women" (nine pages), and Lennox's own "The Trifler" (seven pages).

"The History of Harriot and Sophia" was clearly the centerpiece of *The Lady's Museum.* Though in individual issues (such as this first one) other articles occasionally took up more pages, generally the novel predominated. Furthermore, the periodical opened with the first installment and folded when "The History of Harriot and Sophia" finished, suggesting that Lennox (or her publishers) believed that readers would no longer purchase the periodical after the end of the novel, or that *The Lady's Museum* had run its course for other reasons. Publishing an entire novel by a reasonably well-established author written specifically for periodical publication was a new phenomenon. Tobias Smollett's *The Adventures of Sir Launcelot Greaves* is generally considered to be the first "long piece of original fiction written expressly for publication in a British magazine" (Mayo 277). However, since *Greaves* began publication only two months before "The History of Harriot and Sophia" and ended almost a year later (January 1760–December 1761), it is likely that Lennox came up with the idea of a serial novel independently. Therefore, *Greaves* and "The History of Harriot and Sophia" can both be described as the first novel written for publication in a journal by a major author—a significant milestone in the history of the novel genre and an important step towards professionalizing authorship for men or women.

Another significant innovation in *The Lady's Museum* was the inclusion of illustrations for the text. Illustrations in books or journals were still a relatively new phenomenon in Britain: the first illustrated editions of *The Pilgrim's Progress* and *Paradise Lost* had only appeared in 1680 and 1688, respectively (Hodnett 45), and the first novel edition with a series of illustrations was Richardson's *Pamela*, with engravings by Hubert Gravelot and Francis Hayman, in 1742 (ibid. 75n.).[1] For a journal, illustrations were expensive, but they were an important draw for potential buyers. In periodicals for women these illustrations were usually limited to frontispieces: Manley's *Female Tatler* had no images except for a vignette of the authorial persona Mrs. Crackenthorpe (see below, 39), and Haywood's *Female Spectator* was limited to different frontispieces for each of the four volumes. Beyond frontispieces, only one other text had been illustrated before (or at about the same time): the images for Smollett's *Sir Launcelot Greaves*—by the same Anthony Walker who contributed an engraving to *Sophia*—made it "the first serially published novel ever to be illustrated" (Smollett xvii). But as the production value of periodicals had increased over the last twenty years since *The Female Spectator* and *The Rambler*, so had the expectations of readers.

In keeping with the market's demand for visual images, the first issue of *The Lady's Museum* contained three engravings: a frontispiece, a portrait of the Duchess of Beaufort, and the first illustration for "The History of Harriot and Sophia," all by Anthony Walker.[2] A superscription refers to the passage from the

---

1 There had been editions of earlier texts like *Robinson Crusoe* and *Gulliver's Travels* with illustrations (1719 and 1726, respectively), but these were mostly restricted to frontispieces or portraits of the "authors" Gulliver and Crusoe.

2 While the frontispiece was probably added only when the journal was bound, the other illustrations were possibly included in the original monthly installments of *The Lady's Museum*.

novel being illustrated (see Figure 2): "Saying this, [Harriot] flung out of the room, leaving her mother divided between grief and anger, and Mr. Herbert motionless with astonishment" (74). Anthony Walker (1726–65), the designer and engraver of this illustration, was at the height of his career when Lennox first published "The History of Harriot and Sophia" in *The Lady's Museum*, so his contribution would have given Lennox's periodical some reputation with readers who were aware of the latest fashion in engravings. The second illustration specifically for "The History of Harriot and Sophia," which appeared in the fourth issue of *The Lady's Museum*, was by the younger Alexander Bannerman (see Figure 3). A superscription again directs the reader to a specific page, but this time there is also a caption, "Dolly relating her Story to Sophia." The page reference is specific—"'Come, my dear,' said Sophia, leading her to the root of a large tree, 'let us sit down here, we shall not be called to supper yet, you have time enough to give me some account of this young man'" (104)—but the caption more generally describes the scene for all of what was to become chapters twelve and thirteen, in which Dolly tells Sophia the story of her friendship with William. While Walker's image focuses on a moment of action, Bannerman's presents an emotional tableau.

Three other items appeared in the first issue of *The Lady's Museum*. Since the contributions to the periodical were probably written or selected by Lennox,[1] and since they were no doubt designed to provide reading context for the novel, a brief consideration of these items is worthwhile. Two of them depict the goal of reading as being primarily to teach morality, while the third suggests alternatives to this model. The first two are translations from other authors, while the third was written by Lennox herself.

---

1 There have been suggestions that other writers contributed to *The Lady's Museum*. Alison Adburgham, for instance, writes that the journal "was not all [Lennox's] own work, for at some point she acquired a young collaborator, Hugh Kelly" (118). An early biography of Kelly, published in 1793 when Lennox was still alive, makes a similar claim: "The Booksellers [...] offered him engagements in the *Lady's Museum*, and *Court Magazine*, which he accepted" (Cooke 339). However, Kelly's most recent biographer, Robert Bataille, concludes that "it is doubtful that Kelly did much more than follow Lennox's directions" (5). Kelly's contribution "most probably did not include much writing of the actual material that formed the contents of the magazine" (5). In other words, his input was probably quite limited.

A. Bannerman delin & sculp.

Figure 3: "'Come, my dear,' said Sophia, leading her to the root of
a large tree, 'let us sit down here, we shall not be called to supper yet,
you have time enough to give me some account of this young man'"
(104). © British Library Board. All Rights Reserved (C.175.n.15).

The first two issues of *The Lady's Museum* included an excerpt and abridgement from Lennox's translation of *Sully* published five years before.[1] This was an account of the story of the duchess of Beaufort, Gabrielle d'Estrées (1573–99), the acknowledged mistress of King Henry IV of France (1553–1610). The voice of the translator points to the morality in her otherwise salacious tale at the beginning: "Here [my fair readers] will see grandeur purchased by crimes, and possessed with anxiety; schemes of ambition carried far into futurity, suddenly defeated by an immature and horrible death; and hence they may learn to rejoice in that innocence which is at once their merit and their reward" (Lennox 49n.). D'Estrées became Henry's mistress around 1591 and stayed with him until her premature death in 1599. She had two sons and a daughter with Henry, all of whom were legitimized and given titles.[2] Even though Henry was officially married to Margaret de Valois (1553–1615) and d'Estrées to Nicolas d'Amerval, she considered herself to be, and acted like, Henry's wife and Queen of France.[3] Lennox keeps pointing to the morality of the biography, reminding the reader that "She was interested, vain, and ambitious" (Lennox 51). D'Estrées is punished for her misguided pursuits with a gruesome death that takes place on Good Friday—with no subsequent resurrection. Lennox also insists that evil people such as d'Estrées suffer even in this world, always wrestling with a guilty conscience: "In the midst of all this splendor madame de Beaufort was completely wretched" (Lennox 85). In contrast, the equally adulterous Henry—who is nevertheless besotted with his mistress—comes off fairly well and even manages to formulate a list of positive wifely characteristics: "it is necessary that in her I marry, I should find these seven things, beauty, prudence, softness, wit, fruitfulness, riches, and a royal birth" (Lennox 72). Of course, in the context of the moral/sentimental development of *The Lady's*

---

1 Maximilien de Béthune, duc de Sully, *The Memoirs of Maximilian de Bethune, Duke of Sully, Prime Minister to Henry the Great*, tr. Charlotte Lennox (London: Millar, 1755). In her typical entrepreneurial fashion, Lennox was reusing material she had produced earlier in a new context, namely her periodical.

2 The daughter is not included in Lennox's version, perhaps to avoid the complication of another female character.

3 According to Lennox's narrative, Henry even sought an annulment for his marriage and debated marrying d'Estrées, but this plan never came to fruition.

Museum's readers, these are qualities that eighteenth-century British women readers were being overtly counseled to cultivate for their own successful marriage. There is a quiet relationship with "The History of Harriot and Sophia," where avoiding the temptation of immorality in the search for an appropriate partner is just as much at issue. D'Estrées in some respects is a more extreme version of Harriot, embodying characteristics of vanity and ambition, whereas the suitable wifely qualities Henry lists sound like Sophia's traits. On the one hand, then, this salacious and titillating story is subsumed under the explicit morality Lennox articulates in her translation. At the same time, unlike Charles, Henry does not opt for the Sophia-like character, but for the woman who is more similar to Harriot, so there is the contrary subtext as well.[1]

Another article published in the first issue of *The Lady's Museum* was Lennox's translation of "Of the Studies Proper for Women," by Pierre Joseph Boudier de Villemert (born 1718, death unknown).[2] In Lennox's selection, Villemert discusses female education, concluding that women should be given more education so that relationships between men and women can be more fulfilling for both. Specifically, Villemert recommends that women learn the arts, history, and natural philosophy (what would today be called science) and that this education take place in "mixed-sex social gatherings, in which scholarly subjects are discussed in a relaxed domestic setting" (Italia 201). Such a setting is provided in Lennox's periodical (Batchelor 92). At the same time, Villemert cautions women against too much learning, mocking those who venture into philosophy and religion. Villemert's ambivalent stance towards female education shows admi-

---

1 In "Reading Women Reading History: The Philosophy of Periodical Form in Charlotte Lennox's *The Lady's Museum*," *Historical Reflections/Réflexions Historiques* 18.3 (Fall 1992): 7–27, Judith Dorn argues that "Beaufort" allows Lennox to display criticism of historical sources and to point to the instability of what counts as history—and who decides what counts as history. "Beaufort," Dorn claims, turns a footnote in male history into a main subject and functions as proof that women's actions do have historical and political consequences.

2 This treatise was the second chapter of Villemert's *L'ami des femmes*, which had been published in France in 1758 and was translated in its entirety into English in 1766 as *The Ladies Friend* (London, Nicoll). Villemert's text remained popular, particularly in the new United States, for the rest of the eighteenth century.

ration for some female learning but disgust with too much. The task of a character like Sophia, then, is to situate herself between these two extremes. Villemert's description of women without learning sounds like Harriot:

> But what preservative is there against weariness and disgust in the society of women of weak and unimproved understanding? In vain do they endeavour to fill the void of their conversation with insipid gaiety: they soon exhaust the barren funds of fashionable trifles, the news of the day, and hackneyed compliments; they are at length obliged to have recourse to scandal, and it is well if they stop there: a commerce in which there is nothing solid must be either mean or criminal. (231).

Given that ignorant women have few topics for conversation, they first engage in small talk, which soon devolves into gossip. From there, they either have to turn vicious or engage in "crime" themselves, i.e., immoral activities. Sophia's sister Harriot is exactly this kind of woman—she ridicules her sister for reading; alienates the man who is interested in her; attends parties in order to find a husband; and finally becomes an aristocrat's mistress. Villemert even excuses male behavior in the presence of such women:

> When the woman whose person we admire is incapable of pleasing us by her conversation, languor and satiety, soon triumph over the taste we had for her charms: hence arises the inconstancy with which we are so often reproached; it is that barrenness of ideas which we find in women that renders men unfaithful. (227)

Villemert's discussion foreshadows Lennox's careful distinction between women who merit admiration and those whose behavior leads to trouble. He sees education as giving women a "better hold" over men—but also cautions that they should not be educated *too* much. Like "The History of the Dutchess of Beaufort," Villemert's text suggests a clearly didactic purpose for the novel in *The Lady's Museum*. But there are limitations to this didacticism. With "Beaufort," the improving message criticizing d'Estrées is undercut by Henry's preferring her over his more moral wife. With Villemert, it is that too much learning may be detrimental to women.

The third lengthy contribution to the first issue of *The Lady's Museum* is a character who calls herself "The Trifler." This type of character, an authorial persona introducing the journal to his or her readers, was a convention in most eighteenth-century periodicals.[1] Readers would have conflated this narrative voice with "The Author of The Female Quixote," as the periodical's authorship was announced on the title page. Therefore, it is interesting that the persona of the "Trifler"—the only one of the three voices in the first issue of *The Lady's Museum* written by Lennox herself—most undermines the idea that literature's main purpose should be the moral education of readers.

In the first installment, the "Trifler" character recounts a short narrative about reading and writing, which leads into a discussion of coquetry. Second, the "Trifler" gives a brief history of the narrator's own life, recalling an episode where she was rebuked as a young girl; this episode later inadvertently leads to her education. It would be too simple to equate the "Trifler" with Charlotte Lennox—she would probably have been considering her readers' interests and female propriety as well—but certainly of any voice in *The Lady's Museum*, this is closest to Lennox's own. The installment starts with a quote from "a polite old gentleman" (222), who invites the character to read in order to escape moral corruption—possibly a nod to the rhetoric of Richardson and Fielding. This advice is interesting in itself because it recognizes only one goal for reading at a time when literature was also sometimes considered dangerous, particularly to young women. But the female "Trifler" intentionally misreads the gentleman's comment, "with a small deviation from the sense" (222), to interpret it instead as a suggestion that she should *write*. The "polite old gentleman" wants the woman—who describes herself as "young, single, gay, and ambitious of pleasing" (223)—to read to take her mind off her own vanity; currently, she is "too intent upon pleasing" (222). The most important word here, repeated twice, is "pleasing." Instead of following the advice given by the "gentleman" (and by inference, also the advice given by Richardson and Fielding) to read for moral edification, the "Trifler" decides to write in order to bring pleasure to her readers.

---

1   For instance, Manley's *Female Tatler* had Mrs. Crackenthorpe; Steele and Addison introduced Mr. Spectator; Haywood's authorial persona in *The Parrot* was Mrs. Prattle; and Johnson's eponymous periodical was narrated by the Rambler.

After stating her intention to write for pleasure, the "Trifler" goes on to defend her position against imagined objections, particularly that "forwardness" in women is considered inappropriate. She argues that there is little difference between a woman's longing for recognition (expressed in coquetry) and men's quest for respect via other means: "The desire of fame, or the desire of pleasing," she writes, "in my opinion, are synonimous terms" (222). As Jennie Batchelor summarizes this argument, both the gentleman and the "Trifler" want to please others, but "where a desire for fame or to please others may earn the statesman respect, it leaves women vulnerable to accusations of 'coquetry'" (94), i.e., immorality. This implies an indictment of the eighteenth-century sexual double standard, where the same motivation or action is evaluated differently in men and women.

In the next section, Lennox moves from discussing her own role as a woman writer to situating women as readers. She recounts another fictional anecdote from "her" (i.e., the "Trifler's") youth (224)[1] that provides a kind of lesson in "proper" reading. In this story, the then nine-year-old speaker is one of two daughters; the other daughter is her mother's favorite. After a particular insult from her mother, the author reads Aesop's fable of "The Ape and her Two Brats," where the simian mother accidentally kills her favorite child; the young girl shows this fable to her mother. The mother misreads the fable and the context in which her daughter is demonstrating it, is offended, punishes the child, and tells all visitors of the child's "crime." While the mother realizes that Aesop's fable is supposed to apply to her, her reading skills are so poorly developed that she simply thinks she is being likened to an ape. But really, the story is a metaphor for her unequal treatment of her daughters. In other words, she reads too literally and thus misses the message.[2] The story is also a metaphor for the novel itself, in particular Lennox's own novel: it should be read on a symbolic or metaphorical level to readers who "are childlike in their ignorance and need to be coaxed into learning" (Italia 196), almost like the ape. This is

---

1 Even though that persona is probably similar to Lennox in her opinions, the biographical details given about her are quite different.
2 The mother's failure to grasp the message is symbolized by Lennox's omission of the fable's overt moral, which in her 1740 source reads, "*Fondlings are commonly unfortunate; and the Children that are least indulged make usually the best Men*" (Aesop 146). A "fondling" in eighteenth-century language is a person who is fondly or excessively loved.

interesting in relation to Villemert's "Of the Studies Proper for Women," where an excess of reading and education is also perilous. Finally, the troubled family dynamic indicates that Lennox is preparing her readers for a similar arrangement in the novel to come.

The three items surrounding the serialized version of *Sophia* in *The Lady's Museum* thus construct what Batchelor calls "a moral world that was far from black and white" (93). "The History of the Dutchess of Beaufort" presents a (negative) moral exemplar, but more in the sentimental than in the didactic mode. "Of the Studies Proper for Women" encourages female education, but only to a limited extent. Finally, the "Trifler" presents a character who embraces writing, but who also cautions against misreading. This could be taken as a simple endorsement of reading for moral improvement (because the immoral mother is the "bad" reader), but since the "Trifler" insists on the importance of pleasure in reading, her views do not fit entirely into either the framework of the didactic novel or the principles of sentimental fiction. Lennox uses concepts and rhetoric from those discourses, but her ideas cannot be reduced to their ideologies. Instead, *Sophia* is a heroine who pushes against the gender roles assigned to her by eighteenth-century British society.

Sophia in Context

After *The Lady's Museum* folded in February, Lennox republished "The History of Harriot and Sophia" in book format as *Sophia* with James Fletcher in May 1762. For this publication, she made two major changes in the text (in addition to amending the title): she expanded the first description of the two sisters, and she split the eleven installments into 41 chapters (see Appendix A). The reactions to this novel edition of *Sophia* in contemporary reviews were mostly positive, with *The Critical Review* commenting, "The lesson is instructive, the story interesting, the language chaste, the reflections natural, and the general moral such as we must recommend to the attention of all our female readers" (217), and *The Library* calling the novel "an agreeable love-tale, composed with great purity of sentiment and stile" (218). These reviews allude to the two traditions drawn on by Lennox—moral/didactic fiction and the sentimental novel—but do not pick up on any other more subtle aspects of *Sophia*. *The British Magazine* succinctly reviewed the novel in four words: "Ingenious, delicate, and interesting" (218). *The Gentleman's*

Magazine recognized in the novel "many observations which shew a perfect knowledge of the human heart, and a delicate sense of sublime virtue" (210), and only *The Monthly Review* missed "much of that spirit and variety which this species of composition peculiarly requires, and which are more conspicuous in some of her former works" (219). The reviews also missed one other significant development, which was that Lennox explicitly identified herself on the title page. On the title page of *The Lady's Museum*, she had only named herself as "the Author of The Female Quixote," but now the page announced her full name— only the second time in her career (after the second edition of her *Henrietta* in 1761) she had done so. Perhaps *The Lady's Museum* had given her the confidence to step forward as a female author.

In many ways, *Sophia* is firmly rooted in its context in the middle of the eighteenth century. The text is a conventional sentimental novel with its story of a poor heroine who is endowed with innate sensibility and suffers many difficulties in a cruel world, using a number of conventional details of plot and style. Similarly, in its foregrounding of a purported didactic goal, and in overtly promoting a traditional, patriarchal, eighteenth-century version of sexual virtue, the novel falls into the pattern established for its genre. At the same time, *Sophia* breaks some new ground. Harriot has more freedom and pleasure than Sophia, suggesting that there may be a quiet critique of the didactic novel. In its concern with rank and money, *Sophia* exposes the limitations of the sentimental form (which it simultaneously employs) as well as the difficulties women faced in trying to support themselves independently in eighteenth-century Britain. The novel's original presentation in an innovative periodical format allows Lennox to prepare her readers for "The History of Harriot and Sophia" in surrounding material like an essay by her authorial persona, a translation of part of a contemporary treatise on female education, and a biography of a sixteenth-century French mistress. These texts encourage a reading of *Sophia* within the paradigms of didactic fiction and the sentimental novel, but also allow for the possibility of a slightly more challenging interpretation with regard to eighteenth-century gender roles. In a century that was in many ways very conservative, Charlotte Lennox was thus able to use her skills in writing and marketing literature at least to hint at possible alternatives.

Charlotte Lennox: A Brief Chronology

1729-30	Charlotte Ramsay born, probably in Gibraltar, daughter of James Ramsay
?1739-43	James Ramsay stationed in the New York colony; family moves there
?1743	James Ramsay dies; Charlotte sent to England to live with relative, who dies before she arrives; Charlotte lives in London for the rest of her life
1746-50	Works as actress, performing in Nicholas Rowe's *The Fair Penitent* and William Congreve's *The Mourning Bride*
1747	Marries Alexander Lennox, an employee of the London printer William Strahan; publishes *Poems on Several Occasions* with a dedication to Lady Isabella Finch signed "Charlotte Ramsay"
c.1748-50	Meets and becomes friends with Samuel Johnson and Samuel Richardson
1750	First novel, *The Life of Harriot Stuart*, published
1752	Novel *The Female Quixote* published; Lennox attempts subscription publication of *Poems on Several Occasions*
1753	Critical work *Shakespear Illustrated* (vols. 1 and 2) published; sections of book contributed by Johnson and the Earl of Cork and Orrery
1754	*Shakespear Illustrated* (vol. 3) published
1755	Translation *The Memoirs of Maximilian de Bethune, Duke of Sully* published
1756	Translation *The Memoirs of the Countess of Berci* published
1757	Translation *The Memoirs for the History of Madam de Maintenon* published; pastoral drama *Philander* published after Garrick rejects it for production at Drury Lane Theatre
1758	Novel *Henrietta* published
1760	Translation *The Greek Theatre of Father Brumoy* published; monthly periodical *The Lady's Museum* (including serial novel "The History of Harriot and Sophia") begins publication
c. 1760–82	Alexander Lennox works for the Customs service, giving the family a regular income

1761	*The Lady's Museum* ceases publication after eleven installments; Sir Joshua Reynolds paints portrait of Lennox
1762	"The History of Harriot and Sophia" published as *Sophia*
1765	Daughter Harriot Holles born
1766	Novel *The History of Eliza* published
1769	Drama *The Sister* (based on *Henrietta*) performed once at Covent Garden Theatre, but immediately withdrawn, and then published
c.1770	Son George Louis born
1774	Translation *Meditations and Penitential Prayers, written by the celebrated Dutchess de la Vallière* published
1775	Drama *Old City Manners* (based on George Chapman, Ben Jonson, and John Marston's collaboration *Eastward Ho!*) successfully performed at Drury Lane Theatre and published; after copyright decision of *Donaldson v. Becket* (which strengthens the rights of authors), Lennox produces proposal for subscription publication of her works, written by Johnson and dedicated to the Queen
1778	After negotiation in the wake of *Donaldson v. Becket*, Lennox convinces her publisher to release new edition of the *Memoirs of Sully* for her financial benefit
c.1779	Lennox represented in Richard Samuel's painting *The Nine Living Muses of Great Britain* (with poet and critic Anna Barbauld, translator Elizabeth Carter, actress Elizabeth Griffith, painter Angelica Kauffman, singer Elizabeth Linley, historian Catharine Macaulay, patron and "Queen of the Bluestockings" Elizabeth Montagu, and educator and moralist Hannah More)
1783	Poems supposedly by George Louis Lennox start appearing in the *British Magazine* and the *Edinburgh Weekly Magazine*; around this time, Lennox and her husband separate
c.1783–84	Death of Harriot Holles Lennox
1790	Novel *Euphemia* published
1792	Begins to receive assistance from the newly founded Royal Literary Fund
1793	Attempts to produce subscription publication of revised edition of *Shakespear Illustrated*
1804	January 4 Lennox dies

A Note on the Text

Sophia was published in three versions during Charlotte Lennox's lifetime. It first appeared in eleven installments in Lennox's periodical *The Lady's Museum* between March 1760 and January 1761 under the title "The History of Harriot and Sophia." From this version, the Dublin publisher James Hoey pirated an edition that appeared in one volume titled *Sophia* early in 1762. Finally, the London printer James Fletcher issued a two-volume edition of *Sophia* in May 1762.

While there are hundreds of small differences between the editions—mostly in punctuation and spelling, but sometimes also in word choice (see Appendix A)—there is only one lengthy textual emendation: a passage in the first chapter of the novel was changed from serial publication to Fletcher's edition (see Appendix A), perhaps because the novel was no longer accompanied by the rest of the material in *The Lady's Museum* (see Appendix D1). Chapter titles were also introduced.

I have taken Fletcher's version as the copy text for the present edition. We may assume that Lennox was involved in the preparation of this edition since the title page specified "By Mrs. Charlotte Lennox" and since Lennox was generally quite involved in the publication of her novels (as documented in the correspondence surrounding *The Female Quixote* and her translation *The Memoirs of Maximilian de Bethune, Duke of Sully*). Some silent changes (such as correcting clear typographical errors, changing punctuation, and normalizing running quotation marks) have been made, but other irregularities of the original have been maintained. In the appendix material, the common variation of her name as "Lenox" have been standardized to "Lennox," as has the spelling of "Quixotte."

The following pages offer brief notes on eighteenth-century money, transportation, clergy, rank and titles, and on the topic of women and property. For more information, see Paul Langford, *A Polite and Commercial People: England 1727–1783* (Oxford: Oxford UP, 1989), Kristin Olsen, *Daily Life in Eighteenth-Century England* (Westport, CT: Greenwood, 1999), Roy Porter, *English Society in the Eighteenth Century* (rev. ed., Harmondsworth: Penguin, 1990), and Roy Porter, *London: A Social History* (Cambridge, MA: Harvard UP, 1994).

A Note on Female Property and Education

Eighteenth-century attitudes held that women were best suited to the private sphere of the home, where their role was to run the household and bear children. Most couples did not marry from love; instead, their marriages were arranged by their families for dynastic and financial reasons—which is why novels such as *Sophia*, where the protagonist holds out for true love, were so revolutionary. Women in the eighteenth century were seen in terms of their relationship with men—daughters, wives, or widows. Only widows held substantial property rights. As daughters and wives, women were the legal property of their fathers and husbands. Their only claim to their own property was if a male "settled" money on them in the form of a jointure or "pin" money (197)—this, however, was open to legal challenge—or if they were left a legacy (58). These settlements were usually made as part of a marriage contract (88) to give the woman spending money, or to provide for her in case her husband died. In *Sophia* Sir Charles intends to make one for Sophia as an attempt to help convince her to become his mistress (87).

Women's education was equally up to the men in their lives (see Appendix D). In *Sophia*, Harriot's "polite education" (54) would have consisted of practical topics like manners, music, religion, arts, and French—the accomplishments that raised her value in the marriage market. Learning "French and Italian" (55) was unusual enough, but "Greek and Latin" (122) were rarely part of female education. Unlike Harriot, Sophia apparently relies on her common sense and on what she learns from the books supplied by Mr. Herbert (55). Books, however, could also be used to manipulate learners (66) and at times could entirely mislead undiscerning readers.

A Note on Rank and Titles

The upper ranks of English society in the eighteenth century were divided into five major groups: the royalty, the nobility or peers, the gentry or land-owners, the professions, and the trades. The first three are similar to what today we would call the upper classes or the aristocracy; the last two are similar to today's upper middle class. According to one estimate, made by Joseph Massie in his broadside *A Computation of the Money that hath been exorbitantly Raised upon the People of Great Britain* (London, 1760), there were only about 2070 families in the aristocracy out of almost a million and a half in the country; in other words, the aristocracy made up only about 0.15 percent of the population. Within the aristocracy, the royal family and the peers had titles like Duke, Marquess, Earl, Viscount, and Baron. Barons, the lowest ranks of the peerage, were addressed as "Lord," so Lord L— (64) is actually a baron. As a baronet (60), Charles Stanley is *not* a member of the nobility, but of the gentry—land-owners who did not have to work for a living—and he is addressed as "Sir." Members of the gentry were also called squires (104, 108), though that term was not very specific. The term "gentleman" could apply to a member of the gentry or to a member of the upper middle classes, who could also expect to be addressed as "Sir" or "Madam." Throughout *Sophia*, most older (married) women are addressed as "madam" in direct speech, while younger (unmarried) women are called "miss." These people all worked for a living, but the members of the professions such as lawyers, soldiers, and doctors saw themselves as superior to mere merchants and tradesmen. However, by the second half of the eighteenth century, these fine social distinctions were starting to disappear, and all members of the gentry and upper middle classes were sometimes (with no particular reason or pattern) indiscriminately addressed as "Mr." and "Mrs." For instance, the Barton family seems to be part of the gentry, given that the son is called a squire (163), but at the same time mother and son are known as Mrs. and Mr. Barton. It is important to note that almost all the interaction in *Sophia* happens between the upper ranks of the middle classes and the lower ranks of the upper classes.

A Note on the Clergy

Though various dissenting denominations such as Presbyterians and Methodists were slowly gaining numbers, the English in the eighteenth century overwhelmingly belonged to the Anglican Church, or Church of England. The Anglican Church was divided into parishes, each of which was led by a parson, sometimes also called rector (99). The office of parson usually came with a substantial salary or benefice (99), and sometimes parsons served more than one parish at a time. In that case, they could outsource their duties to curates, clergymen without their own parishes who were often exploited because of their weak position. Mr. Lawson in *Sophia* is such a curate—the innkeeper who calls him a parson (155) is either misinformed or using the word in the more general sense of member of the clergy. At £60 per year (99), Mr. Lawson's salary is actually not bad by the standards of his time, but his position as a country curate carries so little social status that Mrs. Howard feels perfectly comfortable leaving him waiting in her parlor for a significant amount of time (167). Because of his relative poverty, Mr. Lawson would have been happy to take in a paying lodger like Sophia, while for her part Sophia would have maintained her status of respectability by staying with a married curate. Country clergymen like Mr. Lawson were popular figures in eighteenth-century literature.

A Note on British Currency

In the eighteenth century, British money was counted in three main units: pence, shillings, and pounds. One pound (£1) was twenty shillings (20s.), and one shilling was twelve pence (12d.). In addition, a crown was 5s. and a guinea was 21s. (so two guineas were £2 2s.; see p. 190). The value of money is difficult to compare with today's currency. A soldier might have earned around £14 per year in 1759, a sailor £15–£24, and an innkeeper £50–£79. In the 1780s, a shoemaker might have earned 2s. a day and a carpenter 1s.–1s. 6d. In other words, the hundred pounds of profit that Sophia makes by selling the Darnley family's possessions (see p. 178; this was only £50 in the version in *The Lady's Museum*) are quite a substantial amount of money. Mrs. Darnley's annuity of £80 (61) is enough to live in relative comfort, and even Mr. Lawson's salary of £60 (99) is acceptable. A chicken cost 1s. 6d. in London in 1755, and a bed at a gin-shop cost 2d. per night in 1751. Lennox's novel cost between 1s. 7½d. and 2s. 2d. in the pirated Dublin edition (depending on binding) and 5s. to 6s. in Fletcher's edition, which was about the price of one pound of tobacco or a pair of men's calf shoes.

A Note on Transportation

Few members of the middle and upper classes in London in the eighteenth century walked. One option was a sedan chair (usually simply known as "chair"), which consisted of a box made of wood that shielded the passenger from other people as well as the weather. The chair was carried by two men, one in the front and one in the back, with poles attached on either side of the box. A chair could be hailed in the street or from a house—as when Harriot leaves the family residence (78)—and could drop the passenger off inside a house, maintaining complete privacy.

For longer distances, individuals could travel in a variety of coaches. Almost all of these were slow and uncomfortable and made many stops. Their names were sometimes interchangeable, but there were clear differences in quality. The hackney-coach or stage-coach had four to six passengers inside a closed compartment and sometimes more sitting on top. Since anyone could take the stage-coach, it was not considered proper, particularly for young women. In *Sophia*, the rather poor Mr. Herbert travels by stage-coach (194), and Sophia herself takes a coach—with William as an escort (159) or on her own (171). The post-chaise—which Mr. Lawson uses to collect Sophia from Mrs. Howard's house (169) and in which Mrs. Darnley wants to explore the countryside (180)—was more expensive given that it seated only two passengers and was faster. This was driven by a post-boy (99). Mr. Herbert hires a post-chaise to take Sophia to the countryside (98) and takes it himself once (94). Still, traveling times were long by contemporary standards: the trip from London to Bath—where both Sir Charles (89) and Mr. Herbert (160) travel—takes about 90 minutes today; but at the time of the novel, it could take anywhere from 16 to 50 hours. Rich individuals such as Sir Charles (86, 131, 196), Mrs. Barton (164), or Lord L— (181) also owned their own chariots and occasionally lent them to friends (127, 152, 171). However, even they still sometimes traveled by post-chaise (89).

SOPHIA

BY

Mrs. CHARLOTTE LENNOX

In TWO VOLUMES

LONDON:
Printed for JAMES FLETCHER, in St. Paul's
Church-Yard. MDCCLXII

CHAPTER I

The different characters of two sisters.

Harriot and Sophia were the daughters of a gentleman, who, having spent a good paternal inheritance before he was five and thirty, was reduced to live upon the moderate salary of a place[1] at court, which his friends procured him to get rid of his importunities. The same imprudence by which he had been governed in affairs of less importance, directed him likewise in the choice of a wife: the woman he married had no merit but beauty, and brought with her to the house of a man whose fortune was already ruined, nothing but a taste for luxury and expence, without the means of gratifying it.

Harriot, the eldest daughter of this couple, was, like her mother, a beauty, and upon that account, as well as the conformity of her temper and inclinations to hers, engrossed all her affection.

Sophia she affected to despise, because she wanted[2] in an equal degree those personal attractions, which in her opinion constituted the whole of female perfection. Mere common judges, however, allowed her person to be agreeable; people of discernment and taste pronounced her something more. There was diffused throughout the whole person of Sophia a certain secret charm, a natural grace which cannot be defined; she was not indeed so beautiful as her sister, but she was more attractive; her complexion was not so fair as Harriot's, nor her features so regular, but together they were full of charms: her eyes were particularly fine, large, and full of fire, but that fire tempered with a tenderness so bewitching, as insensibly made its way to the heart. Harriot had beauty, but Sophia had something more; she had graces.

---

1 Paid position in the government or in the royal household.
2 Lacked.

One of the most beautiful fictions of Homer, says the celebrated *Montesquieu*,[1] is that of the girdle which gave Venus the power of pleasing. Nothing is more proper to give us an idea of the magick and force of the graces, which seem to be given to a person by some invisible power, and are distinguished from beauty itself.

Harriot's charms produced at the first sight all the effect they were capable of; a second look of Sophia was more dangerous than the first, for grace is seldomer found in the face than the manners; and, as our manner is formed every moment, a new surprise is perpetually creating. A woman can be beautiful but one way, she can be graceful a thousand. *aphorism*

Harriot was formed to be the admiration of the many; Sophia the passion of the few, the sweet sensibility of her countenance, the powerful expression of her eyes, the soft elegance of her shape and motion, a melodious voice, whose varied accents enforced the sensible things she always said, were beauties not capable of striking vulgar[2] minds; and which were sure to be eclipsed by the dazling lustre of her sister's complexion, and the fire of two bright eyes, whose looks were as quick and unsettled as her thoughts.

While Harriot was receiving the improvement of a polite education, Sophia was left to form herself as well as she could; happily for her a just and solid judgment supplied the place of teachers, precept, and example. The hours that Harriot wasted in dress, company, and gay[3] amusements, were by Sophia devoted to reading.

A good old gentleman, who was nearly[4] related to her father, perceiving this taste in her, encouraged it by his praises, and fur-

---

1 In his "Essay on Taste," Montesquieu discusses (among other topics) the subject of grace: "One of the most beautiful fictions in the *Iliad* is that of the Girdle, which imparted to *Venus* the power of pleasing. No image could contribute so happily to give us a notion of the secret magick and influence of those graces which seem to be shed upon certain persons by an invisible hand, and which are intirely distinct from beauty" (Alexander Gerard, *An Essay on Taste, with Three Dissertations on the Same Subject* [by other authors; London: Millar, 1759], 300n.). By quoting almost directly from Montesquieu—in contemporary parlance, plagiarizing— Lennox is demonstrating not only her knowledge of French philosophy, but how current she is in her reading: the first translation into English of Montesquieu's essay for d'Alembert's encyclopedia had appeared less than a year before the beginning of *Sophia* in the *Lady's Museum*.
2 "Vulgar" here means both uneducated and lower-class.
3 Happy, entertaining.
4 Closely.

nished her with the means of gratifying it, by constantly supplying her with such books[1] as were best calculated to improve her
morals and understanding. His admiration encreasing in proportion as he had opportunities of observing her merit, he undertook
to teach her the French and Italian languages,[2] in which she soon
made a surprising progress; and by the time she had reached her
fifteenth year, she had read all the best authors in them, as well
as in her own.

By this unwearied[3] application to reading, her mind became a
beautiful store-house of ideas: hence she derived the power and
habit of constant reflection, which at once enlarged her understanding, and confirmed her in the principles of piety and virtue.

As she grew older the management of the family entirely
devolved upon her; for her mother had no taste for any thing but
pleasure, and her sister was taught to consider herself as a fine
lady,[4] whose beauty could not fail to make her fortune,[5] and
whose sole care it ought to be to dress to the greatest advantage,
and make her appearance in every place where she might
encrease the number of her admirers.

Sophia, in acquitting herself of the duties of a house-keeper to
her mother, shewed[6] that the highest intellectual improvements
were not incompatible[7] with the humbler cares of domestic life:
every thing that went through her hands received a grace and
propriety from the good sense by which she was directed; nor did
her attention to family-affairs break in upon her darling amusement reading.

People who know how to employ their time well are good
economists of it. Sophia laid out hers in such exact proportions,
that she had always sufficient for the several employments she
was engaged in: the business of her life, like that of nature, was
performed without noise, hurry, or confusion.

---

1 A library was part of most gentlemen's houses, but apparently Sophia's
   father was not polite enough to acquire books.
2 These details may be a reference to Lennox's own life. She translated
   several books from French and Italian.
3 Unceasing, never-ending.
4 I.e., an upper-class lady.
5 Harriot means that she wants to marry a rich husband.
6 "Shew" is a widespread eighteenth-century spelling for "show"; hence
   "shewed" for "showed."
7 One of the most widespread objections to female education was that it
   made women unfit to be wives. See Appendix D4, p. 246-48.

The death of Mr. Darnley threw this little family into a deplorable state of indigence, which was felt the more severely, as they had hitherto lived in an affluence of all things, and the debts which an expence so ill proportioned to their income had obliged Mr. Darnley to contract, left the unhappy widow and her children without any resource.[1] The plate,[2] furniture, and every thing valuable were seized by the creditors.[3] Mrs. Darnley and her daughters retired to a private lodging,[4] where the first days were passed in a weak despondence on the part of the mother, in passionate repinings[5] on that of the eldest daughter, and by Sophia in decent sorrow and pious resignation.

Mrs. Darnley however, by a natural consequence of her thoughtless temper,[6] soon recovered her former gaiety. Present evils only were capable of affecting her; reflection and forecast never disturbed the settled calm of her mind. If the wants of one day were supplied, she did not consider what inconveniences the next might produce. As for Harriot she found resources of comfort in the exalted ideas she had of her own charms; and having already laid it down as a maxim, that poverty was the most shameful thing in the world, she formed her resolutions accordingly.

Sophia, as soon as her grief for the loss of her father had subsided, began to consider of some plan for their future subsistence. She forbore however to communicate her thoughts on this subject to her mother and sister, who had always affected to treat every thing she said with contempt, the mean disguise which envy had assumed to hide their consciousness of her superior merit; but she opened her mind to the good old gentleman, to whom she had been obliged for many of her improvements. She told him that being by his generous cares qualified to undertake the education

---

1 Since Mr. Darnley had an appointment at court, his family's source of income dried up entirely when he died.

2 Silverware.

3 Genteel poverty was a huge problem in the eighteenth century. Debt was serious, given that creditors had almost unlimited rights over the property of the debtors, who often ended up in prison. There, they still had to pay for their own upkeep, so there was often no way out of poverty.

4 I.e., the Darnley family moved from a residence of their own to rented accommodations.

5 Expressions of grief.

6 Character, predisposition.

of a young lady, she was desirous of being received into the family of some person of distinction in the quality of governess[1] to the daughters of it, that she might at once secure to herself a decent establishment, and be enabled to assist her mother. She hinted that if her sister could be also prevailed upon to enter into the service of a lady of quality, they might jointly contribute their endeavours to make their mother's life comfortable.

Mr. Herbert praised her design, and promised to mention it to Mrs. Darnley, to whom he conceived he might speak with the greater freedom, as his near relation to her husband, and the long friendship which had subsisted between them, gave him a right to interest himself in their affairs. The first words he uttered produced such an emotion in Mrs. Darnley's countenance, as convinced him that what he had farther to say would not be favourably received. She coloured, drew herself up with an air of dignity, looking at the same time at her eldest daughter with a scornful smile.

Mr. Herbert, however, continued his discourse, when Harriot, with a pertness which she took for wit, interrupted him by a loud laugh, and asked him, if going to service was the best provision he could think of for Mr. Darnley's daughters?

Mr. Herbert, turning hastily to her, replied with a look of great gravity, and in a calm accent, "Have you, miss, thought of any thing better?"

Harriot, without being disconcerted, retorted very briskly, "People who have nothing but advice to offer to their friends in distress, ought to be silent till they are asked for it."

"Good advice, Miss," replied the old gentleman with the same composure, "is what every body cannot, and many will not give; and it is at least an instance of friendship to hazard it, where one may be almost sure of its giving offence. But," continued he, turning to Sophia, "my young pupil here has, I hope, not profited so little by her reading as to be ignorant of the value of good counsel; and I promise her she shall not only command the best that I am capable of giving, but every other assistance she may stand in need of." Saying this, he bowed and went away, without any attempts from Mrs. Darnley to detain him.

---

1 The position of governess (in which one served as a tutor and caretaker for children, particularly young girls), was one of the few professions open to respectable women in the eighteenth century. The position was a precarious one, however: governesses had no rights.

Poor Sophia, who was supposed by her silence to have acquiesced in the old gentleman's proposal, was exposed to a thousand reproaches for her meanness[1] of spirit. She attempted to shew the utility, and even the necessity of following his advice; but she found on this occasion, as she had on many others, that with some persons it is not safe to be reasonable. Her arguments were answered with rage and invective, which soon silenced her, and increased the triumph of her imperious sister.

Mr. Herbert, apprehensive of the ill treatment she was likely to be exposed to, offered to place her in the family of a country clergyman, and to pay for board till such a settlement as she desired could be procured for her; but the tender Sophia, not willing to leave her mother while she could be of any use to her, gratefully declined his offer, still expecting that the increasing perplexity of their circumstances might bring her to relish his reasonable counsels, and that she might have the sanction of her consent to a step which prudence made necessary to be taken.

A legacy of a hundred pounds being left her by a young lady who tenderly loved her, and who died in her arms, she immediately presented it to her mother, by whom it was received with a transport of joy, but without any reflection upon the filial piety of her who gave it.

Sophia's good friend, though he did not absolutely approve of this exalted[2] strain of tenderness, yet did not fail to place the merit of it in the fullest light: but Harriot, who never heard any praises of her sister without a visible emotion, interrupted him, by saying, that Sophia had only done what she ought; and that she herself would have acted in the same manner, if the sum had been twenty times larger.

The same delicacy which induced Sophia to divest herself of any particular right to this small legacy, made her see the misapplication of it without discovering[3] the least mark of dislike. Harriot, who governed her mother absolutely, having represented to her, that the obscurity in which they lived was not the means to preserve their old friends, or to acquire new ones, and that it was their business to appear again in the world, and put themselves in the way of fortune, which could not be done without making a decent appearance at least; Mrs. Darnley, who thought this reasoning unanswerable, consented to their changing their

---

1 Commonness, not in keeping with her class.
2 Exaggerated and overly pious.
3 Showing, demonstrating.

present lodgings for others more genteel, and to whatever expences her eldest daughter judged necessary to secure the success of her scheme.

Sophia lamented in secret this excess of imprudence; and to avoid being a witness of it, as well as to free her mother from the expence of her maintenance,[1] she resolved to accept of the first genteel place[2] that offered; but the natural softness and timidity of her temper, made her delay as long as possible mentioning this design to her mother and sister, lest it should be construed into a tacit reproach of them for a conduct so very different.

Indeed her condition was greatly altered for the worse, since the present she had made of her legacy. Her mother and sister had never loved her with any great degree of affection, and their tenderness for her was now entirely lost in the uneasy consciousness of having owed an obligation to her, for which they could not resolve to be grateful. They no longer considered her as an insignificant person whose approbation or dislike was of no sort of consequence, but as a saucy censurer of their actions, who assumed to herself a superiority, on account of the paultry assistance she had afforded them: every thing she said was construed into upbraidings of the benefit she had conferred upon them. If she offered her opinion upon any occasion, Harriot would say to her with a malicious sneer, "To be sure you think you have a right to give us laws, because we have had the misfortune to be obliged to you." And Mrs. Darnley, working herself up to an agony of grief and resentment for the fancied insult, would lift up her eyes and cry, "How much is that mother to be pitied who lives to receive alms from her child!"

Poor Sophia used to answer no otherwise than by tears: but this was sure to aggravate her fault; for it was supposed that she wept and appeared afflicted only to shew people what ungrateful returns she met with for her goodness.

Thus did the unhappy Sophia, with the softest sensibility of heart, and tenderest affections, see herself excluded from the endearing testimonies of a mother's fondness, only by being too worthy of them, and exposed to shocking suspicions of undutifulness, for an action that shewed the highest filial affection: so true is it, that great virtues cannot be understood by mean and

---

1 As an unmarried daughter, Sophia could only look to her mother for financial support.
2 Position, job.

little minds, and with such, not only lose all their lustre, but are too often mistaken for the contrary vices.

CHAPTER II
The Triumph of the Graces.

While Sophia passed her time in melancholy reflections, Harriot, being by her generous gift enabled to make as shewy an appearance as her mourning habit[1] would permit, again mixed in company, and laid baits for admiration. Her beauty soon procured her a great number of lovers;[2] her poverty made their approaches easy;[3] and the weakness of her understanding, her insipid gaiety, and pert affectation of wit, encouraged the most licentious hopes, and exposed her to the most impertinent addresses.

Among those who looking upon her as a conquest of no great difficulty formed the mortifying design of making a mistress[4] of her, was Sir Charles Stanley, a young baronet of a large estate, a most agreeable person, and engaging address: his fine qualities made him the delight of all who knew him, and even envy itself allowed him to be a man of the strictest honour and unblemished integrity.[5]

Persons who connect the idea of virtue and goodness with such a character, would find it hard to conceive how a man who lives in a constant course of dissimulation[6] with one part of his

---

1 A daughter in the Darnley's social class would have been expected to wear a mourning habit for as long as one year. There was a "first mourning" outfit that was usually black and a "second mourning" costume that was grey. In either case, this outfit was cut according to the reigning fashion, but had no decorations or ornaments. Poorer people sometimes simply had their regular clothes dyed black.

2 In the eighteenth century, "lover" meant someone romantically interested in a woman, not a sexual partner.

3 In the eighteenth century, there was a direct relation between the wealth of a family and the quality of suitors for its daughters.

4 A mistress was a long-term companion or sexual partner outside of marriage, usually set up in an apartment, but without the social status of a wife. By becoming a mistress, one risked social ostracism.

5 I.e., even individuals envious of Sir Charles conceded he was a man of honor and integrity.

6 Dissipated living.

species, and who abuses the advantages he has received from nature and fortune, in subduing chastity, and ensnaring innocence, can possibly deserve, and establish a reputation for honour! but such are the illusions of prejudice, and such the tyranny of custom, that he who is called a man of gallantry, is at the same time esteemed a man of honour, though gallantry comprehends the worst kind of fraud, cruelty, and injustice.

Sir Charles Stanley had been but too successful in his attempts upon beauty, to fear being rejected by Miss Darnley;[1] and knowing her situation, he resolved to engage her gratitude at least before he declared his designs. He had interest[2] enough to procure the place her father enjoyed for a gentleman, who thought himself happy in obtaining it, though charged with an annuity of fourscore pounds a year for the widow of his predecessor.

Sir Charles, in acquainting Miss Darnley with what he had done in favour of her mother, found himself under no necessity of insinuating[3] his motive for the extraordinary interest he took in the affairs of this distrest family. Harriot's vanity anticipated any declaration of this sort, and the thanks she gave him were accompanied with such an apparent consciousness of the power of her charms, as convinced him his work was already more than half done.

He was now received at Mrs. Darnley's in the quality of a declared lover of Harriot; and although amidst all his assiduities he never mentioned marriage, either the mother and daughter did not penetrate into his real designs, or were but too much disposed to favour them.

The innocent heart of Sophia was at first overwhelmed with joy for the happy provision that had been made for her mother, and the prospect of such an advantageous match for her sister, when Mr. Herbert, who knew the world too well to be imposed upon by these fine appearances, gently hinted to his young favourite, his apprehensions of the baronet's dishonourable views.

Her delicacy was so shocked by this suspicion, that she could scarce forbear expressing some little resentment of it; but reflecting that this ardent lover of Harriot's had not yet made any pro-

---

1 "Miss" was the title for a young unmarried woman of the middle class.
2 Influence.
3 Explaining.

posals of marriage, her good sense immediately suggested to her, that such affected delays in a man who was absolutely independent,[1] and with a woman whose situation made it a point of delicacy to be early explicit on the head,[2] could only proceed from intentions which he had not yet dared to own.

Chance had so ordered it, that hitherto she had never seen Sir Charles Stanley; whenever he came, she was either employed in the family affairs,[3] or engaged with her books, which it was no easy matter to make her quit. Besides, as she had no share in his visits, and as her sister never shewed any inclination to introduce her to him, she thought it did not become her to intrude herself upon his acquaintance. Sir Charles indeed, knowing that Mrs. Darnley had another daughter, used sometimes to enquire for her, but was neither surprised nor disappointed that she never appeared.

Sophia, however, was determined to be in the way when he came next, that she might have an opportunity of observing his behaviour to her sister; and fondly flattered herself that she should discover nothing to the disadvantage of a person, whom her grateful heart had taught itself to love and esteem as their common benefactor.[4]

Sir Charles at the next visit found Sophia in the room with her sister. He instantly saw something in her looks and person which inspired him with more respect than he had been used to feel for Mrs. Darnley and Harriot; a dignity which she derived from innate virtue, and exalted understanding. Struck with that inexplicable charm in her countenance which made it impossible to look on her with indifference, he began to consider her with an attention which greatly disgusted Harriot, who could not conceive that where she was present any other object was worthy notice.

Sophia herself was a little disconcerted by the young baronet's so earnestly gazing on her; and, in order to divert his looks,

1   Because he is financially independent, Sir Charles does not have to consult anyone else (parents, guardians) in his choice of a partner. This means that he could have immediately declared his desire to marry Harriot, if he had honorable intentions.
2   To be explicit on the subject.
3   I.e., household management.
4   Sir Charles is considered a benefactor because he has given Mr. Darnley's position to a successor who is required to support the Darnley family.

opened a conversation in which her sister might bear a part. Then it was, that without designing it, she displayed her whole power of charming: that flow of wit which was so natural to her, the elegant propriety of her language, the delicacy of her sentiments, the animated look which gave them new force, and sent them directly to the heart, and the moving graces of the most harmonious voice in the world, were attractions, which, though generally lost on fools, seldom fail of their effect on the heart of a man of sense.

Sir Charles was wrapt in wonder and delight; he had no eyes, no ears, but for Sophia: he scarce perceived that Harriot was in the room.

The insolent beauty, astonished at such unusual neglect, varied her attitude and her charms a thousand different ways to draw his attention; but found all was to no purpose. Had she been capable of serious reflection, she might now have discovered what advantages her sister, though inferior to her in beauty, gained over her, by the force of her understanding: she might now have seen,

How beauty is excelled by *modest* grace,
And wisdom, which alone is truly fair.[1]

But too ignorant to know her own wants, and too conceited to imagine she had any, she was strangely perplexed how to account for so sudden an alteration in Sir Charles.

Her uneasiness, however, grew so great, that she was not able to conceal it. She shifted her seat two or three times in a minute, bit her lips almost through, and frowned so intelligibly, that Sophia at last perceiving her agitation, suddenly recollected herself, and quitted the room upon pretence of business.

---

1 John Milton, *Paradise Lost* (1667). Eve is speaking about her first encounter with Adam, during which she realizes that her physical beauty is insignificant compared with Adam's grace:

> with that thy gentle hand
> Seized mine, I yielded, and from that time see
> How beauty is excelled by manly grace,
> And wisdom, which alone is truly fair. (IV.488–91)

In other words, Lennox is appropriating Eve's moment of submission to Adam to argue that a woman can have the same grace and intelligence as a man and can use it to assert herself over a man.

When she was gone, Harriot drawing herself up, and assuming a look which expressed her confidence in the irresistible power of her charms, seemed resolved to make her lover repent the little notice he had taken of her in this visit by playing off a thousand scornful airs upon him; but she was more mortified than ever, when upon turning her eyes towards him, in full expectation of finding his fixed upon her, she saw them bent upon the ground, and such a pensiveness in his countenance, as all her rigors could never yet occasion.

She was considering what to say to him to draw him out of this reverie, when Sir Charles, on a sudden raising his eyes, turned them towards the door with a look of mingled anxiety and impatience, and then, as if disappointed, sighed and addressed some indifferent conversation to Harriot.

The lady, now quite provoked, had recourse to an artifice which her shallow understanding suggested to her, as an infallible method of awakening his tenderness, and this was to make him jealous. Without any preparation, therefore, she introduced the name of Lord L—,[1] a young nobleman who was just returned from his travels,[2] and lavishing a thousand encomiums[3] upon his person, and his elegant taste in dress, added, "That he was the best bred man in the world, and had entertained her so agreeably one night at the play,[4] when happening to come into a box where

---

1 In addition to praising L—'s appearance ("person" is physical shape), Harriot is insulting Sir Charles since a Lord is higher on the social scale. (See "Note on Titles and Ranks," 46n.)

2 Between the ages of fourteen and twenty, the sons of the gentry and nobility frequently went on an extended trip of continental Europe known as the "Grand Tour." On this trip, the young men, often accompanied by a companion or tutor, visited France, Germany, and Italy for as long as three years. The goal was to learn about the cultures of antiquity and to gain knowledge of other societies, but the travelers were also sometimes sent away from England to get them out of legal or romantic trouble (see 170). There were enough Englishmen on the Grand Tour at any given time to constitute an expatriate community. Some women also went on a Grand Tour, but the practice was mostly male for most of the eighteenth century. It was also very expensive—the cost for three years could be as high as £5000. (See "A Note on British Currency," 48.)

3 Praises.

4 In the eighteenth century, the theater was a place notorious for sexual intrigue. Not listening to the play was common. See for instance, Fanny Burney, *Evelina* (1778), Letter 20.

she was with a lady of her acquaintance, that they did not mind a word the players said, he was so diverting."

Sir Charles coldly answered, "That Lord L— was a very pretty youth, and that he was intimately acquainted with him."

"Oh then," cried Harriot, with a great deal of affected joy, "I vow and protest you shall bring him to see me."

"Indeed you must excuse me, madam," said Sir Charles with some quickness.

Harriot, concluding her stratagem had taken effect, was quite transported, and renewed her attacks, determined to make him suffer as much as possible; but the young baronet, whose thoughts were full of Sophia, and whose emotion at the request Harriot had made him, was occasioned by fears very different from those she suspected, took no further notice of what she said, but interrupted her to ask how old her sister Sophia was?

"I dare engage," replied Harriot, "you would never have supposed her to be younger than I am."

The baronet smiled, and looking at his watch, seemed surprised that it was so late, and took his leave.

Miss Darnley following him to the door of the room, cried, "Remember I lay my commands upon you to bring my Lord L— to see me."

Sir Charles answered her no otherwise than by a low bow, and she returned, delighted at the parting pang which she supposed she had given him. Vanity is extremely ingenious in procuring gratifications for itself.

CHAPTER III
The Young Baronet declares his Passion.

Harriot did not doubt but that she had tormented Sir Charles sufficiently; and it was the unshaken confidence which she had in the power of her charms, that hindered her from discovering the true cause of the new disgust she had conceived for her sister. However, it was so great that she could scarcely speak to her civilly, or endure her in her sight: yet she found an increase of pleasure in talking to her mother when she was present, of the violent passion Sir Charles Stanley had for her, and in giving an exaggerated account of the professions[1] he made her.

---

1 Declarations of love.

Sophia did not listen to this sort of discourse with her usual complaisance. Her mind became insensibly more disposed to suspect the sincerity of the baronet's passion for her sister: she grew pensive and melancholy, sought solitude more than ever, and loved reading less.

This change, which her own innocence hid from herself, was quickly perceived by Mr. Herbert, who loved her with a parent's fondness, and thought nothing indifferent[1] which concerned her. He took occasion one day to mention Sir Charles Stanley to her, and asked her opinion of his person and understanding, keeping his eyes fixed upon her at the same time, which disconcerted her so much that she blushed; and though she commended him greatly, yet it was easy to discover that she forbore to say all the good she thought of him, for fear of saying too much.

Mr. Herbert no longer doubted but this dangerous youth had made an impression on the innocent heart of Sophia, which was still ignorant of its own emotions.

He had perceived for some time that Sir Charles had changed the object of his pursuits: his visits now were always short, unless Sophia was in the way: he brought her all the new books and pamphlets that were published which were worth her reading: he adopted the purity and delicacy of her sentiments, declared himself always of the side she espoused: he talked of virtue like a man who loved and practised it, and set all his own good qualities in the fairest light: he presented Harriot from time to time with fashionable trifles, and sent Sophia books enough to furnish out a little library, consisting of the best authors, in English, French, and Italian, all elegantly bound, with proper cases for their reception: he praised whatever she approved, and appeared to have great respect and consideration for Mr. Herbert, because he observed she loved and esteemed him.

That faithful friend of the virtuous Sophia trembled for her danger, when he considered that by this artful management the baronet was strengthening himself every day in her good opinion, and seducing her affections under the appearance of meriting her esteem; yet he did not think it proper to give her even a hint of her situation. A young maid has passed over the first bounds of reservedness, who allows herself to think she is in love.

Mr. Herbert would not familiarize her with so dangerous an idea: he knew her extreme modesty, her solid virtue; he was

---

1 Unimportant.

under no apprehensions that she would ever act unworthy of her character; but a heart so nicely sensible, so delicately tender as hers, he knew must suffer greatly from a disappointed passion; and this was what he wanted to prevent, not by wounding her delicacy with suggesting to her that she was in love, but by preserving her from the secret encroachments of that passion.

He reminded her of the design she had formerly mentioned to him of entering into the service of a lady, and was rejoiced to find that she still continued her resolution. Harriot's natural insolence and ill temper, irritated by the change she now plainly saw in Sir Charles, made home so disagreeable to Sophia, that she wished impatiently for an opportunity of providing for herself, that she might no longer live upon the bounty of her sister, who often insinuated that their mother's annuity was her gift.

Mr. Herbert, who had other reasons besides those urged, for freeing her from so uneasy a dependence, promised to be diligent in his enquiries for something that would suit her.

Neither Mrs. Darnley nor Harriot now opposed this design, which soon came to the knowledge of Sir Charles, who had bribed a servant of the family to give him intelligence of every thing that passed in it.

Impatient to prevent the execution of it, and tortured by the bare apprehension of Sophia's absence, he resolved to break through that constraint he had so long laid upon himself, and acquaint her with his passion.

But it was not easy to find an opportunity of speaking to her alone.[1] At length having contrived to get Harriot engaged to a play, and prevailing upon a maiden kinswoman of his to invite Mrs. Darnley to a party at whist,[2] he went to the house at his usual hour of visiting this little family, and found Sophia at home, and without any company.

Not all the confidence he derived from his rank and fortune, his fine understanding, and those personal graces which gave him but too much merit in the eyes of many women, could hinder him from trembling at the thought of that declaration he was about to make.

---

1 In the eighteenth century, a young man and a young woman meeting alone would have been considered inappropriate. The mere hint of scandal was almost as effective as an actual scandal in ruining a woman's reputation.

2 Whist was a popular card game featuring players separated into teams of two.

As soon as he came into Sophia's presence he was awed, disconcerted, and unable to speak; such was the power of virtue, and such the force of a real passion! Two or three times he resolved to begin; but when he looked upon Sophia, and saw in her charming eyes that sparkling intelligence which displayed the treasures of the soul that animated them; when he observed the sweet severity of her modest countenance, the composed dignity of her behaviour, he durst not own a passion which had views less pure than the perfect creature that inspired it.

His conversation for near an hour was so confused, so disjointed, and interrupted by such frequent musings, that Sophia was amazed, and thought it so disagreeable, and unlike what it used to be, that she was not sorry when he seemed disposed to put an end to his visit.

Sir Charles indeed rose up to be gone, but with so deep a concern in his eyes as increased Sophia's perplexity. She attended him respectfully to the door of the room, when he suddenly turning back, and taking her hand, "Do not hate me," said he, "nor think ill of me, if I tell you that I love and adore you."

Sophia in the utmost confusion at such a speech, disengaged her hand from his, and retiring a few steps back, bent her eyes on the ground, and continued silent.

Sir Charles, emboldened by her confusion, made a tender, and at the same time, respectful declaration of the passion he had long felt for her.

Sophia, not willing to hear him enlarge upon this subject, raised her eyes from the ground; her cheeks were indeed overspread with blushes, but there was a grave composure in her looks that seemed a bad omen to Sir Charles.

"I have hitherto flattered myself, sir," said she, "that you entertained a favourable opinion of me, how happens it then that I see myself to-day exposed to your raillery?"[1]

The baronet was beginning a thousand protestations, but Sophia stopt him short. "If your professions to me are sincere," said she, "what am I to think of those you made to my sister?"

Sir Charles expected this retort, and was the less perplexed by it, as he needed only to follow the dictates of truth to form such an answer as was proper to be given. "I acknowledge," said he, "that I admired your sister, and her beauty made as strong an impression upon me, as mere beauty can make upon a man who

---

1 Ridicule.

has a taste for higher excellencies. I sought Miss Darnley's acquaintance. I was so happy as to do her some little service. I wished to find in her those qualities that were necessary to fix my heart—Pardon my freedom, Miss Sophia, the occasion requires that I should speak freely. Miss Darnley, upon a nearer acquaintance, did not answer the idea[1] I had formed to myself of a woman whom I could love for life; and the professions I made her, as you are pleased to call them, were no more than expressions of gallantry; a sort of homage which beauty, even when it does not touch the heart, exacts from the tongue. My heart was not so easy a conquest—tell me not of raillery, when I declare that none but yourself was ever capable of inspiring me with a real passion."

The arrival of Mr. Herbert proved a grateful interruption to Sophia, in whose innocent breast the tenderness and apparent sincerity of this declaration raised emotions which she knew not how to disguise.

Sir Charles, though grieved at this unseasonable visit, yet withdrew, not wholly despairing of success. He had heedfully observed the changes in Sophia's face while he was speaking, and thought he had reason to hope that he was not indifferent to her. Loving her as he did with excessive tenderness, what pure and unmixed satisfaction would this thought have given him, had he not been conscious that his designs were unworthy of her! The secret upbraidings of his conscience disquieted him amidst all his flattering hopes of success; but custom, prejudice, the insolence of fortune, and the force of example, all conspired to suppress the pleadings of honour and justice in favour of the amiable Sophia, and fixed him in the barbarous resolution of attempting to corrupt that virtue which made her so worthy of his love.

CHAPTER IV

In which Harriot makes a very contemptible Figure.

Mr. Herbert having, as has been already mentioned, interrupted the conversation between Sir Charles and Sophia, was not surprised at the young baronet's abrupt departure, as he seemed preparing to go when he came in; but upon looking at Sophia, he perceived so many signs of confusion and perplexity in her coun-

---

1 I.e., she did not live up to the image.

tenance, that he did not doubt but the discourse which his entrance had put an end to, had been a very interesting one. He waited a moment, in expectation that she would open herself to him; but finding that she continued silent and abashed, he gently took her hand, and looking tenderly upon her, "Tell me, my child," said he, "has not something extraordinary happened, which occasions this confusion I see you in?"

"Sir Charles has indeed been talking to me," replied Sophia blushing, "in a very extraordinary manner, and such as I little expected."

Mr. Herbert pressed her to explain herself, and she gave him an exact account of Sir Charles's discourse to her, without losing a word; so faithful had her memory been to all he had said.

Mr. Herbert listened to her attentively, and found something so like candor and sincerity in the baronet's declaration, that he could not help being pleased with it. He had never indeed judged favourably of his views upon Harriot, but here the case was very different.

Harriot's ignorance, vanity, and eager desire of being admired, exposed her to the attacks of libertinism,[1] and excited presumptuous hopes.

Sophia's good sense, modesty, and virtue, placed her out of the reach of temptation. No one could think it surprising that a man of sense should make the fortune of a woman who would do honour to his choice, and where there was such exalted merit as in Sophia, overlook the disparity of circumstances.[2]

But justly might it be called infatuation and folly, to raise to rank and affluence a woman of Harriot's despicable turn; to make a companion for life of a handsome ideot,[3] who thought the highest excellencies of the female character were to know how to dress, to dance, to sing, to flutter in a drawing-room, or coquet at a play; who mistook pertness for wit, confidence for knowledge, and insolence for dignity.

While he was revolving these thoughts in his mind, Sophia looked earnestly at him, pleased to observe that what the baronet had said seemed worthy his consideration.

---

1 Though philosophically more complex, "libertinism" as a derogatory term usually referred simply to an indulgence in illicit sexual conduct (see also 81 and 113).

2 I.e., overlook the large differences in wealth and class.

3 Eighteenth-century alternate spelling for "idiot."

Mr. Herbert, who read in her looks that she wished to have his advice on this occasion, but would not ask it, lest she should seem to lay any stress upon Sir Charles's declaration, told her it was very possible the baronet was sincere in what he had said to her; that his manner of accounting for his quitting her sister, was both sensible and candid; that she ought not to be surprised at the preference he gave her over Miss Darnley, since she deserved it by the care she had taken to improve her mind, and to acquire qualities which might procure the esteem of all wise and virtuous persons.

He warned her, however, not to trust too much to favourable appearances, nor to suffer her inclinations to be so far engaged by the agreeable person and specious behaviour of Sir Charles Stanley, as to find it painful to renounce him, if he should here-after shew himself unworthy of her good opinion.

He advised her, when he talked to her in the same strain again, to refer him to her mother and to him for an answer; and told her that he would save her the confusion and perplexity of acquaint-ing her mother and sister with what had happened, by taking that task upon himself.

"You will, no doubt," added he, "be exposed to some sallies of ill temper from Miss Darnley, for robbing her of a lover; for envy is more irreconcileable than hatred: but let not your sensibility suffer much on her account; if you deprive her of a lover, you do not deprive her of one she loves: she is too vain, too volatile, and too greedy of general admiration, to be affected with the loss of Sir Charles, any farther than as her pride is wounded by it: and one would imagine she had foreseen this desertion by the pains she has taken about a new conquest lately."

Mr. Herbert was going on, when Mrs. Darnley knocked at the door. Sophia, in extreme agitation, begged him to say nothing concerning Sir Charles that evening. He promised her he would not, and they all three conversed together upon indifferent things, until Harriot returned from the play.

Mr. Herbert then took leave of them, after inviting himself to breakfast the next morning; which threw Sophia into such terror and confusion, that she retired hastily to her own room to conceal her disorder.

Mr. Herbert came the next morning, according to his promise; and Sophia all trembling with her apprehensions retiring imme-diately after breakfast, he entered upon the business that had brought him thither; but sensible that what he had to say would prove extremely mortifying to miss Harriot, he thought it not amiss to sweeten the bitter pill he was preparing for her, by sacrificing a little flattery to her pride.

"You fine ladies," said he, addressing himself to her with a smile, "are never weary of extending your conquests; but you use your power with so much tyranny that it is not surprising some of your slaves should assume courage at last, to break your chains. Do you know, my pretty cousin, that you have lost Sir Charles Stanley; and that he has offered that heart which you no doubt have despised, to your sister Sophia?"

Miss Darnley, who had bridled up at the beginning of this speech, lost all her assumed dignity towards the end of it: her face grew pale and red by turns; she fixed her eyes on the ground, her bosom heaved with the violence of her agitations, and tears, in spite of her, were ready to force their way.

Sir Charles had indeed for a long time discontinued his addresses to her, and had suffered his inclination for her sister to appear plainly enough; but still her vanity suggested to her that this might be all a feint, and acted only with a view to alarm her fears, and oblige her to sacrifice all her other admirers to him.[1]

What Mr. Herbert had said therefore, struck her at first with astonishment and grief; but solicitous to maintain the fancied superiority of her character, she endeavoured to repress her emotions; and taking the hint which he had designedly thrown out to her to save her confusion,

"Sir Charles has acted very wisely," said she, putting on a scornful look, "to quit me who always despised him, for one who has been so little used to have lovers, that she will be ready to run mad with joy at the thoughts of such a conquest; but, after all, she has only my leavings."

Mr. Herbert, though a little shocked at the grossness of her language, replied gravely, "However that may be, Miss, it is certain that he has made a very open, and to all appearance, sincere declaration of love to Miss Sophia, who not knowing how to mention this affair to her mother herself, commissioned me to acquaint her with it, that she may have directions how to behave to Sir Charles, and what to say to him."

"One would have imagined," interrupted Miss Darnley eagerly, "that she who sets up for so much wit, and reads so many books, might have known what to say to him."

---

1 I.e., in order to oblige Harriot to give up her other suitors in favor of Sir Charles.

"Pray, Miss," said Mr. Herbert, "what would you have had her say to Sir Charles?"

"Why truly," replied she, "I think she ought to have told him that he was very impertinent, and have shewn him the door."

"Sure, Harriot," said Mrs. Darnley, who had been silent all this time, "You forget that Sir Charles is our benefactor, and that I am obliged to him for all the little support I have."

"It is not likely I should forget it," retorted Miss Darnley, "since I am the person who am most obliged to him for what he has done; if I mistake not, it was upon my account that he interested himself in our affairs."

"Well, well, Harriot," replied Mrs. Darnley, "I have been told this often enough; but why should you be angry at this prospect of your sister's advancement?"

"I angry at her advancement, madam!" exclaimed Miss Harriot, "not I really: I wish the girl was provided for by a suitable match with all my heart; but as for Sir Charles, I would not have her set her foolish heart upon him; he is only laughing at her."

"It may be so," said Mr. Herbert, "though I think Miss Sophia the last woman in the world whom a man would chuse to laugh at. However, this affair is worth a little consideration—Miss Sophia, madam," pursued he, addressing himself to Mrs. Darnley, "intends to refer Sir Charles entirely to you. You will be the best judge whether the passion he professes is sincere, and his intentions honourable; and I can answer for my young cousin, that she will be wholly governed by your advice, since it is impossible that you can give her any but what is most advantageous to her honour and happiness."

Harriot, no longer able to suppress her rage and envy, was thrown so far off her guard as to burst into tears. "I cannot bear to be thus insulted," cried she; "and I declare if Sir Charles is permitted to go on with his foolery with that vain girl, I will quit the house."

"Was there ever any one so unreasonable as you are, Miss," said Mr. Herbert; "have you not owned that you despised Sir Charles; and if your sister is a vain girl, will she not be sufficiently mortified by accepting your leavings, as you said just now?"

"I am speaking to my mother, sir," replied Harriot, with a contemptuous frown; "depend upon it, Madam," pursued she, "that I will not stay to be sacrificed to Mr. Herbert's favourite—either she shall be forbid to give Sir Charles any encouragement, who after all, is only laughing at her, or I will leave the house."

Saying this, she flung out of the room, leaving her mother divided between grief and anger, and Mr. Herbert motionless with astonishment.

CHAPTER V

Sir Charles, by a proper Degree of Address and Assurance,
extricates himself from a very pressing difficulty.

Mr. Herbert having recovered from the astonishment into which he had been thrown by the strange behaviour of Miss Darnley, endeavoured to comfort her mother, whose weak mind was more disposed to be alarmed at the threat she had uttered upon her quitting the room, than to resent such an insult to parental tenderness.

After gently insinuating to her, that she ought to reduce[1] her eldest daughter to reason, by a proper exertion of her authority, he earnestly recommended to her to be particularly attentive to an affair which concerned the happiness of her youngest child, from whose piety and good sense she might promise herself so much comfort.

He advised her to give Sir Charles Stanley an opportunity of explaining himself to her as soon as possible; and to make him comprehend, that he must not hope for permission to pay his addresses to Sophia, till he had satisfied her that his intentions were such, as she ought to approve.

Mrs. Darnley appeared so docile and complaisant upon this occasion, so ready to take advice, and so fully determined to be directed by it, that Mr. Herbert went away extremely well satisfied with her behaviour, and full of pleasing hopes for his beloved Sophia.

Harriot, in the mean time, was tormenting her sister above stairs:[2] she had entered her room with a heart full of bitterness, and a countenance inflamed with rage, throwing the door after her with such violence, that Sophia letting fall her book, started up in a great terror, and, in a trembling accent, asked what was the matter with her?

Her own apprehensions had indeed already suggested to her the cause of the disorder she appeared to be in, which it was not

---

1 Return, bring back.
2 I.e., upstairs.

easy to discover, in that torrent of reproach and invective with which she strove to overwhelm her. Scornful and unjust reflections upon her person, bitter jests upon her pedantic affectation, and malignant insinuations of hypocrisy, were all thrown out with the utmost incoherence of passion; to which Sophia answered no otherwise than by a provoking serenity of countenance, and the most calm attention.

That she was able to bear with such moderation the cruel insults of her sister, was not more the effect of her natural sweetness of temper, than her good sense and delicate turn of mind. The upper region of the air, says a sensible French writer, admits neither clouds nor tempests; the thunder, storms, and meteors, are formed below: such is the difference between a mean, and an exalted understanding.[1]

Harriot, who did not find her account[2] in this behaviour, sought to rouse her rage by reproaches still more severe, till having ineffectually railed herself out of breath, she aukwardly imitated her sister's composure, folded her hands before her, and seating herself, asked her in a low but solemn tone of voice, whether she would deign to answer her one plain question?

Sophia then resuming her seat, told her with a look of mingled dignity and sweetness, that she was ready to answer her any question, and give her any satisfaction she could desire, provided she would repress those indecent transports of anger, so unbecoming her sex and years.

"Why, you little envious creature," said Harriot, "you do not surely, because you are two or three years younger than I am, pretend to insinuate that I am old?"

"No certainly," replied Sophia, half smiling; "my meaning is, that you are too young to adopt, as you do, all the peevishness of old age; but your question, sister," pursued she—

"Well then," said Harriot, "I ask you, how you have dared to

---

1 The "French writer" Lennox refers to here is probably Roger L'Estrange (1616–1704), who was not actually French but a British journalist. L'Estrange translated many works, including *Seneca's Morals* (1678), from which this quotation is taken. In the original, it reads, "The upper Region of the Air, admits neither Clouds, nor Tempests; The Thunder, Storms, and Meteors, are form'd Below; and this is a Difference betwixt a mean, and an exalted Mind" (8th edn. [London: Bowyer, 1702], 148n.). *Seneca's Morals* was available throughout the eighteenth century in a variety of editions.

2 I.e., who did not find the response she expected.

say that Sir Charles Stanley was tired of me, and preferred you to me?"

"Tired of you!" repeated Sophia, shocked at her coarseness and falshood, "I never was capable of making use of such an expression, nor do I familiarize myself with ideas that need such strange language to convey them."

Harriot, provoked almost to frenzy by this hint, which her indiscreet conduct made but too just, flew down stairs to her mother, and with mingled sobs and exclamations, told her, that Sophia had treated her like an infamous creature,[1] who had dishonoured herself and her family.

Mrs. Darnley, though more favourably disposed towards her youngest daughter, since she had been made acquainted with the baronet's affection for her, yet was on this occasion governed by her habitual preference of Harriot; and sending for Sophia, she reproved her with great asperity for her insolent behaviour to her sister.

Sophia listened with reverence to her mother's reproofs; and after justifying herself, as she easily might, from the accusation her sister had brought against her, she added, that not being willing to be exposed to any farther persecutions on account of Sir Charles Stanley, whose sincerity she thought very doubtful, she was resolved not to wait any longer for a place, such as Mr. Herbert's tenderness was in search of for her, but to accept the first reputable one that offered.

"I have not the vanity, madam," pursued she, "to imagine that a man of rank and fortune can seriously resolve to marry an indigent young woman like me; and although I am humble enough to go to service, I am too proud to listen to the addresses of any man who, from his superiority of fortune, thinks he has a right to keep me in doubt of his intentions, or, in a mean dependance upon a resolution which he has not perhaps regard enough for me to make."

This discourse was not at all relished by Mrs. Darnley, who conceived that many inconveniencies were to be submitted to, for the enjoyment of affluence and pleasure; but Sophia, who had revolved in her mind all the mortifications a young woman is exposed to, whose poverty places her so greatly below her lover; that she is to consider his professions as an honour, and be rejoiced at every indication of his sincerity; her delicacy was so

---

1 I.e., like a whore or other unworthy woman.

much wounded by the bare apprehension of suffering what she thought an indignity to her sex, that she was determined to give Sir Charles Stanley no encouragement, but to pursue her first design of seeking a decent establishment, suitable to the depressed state of her fortune.

Mrs. Darnley, however, combated her resolution with arguments which she supposed absolutely conclusive; and added to them her commands not to think any more of so humiliating a design, which so offended Harriot, that she broke out again into tears, exclamations, and reproaches.

Her mother would have found it a difficult task to have pacified her, had not a message from a lady, inviting her to a concert that evening, obliged her to calm her mind, that her complexion might not suffer from those emotions of rage which she had hitherto taken no pains to repress.

As soon as Harriot retired, to begin the labours of the toilet,[1] Mrs. Darnley, with great mildness, represented to Sophia, that it was her duty to improve the affection Sir Charles expressed for her, since by that means it might be in her power to make her mother and her sister easy in their circumstances, and engage their love for her.

This was attacking Sophia on her weak side; she answered with the softest tenderness of look and accent, "That it was her highest ambition to make them happy."

"Then I do not doubt, my child," said Mrs. Darnley, "but you will employ all your good sense to secure the conquest you have made."

Sophia, melted almost to tears by these tender expressions, to which she had been so little used, assured her mother she would upon this occasion act in such a manner as to deserve her kindness.

Mrs. Darnley would have been better pleased if she had been less reserved, and had appeared more affected with the fine prospect that was opening for her; but it was not possible to press her farther. Nature here had transferred the parent's rights to the child, and the gay, imprudent, ambitious mother, stood awed and abashed in the presence of her worthier daughter.

Sophia, who expected Sir Charles would renew his visit in the evening, past the rest of the day in uneasy perturbations. He entered the house just at the time that Harriot, who had ordered

---

1 I.e., to get dressed and put on make-up.

a chair to be got for her, came fluttering down the stairs in full dress. As soon as she perceived him, her cheeks glowed with resentment; but affecting a careless inattention, she shot by him with a half courtesy, and made towards the door: he followed, and accosting her with a grave but respectful air, desired she would permit him to lead her to her chair. Harriot, conveying all the scorn into her face which the expression of her pretty but unmeaning features were capable of, and rudely drawing away her hand, "Pray, Sir," said she, "carry your *devores*[1] where they will be more acceptable; I am not disposed to be jested with any longer."

Sir Charles, half-smiling, and bowing low, told her, that he respected her too much, as well upon her own account as upon Miss Sophia's, for whom indeed he had the most tender regard, to be guilty of the impertinence she accused him of.

Harriot did not stay to hear more: offended in the highest degree at the manner in which he mentioned Sophia, she darted an angry look at him, and flung herself into her chair.

It must be confessed that Sir Charles discovered upon this occasion a great share of that easy confidence which people are apt to derive from splendid fortunes and undisputed rank; but as he wanted neither good sense, generosity, nor even delicacy, he would have found it difficult to own to a lady whom he had been used to address in the style of a lover, that his heart had received a new impression, if the contemptible character of Harriot had not authorized his desertion of her. Pride, ignorance, folly, and affectation, sink a woman so low in the eyes of men, that they easily dispense with themselves from a strict observance of those delicate attentions, and respectful regards, which the sex in general claim by the laws of politeness, but which sense and discernment never pay to the trifling part of it.

Sir Charles was likewise glad of an opportunity to shew Miss Darnley, that he did not think the little gallantry which had passed between them, entitled her to make him any reproaches; or to consider the passion he professed for her sister as an infidelity to her; and now finding himself more at ease from the frank acknowledgement he had made, he sent up his name,[2] and was received by Mrs. Darnley with all the officious civility she was used to shew him.

---

1 French: service, duty.
2 The common practice of visiting in the eighteenth century—one of the middle class's major pastimes—was to announce one's presence through a servant with a card and wait to be invited into the house.

Sophia was in the room, and rose up at his entrance in a sweet confusion, which she endeavoured to conceal, by appearing extremely busy at a piece of needle-work.[1]

Sir Charles, after some trifling conversation with her mother, approached her, and complimented her with an easy air upon her being so usefully employed, when most other young ladies were abroad in search of amusement.

Sophia, who was now a little recovered, answered him with that wit and vivacity which was so natural to her; but looking up at the same time, she saw his eyes fixed upon her with a look so tender and passionate, as threw her back into all her former confusion, which encreased every moment by the consciousness that it was plain to his observation.

The young baronet, though he was charmed with her amiable modesty, yet endeavoured to relieve the concern he saw her under, by talking of indifferent matters, till Mrs. Darnley seeing them engaged in discourse, prudently withdrew, when he instantly addressed her in language more tender and particular.

Sophia, shocked at her mother's indiscretion,[2] and at his taking advantage of it so abruptly, let all the weight of her resentment fall on him; and the poor lover was so awed by her frowns, and the sarcastic raillery which she mingled with expressions that shewed the most invincible indifference, that not daring to continue a discourse which offended her, and in too great concern to introduce another subject, he stood fixed in silence for several minutes, leaning on the back of her chair, while she plied her needle with the most earnest attention, and felt her confusion decrease in proportion as his became more apparent.

At length he walked slowly to the other end of the room, and taking up a new book which he had sent her a few days before, he asked her opinion of it in a faultering accent; and was extremely mortified to find she was so much at ease, as to answer him with all the readiness of wit and clearness of judgment imaginable.

Another pause of silence ensued, during which Sophia heard

---

1 Needle-work was one of the few ways women of some social standing could earn money, but it was not a lucrative profession.

2 Sophia calls her mother's absenting herself an "indiscretion": unmarried men and women were not supposed to be alone in each other's company. Sir Charles, for his part, demonstrates his inattention to proper etiquette because he does not leave when he finds himself alone with Sophia.

him sigh softly several times, while he turned over the leaves of the book with such rapidity as shewed he scarce read a single line in any page of it.

He was thus employed when Mrs. Darnley returned, who stood staring first at one, then at the other, strangely perplexed at their looks and silence, and apprehensive that all was not right. Sophia now took an opportunity to retire, and met an angry glance from her mother as she passed by her.

Her departure roused Sir Charles out of his revery, he looked after her, and then turning to Mrs. Darnley, overcame his discontent so far as to be able to entertain her a quarter of an hour with his usual politeness; and finding Sophia did not appear again he took his leave.

As soon as he was gone Mrs. Darnley called her daughter, and chid her severely for her rudeness in leaving the baronet.

Sophia defended herself as well as she could, without owning the true cause of her disgust, which was her mother's so officiously quitting the room; but Mrs. Darnley was so ill satisfied with her behaviour, that she complained of it to her friend Mr. Herbert, who came in soon afterwards, telling him that Sophia's pride and ill temper would be the ruin of her fortune.

The good man having heard the story but one way, thought Sophia a little to blame, till having an opportunity to discourse with her freely, he found the fault she had been charged with was no more than an excess of delicacy, which was very pardonable in her situation: he warned her, however, not to admit too readily apprehensions injurious to herself, which was in some degree debasing the dignity of her sex and character; but to make the baronet comprehend that esteeming him as a man of honour, she considered his professions of regard to her as a claim upon her gratitude; and that, in consequence, she should without any reluctance receive the commands of her mother, and the advice of her friends in his favour.

CHAPTER VI
Sophia entertains Hopes, and becomes more unhappy.

Poor Sophia found herself but too well disposed to think favourably of Sir Charles; her tenderness had suffered greatly by the force she had put upon herself to behave to him in so disobliging a manner, and the uneasiness she saw him under, his silence, and confusion, and the sighs that escaped him, apparently without design, had affected her sensibly, and several days passing away without his appearing again, she concluded he was irrecoverably prejudiced against her; the uneasiness this thought gave her, first hinted to herself the impression he had already made on her heart.

Sir Charles indeed had been so much piqued by her behaviour as to form the resolution of seeing her no more; but when he supposed himself most capable of persisting in this resolution, he was nearest breaking through it, and suddenly yielding to the impulse of his tenderness, he flew to her again more passionate than ever; this little absence having only served to shew him how necessary she was to his happiness. When Sophia saw him enter the room, the agitations of her mind might be easily read in her artless countenance; a sentiment of joy for his return gave new fire to her eyes, and vivacity to her whole person; while a consciousness of the effect his presence produced, and a painful doubt of his sincerity, and the rectitude of his intentions, alternately dyed her cheeks with blushes and paleness.

The young baronet approached her trembling; but the unexpected softness with which she received him, increasing at once his passion and his hopes, he poured out his whole soul in the tenderest and most ardent professions of love, esteem, and admiration of her.

Sophia listened to him with a complaisant attention; and having had sufficient time, while he was speaking, to compose and recollect herself, she told him in a modest but firm accent, that she was obliged to him for the favourable opinion he entertained of her; but that she did not think herself at liberty to hear, much less to answer to such discourse as he had thought proper to address to her, till she had the sanction of her mother's consent, and Mr. Herbert's approbation, whose truly parental regard for her, made her look upon him as another father, who supplied the place of him she had lost.

Sir Charles, more charmed with her than ever, was ready in his present flow of tender sentiments for her, to offer her his hand with an unreservedness that would have satisfied all her delicate scruples; but carried away by the force of habit, an insurmountable aversion to marriage, and the false but strongly impressed notion of refinements in an union of hearts, where love was the only tye, he could not resolve to give her a proof of his affection, which in his opinion was the likeliest way to destroy all the ardor of it; but careful not to alarm her, and apprehending no great severity of morals from the gay interested mother, he politely thanked her for the liberty she gave him to make his passion known to Mrs. Darnley, and to solicit her consent to his happiness.

Sophia observed with some concern, that he affected to take no notice of Mr. Herbert upon this occasion; but she would not allow herself to dwell long upon a thought so capable of raising doubts injurious to his honour; and satisfied with the frankness of his proceeding thus far, she suffered no marks of discontent or apprehension to appear in her countenance and behaviour.

Sir Charles did not fail to make such a general declaration of his sentiments to Mrs. Darnley as he thought sufficient to satisfy Sophia, without obliging himself to be more explicit; and in the mean time, having acquired a thorough knowledge of Mrs. Darnley's character, he sought to engage her in his interest by a boundless liberality, and by gratifying all those passions which make corruption easy. She loved dissipation; and all the pleasures and amusements that inventive luxury had found out to vary the short scene of life were at her command; she had a high taste for the pleasures of the table, and therefore the most expensive wines, and choicest delicacies that earth, sea, and air could afford, were constantly supplied by him in the greatest profusion. No day ever passed without her receiving some considerable present, the value of which was inhanced by the delicacy with which it was made.

The innocent Sophia construed all this munificence into proofs of the sincerity of his affection for her; for the young baronet, whether awed by the dignity of her virtue, or that he judged it necessary to secure the success of his designs, mingled with the ardor of his professions a behaviour so respectful and delicate, as removed all her apprehensions, and left her whole soul free to all the tender impressions a lively gratitude could make on it.

Mr. Herbert, however, easily penetrated into Sir Charles's views; he saw with pain the progress he made every day in the affection of Sophia; but, by the speciousness of his conduct, he had established himself so firmly in her good opinion, that he judged any attempt to alarm her fears, while there seemed so little foundation for them, would miss its effect; and not doubting but ere it was long her own observation would furnish her with some cause for apprehension, he contented himself for the present with keeping a vigilant eye upon the conduct of Sir Charles and Mrs. Darnley, and with being ready to assist Sophia in her perplexities, whenever she had recourse to him.

The change there was now in the situation of this amiable girl, afforded him many opportunities of admiring the excellence of her character: she who formerly used to be treated with neglect and even harshness by her mother, was now distinguished with peculiar regard; her opinion always submitted to with deference, her inclinations consulted in all things, and a studious endeavour to please her was to be seen in every word and action of Mrs. Darnley's, who affected to be as partially fond of her as she had once been of her sister.

Even the haughty insolent Harriot, keeping her rage and envy concealed in her own breast, condescended to wear the appearance of kindness to her, while she shared with her mother in all those gratifications which the lavish generosity of Sir Charles procured them, and which Sophia, still continuing her usual simplicity of life, could never be persuaded to partake of. Yet all this produced no alteration in Sophia; the same modesty and humility, the same sweetness of temper, and attention to oblige, distinguished her now as in her days of oppression.

Mr. Herbert contemplated her with admiration and delight, and often with astonishment reflected upon the infatuation of Sir Charles, who could allow himself to be so far governed by fashionable prejudices, and a libertine turn of mind, as to balance one moment whether he should give himself a lawful claim to the affections of such a woman.[1]

Affairs continued in this state during three months, when the good old man, who watched over his young favourite with all the pious solicitude of her guardian angel, perceived she was grown more melancholy and reserved than usual; he often heard her sigh, and fancied she had been weeping, and her fine eyes would appear sometimes suffused with tears, even when she endeavoured to appear most chearful.

He imagined that she had something upon her mind which she wished to disclose to him; her looks seemed to intimate as much, and she frequently sought opportunities of being alone with him, and engaged him to pass those evenings with her, when her mother and sister were at any of the public entertainments. Yet all those times, though her heart seemed labouring with some secret uneasiness which she would fain impart to him,[2] she had not resolution enough to enter into any explanation.

Mr. Herbert, who could have wished she had been more com-

---

1 Sir Charles can only have "a lawful claim" if he and Sophia are married.
2 I.e., she would really like to tell him.

municative, resolved at length to spare her any farther struggles with herself; and one day when he was alone with her, taking occasion to observe that she was not so chearful as usual, he asked her tenderly if any thing had happened to give her uneasiness; "Speak freely my child," said he to her, "and think you are speaking to a father."

Sophia made no other answer at first than by bursting into tears, which seeming to relieve her a little, she raised her head, and looking upon the good man, who beheld her with a fixed attention, "May I hope, sir," said she, "that you are still disposed to fulfil the kind promise you once made me—Oh take me from hence," pursued she, relapsing into a new passion of tears, "place me in the situation to which my humble lot has called me; save me from the weakness of my own heart—I now see plainly the delusion into which I have fallen; but, alas! my mother does not see it—every thing here conspires against my peace."

CHAPTER VII
Sophia takes a very extraordinary resolution.
Mr. Herbert encourages her in it.

Sophia, as if afraid she had said too much, stopped abruptly, and, fixing her eyes on the ground, continued silent, and lost in thought.

Mr. Herbert, who had well considered the purport of her words, passed over what he thought would give her too much pain to be explicit upon, and answered in great concern, "Then my fears are true! Sir Charles is not disposed to act like a man of honour."

A sudden blush glowed in the cheeks of Sophia at the mention of Sir Charles's name; but it was not a blush of softness and confusion. Anger and disdain took the place of that sweet complacency, which was the usual expression of her countenance, and with a voice somewhat raised, she replied eagerly,

"Sir Charles I believe has deceived me; but him I can despise—Yet do not imagine, Sir, that he has dared to insult me by any unworthy proposals: if he has any unjustifiable views upon me, he has not had presumption enough to make me acquainted with them, otherwise than by neglecting to convince me that they are honourable; but he practices upon the easy credulity of my mother. He lays snares for her gratitude by an interested generosity, as I now too plainly perceive; and he has the art to make her so much his friend, that she will not listen to any thing I say, which implies the least doubt of his honour."

Mr. Herbert sighed, and cast down his eyes. Sophia continued in great emotion: "It is impossible for me, Sir, to make you comprehend all the difficulties of my situation. A man who takes every form to ensnare my affections, but none to convince my judgment, importunes me continually with declarations of tenderness, and complaints of my coldness and indifference: what can I do? what ought I to answer to such discourse? In this perplexity, why will not my mother come to my assistance? her years, her authority as a parent, give her a right to require such an explanation from Sir Charles as may free me from doubts, which although reason suggests, delicacy permits me not to make appear; but such is my misfortune, that I cannot persuade my mother there is the least foundation for my fears. She is obstinate in her good opinion of Sir Charles; and I am reduced to the sad necessity of either acting in open contradiction to her sentiments and commands, or of continuing in a state of humiliating suspence, to which my character must at last fall a sacrifice."

"That, my dear child," interrupted Mr. Herbert, "is a point which ought to be considered. I would not mention it to you first; but since your own good sense has led the way to it, I will frankly own that I am afraid, innocent and good as you are, the censures of the world will not spare you, if you continue to receive Sir Charles's visits, doubtful as his intentions now appear to every one: I know Mrs. Darnley judges of the sincerity of his professions to you, by the generosity he has shewn in the presents he has heaped upon her:—but, my dear child, that generosity was always suspected by me."

"I confess," said Sophia, blushing, "I once thought favourably of him, for the attention he shewed to make my mother's life easy; but if his liberality to her be indeed, as you seem to think, a snare, what opinion ought I to form of his motives for a late offer he has made her, and which at first dazzled me, so noble and so disinterested did it appear!"

"I know no offer but one," interrupted Mr. Herbert hastily, "which you ought even to have listened to."

"Then the secret admonitions of my heart were right!" cried Sophia with an accent that at once expressed exultation and grief.

"But what was this offer, child?" said Mr. Herbert, "I am impatient to know it."

"I will tell you the whole affair as it happened," resumed

Sophia; "but you must not be surprised, that my mother was pleased with Sir Charles's offer. He has been her benefactor, and has a claim to her regard: it would be strange if she had not a good opinion of him. You know what that celebrated divine says, whose writings you have made me acquainted with: *Charity itself commands us where we know no ill, to think well of all; but friendship, that goes always a pitch higher, gives a man a peculiar right and claim to the good opinion of his friend.*[1] My mother may be mistaken in the judgment she has formed of Sir Charles; but it is her friendship for him, a friendship founded upon gratitude for the good offices he has done her, that has given rise to this mistake."

Sophia, in her eagerness to justify her mother, forgot that she had raised Mr. Herbert's curiosity, and left it unsatisfied; and the good old man, charmed with the filial tenderness she shewed upon this occasion, listened to her with complacency, though not with conviction. At length she suddenly recollected herself, and entered upon her story; but a certain hesitation in her speech, accompanied with a bashful air that made her withdraw her eyes from him, to fix them upon the ground, intimated plainly enough her own sentiments of the affair she was going to acquaint him with.

"You know, Sir," said she, "Sir Charles has had a fit of illness lately, which alarmed all his friends. My mother was particularly attentive to him upon this occasion, and I believe he was sensibly affected with her kind concern for him. When he recovered, he begged my mother, my sister, and myself, would accompany him in a little excursion to Hampstead[2] to take the air. We dined there, and returning home early in the evening, as we passed through Brook-street,[3] he ordered the coach to stop at the door

---

1   Robert South (1634–1716), *Twelve Sermons Preached Upon Several Occasions: The Second Volume* (London: Bennet, 1694), 57. South was a preacher at the court of Charles II. His sermons were popular throughout the eighteenth century and were republished several times.

2   Today, Hampstead Heath is part of Greater London; in the eighteenth century, it was a popular destination for short trips north of the city. By the 1750s, Hampstead was a popular village and even began to have an intellectual community.

3   There were several Brook Streets in eighteenth-century London, but Lennox was probably referring to Brook Street in Holborn in northern London rather than Brook Street off Grosvenor Square, which would have been too fashionable for a mistress and too far to the east of London.

of a very genteel house, which appeared to be newly painted and fitted up. Sir Charles desired us to go in with him and look at it, and give him our opinion of the furniture. Nothing could be more elegant and genteel, and we told him so; at which he appeared extremely pleased, for all had been done, he said, according to his directions.

"He came home with us, and drank tea; after which he had a private conversation with my mother, which lasted about a quarter of an hour; and when they returned to the room where they had left my sister and I, Sir Charles appeared to me to have an unusual thoughtfulness in his countenance, and my mother looked as if she had been weeping; yet there was at the same time, an expression of satisfaction in her face.

"He went away immediately, when my mother, eager to give vent to the emotions which filled her heart, exclaimed, 'Oh, Sophia, how much are you obliged to the generous affection of that man!'

"You may imagine, Sir," pursued Sophia, in a sweet confusion, "that I was greatly affected with these words. I begged my mother to explain herself. 'Sir Charles,' said she, 'has made you a present of that house which we went to view this afternoon; and here,' added she, giving me a paper, 'is a deed by which he has settled three hundred pounds a year upon you.'

"I was silent, so was my sister, who looked at me as if impatient to know my thoughts of this extraordinary generosity. My thoughts indeed were so perplexed, my notions of this manner of acting so confused and uncertain, that I knew not what to say. My mother told us Sir Charles had declared to her, that his late illness had given him occasion for many uneasy reflections upon my account; that he shuddered with horror when he considered the unhappy state of my fortune, and to what difficulties I should have been exposed if he had died; and that, for the satisfaction of his own mind, he had made that settlement upon me, that whatever happened I might be out of the reach of necessity.

"I am afraid, Sir," pursued Sophia with a little confusion in her countenance, "that you will condemn me when I tell you I was so struck at first with the seeming candor and tenderness of Sir Charles's motives for this act of generosity, that none but the most grateful sentiments rose in my mind."

"No, my dear," replied Mr. Herbert, "I do not condemn you: this snare was artfully laid; but when was it that your heart, or rather your reason, gave you those secret admonitions you spoke of?"

"Immediately," said Sophia: "a moment's reflection upon the conduct of Sir Charles served to shew me that some latent design lay concealed under this specious offer; but I am obliged to my sister for giving me a more distinct notion of it than my own confused ideas could furnish me with."

"Then you desired to know her opinion," said Mr. Herbert.

"Certainly," resumed Sophia, "this conversation passed in her presence, and as my elder sister she had a right to be consulted."

"Pray what did she say?" asked Mr. Herbert impatiently.

"You know, Sir," said Sophia, with a gentle smile, "my sister takes every opportunity to rally me about my pretensions to wit: she told me it was a great condescension in me, who thought myself wiser than all the world besides, to ask her advice upon this occasion; and that she would not expose herself to my contempt, by declaring her opinion, any farther than that she supposed Sir Charles did not consider this as a marriage-settlement.

"These last words," pursued Sophia, whose face was now covered with a deeper blush, "let in so much light upon my mind, that I was ashamed and angry with myself for having doubted a moment of Sir Charles's insincerity. I thanked my sister, and told her she should see that I would profit by the hint she had given me."

"I wish," interrupted Mr. Herbert, "that she may profit as much by you: but people of good understanding learn more from the ignorant than the ignorant do from them, because the wise avoid the follies of fools, but fools will not follow the example of the wise: but what did Mrs. Darnley say to this?"

"I never saw her so angry with my sister before," replied Sophia: "she said several severe things to her, which made her leave the room in great emotion; and when we were alone, I endeavoured to convince my mother that it was not fit I should make myself a dependant upon Sir Charles, by accepting such considerable presents: she was, however, of a different opinion, because Sir Charles's behaviour had been always respectful in the highest degree to me, and because the manner in which he made this offer, left no room to suspect that he had any other design in it but to secure a provision for me, in case any thing should happen to him."

"Your mother imposes upon herself,"[1] replied Mr. Herbert; "but I hope, my dear child, you think more justly."

---

1 I.e., she deceives herself.

"You may judge of my sentiments, Sir," answered Sophia, "by the resolution I have taken: I wished to consult you; but as I had no opportunity for it, I satisfied myself with doing what I thought you would approve. My mother, prest by my arguments, told me in a peevish way that I might act as I thought proper: upon which I retired, and, satisfied with this permission, I enclosed the settlement in a cover directed to Sir Charles. I had just sealed it, and was going to send it away, when my mother came into my room: I perceived she was desirous to renew the conversation about Sir Charles; but I carefully avoided it, for fear she should retract the permission she had given me to act as I pleased upon this occasion. My reserve piqued her so much, that she forbore to enter upon the subject again; but as I had no opportunity of sending any letter[1] that night without her knowledge, I was obliged to go to bed much richer than I desired to be; and the next morning, when we were at breakfast, a letter was brought me from Sir Charles, dated four o'clock, in which he informed me that he was just setting out in a post-chaise for Bath.[2] His uncle, who lies there at the point of death, has it seems earnestly desired to see him, and the messenger told him he had not a minute to lose."

"I am sorry," interrupted Mr. Herbert, "that he did not get your letter before he went."

Sophia then taking it out of her pocket, gave it to him, and begged he would contrive some way to have it safely delivered to Sir Charles; "and now," added she, "my heart is easy on that side, and I have nothing to do but to arm myself with fortitude to bear the tender reproaches of a mother, whose anxiety for my interest makes her see this affair in a very different light from that in which you and I behold it."

Mr. Herbert put the letter carefully into his pocket-book,[3] and promised her it should be conveyed to Sir Charles; then taking

---

1 Mailing letters was a rather haphazard and expensive affair in the first half of the eighteenth century, unless individuals were rich enough (like Sir Charles) to send their own servants. A letter within London cost at least 3d., and it could take up to two days for mail from London to arrive in Bath via post-boy, if it arrived at all.

2 Bath was the most important spa in England because of its mineral waters. Since many ailing people bathed in the same water, it was quite possibly unhygienic and/or ineffective, but Britons believed that the waters had salutary effects. Bath was also a popular social venue.

3 Small paper book carried in one's pocket, usually for jotting down notes.

her hand, which he pressed affectionately, "You have another sacrifice yet to make, my dear good child," said he, "and I hope it will not cost you much to make it. You must resolve to see Sir Charles no more: it is not fit you should receive his visits, since you suspect his designs are not honourable, and you have but too much cause for suspicion. It is not enough to be virtuous: we must appear so likewise; we owe the world a good example, the world, which oftener rewards the appearances of merit, than merit itself. It will be impossible for you to avoid seeing Sir Charles sometimes, if you continue with your mother: you have no authority to forbid his visits here; and whether you share them or not, they will be all placed to your account. Are you willing, Miss Sophia, to go into the country, and I will board you in the family of a worthy clergyman, who is my friend? His wife and daughters will be agreeable companions for you; you will find books enough in his study to employ those hours which you devote to reading, and his conversation will be always a source of instruction and delight."

Sophia, with tears in her eyes, and a look so expressive that it conveyed a stronger idea of the grateful sentiments which filled her heart, than any words could do, thanked the good old man for his generous offer, and told him she was ready to leave London whenever he pleased: but unwilling to be an incumbrance upon his little fortune, she intreated him to be diligent in his enquiries for a place for her, that she might early inure herself to the humble condition which Providence thought fit to allot for her.

Mr. Herbert, entering into her delicate scruples, promised to procure her a proper establishment; and it was agreed between them that he should acquaint her mother the next day with the resolution she had taken, and endeavour to procure her consent to it.

CHAPTER VIII

Mr. Herbert and Sophia carry their Point with great Difficulty.

Mr. Herbert well knew all the difficulties of this task, and prepared himself to sustain the storm which he expected would fall upon him. He visited Mrs. Darnley in the morning, and finding her alone, entered at once into the affair, by telling her that he had performed the commission Miss Sophia had given him; that a friend of his who was going to Bath would take care to deliver her letter to her unworthy lover, who, added he, will be convinced, by her returning his settlement, that she has a just notion of his base designs, and despises him as well for his falshood and presumption, as for the mean opinion he has entertained of her.

The old gentleman, who was perfectly well acquainted with Mrs. Darnley's character, and had studied his part, would not give her time to recover from the astonishment his first words had thrown her into, which was strongly impressed upon her countenance, and which seemed to deprive her of the power of speech; but added, with an air natural enough, "Your conduct, Mrs. Darnley, deserves the highest praises; indeed I know not which to admire most, your disinterestedness, prudence, and judgment; or Miss Sophia's ready obedience, and the noble sacrifice she makes to her honour and reputation. You knew her virtue might be securely depended upon, and you permitted her to act as she thought proper with regard to the insidious offer Sir Charles made her: thus, by transferring all the merit of a refusal to her, you reflect a double lustre upon your own, and she has fully answered your intentions by rejecting that offer with the contempt it deserved."

While Mr. Herbert went on in this strain, Mrs. Darnley insensibly forgot her resentment; her features assumed all that complacency which gratified vanity and self-applause could impress upon them: and although she was conscious her sentiments were very different from those which Mr. Herbert attributed to her, yet, as she had really spoke those words to Sophia which had given her a pretence to act as she had done, she concluded his praises were sincere, and enjoyed them as much as if she had deserved them.

It was her business now, however vexed at her daughter's folly, as she conceived it, to seem highly satisfied with her conduct, since what she had done could not be recalled; yet inwardly fretting at the loss of so noble a present, all her dissimulation could not hinder her from saying, that although she approved of Sophia's refusal, yet she could not help thinking she had been very precipitate, and that she ought to have waited till Sir Charles returned; and not have sent, but have given him back his settlement.

Mr. Herbert, without answering to that point, told her, that what now remained for her prudence to do was, to take away all foundation for slander, by peremptorily forbidding Sir Charles's future visits; (here Mrs. Darnley began to frown) "for since it is plain to us all, madam," pursued he, without seeming to perceive her emotion, "that marriage is not his intention, by being allowed to continue his addresses, miss Sophia's character will suffer greatly in the opinion of the world; and the wisdom and discretion by which you have hitherto been governed in this affair, will not secure you from very unfavourable censures. To shew therefore how much you are in earnest to prevent them, I think it is absolutely necessary that you should send your daughter out of this man's way."

Mrs. Darnley, who thought she had an unanswerable objection to make to this scheme, interrupted him eagerly, "You know my circumstances, Mr. Herbert, you know I cannot afford to send my daughter from me; how am I to dispose of her, pray?"

"Let not that care trouble you, madam," replied Mr. Herbert, "I will take all this expence upon myself: I love Miss Sophia as well as if she was my own child; and slender as my income is, I will be at the charge of her maintenance till fortune and her own merit place her in a better situation."

Mr. Herbert then acquainted her with the name and character of the clergyman in whose family he intended to place Sophia: he added, that the village to which she was going being at no great distance, she might hear from her frequently, and sometimes visit her, without much expence or inconvenience.

Mrs. Darnley having nothing that was reasonable to oppose to these kind and generous offers, had recourse to rage and exclamation. She told Mr. Herbert that he had no right to interpose in the affairs of her family; that he should not dispose of her daughter as he pleased; that she would exert the authority of a parent, and no officious meddler should rob her of her child.

Mr. Herbert now found it necessary to change his method with this interested mother. "Take care, madam," said he, with a severe look, "how far you carry your opposition in this case: the world has its eyes upon your conduct; do not give it reason to say that your daughter is more prudent and cautious than you are; nor force her to do that without your consent which you ought to be the first to advise her to."

"Without my consent!" replied Mrs. Darnley, almost breathless with rage; "will she go without my consent, say you; have you alienated her affections from me so far? I will soon know that."

Then rising with a furious air, she called Sophia, who came into the room, trembling, and in the utmost agitation. The melancholy that appeared in her countenance, the paleness and disorder, the consequences of a sleepless night, which she had passed in various and afflicting thoughts, made Mr. Herbert apprehensive that her mother's obstinacy would prove too hard for her gentle disposition; and that her heart, thus assaulted with the most powerful of all passions, love and filial tenderness, would insensibly[1] betray her into a consent to stay.

Mrs. Darnley giving her a look of indignation, exclaimed with the sarcastic severity with which she used formerly to treat her; "So my wise, my dutiful daughter! you cannot bear, it seems, to live with your mother; you are resolved to run away from me, are you?"

"Madam," replied Sophia, with a firmness that disconcerted Mrs. Darnley, as much as it pleasingly surprised Mr. Herbert, "it is not you I am running away from, as you unkindly say, I am going into the country to free myself from the pursuits of a man who has imposed upon your goodness, and my credulity; one who I am convinced, seeks my dishonour, and whose ensnaring addresses have already, I am afraid, given a wound to my reputation, which nothing but the resolution I have taken to avoid him can heal."

Poor Sophia, who had with difficulty prevailed over her own softness to speak in this determined manner, could not bear to see the confusion into which her answer had thrown her mother; but sighing deeply, she retired towards the window, and wiped away the tears that fell from her charming eyes.

Mrs. Darnley, who observed her emotion, and well knew how to take advantage of that amiable weakness in her temper, which made any opposition, however just and necessary, painful to her, desired Mr. Herbert to leave her alone with her daughter, adding that his presence was a constraint upon them both.

Sophia, hearing this, and dreading lest he should leave her to sustain the storm alone, went towards her mother, and with the most persuasive look and accent, begged her not to part in anger from Mr. Herbert.

"I cannot forgive Mr. Herbert," said Mrs. Darnley, "for supposing I am less concerned for your honour than he is. I see no necessity for your going into the country; your reputation is safe while you are under my care; it is time enough to send you out of Sir Charles's way when we are convinced his designs are not honourable. Mr. Herbert, by filling your head with groundless apprehensions, will be the ruin of your fortune."

---

1 Against common sense.

"Sir Charles's dissembled affection for me," interrupted Sophia, "will be the ruin of my character. There is no way to convince the world that I am not the willing dupe of his artifices, but by flying from him as far as I can: do not, my dear mamma," pursued she, bursting into tears, "oppose my going; my peace of mind, my reputation depend on it."

"You shall go when I think proper," replied Mrs. Darnley; "and as for you, Sir," turning to Mr. Herbert, "I desire you will not interpose any farther in this matter."

"Indeed I must, madam," said the good old man, encouraged by a look Sophia gave him; "I consider myself as guardian to your daughter, and in that quality I pretend to some right to regulate her conduct on an occasion which requires a guardian's care and authority."

"Ridiculous!" exclaimed Mrs. Darnley, with a malignant sneer, "what a jest! to call yourself guardian to a girl who has not a shilling to depend upon."[1]

"I am the guardian of her honour and reputation," said Mr. Herbert: "these make up her fortune: and with these she is richer than if she possessed thousands without them."

"And do you, Miss," said Mrs. Darnley to her daughter, with a scornful air, "do you allow this foolish claim? Are you this gentleman's ward, pray?"

"Come, madam," said Mr. Herbert, willing to spare Sophia the pain of answering her question, "be persuaded that I have the tenderness of a parent, as well as guardian, for your daughter: it is absolutely necessary she should see Sir Charles no more; and the most effectual method she can take to shun him, and to preserve her character, is to leave a place where she will be continually exposed to his importunity. I hope she will be able to procure your consent to her going tomorrow. I shall be here in the morning with a post-chaise, and will conduct her myself to the house of my friend, whom I have already prepared by a letter to receive her."

Mr. Herbert, without waiting for any answer, bowed and left the room. Sophia followed him to the door, and by a speaking glance assured him he might depend upon her perseverance.

---

1 Mrs. Darnley is mocking Mr. Herbert: usually, guardians would be put in place to watch over young men and women until they reached their majority, at which point they would inherit a fortune. But of course there is no money waiting for Sophia.

CHAPTER IX
In which Sophia shews less of the Heroine than the Woman.

As soon as Mr. Herbert went away, Harriot, who had been listening, and had heard all that past, entered the room. The virtue and strength of mind her sister shewed in the design she had formed of flying from Sir Charles Stanley excited her envy; and she would have joined with her mother in endeavouring to prevail upon her to stay, to prevent the superiority such a conduct gave her, had not that envy found a more sensible gratification in the thought that Sophia would no longer receive the adorations of the young baronet; and that all her towering hopes would be changed to disappointment and grief.

The discontinuance of those presents which Sir Charles so liberally bestowed on them, evidently on Sophia's account, and which had hitherto enabled them to live in affluence, affected her but little; for vanity is a more powerful passion than interest in the heart of a coquet; and the pleasure of seeing her sister mortified and deserted by her lover, outweighed all other considerations: besides, she was not without hopes that when Sophia was out of the way, her own charms would regain all their former influence over the heart of Sir Charles.

She came prepared, therefore, to support her in her resolution of going into the country; but Mrs. Darnley, who did not enter into her views, and who had no other attention but to secure to herself that ease and affluence she at present enjoyed, expected Harriot would use her utmost efforts to prevent her sister from disobliging a man whose liberality was the source of their happiness.

She complained to her in a tender manner of Sophia's unkindness; she exaggerated the ill consequences that might be apprehended from the affront she put on Sir Charles, by thus avowing the most injurious suspicions of him; and declared she expected nothing less than to be reduced by the loss of her pension to that state of misery from which he had formerly relieved her.

Sophia melted into tears at these words; but a moment's reflection convinced her, that her mother's apprehensions were altogether groundless: Sir Charles was not capable of so mean a revenge; and Sophia, on this occasion, defended him with so much ardor, that Miss Darnley could not help indulging her malice, by throwing out some severe sarcasms upon the violence of her affection for a man whom she affected to despise.

Sophia blushed; but answered calmly, "Well, sister, if I love Sir Charles Stanley, I have the more merit for leaving him."

"Oh, not a bit the more for that," replied Harriot; "for, as I read in one of your books just now, *Virtue would not go so far, if pride did not bear her company.*"[1]

"You might also have read, sister," said Sophia, "that no woman is envious of another's virtue who is conscious of her own."[2]

This retort threw Harriot into so violent a rage, that Sophia, who knew what excesses she was capable of, left the room, and retired to pack up her cloaths, that she might be ready when Mr. Herbert called for her.

In this employment Mrs. Darnley gave her no interruption; for Harriot having quitted her mother in a huff, because she did not join with her against Sophia, she was left at liberty to pursue her own reflections. After long doubt and perplexity in what manner to act, she resolved to consent that Sophia should depart; for she saw plainly that it would not be in her power to prevent it, and she was willing to derive some merit from the necessity she was under of complying. She considered that if Sir Charles really loved her daughter, her flight on such motives would rather increase than lessen his passion; and that all his resentment for being deprived of her sight would fall upon Mr. Herbert, who alone was in fault.

Mrs. Darnley, as has been observed before, was not of a temper to anticipate misfortunes, or to give herself much uneasi-

---

1   Actually, the sentence in the *Moral Maxims* (1665) by François VI, Duke de la Rochefoucauld (1613–80) reads, "Virtue would not go so far, if Vanity did not bear her Company." Rochefoucauld's book was translated into English for the first time in 1694 and remained available throughout the eighteenth century in many editions, but Lennox quotes directly from John Exshaw's version. Harriot's misquotation points to her own blind spot: her vanity.

2   This quotation is a gender-specific adaptation of a sentence in *The History of the Life of Marcus Tullius Cicero*, 2 vols. (London: Printed for the Author, 1741) by Conyers Middleton (1683–1750). The original quotation reads, "*no man could be envious of another's virtue, who was conscious of his own*" (2:515). Middleton's work was quite popular in the eighteenth century. By the time Lennox was writing *Sophia*, six editions had appeared, and another three were published before the end of the century.

ness about evils in futurity: she always hoped the best, not because she had any well-grounded reasons for it, but because it was much more pleasing to hope than to fear.

Sophia, when she saw her next, found her surprisingly altered: she not only no longer opposed her departure, but even seemed desirous of it; and this she thought a master-piece of cunning which could not fail of gaining Mr. Herbert's good opinion; never once reflecting that her former opposition deprived her of all the merit of a voluntary compliance.

This change in Mrs. Darnley left Sophia no more difficulties to encounter but what she found in her own heart. Industrious to deceive herself, she had imputed all the uneasy emotions there to the grief of leaving her mother contrary to her inclination: she had now her free consent to go, yet still those perturbations remained. She thanked her mother for her indulgence: she took her hand, and tenderly pressed it to her lips, tears at the same time flowing fast from her eyes.

Mrs. Darnley was cruel enough to shew that she understood the cause of this sudden passion. "What," said she, to the poor blushing Sophia, "after all the clutter you have made about leaving Sir Charles, does your heart fail you now you come to the trial?"

Sophia, abashed and silent, hid her glowing face with her handkerchief; and having with some difficulty represt another gush of tears, assumed composure enough to tell her mother that she hoped she should never want fortitude to do her duty.

"To be sure," replied Mrs. Darnley, with a sneer, "one so wise as you can never mistake your duty."

Sophia however understood hers so well that she did not offer to recriminate upon this occasion; for Mrs. Darnley was but a shallow politician, and was thrown so much off her guard by the vexation she felt, that an affair on which she built such great hopes had taken so different a turn, that she gave plain indications of her displeasure, and that her consent to her daughter's going was indeed extorted from her.

Sophia had many of these assaults to sustain, as well from Harriot as Mrs. Darnley, during the remainder of that day; but they were of use to her. Her pride was concerned to prevent giving a real cause for such sarcasms as her sister in particular threw out: opposition kept up her spirits, and preserved her mind from yielding to that tender grief which the idea of parting for ever from Sir Charles excited.

CHAPTER X
The Description of two Rural Beauties.

When Mr. Herbert came the next morning, Mrs. Darnley, who had no better part to play, had recourse again to dissimulation, and expressed great willingness to send her daughter away; but the good man, who saw the feint in her overacted satisfaction, suffered her to imagine that she had effectually imposed upon him.[1]

Sophia wept when she took leave of her mother, and returned the cold salute[2] her sister gave her with an affectionate embrace. She sighed deeply as Mr. Herbert helped her into the post-chaise; and continued pensive and silent for several minutes, not daring to raise her eyes up to her kind conductor, lest he should read in them what passed in her heart.

Mr. Herbert, who guessed what she felt on this occasion, was sensibly affected with that soft melancholy, so easy to be discovered in her countenance, notwithstanding all her endeavours to conceal it. He wished to comfort her, but the subject was too delicate to be mentioned: kind and indulgent as he was, he began to think his admired Sophia carried her concern on this occasion too far; so true that observation is, that the case of tried virtue is harder than that of untried:[3] we require from it as debts continual exertions of its power, and if we are at any time disappointed in our expectations, we blame with resentment as if we had been deceived.

Sophia's sensibility, however, was very excusable; in flying from Sir Charles she had done all that the most rigid virtue could demand; for as yet she had only suspicions against him; and this man, whose generous gift she had returned with silent scorn, whom she had avoided as an enemy, had hitherto behaved to her with all the tenderness of a lover, and all the benevolence of a friend. It was under that amiable idea that he now presented himself to her imagination; her pride and her resentment were appeased by the sacrifice she had made in her abrupt departure, and every unkind thought of him was changed to tender regret for his loss.

---

1 I.e., that she has tricked him into believing she was sincere.
2 "Salute" could mean any kind of salutation or greeting, from a wave of a hand to a kiss.
3 Conyers Middleton, *History of the Life of Marcus Tullius Cicero* : "The case of tried virtue, I own, is harder than of untried" (2:486).

Mr. Herbert, by not attempting to divert the course of her reflections, soon drew her out of her revery: his silence and reserve first intimated to her the impropriety of her behaviour. She immediately assumed her usual composure, and during the remainder of their little journey, she appeared as chearful and serene as if nothing extraordinary had happened.

The good curate with whom she was to lodge having rode out to meet his friend and his fair guest, joined them when they had come within three miles of his house. Mr. Herbert, who had descried him at a little distance, shewed him to Sophia: "There, my dear," said he, "is a man who, with more piety and learning than would serve to make ten bishops, is obliged to hire himself out at the rate of sixty pounds a year, to do the duty of the parish church, the rector of which enjoys three lucrative benefices, without praying or preaching above five times in a twelve-month."[1]

Mr. Lawson, for that was the curate's name, had now galloped up to the chaise, which Mr. Herbert had ordered the post-boy to stop, and many kind salutations passed between the two friends.

Sophia was particularly pleased with the candor and benevolence which appeared in the looks and behaviour of the good clergyman; who gazed on her attentively, and found the good opinion he had entertained of her from Mr. Herbert's representations fully confirmed. The bewitching sweetness in her voice and eyes, the spirit that animated her looks, and the peculiar elegance of her person and address, produced their usual effects, and filled Mr. Lawson's heart with sentiments of tenderness, esteem, and respect for her.

Mrs. Lawson and her two daughters received her with that true politeness which is founded on good sense and good nature. Both the young women were extremely agreeable in their persons, and Sophia contemplated with admiration the neat simplicity of their dress, their artless beauty, and native sweetness of manners. Health dyed their cheeks with blushes more beautiful than those the fine lady borrows from paint;[2] innocence and chearfulness lighted up smiles in their faces, as powerful as those of the most finished coquet; and good humour and a sincere desire of obliging, gave graces to their behaviour which ceremony but poorly imitates.

---

1 See the "Note on the Clergy," 47.
2 Make-up.

These were Sophia's observations to Mr. Herbert, who seized the first opportunity of speaking to her apart, to ask her opinion of her new companions. He was rejoiced to hear her express great satisfaction in her new situation, and not doubting but time and absence, assisted by her own good sense and virtue, would banish Sir Charles Stanley entirely from her remembrance; he scrupled not to leave her at the end of three days, after having tenderly recommended her to the care of this little worthy family, every individual of which already loved her with extreme affection.

Sophia was indeed so much delighted with the new scene of life she had entered upon, and her fancy was at first so struck with the novelty of all the objects she beheld, that the continual dissipation of her thoughts left no room for the idea of the baronet: but this deceitful calm lasted not long. She soon found by experience, that the silence and solitude of the country were more proper to nourish love than to destroy it; and that groves and meads, the nightingale's song, and the rivulet's murmur, were food for tender melancholy, and the soft reveries of imagination.

Mr. Lawson's house was most romantically situated on the borders of a spacious park; from whose opulent owner he rented a small farm, which supplied his family with almost all the necessaries of life.[1] Mrs. Lawson his wife, brought him a very small fortune, but a great stock of virtue, good sense, and prudence. She had seen enough of the world to polish her manners without corrupting her heart; and having lived most part of her time in the country, she understood rural affairs[2] perfectly well, and superintended all the business of their little farm. Their two daughters were at once the best house-wives,[3] and the most accomplished young women in that part of the country. Mr. Lawson took upon himself the delightful task of improving their minds, and giving them a taste for useful knowledge: and their mother, besides instructing them in all the economical duties suitable to their humble fortunes, formed them to those decencies of manners and propriety of behaviour, which she had acquired by a genteel education, and the conversation of persons of rank. In the affairs of the family, each of the young women had

---

1 That Mr. Lawson must rent this small farm to supply for his family suggests that his sixty-pound income as a parson is insufficient.
2 I.e., the management of a farm.
3 I.e., they are good at work in the house.

their particular province assigned them. Dolly, the eldest, presided in the dairy; and Fanny, so was the youngest called, assisted in the management of the house. Sophia soon entertained a friendship for them both; but a powerful inclination attached her particularly to Dolly. There was in the countenance of this young woman a certain sweetness and sensibility that pleased Sophia extremely; and though she had all that chearfulness which youth, health, and innocence inspire, yet the pensiveness that would sometimes steal over her sweet features, the gentle sighs that would now and then escape her, excited a partial tenderness for her in the heart of Sophia.

She took pleasure in assisting her in her little employments. Dolly insensibly lost that awe which the presence of the fair Londoner first inspired, and repaid her tenderness with that warmth of affection which only young and innocent minds are capable of feeling.

CHAPTER XI
Sophia makes an interesting Discovery.

Sophia, instructed by her own experience, soon discovered that her young friend was in love; but neither of them disclosed the secret of their hearts to each other. Dolly was with-held by bashful timidity, Sophia by delicate reserve. Fond as they were of each other's company, yet the want of this mutual confidence made them sometimes chuse to be alone. Sophia having one evening strayed in the wood, wholly absorbed in melancholy thoughts, lost her way, and was in some perplexity how to recover the path that led to Mr. Lawson's house; when looking anxiously around her, she saw Dolly at a distance, sitting under a tree. Overjoyed to meet her so luckily, she was running up to her, but stopped upon the appearance of a young man, who, seeing Dolly, flew towards her with the utmost eagerness, and with such an expression of joyful surprize in his countenance, as persuaded her this meeting was accidental.

Sophia, not willing to interrupt their conversation, passed on softly behind the trees, unobserved by Dolly, who continued in the same pensive attitude; but being now nearer to her, she perceived she was weeping excessively.

Sophia, who was greatly affected at this sight, could not help accompanying her tears with some of her own; and not daring to stir a step farther, for fear of being seen by the youth, she resolved to take advantage of her situation, to know the occasion of Dolly's extraordinary affliction.

The poor girl was so wrapt in thought, that she neither saw nor heard the approach of her lover, who called to her in the tenderest accent imaginable, "My dear Dolly, is it you? Won't you look at me? Won't you speak to me? What have I done to make you angry, my love? Don't go," (for upon hearing his voice she started from her seat, and seemed desirous to avoid him) "don't go, my dear Dolly," said he, following her, (and she went slowly enough) "don't drive me to despair."

"What would you have me do, Mr. William," said she, stopping and turning gently towards him; "you know my father has forbid me to speak to you, and I would die rather than disoblige him: you may thank your proud rich aunt for all this. Pray let me go," pursued she, making some faint efforts to withdraw her hand, which he had seized and held fast in his, "you must forget me, William, as I have resolved to forget you," added she sighing, and turning away her head, lest he should see the tears that fell from her eyes.

Cruel as these words sounded in the ears of the passionate William, yet he found something in her voice and actions that comforted him; "No, my dear Dolly," said he, endeavouring to look in her averted face, "I will not believe that you have resolved to forget me; you can no more forget me, than I can you, and I shall love you as long as I live—I know you say this only to grieve me; you do not mean it."

"Yes, I do mean it," replied Dolly, in a peevish accent, vexed that he had seen her tears. "I know my duty, and you shall find that I can obey my father." While she spoke this, she struggled so much in earnest to free her hand from his, that fearing to offend her, he dropped it with a submissive air.

Dolly having now no pretence for staying any longer, bid him farewell in a faltering voice, and went on, though with a slow pace, towards her father's house. The youth continued for a moment motionless as a statue, with a countenance pale as death, and his eyes, which were suffused with tears, fixed on the parting virgin.

"What," cried he at last, in the most plaintive tone imaginable, "can you really leave me thus? go then, my dear unkind Dolly, I will trouble you no more with my hateful presence; I wish you happy, but if you hear that any strange mischief has befallen me, be assured you are the cause of it."

He followed her as he spoke, and Dolly no longer able to continue her assumed rigour, stopped when he approached her, and burst into tears. The lover felt all his hopes revive at this sight, and taking her hand, which he kissed a thousand times, he uttered the tenderest vows of love and constancy; to which she listened in silence, only now and then softly sighing; at length she disengaged her hand, and gently begged him to leave her, lest he should be seen by any of the family. The happy youth, once more convinced of her affection for him, obeyed without a murmur.

Dolly, as soon as he had quitted her, ran hastily towards home; but he, as if every step was leading him to his grave, moved slowly on, often looking back, and often stopping: so that Sophia, who was afraid she would not be able to overtake her friend, was obliged to hazard being seen by him, and followed Dolly with all the speed she could. As soon as she was near enough to be heard, she called out to her to stay. Dolly stopt, but was in so much confusion at the thought of having been seen by Miss Darnley, with her lover, that she had not courage to go and meet her. "Ah, Miss Dolly," said Sophia smiling, "I have made a discovery; but I do assure you it was as accidental as your meeting with the handsome youth, who I find is your lover."

"Yes, indeed," replied Dolly, whose face was covered with blushes, "my meeting with that young man was not designed, at least on my part: but surely you jest, Miss Darnley, when you call him handsome: do you really think him handsome?"

"Upon my word I do," said Sophia; "he is one of the prettiest youths I ever saw; and if the professions of men may be relied on," added she, with a sigh, "he certainly loves you; but, my dear Dolly, by what I could learn from your conversation, he has not your father's consent to make his addresses to you; I was sorry to hear that, Dolly, because I perceive, my dear, that you like him."

Dolly now held down her head, and blushed more than before, but continued silent. "Perhaps you will think me impertinent," resumed Sophia, "for speaking so freely about your affairs; but I love you dearly, Miss Dolly."—"And I," interrupted Dolly, throwing one of her arms about Sophia's neck, and kissing her cheek, "love you, Miss Darnley, better a thousand times than ever I loved any body, except my father and mother and my sister."

"Well, well," said Sophia, "I won't dispute that point with you now; but if you love me so much as you say, my dear Dolly, why have you made a secret of this affair? friends do not use to be so reserved with each other."

"Perhaps," said Dolly, smiling a little archly, "you have taught me to be reserved by your example; but indeed," added she, with a graver look and accent, "I am not worthy to be your confidant; you are my superior in every thing: It would be presumption in me to desire to know your secrets."

"You shall know every thing that concerns me," interrupted Sophia, "which can be of use to you, and add weight to that advice I shall take the liberty to give you upon this occasion: I am far from being happy, my dear Dolly, and I blush to say it; it has been in the power of a deceitful man greatly to disturb my peace."

Sophia here wiped her charming eyes, and Dolly who wept sympathetically for her, and for herself, exclaimed, "Is there a man in the world who could be false to you? alas! what have I to expect?"

"Come, my dear," said Sophia, leading her to the root of a large tree, "let us sit down here, we shall not be called to supper yet, you have time enough to give me some account of this young man, whom I should be glad to find worthy of you: tell me how your acquaintance began, and what are your father's reasons for forbidding your correspondence."

CHAPTER XII
The Beginning of a very simple Story.

Dolly, though encouraged by the sweet condescension of Sophia, who, to inspire her with confidence, freely acknowledged the situation of her own heart, blushed so much, and was in such apparent confusion, that Sophia was concerned at having made her a request which gave her so much pain to comply with.

At length the innocent girl, looking up to her with a bashful air, said, "I should be ashamed, dear miss, to own my weakness to you, if I did not know that you are too generous to think the worse of me for it: to be sure I have a great value for Mr. William; but I was not so foolish as to be taken with his handsomeness only, tho' indeed he is very handsome, and I am delighted to find that you think him so; but Mr. William, as my father can tell you, madam, is a very fine scholar: he was educated in a great school at London,[1] and there is not a young squire in all this country

---

1 England's only universities in the eighteenth century were in Oxford and Cambridge.

who has half his learning, or knows how to behave himself so genteely as he does, though his father is but a farmer: however, he is
rich, and he has but one child besides Mr. William, and that is a
sickly boy, and not likely to live;[1] so that Mr. William, it is
thought, will have all."

"I should imagine then," said Sophia, "that this young man
would not be a bad match for you?"

"A bad match!" replied Dolly, sighing: "no certainly; but his
aunt looks higher for him: yet there was a time when she was well
enough pleased with his liking me."

"What is his aunt," said Sophia, "and how does it happen that
she has any authority over him?"

"Why you must know, madam," answered Dolly, "that his aunt
is very rich; when she was a young woman, a great lady took a
fancy to her, and kept her as her companion[2] a great many years,
and when she died, she left her all her cloaths and jewels, and a
prodigious deal of money: she never would marry, for she was
crossed in love they say in her youth, and that makes her so ill-
natured and spiteful, I believe, to young people; but notwithstanding that, I cannot help loving her, because she was always so
fond of Mr. William: she is his god-mother, and when he was
about ten years old she sent for him to London, and declared she
would provide for him as her own; and indeed she acted like a
mother towards him: she put him to school, and maintained him
like a gentleman; and when he grew up, she would have made a
gentleman of him; for she had a great desire that he should be an
officer.[3]

---

1 Child mortality was high in eighteenth-century England; approximately
   20 per cent of infants died in their first year.

2 Young impoverished women of genteel birth often took positions as
   companions to richer ladies. In this position, they helped with work
   around the house and, if they were lucky, were treated as members of
   the family. On the other hand, they could easily be exploited as cheap
   labor by their host families, as happens with Sophia when she stays with
   Mrs. Howard (see 161-71).

3 In order to become officers, individuals (or, as in this case, their rela-
   tives) had to buy commissions from retired or promoted officers. These
   commissions could be expensive (it cost about £400 to become an
   ensign, for instance, which was a rather low rank—see 198). Usually
   only the rich (the gentry and nobility) could afford to become officers.
   Later in the century, more members of the middle class joined the ranks
   of officers.

"Mr. William at that time was very fond of being an officer too; but as he was very dutiful and obedient to his father, (indeed Miss Sophia he is one of the best young men in the world,) he desired leave to consult him first; so about a year ago he came to visit his father, and has never been at London since; and he had not been long in the country before he changed his mind as to being an officer, and declared he would be a farmer like his father, and live a country life."

"Ah Dolly," said Sophia smiling, "I suspect you were the cause of this change, my friend."

"Why indeed," replied Dolly, "he has since told me so: but perhaps he flattered me when he said it; for, ah my dear Miss, I remember what you said just now about the deceitfulness of men, and I tremble lest Mr. William should be like the rest."

"Well, my dear," interrupted Sophia, "go on with your story; I am impatient to know when you saw each other first, and how your acquaintance began."

"You know, madam," said Dolly, "my father keeps us very retired: I had no opportunity of seeing Mr. William but at church; we had heard that farmer Gibbons had a fine son come from London, and the Sunday afterwards when we were at church, my sister, who is a giddy wild girl, as you know, kept staring about, in hopes of seeing him. At last she pulled me hastily, and whispered, 'look, look, Dolly, there is farmer Gibbons just come in, and I am sure he has got his London son with him, see what a handsome young man he is, and how genteely he is drest!'

"Well, madam, I looked up, and to be sure I met Mr. William's eye full upon me; I felt my face glow like fire; for as soon as I looked upon him, he made me a low bow. My sister courtesied; but for my part, I don't know whether I courtesied or not: I was never so confused in my life, and during the whole time we were at church, I scarce ever durst raise my eyes; for I was sure to find Mr. William looking into our pew."[1]

"I supposed you was[2] not displeased with him," said Sophia, "for taking so much notice of you?"

"I do not know whether I was or not," replied Dolly; "but I know that I was in a strange confusion during all church-time; yet I observed that Mr. William did not go out when the rest of the

---

1 Usually, only wealthy families had private pews. In this case, however, the family of the curate would sit in a specially designated pew.

2 This grammatical construction, though incorrect in the twenty-first century, was frequently used in the eighteenth.

congregation did, but staid behind, which made my sister laugh, for he looked foolish enough standing alone. But he staid to have an opportunity of making us another bow; for it is my father's custom, as soon as he has dismissed the people, to come into our pew and take us home with him. I never shall forget how respect-fully Mr. William saluted my father as he passed him. I now made amends for my former neglect of him, and returned the bow he made with a very low courtesy.

"Fanny and I talked of him all the way home: I took delight in hearing her praise him; and although I was never used to disguise my thoughts before, yet I knew not how it was, but I was ashamed to speak so freely of him as she did, and yet I am sure I thought as well of him."

"I dare say you did," said Sophia, smiling; "but my dear," pursued she in a graver accent, "this was a very sudden impres-sion. Suppose this young man whose person captivated you so much, had been wild and dissolute, as many young men are; how would you have excused yourself for that early prejudice in his favour, which you took in so readily at your eyes, without con-sulting your judgment in the least?"

CHAPTER XIII
Dolly continues her Story.

Dolly, fixing her bashful looks on the ground, remained silent for a moment; then sighing, answered, "I am sure if I had not believed Mr. William good and virtuous, I should never have liked him, though he had been a hundred times handsomer than he is; but it was impossible to look on him and think him other-wise; and if you had observed him well, Miss Darnley, his coun-tenance has so much sweetness and candor in it, as my father once said, that you could not have thought ill of him."

"It is not always safe," said Sophia, sighing likewise, "to trust appearances: men's actions as well as their looks often deceive us; and you must allow, my dear Dolly, that there is danger in these sudden attachments; but when did you see this pretty youth again?"

"Not till the next Sunday," replied Dolly; "and though you should chide me never so much, yet I must tell you that this seemed the longest week I ever knew in my life. I did not doubt but he would be at church again, and I longed impatiently for Sunday. At last Sunday came; we went with my father as usual to church, and would you believe it, Miss Darnley, though I wished so much to see Mr. William, yet now I dreaded meeting him, and trembled so when I came into church, that I was obliged to take hold of Fanny to keep me from falling. She soon discovered him, and pulled me in order to make me look up: he had placed himself in our way, so that we passed close by him. He made us a very low bow, and my mother, who had not seen him before, smiled and looked extremely pleased with him; for to be sure, Madam, she could not help admiring him.

"Well, I was very uneasy all the time we were in church; for Fanny whispered me that my sweet-heart, for so she called Mr. William, minded nothing but me. This made me blush excessively, and I was afraid my mother would take notice of his staring and my confusion; so that (heaven forgive me) I was glad when the sermon was ended. He made his usual compliment at our going out, but I did not look up: however, I was impatient to be alone with Fanny, that I might talk of him, and in the evening we walked towards the Park. Just as we had placed ourselves under a tree, we saw a fine drest gentleman, a visiter of the Squire's as we supposed, coming up to us: upon which we rose and walked homewards; but the gentleman followed us, and coming close to me, stared impudently under my hat, and swearing a great oath, said I was a pretty girl, and he would have a kiss. Fanny seeing him take me by the arm, screamed aloud; but I, pretending not to be frightened, though I trembled sadly, civilly begged him to let me go. He did not regard what I said, but was extremely rude: so that I now began to scream as loud as Fanny, struggling all the time to get from him, but in vain, and now who should come to my assistance but Mr. William: I saw him flying across a field, and my heart told me it was he, before he came near enough for me to know him.

"As soon as Fanny perceived him, she ran to him, and begged him to help me; but he did not need intreaty;[1] he flew like a bird to the place where I was, and left Fanny far behind. The rude gentleman bad him be gone,[2] and threatened him severely; for he had taken the hand I had at liberty, which I gladly gave him, and insisted upon his letting me go: and now, my dear Miss Darnley, all my fears were for him, for the gentleman declared that if he did not go about his business, he would run him through the

---

1 A request.
2 I.e., he asked him to leave.

body, and actually drew his sword; I thought I should have died at that terrible sight; my sister run towards home crying like one distracted; and as for me, though the man had let go my hand, and I might have run away, yet I could not bear to leave Mr. William to the mercy of that cruel wretch; and I did what at another time I should have blushed to have done. I took his hand and pulled him with all my force away; but he, enraged at being called puppy by the gentleman, who continued swearing, that he would do him a mischief, if he did not leave the place, begged me to make the best of my way home; and turning furiously to him who was brandishing his sword about, he knocked him down with one stroke of a cudgel[1] which he fortunately had in his hand, and snatching his sword from him, he threw it among the bushes."

"Upon my word" (said Sophia) "your William's character rises upon me every moment: this was a very gallant action, and I do not wonder at your liking him now."

"Ah, Miss" (cried Dolly) "if you had seen how he looked when he came back to me, if you had heard the fine things he said— Well, you may imagine I thanked him for the kindness he had done me, and he protested he would with pleasure lose his life for my sake. I think I could have listened to him for ever; but now my father appeared in sight. My sister had alarmed him greatly with her account of what had happened, and he was coming hastily to my assistance, followed by my mother and all the family. As soon as we perceived them coming we mended our pace; for we had walked very slowly hitherto: then it was that Mr. William, who had not spoke so plainly before, told me how much he loved me, and begged me I would give him leave to see me sometimes. I replied, that depended upon my father, and this was prudent, was it not, my dear Miss Darnley?"

"Indeed it was," answered Sophia, "but what said your lover?"

"He sighed, Madam," resumed Dolly, "and said he was afraid my father would not think him worthy of me: he owned he was no otherwise worthy of me than from the great affection he bore me, and then—But here I fear you will think him too bold and perhaps blame me."

"I hope not," said Sophia.

"Why, Madam," continued Dolly, "he took my hand and kissed it a thousand times; and tho' I did all I could to be sure to

---

1 Heavy stick.

pull it away, yet he would not part with it, till my father was so near that he was afraid he would observe him; and then he let it go, and begged me in a whisper not to hate him. Bless me, what a strange request that was, Miss Darnley! how could I hate one to whom I had been so greatly obliged! I was ready to burst into tears at the very thought, and told him I was so far from hating him, that—"

"Pray go on, my dear" (said Sophia) observing she hesitated and was silent.

"I told him, Madam," resumed she, "that I would always regard him as long as I lived.—I did not say too much, did I?"

"I supposed," said Sophia, "you gave him to understand that it was in gratitude for the service he had done you."

"To be sure," said Dolly, "I put it in that light. Well I am glad you approve of my behaviour, Miss Darnley; so, as I was telling you, my father came up to us, and thanked Mr. William for having rescued his daughter; he then asked him what he' had done with the rude fellow? Mr. William told him he had given him a lucky stroke with his cudgel, which made him measure his length on the ground; 'but,' said he (and sure[1] that shewed excessive good nature) 'I hope I have not hurt him too much:'

"My father said he would go and see; and then shaking Mr. William kindly by the hand, he called him a brave youth, and said he hoped they should be better acquainted—Oh! how glad was I to hear him say so: My mother too was vastly civil to him; and as for Fanny, I thought she would have hugged him, she was so pleased with him for his kindness to me. My mother insisted upon his staying to drink tea with us, and as soon as my father came back, we all went in together."

"Pray what became of the poor vanquished knight?" said Sophia, smiling.

"Oh, I forgot to tell you," resumed Dolly, "that my father said he saw him creeping along as if he was sorely bruised with his fall, supporting himself with his sword, which it seems he had found. We were all glad it was no worse, and Mr. William having accepted my mother's invitation, he staid with us till the evening was pretty far advanced; and then my father accompanied him part of his way home, and at parting, as he told us, desired to see him often.

"He was not backward, you may be sure, in complying with his

---

1 Certainly.

request: he came so often, that my father was surprised; and besides, my sister and I scarce ever went out to walk but we met him; so that one would have imagined he lived in the fields about our house. My mother at last suspected the truth, and questioned me about him, and I told her all that he had ever said to me; and not long afterwards he took an opportunity to open his heart to my father, and asked his permission to make his addresses to me. With such modesty and good sense he spoke, that my father was extremely pleased with him: but told him that he must consult his friends, and know whether they approved of it, and then he would consider of his proposal. Mr. William, as he afterwards told me, wrote to his aunt first; for he was well assured that his father would agree to any thing which she thought for his advantage.

"He had a very favourable answer from Mrs. Gibbons, for she had changed her mind also, with regard to his being an officer, as war was then talked of;[1] and she was afraid of his being sent abroad. He shewed me her letter, and she told him in it, that since he was resolved to settle in the country, she approved of his marrying; and was glad he had not fixed his affections upon some homespun farmer's daughter, but had chosen a gentle-woman, and one who was well brought up. She added, that she intended to come into the country, in a few weeks; and if she found the young lady (so she called me) answered[2] his description, she would hasten the marriage, and settle us handsomely.— Oh! how pleased was I with this letter, and how did it rejoice Mr. William!

"I should never have done, were I to tell you all the tender things he said to me. Mr. Gibbons, at his son's desire, came to my father, and begged him to give his consent, which he obtained; for my father had well considered the affair before: and nothing was wanting but Mrs. Gibbons' arrival to make us all happy. Mr. William thought every hour an age till she came, and prest her continually in his letters to hasten her journey.

---

1 Wars were a source of constant discussion throughout the eighteenth century. Some of the wars of the (extended) century include the Nine Years' War (1688–97), the War of the Spanish Succession (1701–14), the War of the Austrian Succession (1740–48), the Seven Years' War (1756–63), and the American Revolution (1775–83)—and this list does not even include the Jacobite uprisings (by French, Britons, and Scots loyal to the ousted King James and his heirs) in 1690, 1708, 1715, 1719, and 1745.

2 Met.

"Alas! if he had known what was to happen, he would not have been so impatient; for soon after she came, all our fine hopes were blasted; and I have now nothing to expect but misery."

CHAPTER XIV
Sir Charles makes his appearance again.

Poor Dolly was so oppressed with grief, when she came to this part of her story, that she was unable to proceed, and burst into tears. The tender Sophia, who was greatly affected with the anguish she saw her in, employed every soothing art to comfort her. And Dolly being a little composed, was going to continue her story, when she saw her sister looking about for them; Sophia and she immediately rose up and joined Fanny, who rallied them both upon their fondness for lonely places; but perceiving that Dolly had been weeping, she immediately became grave, and accommodated her looks and behaviour to the gentle melancholy of her sister.

Sophia, from the state of her own mind, was but too much disposed to sympathize with the love-sick Dolly: these softening conversations were ill calculated to banish from her remembrance the first object of her innocent affections; and who, with all his faults, she still loved. Dolly's story awakened a thousand tender ideas, and recalled to her memory every part of Sir Charles's conduct which had any resemblance to that of the faithful and passionate William.

She dwelt with tender regret upon these pleasing images, and for a while forgot how necessary it was for her peace, to suppress every thought of Sir Charles, that tended to lessen her just resentment against him.

But, good and pious as she was, the passion she could not wholly subdue, she regulated by reason and virtue; for, as an eminent Divine says, "Although it is not in our power to make affliction no affliction; yet we may take off the edge of it, by a steady view of those divine joys prepared for us in another state."[1]

It was quite otherwise with Sir Charles: for the guilty, if unhappy, are doubly so; because they are deprived of those

---

1 The "eminent Divine" is Francis Atterbury (1663–1732), an Anglican bishop, defender of the traditional church at the beginning of the eighteenth century, and later supporter of Jacobite pretender James (1688–1766), who challenged the then kings of England. Atterbury was considered the best preacher of his time and was friends with authors

resources of comfort, which the virtuous are sure to find in the consciousness of having acted well.

Sir Charles, upon finding his settlement sent back to him, in such a manner, as shewed not only the most obstinate resolution to reject his offers, but also a settled contempt for the offerer, became a prey to the most violent passions: rage, grief, affronted pride, love ill requited, and disappointed hope, tormented him by turns; nor was jealousy without a place in his heart; the chaste, the innocent, the reserved Sophia, became suspected by the man, who in vain attempted to corrupt her; so true it is, that libertinism gives such a colour to the actions of others, as takes away all distinction between virtue and vice.

Love, he argued, is either rewarded with a reciprocal affection, or with an inward and secret contempt; therefore he imputed Sophia's rejection of his offers, not to her disapprobation of the intention of them, but to want of affection for his person; and from her youth, and the tender sensibility of her heart, he concluded, that since he had failed in making an impression on it, it was already bestowed upon another; one[1] while he resolved to think no more of her, and repay her indifference and disdain with silence and neglect; the next moment, dreading lest he had lost her for ever, he regretted his having alarmed her with too early a discovery of his intentions, and sometimes his passion transported him so far, as to make him think seriously of offering her his hand: then starting at his own weakness, and apprehensive of the consequences, he sought to arm himself against that tenderness which suggested so mad a design, by reflecting on her indifference towards him, and accounting for it in such a manner, as fixed the sharpest stings of jealousy in his mind.

Thus various and perplexed were his thoughts and designs; and he was incapable of resolving upon any thing, except to see her; and so great was his impatience, that he would have set out for London the moment he received the fatal paper, but decency would not permit him to leave his uncle, who was in a dying condition, and wished only to expire in his arms.

The poor man, however, lingered a week longer, during which Sir Charles passed some of the most melancholy hours he had ever known; at length his uncle's death left him at liberty to

---

such as Alexander Pope (1688–1744) and Jonathan Swift (1667–1745) (see note 2, p. 206). The quotation is taken (with a few words changed) from his *Sermon Preach'd in the Cathedral Church of St. Paul; at the Funeral of Mr. Tho. Bennet, Aug. 30. MDCCVI* (London: Bowyer, 1706).

1 I.e., once in a while, for a while.

return to London, which he did immediately, and alighted at Mrs. Darnley's house. Upon hearing she was at home, he did not send in his name, but walked up stairs with a beating heart; he found Mrs. Darnley and Harriot together, but not seeing the person whom he only wished to see, he cast a melancholy look round the room, and answering, in a confused and dejected manner, the mother's excessive politeness, and the cold civility of the daughter, he threw himself into a chair with a deep sigh, and was silent.

So evident a discomposure pleased Mrs. Darnley as much as it mortified Harriot. As for Sir Charles, pride and resentment hindered him at first from enquiring for Sophia; but his anxiety and impatience to hear of her, soon prevailed over all other considerations; and though he asked for her with an affected carelessness, yet his eyes, and the tone of his voice betrayed him.

Mrs. Darnley told him, that she was gone into the country: "Very much against my inclination," said she: "but Mr. Herbert, who you know, Sir, has great power over her, more I think than I have, would have it so."

Sir Charles growing pale as death, replied, in great emotion, "What! gone into the country? Where is she gone? to whom? why did she go? Against your inclination, did you say, Madam? what could possibly induce her to this? You surprize me excessively."

Harriot, who did not chuse to be present at the explanation of this affair, now rose up, and went out of the room, smiling sarcastically, as she passed by Sir Charles, and bridling with all the triumph of conscious beauty. He, who was in a bad humour, beheld her airs not only with indifference but contempt, which he suffered to appear pretty plain in his countenance; for he thought it but just to mortify her for her ill usage of her sister, without considering that he himself was far more guilty, in that respect, towards the amiable Sophia, and equally deserved to be hated by her.

When Harriot was gone, Mrs. Darnley instantly renewed the conversation concerning Sophia; and finding that the young baronet listened to her, with eager attention, she gave him a full account of all that had happened during his absence: she represented Sophia as having followed implicitly the directions of Mr. Herbert, whom she called a busy, meddling, officious, old man; and as the behaviour of her daughter, at her going away, gave sufficient room to believe, that her heart suffered greatly by the effort she made, she dwelt upon every circumstance that tended to shew the concern she was under; and did not scruple to exaggerate, where she thought it would be pleasing.

Sir Charles, though he inwardly rejoiced at what he heard, yet dissembled so well, that no signs of it appeared in his countenance. He now seemed to listen with much indifference, and coldly said, he was sorry Miss Sophia would not permit him to make her easy.

The tranquillity he affected, alarmed Mrs. Darnley: she who was ever ready to judge by appearances, concluded that all was over, and that the baronet was irrecoverably lost; but had her judgment been more acute, she would have perceived, that he was still deeply interested in every thing that related to Sophia. The questions he asked were not such as curiosity suggests, but the tender anxiety of doubting love. Mrs. Darnley informed him of all he wished to hear; Sophia had indeed fled from him, but not without reluctance and grief: she was at present removed from his sight, but she was removed to silence and solitude; and she carried with her a fond impression, which solitude would not fail to increase.

Thus satisfied, he put an end to his visit, with all imaginable composure, leaving Mrs. Darnley in doubt, whether she should see him again, and more enraged than ever with Mr. Herbert, whose fatal counsels had overthrown all her hopes.

CHAPTER XV
Dolly meets her Lover unexpectedly.

It was not long before Sophia had an account of Sir Charles's visit from her mother, who, forgetting the part she had acted before, wrote her a letter full of invectives against her obstinacy and disobedience, and bitter upbraidings of her folly, for losing by her ill-timed pride the heart of such a man as Sir Charles.

She told her, with a kind of exultation, that he had entirely forgotten her, and repeated every circumstance of his behaviour while he was with her, and every word he had spoke, as all tending to shew his indifference; but though this was done to mortify Sophia, and make her repent of her precipitate departure, yet her discernment, and that facility which lovers have, in flattering their own wishes, pointed out to her many things in this minute relation, which served rather to nourish hope than destroy it.

Mrs. Darnley added, as the finishing stroke, that Sir Charles looked pale and thin; she attributed this alteration in his health to efforts he had made to banish her from his heart, and thence inferred that a resolution which had cost him so much trouble to confirm, would not be easily broke through; and that she had no reason to expect he would ever desire to see her more.

Sophia could not read this part of the letter without tears, tears that flowed from tender sensibility, accompanied with a sensation which was neither grief nor joy, but composed of both: that Sir Charles should resolve to forget her was indeed afflicting, but that this resolution should cost him struggles so painful as to affect his health, could not but raise her depressed hopes, since it shewed the difficulty of the attempt, and consequently that the success was doubtful.

This letter gave so much employment to her thoughts, that to be at liberty to indulge them she took her evening walk without solliciting the company of her beloved Dolly, and wandered far into the wood, attracted by those romantic shades which afford such soothing pleasure to a love-sick mind. Here, while she meditated on her mother's letter, and read it over and over, still seeking, and still finding something new in it to engage her attention, she heard the voices of some persons talking behind her, and suddenly recollecting Dolly's adventure, she began to be alarmed at the distance to which she had unwarily strayed, and turned her steps hastily towards home.

Mean time a sudden gust of wind blew off her hat, and carried it several paces back: she turned, in order to recover it, and saw it taken up by a genteel young man, who on a nearer approach she knew to be the lover of her young friend. Pleased at this encounter, she advanced to receive her hat from him, which he gave her with a blushing grace, awed by the dignity of her mein,[1] and that sparkling intelligence which beamed in her eyes, and seemed to penetrate into his inmost soul; for Sophia, who was deeply interested for her innocent and unhappy friend, considered him attentively, and was desirous of entering into some conversation with him, that she might be enabled to form a more exact judgment of his understanding and manners than she could from the accounts of the partial Dolly.

While she was talking to him they were joined by an ancient gentlewoman, who accosting Sophia, told her in an affected style and formal accent, that her nephew was very happy in having had an opportunity to do her this little piece of service.

---

1 Look, bearing, manner.

Sophia, who saw an old woman, apparently opprest with the infirmities of years, drest in all the ridiculous foppery of the last age, was so little pleased with her, that she would have answered this compliment with great coldness, had not the desire and hope of being serviceable to her friend made her conquer her growing disgust; she therefore resolved to improve[1] this opportunity of commencing an acquaintance with the aunt of young William, and met her advances with her usual sweetness and affability, so that the old woman was quite charmed with her; and being very desirous to gain her good opinion, and to shew her breeding, of which she was extremely vain, overwhelmed her with troublesome ceremony; and, to display her understanding, of which she was equally proud, murdered so many hard words, that her discourse was scarcely intelligible.

Sophia would fain have drawn in the youth to partake of their conversation, but his aunt's volubility left him very little to say; yet in that little Sophia thought she discovered both good sense and politeness.

The evening being now pretty far advanced, Sophia thought it time to separate, and took leave of her new acquaintance. Their parting was protracted by so many courtesies and compliments from the old lady, that her patience was almost wearied out; at last she got free from her, and quickened her pace towards home, when on a sudden she heard her in a tremulous voice calling out, "Madam, madam, pray stop one moment." Sophia looked back, and seeing Mrs. Gibbons come tottering up to her with more speed than was consistent with her weakness, she met her half way, and smiling, asked her why she had turned back.

"Oh, madam," replied she, "I am ready to sink with confusion! what a *solism*[2] in good breeding have I committed! to be sure you will think I have been used to converse with savages only." Sophia, not able to guess what this speech tended to, looked at Mr. Gibbons as if she wished for an explanation.

"My aunt, madam," said the youth, (blushing a little at the old woman's affection,) "is concerned that you should walk home

---

1 Take advantage of.
2 Here and in her subsequent comments, Mrs. Gibbons butchers the English language by misusing or inventing words. This first instance shows her mangling the word "solecism" both in spelling and in definition, which is appropriate, given that a "solecism" is "an impropriety or irregularity in speech or diction; a violation of the rules of grammar or syntax" (*OED*).

alone, and that I cannot offer my service to attend you, being obliged to lead her, as you see."

"That is not all, nephew," said the ceremonious gentlewoman: "you do not tell the young lady the true cause of the *dilemnia* I am in: I would not leave you, madam," pursued she, "till I saw you safe home, but you live with a family who has affronted me, and I cannot endure to come within sight of the house. I never can forgive an affront, that would be to shew I do not understand the laws of good breeding: but I thank heaven no body can charge me with that, I was early *instituted* into polite life; but some people are not to be *assessed* with."

"I hope," said Sophia (scarce able to compose her countenance to any tolerable degree of seriousness) "that none of Mr. Lawson's family have given you cause of complaint; they seem to me incapable of affronting any one, much more a person that"—

"Oh, dear madam," interrupted the old lady, courtesying low, "you do me a great deal of honour; but you will find, nay you must have observed already, that Mrs. Lawson is vulgar, very vulgar, she knows nothing of decorums."

"I am very sorry for this misunderstanding between you," said Sophia, "and I should think it a very great happiness if I could be any way useful in renewing your friendship."

"Oh," cried Mrs. Gibbons, "you might as well think of joining the *Antipoles*,[1] madam, as of bringing us together again; and I am grieved beyond measure when I think that it is impossible for me to wait on you."

"However," answered Sophia, "you will have no objection, I hope, to my coming to see you."

"Oh! I must not admit of that by any means, madam," replied Mrs. Gibbons, "you came last into the country, and you are entitled to the first visit; I would not for the world break through the laws of politeness; I am sorry you have so indifferent an opinion of my breeding."

Sophia perceiving that the old gentlewoman was a little discomposed, for this article of good breeding was a tender point with her, endeavoured to bring her into good humour, by some well-timed compliments, and once more took leave of her; but Mrs. Gibbons now insisted upon her nephew's seeing her safe

---

1 By "*Antipoles*," Mrs. Gibbons means "Antipodes," i.e., people on the other side of the earth (literally, people with their feet opposed, since they are on the opposite side of the globe).

home, saying, "She would rest herself under a tree till he came back."

Sophia but faintly declined this civility, for she feared to offend her again; and the joy that sparkled in William's eyes when his aunt made this offer of his attendance, made her unwilling to disappoint him of the hope of seeing his mistress; so after much ceremony on the part of Mrs. Gibbons, they separated.

As they walked, Sophia took occasion to express her concern for the violent resentment his aunt had entertained against Mr. Lawson's family, and which seemed to make a reconciliation hopeless.

The youth told her, that nothing could be more trivial than the accident that had occasioned it; "and yet," pursued he, sighing deeply, "slight as it is, the consequences are likely to be fatal enough."

During their conversation Sophia discovered so much good sense and delicacy of sentiment in the young William, that she more than ever pitied the fate of these poor lovers, whose happiness was sacrificed to the capricious temper of an affected old woman: she assured him she would neglect no opportunity to improve her acquaintance with his aunt: "And perhaps," said she, with an inchanting smile, that expressed the benevolence of her heart, "I may be so fortunate as to effect a reconciliation between her and my Dolly's family."

Mr. Gibbons thanked her in transports of joy and gratitude; and now Dolly and her sister, who had walked out in search of Sophia, appearing in sight, she mended her pace, in order to come up with them soon; for in the ardent glances that William sent towards his mistress, she read his impatience to speak to her.

Dolly, who was in the utmost surprise, to see Sophia thus accompanied, took no notice of William; but avoiding, with a sweet bashfulness, his earnest and passionate looks, she fixed her eyes on Miss Darnley, as if she wished to hear from her by what chance they had met.

"I know," said Sophia to her smiling, "that you did not expect to see me so agreeably engaged; but Mr. Gibbons can inform you how his aunt, whom we left in the forest yonder, and I became acquainted." She then addressed some discourse to Fanny, to give the lovers an opportunity of talking to each other.

Dolly asked a thousand questions concerning their meeting, and his aunt's behaviour to Miss Darnley; but the passionate youth leaving it to Sophia to satisfy her curiosity, employed the few moments he had to stay with her in tender assurances of his own unaltered affection, and complaints of her indifference.

"Surely," said Dolly, with tears in her eyes, "I ought not to be blamed for obeying my father."

"Ah, my dear Dolly," replied William, "our affections are not in the power of our fathers; and if you hate me now because your father commands you to do so, you never loved me."

"Hate you," cried Dolly; "no, Mr. William, my father never bid me hate you; and if he had I am sure I could not have obeyed him: he only commanded me to forget you."

"Only to forget me!" repeated William in a melancholy tone: "then you think that little, Dolly; and perhaps you will be able to obey him; but be assured I would rather be hated by you than forgotten."

"That is strange, indeed," said Dolly, smiling through her tears.

"You would not think it strange," replied the youth, in an accent that expressed at once grief and resentment, "if you had ever loved. Ah Dolly! are all your tender promises come to this! little did I imagine I should ever see you altered thus! but I will trouble you no more," added he, sighing, as if his heart would break; "I will endeavour to follow your example: perhaps it is not so difficult a thing as I imagined to cure one's self of love; you have shewn me it is possible, and if I fail in the attempt, I can be but miserable, and that you have made me now." As he spoke these words, he turned half from her, and let fall some tears.

Dolly, who had no intention to make him uneasy, was excessively affected with this sight, and not a little alarmed at what he had said: "And will you," said she, in the most moving tone imaginable; "will you try to forget me? then indeed you will be false and perjured too, for you have sworn a thousand times that you would love me for ever."

"Why should you wish to see me wretched," said he; "you have resolved to love me no longer, and it is but reasonable that I should try to forget you."

He would have proceeded in this strain; but turning to look on her, he saw her sweet face overspread with tears. "Oh my Dolly," cried he, "we are very cruel to each other; but I am most to blame: can you pardon me, my dearest: say you can; alas, I know I do not deserve it."

Dolly's heart was so opprest, that she was not able to speak; but she held out her hand to her young lover, who seizing it eagerly, prest it to his lips, "Yes, I will love you," said he, "though you should hate me; I will love you to my latest[1] breath."

Dolly perceiving Sophia and her sister coming up to them, drew away her hand hastily; but looked on him at the same time, with inexpressible tenderness: Sophia told him with a smile, that she was afraid his aunt would be impatient: upon which he made his bow, and hastened back to her.

CHAPTER XVI
Dolly concludes her Story.

Fanny now left her sister alone with Miss Darnley, who perceiving that she had been weeping, asked her tenderly the cause. "Oh my dear miss," said the poor girl blushing and pressing her hand, "if I had but a little of your prudence and good sense, I should obey my father better; but when one has once given one's heart, it is very difficult to recal it."

"Very true, my dear," said Sophia; "therefore one ought not to be in haste to give it."

"I hope," interrupted Dolly with an anxious look, "you have observed nothing in Mr. William to make you change your good opinion of him."

"Quite the contrary," said Sophia, "I believe him to be a good, and I am sure he is a sensible youth: nay more, I believe he has a sincere regard for you; and that," pursued she, sighing, "is saying a great deal, considering what reason I have to judge unfavourably of men: but, my dear, I would have you keep your passion so far subjected to your reason, as to make it not too difficult for you to obey your father, if he is fully determined to refuse his consent. I know," added she, with a gentle smile, "That it is easier to be wise for others than for ourselves; but I know it is not impossible for a heart in love to follow the dictates of reason: I think so highly of Mr. Lawson's understanding and goodness, that I am persuaded he would not lay an unreasonable command upon you, and by what I could collect from some hints dropt by Mrs. Gibbons, and the little discourse I had with your lover, the old gentlewoman is wholly to blame."

"Did Mr. William tell you," said Dolly, "what was the occasion of their quarrel?"

1 Last.

"No," replied Sophia: "I should be glad to hear it from your-self."

"Well," resumed Dolly, taking her under the arm, "let us go to our dear oak then, and there we shall be out of sight; but I am impatient to know how you met, and what conversation you had." Sophia satisfied her curiosity, diverting herself a little with the old lady's hard words, and her strict regard to ceremony.

"Ah," said Dolly, "it was those hard words, and the clutter she made about ceremony and decorum, that occasioned all our unhappiness; for as I told you, miss, she was well enough pleased with her nephew's choice, saying, that he was in the right to marry like a gentleman, and prefer person and breeding to money: however, soon after she came into the country, she shewed herself a little dissatisfied with my education, and said, that as my father was a gentleman and a scholar, he ought to have taught his daughters a little Greek and Latin,[1] to have distinguished them from meer country girls."

"Your mother, I suppose," said Sophia, "laughed at this notion."

"It does not become me," said Dolly, "to blame my mother; but to be sure she took great delight in ridiculing Mrs. Gibbons: indeed it was scarce possible to help smiling now and then at her hard words, and her formal politeness; but my mother, as Mr. William often told me with great concern, carried her raillery so far that his aunt would certainly be offended with it at last; and so indeed she was, and grew every day cooler, with regard to the marriage. This disgusted my mother more, so every thing wore a melancholy appearance: at length Mrs. Gibbons broke out one day violently, upon my mother's sending a dish of tea to another gentlewoman before her. I saw a storm in her countenance, and dreading the consequence, I made haste to carry her, her dish myself, but she refused it scornfully, and then began to attack my mother in her strange language, upon her want of breeding, and ignorance of the rules of *precendency*, that was her word. My mother at first only laughed, and rallied; but when the rest of our visitors was gone, and Mrs. Gibbons only remained, the quarrel grew serious. My mother, who was out of patience with her folly, said some severe things, which provoked Mrs. Gibbons so much, that she rose up in a fury, and declared she would never more

---

1 This form of education would have been highly unusual for a woman in the eighteenth century.

have any *collection* with such vulgar creatures. At that moment my father and Mr. William, who had been walking together, came into the room: they both were excessively surprised at the disorder which appeared among us: and poor Mr. William, who was most apprehensive, turned as pale as death: he gave me a melancholy look, as fearing what had happened, and had scarce courage enough to ask his aunt what was the matter? Mean time, my mother, in a laughing way gave my father an account of what had happened, repeating some of Mrs. Gibbons's strange words, and made the whole affair appear so ridiculous, that Mrs. Gibbons in a great fury, flung out of the house, declaring that from that moment she broke off any *treatise*[1] of marriage between her nephew and me; and that if he continued to make his addresses to me, she would make a will, and leave all her money to a distant relation. Mr. William was obliged to follow his aunt; but he begged my father's leave to return as soon as he had seen her safe home. When he came back, he implored my father, with tears in his eyes, not to forbid his seeing me: he said the loss of his aunt's fortune would give him no concern if he durst hope that it would make no alteration in my father's resolutions, since his own little inheritance was sufficient to maintain us comfortably. My father was pleased with his generous affection for me, and said a great many obliging things to him, as did my mother likewise: so that we thought our misfortune not so bad; but the next day old farmer Gibbons came plodding to our house, and with a great deal of confusion and aukwardness, told my father that he was very sorry for what had happened; but sister had changed her mind, and would not let her nephew marry, and he was afraid if he disobliged her she would leave all her money to strangers; so he begged him to give his son no encouragement, but to tell him plainly he must obey his aunt and his father; and he said he was sure his son would mind what my father said to him more than any body else."

"I am in pain for poor Mr. Lawson," said Sophia. "What a boorish speech was this!"

"My father," resumed Dolly, "said afterwards, that if it had not been for the concern he felt for me and Mr. William, he should have been excessively diverted with the old man's simplicity; but he answered him gravely, and with great civility: he promised him

---

1 Here, Mrs. Gibbons means "treaty of marriage," i.e., a marriage contract.

that the affair should go no farther; that I should receive no more visits from his son; and that he would talk with him, and endeavour to make him submit patiently to what his father and his aunt had determined for him. The old man thanked my father a thousand times over for his kindness, and after a great many bows and scrapes he went away. My father was as good as his word: he laid his commands on me to think no more of Mr. William, and forbad me to see or speak to him; and when Mr. William came next, he took him with him into his study, and talked to him a long time. He acknowledged that Mr. William had oftener than once moved him even to tears; but for all that he did not relent, and we were not allowed so much as to speak to each other alone, for fear we should take any measures to meet in private. This I thought very severe," pursued Dolly, sighing, "we might at least have been indulged in taking leave, since we were to be separated for ever."

"I cannot blame your father," said Sophia, "he was indispensably obliged to act as he did: it is to be wished, indeed, that Mrs. Lawson had passed over the poor woman's follies with more temper; but this cannot be helped now: perhaps I may be able to serve you. The old gentlewoman seems to have taken a liking to me; I shall endeavour to improve it, that I may have an opportunity to soften her: it is not impossible but this matter may end well yet."

CHAPTER XVII

Mrs. Darnley and Harriot resolve to visit Sophia.

Poor Dolly was ready enough to admit a hope so pleasing, and felt her heart more at ease than it had been a long time. As for William, his aunt's extravagant praises of Sophia, and some expressions which she dropped, intimating that she should be pleased if he could make himself acceptable to so fine a lady, hinted to him a scheme which might afford him the means of seeing his mistress sometimes: he seemed therefore to listen with satisfaction to these dark overtures made by his aunt, and upon her speaking still plainer, he said it would be presumption in him to think that a young lady so accomplished as Miss Darnley would look down upon him; and besides, he had no opportunity of improving an acquaintance with her, being forbid Mr. Lawson's house, at her request.

The old woman, pleased to find he made so little opposition

to her desire, told him, "That he would have opportunities enough of seeing and conversing with the lady; she often walks out," said she, "either in the forest or the fields about the house: cannot you throw yourself in her way, and accost her politely, as you very well know how; and, to *felicitate*[1] your success, I will let her know that I am willing to receive the honour of a visit from her, though this is against all the rules of decorum, for it is my part to visit her first, she being the greatest stranger here: you shall deliver my message to her to-morrow yourself."

The youth replied, coldly, "that it was possible he might not meet with her to-morrow: nevertheless, he would go every day to the forest, and wherever it was likely she would walk, in hopes of seeing her."

Mrs. Gibbons, exulting in the hope of mortifying Mrs. Lawson, told her nephew, "That if he could succeed in his addresses to miss Darnley, and give her so fine a lady for a niece, she would settle the best part of her fortune on him immediately."

William suffered her to please herself with these imaginations, having secured the liberty of going unsuspected, and as often as he pleased, to those places where he could see his beloved Dolly; hitherto he had not dared indulge himself frequently in these stolen interviews, lest his aunt being informed of them should take measures to engage Mr. Lawson to keep his daughter under a greater restraint; but now he continually haunted the park, the wood, and the fields about Mr. Lawson's house: here he could not fail of often seeing his mistress, and sometimes speaking to her unobserved by any one.

Dolly never failed to chide him as often as this happened, for thus laying her under a necessity of disobeying her father's injunctions; but she took no pains to shun those places where she was almost sure of meeting him; and her chiding was so gentle, that he was convinced she was not greatly offended.

Sophia happening to meet him one morning, while he was thus sauntering about, she enquired for his aunt, and hearing from him how desirous the old gentlewoman was of seeing her, she who was full of her benevolent scheme, and eager to put it in execution, delayed her visit no longer than till the afternoon.

Mrs. Gibbons considered this as a proof of her nephew's sincerity, and was in so good a humour, that she listened without any signs of displeasure, to the praises which Sophia artfully

---

1 Facilitate.

introduced of Dolly; and even sometimes joined in them. Sophia thought this a very favourable beginning, and went away full of hope that she should succeed in her design: but while she was thus endeavouring to make others happy, her sister was preparing a new mortification for her.

Sir Charles continued to visit Mrs. Darnley as usual: he passed some hours every day at her house, and while he applauded himself for the steadiness of his resolution, not to follow his mistress, he perceived not his own weakness in seeking every alleviation of her absence. He went to the house where she had formerly dwelt, because every object he saw in it brought her dear idea to his mind: he loved to turn over the books he had seen her read, to sit in those places where she used to sit: he was transported when he saw any thing that belonged to her; and when he was not observed by the inquisitive eyes of Harriot, he indulged his own in gazing upon Sophia's picture, faintly as it expressed the attractive graces of the original; he endured the trifling discourse of Mrs. Darnley, and the insipid gaiety of Harriot, and left all other company and amusements to converse with them, that he might hear something concerning Sophia; for he had the art, without seeming to design it, to turn the discourse frequently upon her, and thus drew from the loquacious mother all he desired to know, without appearing to be interested in it.

Mrs. Darnley knew not what judgment to form of his assiduity in visiting her, and vainly endeavoured to penetrate into his views. As for Harriot, who had no idea of those refinements of tenderness, which influenced Sir Charles's conduct on this occasion, she concluded that her charms had once more enslaved him, and exulted in her fancied conquest the more, as it was a triumph over her sister, who had been the occasion of so many mortifications to her.

Nothing is so easy or so fallacious as the belief that we are beloved and admired; our own vanity helps the deceit, where a deceit is intended: and a coquet who has a double portion of it, willingly deceives herself.

Harriot was now fully persuaded that Sir Charles had forgot Sophia, and was wholly devoted to her. Impatient to insult her with the news of his change, she proposed to her mother to make her a visit: Mrs. Darnley immediately consented, not because she was very desirous to see her daughter, but because every thing that wore the face of amusement was always acceptable to her. Sir

Charles, upon being made acquainted with their intention, offered to accommodate them with his chariot; and although he only desired them coldly to present his compliments to Sophia, yet when he reflected that they would soon see and converse with her, he could not help envying their happiness; and it was with great difficulty he conquered himself so far as to forbear going with them.

END of the FIRST VOLUME.

CHAPTER XVIII
*Harriot's Artifices produce the desired Effect on the unsuspecting
Sophia.*

When they arrived at Mrs. Lawson's, Sophia, who little expected such a visit, had wandered, as usual, in the wood, accompanied with Dolly: Mrs. Lawson immediately sent Fanny in search of her: and Harriot, expressing impatience to see her sister, went along with her.

They found Sophia sitting under an oak, with Mrs. Gibbons on one side of her, and Dolly on the other; for the old gentlewoman was prevailed upon by Sophia to endure the company of the innocent girl, who had never offended her; and Dolly, instructed by her lovely friend, made good use of these opportunities to recover her favour.

William leaned on a branch close by Sophia, to whom he addressed his discourse, while his eyes often stole tender glances at his beloved Dolly. Harriot, when she approached, cried out affectedly, "Upon my word, sister, you have a brilliant assembly here; I did not expect to find you in such good company."

Sophia, surprised to see her sister, ran hastily to meet her, and embracing her kindly, enquired with a sweet anxiety for her mother, and whether she also had been so good as to visit her. Harriot scarce answered her question; her attention was all fixed upon William: so handsome a youth seemed worthy to feel the influence of her charms; and all the artillery of her eyes was instantly levelled against him. Having returned his respectful bow with an affected courtesy, and the fashionable toss of the head, she deigned to take some little notice of Mrs. Gibbons, and honoured Dolly with a careless glance, whose amiable figure, however, attracted a second look; and after examining her with an inquisitive eye, she turned away with a little expression of scorn in her countenance, and again attacked William, practising a thousand airs to strike him; all which he beheld with the utmost indifference.

Sophia, being impatient to see her mother, took leave of Mrs. Gibbons; but Harriot, who had a new conquest in view, was unwilling to go so soon, professing herself inchanted with the place, and declaring she would turn shepherdess.[1]

Sophia told her, smiling, that she was sure that sort of life would not please her.

"Oh, how can you think so," cried Harriot, "is not the dress excessively becoming? then love in these woods is so tender and sincere! I will engage[2] there is not a nymph in this hamlet whose frown would not drive her lover to despair: own the truth now," said she, turning with a lively air to William, "are you not violently in love?"

The youth bowed, blushed, and sighed; and not daring to look at his mistress, he suffered his eyes, full as they were of tender expression, to direct their glances towards Sophia. "I am proud to own, madam," said he to Harriot, "that I have a heart capable of the most ardent passion."

"And mighty constant too! no doubt," interrupted Harriot with a malignant sneer; for she had observed the sigh and the look, and was ready to burst with vexation and disappointment, to find her conquest obstructed already by her sister, as she supposed; and being now as impatient as she was before unwilling to be gone, "Come, Sophy," said she, taking her under the arm, "my mamma will take it ill that you make no more haste to see her, for we shall return to town immediately."

"Sure you will stay one night," said Sophia.

"Oh not for the world!" exclaimed Harriot affectedly; "How can you imagine I would stay so long in an odious village, to be rusticated into aukwardness," pursued she with a spiteful laugh, "and ashamed to shew my face in any assembly in town afterwards." Saying this, she courtesied disdainfully to Mrs. Gibbons and her nephew, and tripped away, pulling her sister away with her.

Dolly joined the two ladies, but walked by the side of Sophia, not aiming at any familiarity with the insolent and affected Harriot; and as they pursued their way home, she had the mortification to hear her lover ridiculed and despised by the disap-

---

1 The pastoral ideal, which was popular particularly in seventeenth- and early eighteenth-century England, opposed the beauty of the countryside and imagined simplicity of country life to the filth and corruption of the city.

2 Wager, bet.

pointed coquet, who supposed she mortified her sister by the contempt she expressed for a man who had so little taste as to like her.

Sophia, as well in compassion to poor Dolly, who suffered greatly upon this occasion, as in justice to the amiable youth, defended him warmly, which drew some coarse raillery upon her from Harriot.

When they came near to Mr. Lawson's house, the sight of Sir Charles's chariot threw her into a fit of trembling; Harriot perceived it, and, willing to undeceive her, if she hoped to find the young baronet there, "I am charged with Sir Charles's compliments to you," said she; "he insisted upon our using his chariot for this little excursion; my mamma and I would fain have persuaded him to accompany us, but he pleaded an engagement, and would not come."

Dolly now looked with great concern upon her fair friend, who, suppressing a sigh, asked if Sir Charles was quite recovered.

"I do not know that he has been ill," replied Harriot. "Indeed when he came from Bath, the fatigue he had endured with his sick uncle, whom he had sat up with several nights before he died, made him look a little pale and thin; but he is now extremely well, and more gay than ever: and it is well he is so," pursued she, "for we have so much of his company, that if he was not entertaining, we should find him very troublesome."

All this was daggers to the heart of poor Sophia: those pleasing ideas which she had indulged upon reading her mother's letter, that represented Sir Charles as having suffered in his health, from his endeavours to vanquish his passion for her, now vanished, and left in their room a sad conviction that she was become wholly indifferent to him.

She might indeed, knowing her sister's malice, have attributed what she said to artifice; but her manner of accounting for the alteration in Sir Charles's looks, which her fond fancy had dwelt upon so much, was so natural, and so full of probability, that she could expect no artifice there.

Every thing Harriot said was confirmed by facts, which left no room for doubt: his assiduity to Harriot, his neglect of her, appeared but too plain. Did he not lend his chariot for a visit in which he would not share? Did he not send his compliments in a manner that shewed his heart was so much at ease, that he felt not even any resentment for her leaving him? Could there be stronger proofs of indifference than these?

Such were her thoughts, and her heart was so oppressed by this sudden and unexpected shock, that it was with difficulty she restrained her tears. Dolly, who looked at her with tender anxiety, and saw her colour come and go, and her charming eyes bent on the ground, as if she feared to look up, lest they should betray her anguish, cast many an angry glance at her envious sister, and wished her a thousand miles off.

Sophia having a little recovered herself, hastened towards her mother, who, with a face of ignorant wonder, was following Mrs. Lawson about her little farm, asking a thousand questions, without heeding the answers she received. Sophia approaching, paid her duty to her with her usual tenderness and respect, which Mrs. Darnley returned with slightly kissing her cheek, telling her that she thought her complexion was greatly improved, and appealed to Harriot for the truth of her observation.

Harriot answered, "That indeed she could not flatter her sister so much as to say she thought so; for if there was any alteration, it was rather for the worse."

Sophia, without attending to this difference of opinion, with regard to her complexion, was only sollicitous to know if her mother had been well; and while she was making some tender enquiries concerning her health, Mrs. Darnley, who never consulted either time or place, suddenly interrupted her, to draw her aside from the company, and asked her abruptly, "Whether she was not surprised at Sir Charles's indifference?"

Sophia, still smarting with the pangs her sister's discourse had given her, replied, in a tone of resentment, "That nothing now could surprise her with regard to Sir Charles."

"Why, to say the truth, Sophia," replied Mrs. Darnley, "I believe he has quite forgot you; but there was a time when you might have been happy.—Oh, girl, girl," pursued she, kindling with anger as she spoke, "you were always obstinate and conceited; what a foolish part have you played with all your wit! but I am to blame to trouble myself about you."

Sophia now eased her loaded heart by a shower of tears. "It is to little purpose now," said Mrs. Darnley, "to repent of your imprudent behaviour; you were too wise to take a parent's advice, when it might have been useful: when a man of rank and fortune makes his addresses to a woman who is inferior to him in both, he expects a thousand little complacencies and attentions from her, which, without wounding her honour, may convince him that it is not to his riches she sacrifices herself."

"Ah, madam," cried Sophia, "that is a snare which has been

fatal to many young women in my circumstances. Who sees not the advantages this gives a man whose aim is to seduce? I am persuaded these pernicious maxims are not yours, but his, for whose ungenerous purpose they are so well calculated."

Sophia guessed truly; the young baronet had often had discourses of this sort with Mrs. Darnley, who nevertheless took it ill that her daughter should offer such an affront as to suppose she did not understand maxims as well as Sir Charles.

Nothing is more certain than that we are never made so ridiculous by the qualities we have, as by those we affect to have. Mrs. Darnley, with all her ignorance, aspired to be thought witty: she therefore vindicated her claim to what Sophia had called maxims; no matter whether they were pernicious or not. The word maxim sounded learnedly in her ears: she told her daughter, with great asperity, that she was so conceited and vain of her own wit, that she would allow no one else to have any. Sophia found it difficult enough to appease her, but she succeeded at length, and they joined the rest of the company.

CHAPTER XIX
Sophia is agreeably surprized.

Mrs. Lawson easily prevailed upon her guests to stay that night and the following day, which, being Sunday, Harriot could not resist the temptation of displaying her charms and her fine cloaths in a country church, which was so new a triumph, that the thoughts of it kept her waking almost the whole night.

The ridiculous airs she assumed to draw the admiration of the simple villagers, who never saw any thing so fine and so gay before, and who stared at her with stupid surprize, made Sophia often blush for her: but her affected glances were chiefly directed to the beautiful youth, whose insensibility had so greatly mortified her pride: she saw his eyes constantly turned towards the pew where she sat; but she saw plainly that it was not her charms that drew them thither. She had no suspicion that Dolly was the object of his affection, and sensible, to her great grief, of her sister's power to charm, she no longer doubted that this envied conquest was hers.

Thus disappointed, she appeared so much out of humour, and so impatient to return to town, that Mrs. Darnley, over whom her power was absolute, complied with her importunity, and set out with her for London, as soon as they returned from church;

notwithstanding all the endeavours of the good curate and his wife to detain them to dinner.

Sophia was now left alone to her own melancholy reflections; this visit from her mother and sister had produced a sad reverse in her situation: hitherto hope had not quite forsaken her: the idea of being still beloved by Sir Charles lessened all her griefs, and supported her amidst the doubt and anxiety which his mysterious conduct had involved her in: his indifference, so apparent in her sister's account of him, gave her pangs unfelt before: and never till now did she think herself unhappy; for, unperceived by herself, she had encouraged a secret hope that the passion she had inspired him with, would not be easily subdued; and that perhaps all which she had thought exceptionable in his conduct, proceeded not from a settled design to the prejudice of her honour, but from that irresolution and slowness with which a man, too sensible of his superiority in birth and fortune, proceeds in an affair of marriage, where he has no obstacles to fear, and where every thing depends upon himself.

She now perceived the necessity of banishing Sir Charles from her heart; but at the same time, she perceived all the difficulty of the task. Though ashamed of her tears, she wept, and passionately exclaimed against her own weakness, which had kept her in a delusion so fatal to her peace. She continued the whole day in her chamber, wholly absorbed in melancholy thoughts.

Dolly, who knew enough of her situation to guess the cause of this new affliction, was grieved to find herself excluded as well as the rest of the family; and although she ardently wished to console her, yet she durst not intrude uncalled upon her retirement. While she waited impatiently for her appearance, a visitor appeared, who she knew would be welcome to her charming friend. As soon as she perceived him, she flew with eager haste to inform Sophia, and, tapping at her door, told her in a joyful voice, that Mr. Herbert was just alighted.

Sophia, surprised at the news, instantly opened her chamber-door, and smiling tenderly upon the charming girl, to whom she excused herself for her long absence, hastened to receive the good old man, who, after some affectionate enquiries concerning her health, rallied her upon the melancholy that appeared in her countenance.

Sophia blushed and fixed her eyes on the ground, not a little surprised at his talking to her in that manner; and when with a bashful air, she looked up again, and saw a more than usual chearfulness in his eyes, her confusion encreased, and for a few moments she could not help feeling some resentment against her benefactor, for thus diverting himself with her uneasiness.

Mr. Herbert, whose thoughts were wholly employed on the pleasing news he brought, did not perceive how much his behaviour embarrassed her: to prevent his renewing a subject so disagreeable, she talked of the visit her mother and sister made her.

Mr. Herbert asked her, "If they had mentioned Sir Charles, and what she thought of him now?"

"I think of him as I ought to do," replied Sophia, with some warmth, "I despise him."

"Be not too rash, my dear child," said Mr. Herbert; "if your sister, whose malice I well know, has suggested any thing to Sir Charles's disadvantage, be assured she deceives you; for I am convinced he not only loves you, but loves you with honour."

Sophia, who from the first words Mr. Herbert uttered, had been in great agitation, as expecting something extraordinary, was so overwhelmed with surprize at what she heard, that her speech and colour forsaking her, she remained pale, silent, and motionless in her chair.

Mr. Herbert, perceiving how powerfully this news operated on her spirits, began to be apprehensive of the consequences, and was rising hastily to give her some assistance, when Sophia, roused to recollection by this motion of her venerable friend, and ashamed of the extreme sensibility she had discovered, apologised for it with a charming modesty, that greatly affected the good old man, who, if he had known in what melancholy thoughts she had passed the day, would have told her with more caution, a circumstance that raised her at once from despair to hope, and produced so great a change in her situation.

As we are never so ready to fear a disappointment as when we are nearest the completion of our wishes, Sophia, with a sweet apprehensiveness, which yet she laboured to conceal, hinted her doubts of the baronet's sincerity; Mr. Herbert answering explicitly to these half expressed doubts, told her, that he was fully persuaded Sir Charles would act like a man of honour. "I will give you an exact account," said he to her, "of what has passed between us, from which you may judge yourself of his conduct:" he then took a letter out of his pocket, and desired her to read it.

CHAPTER XX

*Mr. Herbert acquaints Sophia with the Result of the Interview
between Sir Charles and him.*

Sophia, trembling a little at the sight of Sir Charles's handwriting, took the billet, and found it contained a message from him to Mr. Herbert, requesting in very earnest terms, the favour of an interview, and an offer to wait upon him at any hour he should appoint.

"You may be sure," said Mr. Herbert, receiving back the billet which Sophia gave him without speaking a word, "that I did not suffer Sir Charles to come to me; hearing from the messenger that his master was at home waiting for my answer, I attended him immediately. I perceived a little embarrassment in his countenance upon my first entrance, but that soon wore off: he welcomed me with great politeness, and after thanking me for the honour I did him, in preventing his visit,[1] he entered immediately upon the affair which had occasioned his sending to me.

"'You have, Sir,' said he, 'shewn so truly a paternal affection for the young lady to whom I have paid my addresses, and are so much esteemed and reverenced by her, that I think I may without any impropriety, address myself to you upon this occasion—'

"Here he paused, and seemed a little perplexed.

"'To be sure,' added he, 'I ought to have done this before; my conduct must have appeared capricious both to her and you, and indeed it was capricious,—but—'

"Here he paused again, and fixed his eyes on the ground. His frankness," pursued Mr. Herbert, "pleased me greatly, and disposed me to give him a favourable attention.

"'I cannot blame Miss Sophia,' resumed he, 'for acting as she has done; my heart did homage to her virtue at the time that I suffered most from the contemptuous behaviour it suggested to her. Fain would I hope,' added he sighing, 'that the prejudices she has conceived against me have not entirely banished me from her remembrance; the delicacy of my passion would be but ill satisfied by calling so deserving a woman my own, unless I could likewise boast a preference in her heart that left me no room to doubt my fortune had any share in determining her in my favour.'

---

1 Sir Charles, who is higher on the social scale, would have lowered himself by paying a visit to Mr. Herbert. Mr. Herbert anticipates this and chooses to visit Sir Charles first. Earlier, Sophia is confronted with a similar problem with Mrs. Gibbons (see 118).

"I know not," pursued Mr. Herbert, "whether Sir Charles expected any answer to this declaration; it is certain he looked on me with a kind of anxious timidity, and stopped a moment; I continued silent, and he proceeded in this manner.

"'I know Miss Sophia has an understanding too solid, and a mind too noble to suffer any considerations of rank and fortune to determine her solely in an affair upon which the happiness of her life depends: she would not surely give her hand where her heart did not acknowledge a preference. 'Tis thus I answer all those doubts which my situation, and perhaps an overstrained delicacy suggest: I am impatient to convince her of the purity of my passion; and considering you as her friend, her guardian, and one who is in the place of a father to her, I will take no steps in this affair but such as have the sanction of your approbation; I will not even presume to visit her without your permission: be you my advocate with her, tell her I lay myself and fortune at her feet, and will receive her from your hand as the greatest blessing that heaven can bestow on me.'

"Now, my child," pursued Mr. Herbert, looking on Sophia with a smile, "how would you have had me answer this discourse? was it necessary, think you, to play off a few female artifices here, and keep Sir Charles in doubt and anxious suspense, or did the apparent openness and candor of his procedure deserve an equal degree of frankness on my part?"

"It is not to be doubted," said Sophia blushing, "but that on this occasion, as on every other, you acted with the utmost prudence."

"I find," resumed Mr. Herbert, "that you are resolved beforehand, to approve of whatever I said: well then, I told Sir Charles, that his present declaration entirely satisfied me; that being fully convinced of his sincerity, I looked upon his offer as highly honourable and advantageous to you; and that I was very sure you would have all the sense you ought to have of so generous an affection.

"He then begged me to set out immediately for this place, and prepare you to receive a visit from him. This request I could not possibly comply with, having business in town, which would necessarily detain me for some hours; but I promised him to go as soon as that was dispatched, which probably might be in the afternoon.

"He modestly asked my leave to accompany me; but this I declined, as fearing his sudden appearance, without your being previously acquainted with what had past, might occasion some perplexity and uneasiness to you; so it was agreed that he should come to-morrow."

"To-morrow," replied Sophia, with an emotion she was not able to suppress.

"Yes, my child," replied the good old man, "have you any objections to this?"

"I know not," replied Sophia, with downcast eyes and a faultering accent, "what I ought to do; I have been so used to consider Sir Charles's professions in an unfavourable point of view; my heart has been so accustomed to suspect him—to guard itself against delusive hopes—perhaps I ought not to admit his visit so easily;—perhaps I ought to resent his former behaviour. I own I am greatly perplexed, but I will be determined wholly by your advice."

Mr. Herbert saw her delicate scruples, and, to favour her modesty, answered, with the authority of a guardian, "When Sir Charles visits you next, Miss Sophia, he comes to offer you his hand; he has asked my consent as your guardian and your friend; and I, presuming on my influence over you in both these characters, have given it freely; and how indeed, having your interest and happiness sincerely at heart, could I do otherwise? but if you think his former behaviour, in which however there were only suspicions against him, deserves to be resented, at a time when those suspicions are absolutely destroyed, you must go through with your heroism, and see him no more; for as the poet says,

He comes too near who comes to be denied.[1]

so he has offended too much who needs a pardon."

---

1   The poet in question is Lady Mary Wortley Montagu (1689–1762), best known today for her letters written during her travels in Eastern Europe and Turkey and for her part in the introduction of the smallpox vaccine to England. This quotation is from the last line of her "The Resolve," a poem about the dangers of coquetry. In the original publication in the periodical *The Plain Dealer* of 27 April 1724, the line reads, "He comes *too near*, that comes to be *Deny'd*." In the manuscript, where the poem bears the title, "Written ex tempore in Company in a Glass Window the first year I was marry'd," Montagu actually wrote, "Too near he has approach'd, who is deny'd" (*Essays and Poems*, ed. Robert Halsband and Isobel Grundy [Oxford: Clarendon Press, 1977], 179). The poem was also printed in Montagu's *Six Town Eclogues* as "The Lady's Resolve" (London: Cooper, 1747) and was frequently anthologized.

Sophia, who felt all the force of this reasoning, answered only by a blushing silence. Mr. Herbert then told her, that Sir Charles had declared to him that he would make the same settlements on her as had been stipulated for his mother; for he added, with equal delicacy and tenderness, "Miss Sophia, in virtue, wit, good-sense, and every female excellence, brings me an immense portion.[1]

"Sir Charles," pursued Mr. Herbert smiling, "by a strange contradiction, which is, I supposed, always found in lovers, though he was impatient to have me with you, yet could not help detaining me to have the pleasure of talking of you: he painted to me very naturally, the uneasiness he had suffered from your sup-posed contempt of him: he told me, that he was at one time determined to travel, in order to efface you from his remem-brance; 'but,' (said he, rising and unlocking a cabinet, from which he took out a paper and put into my hands,) 'you shall judge whether amidst all my resentment I did not still love Miss Sophia; that is my will, which I ordered to be drawn up previous to my intended journey.'

"He then, to spare me the trouble of reading it all through, pointed to the place where you was mentioned, and I found he had bequeathed you an estate of four hundred pounds a-year for life, and five thousand pounds to be disposed of as you pleased."

This last circumstance touched Sophia so much that tears filled her eyes; she sighed, and turned her head aside to conceal her emotion, while Mr. Herbert, without seeming to observe it, continued to repeat to her several expressions used by Sir Charles, which shewed the greatness of his affection, and his ven-eration for her virtues.

"We parted at length," pursued Mr. Herbert, "extremely well satisfied with each other, and to-morrow, or next day at farthest, you may expect to see Sir Charles here; for he told me, that if he received no ill news from me, he would conclude I had prepared him a favourable reception; and, presuming on this hope, he would immediately set his lawyer to work to prepare the writ-ings,[2] that nothing might be left undone which could convince you of the sincerity of his affections; therefore, my dear child, set your heart at rest; and since providence has thought fit to reward

---

1 Dowry.
2 Legal writ, i.e., marriage contract.

your piety and virtue,[1] receive with humble gratitude that fortune to which you are raised, and which puts it so largely in your power to do good. I will now leave you," said the old man rising, "to your own reflections; I have scarce spoke a word yet to our kind friends here, for I was so impatient to see you, that I left them very abruptly."

CHAPTER XXI
Sophia is threatened with a new Disappointment.

Mr. Herbert had no sooner left the room, than Sophia, in an ardent ejaculation, thanked heaven for thus relieving her from her distress: but it was long ere the tumult in her mind raised by such unhoped for happy news subsided, and gave place to that calm recollection which supplied a thousand pleasing ideas, and filled her with the softest emotions of gratitude, tenderness, and joy.

She was now freed from those tormenting doubts, which made her consider her tenderness for Sir Charles as a crime, and occasioned so many painful struggles in her mind. What joy to reflect that the man she loved was worthy of her affection! how pleasing was the prospect that opened to her view; to be blest with the power of shewing her gratitude to her friends, her piety to her mother; to repay her sister's unkindness with acts of generosity; and indulge the benevolence of her heart in relieving every distress which fell within her power to relieve!

These were the advantages which she promised herself in the change of her fortune, and for these her grateful heart lifted itself up every moment in thanks and praise to that providence that bestowed them on her.

While Sophia was thus absorbed in thought, Dolly opened the door, and running up to her, eagerly cried, "Tell me true, my dear miss, has not Mr. Herbert brought you some good news? I am sure he has; I never saw him so joyful in my life: and you look glad too," pursued she, peering in her face with a sweet earnestness. "May I not ask you, Miss Darnley, what this good news is?"

"You may, my dear," said Sophia smiling, "but not now; you shall know all soon. At present I would rather talk of your affairs."

---

1 This may be an allusion to the subtitle of Richardson's *Pamela; or, Virtue Rewarded* (1741), which is also similar to *Sophia* in some of its plot.

"Indeed I am greatly obliged to you, miss," said Dolly, "for what you have done for me. Mrs. Gibbons seems almost as kind to me as ever she was, and you have talked so sensibly to my mother, that she repents of her behaviour to Mrs. Gibbons: and she likes Mr. William so well, that I am sure she would be glad to be reconciled to her."

"That is what I have been labouring at all this time," resumed Sophia. "If Mrs. Lawson can be persuaded to make some concessions to the fantastick old gentlewoman, all may go well yet: it shall be my care to bring them together; and if my endeavours to produce a reconciliation fail, perhaps I may be able to engage a more powerful mediator in your interest."

Sophia had Sir Charles in her thoughts, who she doubted not would readily undertake the cause of the distressed lovers, and possibly add something to her Dolly's portion, to lessen the inequality there was between them in that point. She spoke with such a chearful confidence, that Dolly, full of hope and joy, thanked her with artless transports of gratitude that moved her even to tears.

The next day, though in expectation of seeing Sir Charles, her heart laboured with a thousand emotions; yet kindly attentive to the affairs of her friend, she resolved to make Mrs. Gibbons a visit, to prepare the way for the hoped for interview between her and Mrs. Lawson. As soon as she had disengaged herself from Mr. Herbert, she set out alone for Mrs. Gibbons's house; but scarcely had she crossed the first field when she saw William, who was as usual, sauntering about Mr. Lawson's grounds, in hopes of seeing his mistress.

Sophia beckoned to him, and he eagerly flew to meet her; for, next to Dolly, he thought her the most charming woman in the world; and he adored her for the goodness with which she interested herself in his and his Dolly's happiness.

When he drew near, Sophia told him she was going to visit his aunt; the youth respectfully expressed his concern that his aunt could not have that honour; she was gone, he said, to visit a relation who lived a few miles up the country.

Sophia then told him the design upon which she was going, and the favourable disposition Mrs. Lawson was in. "I am persuaded," said she, "all might be made up, if we could but bring them together. Mrs. Lawson only wants opportunity to repair her fault; but how shall we contrive to give her this opportunity? what expedient can we find out to overcome your aunt's obstinacy, and prevail upon her to enter Mrs. Lawson's door again?"

"I know one, madam," said the youth, "which I think would do."

Sophia concluding from the timidity of his look, that she was concerned in this expedient, prest him to speak freely, assuring him she would assist to the utmost of her power.

"My aunt, madam," said he, "is as you know a great observer of forms: she would not for the world fall under the censure of having failed in any part of ceremony or good breeding; now, madam, if you would be pleased to make a point of her returning your visit, and permit me to tell her that you are offended with her neglect, and that you insist upon this proof of her politeness, I am persuaded she will come."

"Well," said Sophia, smiling, "if you are of opinion this will do, you have my consent to say whatever you think will affect her most; make me as angry and as ceremonious as you please.

"Nothing shall be wanting on my part to promote the success of this affair," added she, with a graver look and accent; "for I believe you have a sincere affection for my young friend, and I shall not be at rest till I see you both happy."

The youth, in whose breast the sweet benevolence of her looks and words excited the strongest transports of gratitude, not able to find words to express his sense of her goodness, suddenly threw himself at her feet, and kissed her hand with a mixture of tenderness and awe.

Sophia, smiling at this sally, stepped back a little; upon which he rose up, and, with a graceful confusion, paid her his thanks: she again repeated her promise of serving him, and took leave: he bowed low, following her for some time with his eyes, and sent a thousand kind wishes after her.

Sophia, at her return, acquainted Dolly with what had passed between her lover and her, and filled her with pleasing hopes of the success of his scheme: but now the day wore away, she was in continual expectation of seeing Sir Charles; her heart throbbed with anxiety; every noise she heard, sounded like the trampling of horses, and then an universal trembling would seize her. She dreaded, yet wished for his arrival; and at every disappointment she sighed, and felt her heart sink with tender despondency.

Such were her agitations, till the evening being far advanced, she gave up all hope of his coming that night. Mr. Herbert had assigned a very pleasing reason for his visit being deferred till the next day; and, her mind growing more composed, she went in search of the good old man, who, Dolly told her, was gone to walk in the meadows behind the house; for she had kept herself out of his sight as much as possible, unwilling that he should observe her emotions. She saw him at a distance, walking with a slow pace, and she perceived he observed her; but to her great surprize, she saw him cross into another field, and take a quite contrary way, on purpose to avoid her.

Struck with this little accident, she stood still, and paused a few moments: she felt herself strangely alarmed, yet wondered why she should be so, and took her way back again to the house with sad forebodings on her mind.

CHAPTER XXII
Sophia suspects the Cause of her Lover's mysterious Conduct.

When Mr. Herbert returned from his walk, and met the curate and his little family at supper, Sophia, who heedfully observed him, saw an alteration in his countenance, which realized all her melancholy apprehensions, and convinced her that some new misfortune awaited her: his eyes, which studiously avoided her's, expressed nothing but grief and confusion; but he retired so early to his chamber, that Sophia, finding there was no hopes of explaining himself that night, passed it in an anxiety of mind, which suffered her not to taste the least repose. Early in the morning he knocked at her door, and desired her to join him in the garden; she was already drest, and instantly complied.

As soon as she came up to him, he took her hand, and pressed it affectionately, but spoke not a word.

Sophia, who feared as much as she wished to know what had happened, had not power to ask for an explanation; so they both continued silent for some minutes.

At length Mr. Herbert told her he was going to London; Sophia, in a faultering accent, asked him what had happened to occasion this sudden resolution?

"Alas! my dear child," said the good old man, in great emotion, "I am ashamed and grieved to tell you that—Sir Charles has, I fear, deceived me."

Although Sophia had reason to expect some sad reverse of fortune, and had endeavoured to prepare herself for it, yet this fatal confirmation of her fears shocked her so much, that Mr. Herbert, who saw a death-like paleness overspread her face, and felt her hand cold and trembling, fearing she would faint, made haste to lead her to a little bench of turf which was near them.

Sophia recovering, saw so much concern in his looks, that

struggling to repress her own anguish, she endeavoured to comfort him, and, smiling through the tears that filled her charming eyes, "Let not this instance of my weakness alarm you, sir," said she; "and doubt not but, with the assistance of heaven, I shall bear this strange insult with proper fortitude."

"How worthy are you, my good child, of better fortune!" said Mr. Herbert; then taking a letter out of his pocket, "My first design," pursued he, "was to seek some explanation of this mysterious letter, before I made you acquainted with it, but I perceived that my too apparent uneasiness had alarmed you, and I thought it would be less cruel to inform you of the whole matter than to leave you in doubt and uncertainty: this letter was delivered to me yesterday in the evening, by one of Sir Charles's servants, just as I was walking out towards the road, in hopes of meeting his master. My surprise at receiving a letter, when I expected to see himself, made me open it instantly, without asking the servant any questions, and while I was reading it he went away, doubtless being directed to do so."

Mr. Herbert then gave the letter to Sophia, who, unfolding it with trembling emotion, found it was as follows:

"SIR,

Since it is impossible my marriage with Miss Sophia can ever take place, I could wish you would look upon all that passed between us upon that subject, as a dream: I dreamt indeed, when I imagined there was a woman in the world capable of a sincere attachment; and I ought to be ashamed to own, that upon so delusive a hope I was ready to act in opposition to the general maxims of the world, and be pointed at as a silly romantic fellow. However, I beg you will assure the young lady, that as I have no right to blame her conduct, so I have not the least resentment for it, and am so perfectly at ease on this occasion, that I can with great sincerity congratulate her on her approaching happiness.

I am, Sir,
Your humble servant,
CHARLES STANLEY."

Although this letter gave Sophia a sad certainty of her misfortune, yet it relieved her from those worst pangs which a heart in love can feel, the belief of being abandoned through indifference, or inconstancy. Unperceived by ourselves, pride mixes with our most tender affections, and either aggravates or lessens the sense of every disappointment, in proportion as we feel ourselves humbled by the circumstances that attend it.

The ill-disguised jealousy, the personated[1] calmness, the struggling resentment that appeared in this letter, convinced Sophia that Sir Charles was far from being at ease, and that to whatever cause his present unaccountable behaviour was owing, yet she was sure at least of not being indifferent to him.

It was not difficult to perceive that he had been deceived by some malicious reports, and her suspicions fell immediately upon Harriot; but rejecting this thought, as too injurious to her sister, she returned the letter to Mr. Herbert without speaking a word, but with a look much more serene and composed than before.

Mr. Herbert, who saw nothing in this letter like what her penetration had discovered, and who conceived it to be only a poor artifice to disengage himself from promises which he now repented of, was surprised to find her so much less affected with it than expected, and asked her what she thought of it?

Sophia told him, that she was fully persuaded Sir Charles had been prejudiced against her.

"Do you think so, my dear," said he, after a little pause; "then it is your sister to whom you are obliged for this kind office."

"I hope not, sir," replied Sophia, sighing; "that circumstance would aggravate my concern—indeed I think it would be a crime in me to suspect her of being capable of such unkindness."

"Well," resumed Mr. Herbert, "I will, if possible, discover this mystery before night; you shall hear from me to-morrow; in the mean time calm your mind, and resign yourself entirely to that Providence, which, while you continue thus good and virtuous, will never forsake you."

CHAPTER XXIII
Sophia is visited by Mrs. Gibbons, and makes new Discoveries.

Mr. Herbert now left her, to go and take leave of the curate and his family; and Sophia, whose fortune had undergone so many revolutions in so short a time, retired to her chamber, where she passed a great part of the day alone, at once to indulge her melancholy, and to conceal it from observation.

---

1 Pretended.

In the afternoon Dolly came up, in a great hurry of spirits, to acquaint her that Mrs. Gibbons was come to wait upon her; that she had been met at the door by her mother, and that several courtesies had passed between them.

The poor girl, though transported with joy at this favourable beginning, no sooner perceived, by the pensive air in Sophia's countenance, and the sighs that escaped her, that her suspicions of some new disappointment having happened to her were true, than instantly forgetting the prosperous situation of her own affairs, her sweet face was overspread with tender grief, and a tear stole from her eyes; but Sophia, whom nothing could have awakened from that stupifying sorrow in which any great and sudden misfortune plunges the mind, but the desire of being useful to her friends, soon assumed a more chearful look, and hastened to receive her visitor.

Mrs. Gibbons was in full dress, and had omitted no superfluous ornament that could serve to shew Sophia how well she understood every sort of punctilio.[1] As soon as the first compliments were over, "You see, madam," said she, "what *affluence* your commands have over me: I once little thought that I should ever have entered this impolished house again; my nephew attended me to the door, but I would not suffer him to come in, because I am not sure that you are willing to let these people know the honour you do him by receiving his adorations."

Sophia, though a little startled at these words, yet supposed she had no particular meaning in them, and ascribed all to her fantastick manner of expressing herself; but Mrs. Gibbons being resolved to hasten the conclusion of an affair which she had very much at heart, spoke so intelligibly at last, that Sophia could no longer be ignorant of her design, all the ill consequences of which suddenly striking her imagination, she exclaimed in a tone of surprise and terror, "Sure I am the most unfortunate creature in the world! is it possible, Mrs. Gibbons, that you can be serious? have you really given any cause for a report, that I receive your nephew's addresses? if you have, you have done me an irreparable injury."

Sophia's spirits were so greatly agitated that she did not perceive how much of her situation these words discovered; so that Mrs. Gibbons, who saw the tears flow fast from her eyes, immediately comprehended the whole truth.

---

1 Correct social custom, precise way of behavior.

"I see plainly," said she, in great concern, "that I have been deceived, and others perhaps have been so too; I shall never *discapitulate* myself for being the cause of any misfortune to you: some more advantageous *treatise* has been on the *tapestry*, and this unlucky affair has done mischief."

"Give me leave to ask you, madam," interrupted Sophia with some peevishness, "what foundation had you for believing that I considered your nephew as my lover? you know his heart has been long since engaged."

"I acknowledge I have been to blame, my dear miss," resumed Mrs. Gibbons, "I was too *sanguinary* in my hopes; but I beg you will *disclaim* no more, this will do no good; only tell me if it is possible to repair the harm I have done by my foolish schemes."

To this Sophia made no answer; but Mrs. Gibbons, who wanted neither tenderness nor candour, and who was greatly concerned at the uneasiness she saw her under, urged her so frequently, and with so much earnestness, to tell her if she could be of any use in clearing up a mistake that had possibly been disadvantageous to her, that Sophia, still attentive amidst all her own distresses to the interest of her friend, thought this a favourable opportunity to serve her; and therefore told Mrs. Gibbons, that if she was really sincere in her offers, there was one way.

"I understand you, madam," interrupted Mrs. Gibbons, "and I believe I may venture to say that I thought of this *expedition* before you did. I cannot, indeed, Miss Darnley, I cannot consent to my nephew's marriage with the young woman here; you know I have been affronted."

Sophia now urged some arguments in favour of Mrs. Lawson, but chiefly rested her defence upon her ignorance of those forms of politeness and good breeding which Mrs. Gibbons was so perfectly mistress of.

This compliment put the old lady into so good a humour, that she cried out, "Well, my dear Miss Darnley, in regard to you, I will take off the *probition* I laid on my nephew to visit here no more; and this I hope," added she smiling, "will set matters right in another place; as for the rest, I shall take no resolution till I see how they behave."

Sophia, in her transport at having succeeded so well with the old lady, felt all her own griefs suspended; and indeed, when she reflected upon what had happened with regard to herself, she found she had less cause for reflection than Mr. Herbert, or her own fears, had suggested.

Mrs. Gibbons acknowledged that she had flattered herself with the hope of her nephew's being well received by her; and that, in consequence of it, she had talked of their marriage as an event which was very likely to happen, and which would give her great joy. Sophia, being fully persuaded that these reports had reached Sir Charles, though by what means she was not so well able to determine, easily accounted for that jealousy and resentment which had produced so strange an inconsistency in his behaviour, and which Mr. Herbert considered as a piece of artifice to palliate his lightness and inconstancy.

The good old man, animated by his affection for the poor afflicted Sophia, rode with the utmost speed to town, and alighted at the house of the young baronet. The servants informed him, that their master was in the country, which was all the intelligence they could give him: for they neither knew where he was, nor when he would return. Mr. Herbert, perplexed and concerned at this new disappointment, repaired[1] immediately to Mrs. Darnley's, hoping to hear some news of him there.

Harriot, in answer to his enquiries, told him with an air of triumph, that the same day they returned from visiting Sophia, Sir Charles had waited on her mamma and her, and had as usual past a great part of the afternoon with them.

Mr. Herbert, who was struck with this incident, endeavoured to make some discoveries concerning their conversation, and Harriot's malice made this no difficult matter: for she could not forbear throwing out some sarcasms against her sister, whose extreme sensibility, she insinuated, had already found out a new object.

Mr. Herbert, by his artful questions, drew her into a confession of all that had passed between her and the baronet upon this subject; and was convinced that her malignant hints had poisoned his mind with suspicions unfavourable to Sophia.

He went away full of indignation at her treachery, and still doubtful of Sir Charles's sincerity, who he could not suppose would have been so easily influenced by Harriot's suggestions, (whose envious disposition he well knew,) if his intentions had been absolutely right.

The next morning he received a letter from Sophia, in which she acquainted him with the discoveries she had made; and modestly hinted her belief that Sir Charles had been imposed

1 Returned.

upon by this report of her intended marriage, which she found was spread through the village; and which, as it was very probable, he had intelligence from thence, had confirmed any idle raillery to that purpose, which her sister might have indulged herself in.

Mr. Herbert reflecting upon all these unlucky circumstances, began to suppose it possible that Sir Charles had been really deceived. He went again to his house, but had the mortification to hear from a servant whom he had not seen the day before, that the baronet was at his seat in—

Thither the good old man resolved to go; the inconveniencies and expence of such a journey, which in his years, and narrow circumstances were not inconsiderable, had not weight enough with him to make him balance a moment whether he should transact this affair by letter, or in person. The happiness of his dear and amiable charge depended upon his success: he therefore delayed no longer than to make the necessary preparations for his journey, and, after writing to Sophia to acquaint her with his design, he set out for Sir Charles's seat, where he met with a new and more severe disappointment. The first news he heard was, that the baronet was not in that part of the country; and upon a fuller enquiry of his servants, he was informed that their master had the morning before set out for Dover with an intention to go to Paris.

Mr. Herbert, dispirited with this news, and fatigued with his fruitless journey, retired to his inn, where he passed the lonely hours in melancholy reflections upon the capricious behaviour of Sir Charles, and the undeserved distress of the innocent Sophia.

CHAPTER XXIV
Displays certain singularities in the character of Sophia, and their effects on the heart of Sir Charles.

Sir Charles, however, notwithstanding appearances, was at present more unhappy than guilty. His resolution to marry Sophia, though suddenly formed, was not the less sincere: he had always loved her with the most ardent passion, and had not the light character of her mother and sister concurred with those prejudices his youth, his fortune, and his converse with the gay world led him into, his heart, which had never ceased to do homage to her virtue, would have sooner suggested to him the only means of being truly happy.

An overstrained delicacy likewise proved another source of disquietude to him. The inequality of their circumstances gave rise to a thousand tormenting doubts: he was afraid, that dazzled with the splendor of his fortune, she would sacrifice her inclinations to her interest, and give him her hand without her heart; and when doing justice to the greatness of her mind, and the real delicacy of her sentiments, he rejected this supposition as injurious to her, his busy imagination conjured up new forms of distrust: he trembled lest, mistaking gratitude for love, she should be deceived by her own generosity and nice sense of obligation, and imagine it was the lover she preferred, when the benefactor only touched her heart.

Such was the perplexed state of his mind, when Mrs. Darnley and Harriot proposed making her a visit. With some difficulty he conquered his desire of accompanying them; but his impatience to hear of her, carried him again to Mrs. Darnley's much earlier in the evening than it was likely they would return; presuming on his intimacy in the family, he scrupled not to go up the stairs, telling the servant he would wait till the ladies came home.

He sat down in the dining-room, where he gazed on Sophia's picture a long time. At last a sudden fancy seized him to visit her apartment, which he knew was on the second floor: he ascended the stairs without being perceived, and with a tender emotion entered the room where his beloved Sophia used to pass so many of her retired hours.

It was still elegantly neat, as when its lovely inmate was there; for Harriot, who hated this room because it contained so many monuments of her sister's taste and industry, never went into it; and it remained in the same order that she had left it.

The first thing that drew the young baronet's attention, was a fire-screen of excellent workmanship; it was a flower-piece, and executed with peculiar[1] taste and propriety: the wainscot[2] was adorned with several drawings, neatly framed and glassed. In this art Sophia took great delight, having while her father lived appropriated all her pocket money to the payment of a master to instruct her in it. Sir Charles considered the subjects of these drawings with a peculiar pleasure. The delicate pencil of Sophia had here represented the Virtues and the

---

1 Particularly good.
2 Wooden paneling inside the walls.

Graces,[1] from those lively ideas which existed in her own charming mind.

Her little library next engaged his notice: many of the books that composed it he had presented her; but he was curious to see those which her own choice had directed her to, and in this examination he met with many proofs of her piety as well as of the excellence of her taste.

Several compositions of her own now fell into his hands: he read them with eagerness, and, charmed with this discovery of those treasures of wit, which she with modest diffidence so carefully concealed, he felt his admiration and tenderness for her encrease every moment.

While he was anxiously searching for more of her papers, a little shagreen[2] case fell from one of the shelves upon the ground. He took it up, and as every thing that belonged to her excited his curiosity, he opened it immediately, and with equal surprise and pleasure, saw his own miniature in water colours,[3] which was evidently the performance of Sophia herself.

Had it been possible for her to imagine the sudden and powerful effect the sight of this picture would have upon the heart of Sir Charles, she would not have suffered so much uneasiness for the loss of it as she really had; for, forgetting where she had laid it, she supposed it had dropt out of her pocket, and was apprehensive of its having fallen into her sister's hands, who she knew would not fail to turn this incident to her disadvantage.

While Sir Charles gazed upon this artless testimony of Sophia's affection for him, the softest gratitude, the tenderest compassion, filled his soul. "Oh, my Sophia," said he, "do you then truly love me! and have I cruelly trifled with your tenderness!"

This thought melted him even to tears; he felt in himself a detestation of those depraved principles which had suggested to

---

1 Since they are capitalized (a change from the periodical edition; see Appendix A, p. 203), this probably means the Greek goddesses who embodied the virtues and graces. The Graces were Aglaia (brightness), Euphrosyne (joyfulness), and Thalia (bloom). The virtues of antiquity (the "natural" virtues) were prudence, temperance, fortitude, and justice, to which the Christian tradition added the "theological" virtues of faith, hope, and love. Sophia would have painted or drawn personifications of these.

2 I.e., a case made of fish skin.

3 Painting in water color was a popular and appropriate hobby for young women in the eighteenth century.

him a design of debasing such purity! he wondered at the hardness of his own heart, that could so long resist the influence of her gentle virtues, and suffer such sweet sensibility to waste itself in anxious doubts, and disappointed hope.

Being now determined to do justice to her merit, and make himself happy, his first design was to go immediately to Mr. Lawson's; but, reflecting that Sophia had great reason to be dissatisfied with his conduct; and that, to remove her prejudices, the utmost caution and delicacy was to be observed, he conceived it would be more proper to make a direct application to Mr. Herbert, whom she loved and reverenced as a father, than to present himself before her, while her mind yet laboured with those unfavourable suspicions for which he had given but too much cause; and hence new fears and doubts arose to torment him. He dreaded lest her just resentment for his injurious designs should have weakened those tender impressions she had once received; and that, in the pride of offended virtue, every softer sentiment would be lost.

Impatient of this cruel state of suspense and inquietude, he left Sophia's apartment, and repairing to the dining-room, rang the bell for the servant, of whom he enquired where Mr. Herbert lodged. Having obtained a direction, he went immediately to the house; Mr. Herbert was not at home, and Sir Charles, grieved at this disappointment, and at Mrs. Darnley's not returning that night, from whom he hoped to have heard some news of Sophia; the agitation of his mind made him think it an age till the next day, in which he determined to put an end to all his perplexities, and to fix his fate.

After his interview with Mr. Herbert, and the good old man's departure, to prepare Sophia for his intended visit, the young baronet resigned his whole soul to tenderness and joy. His impatience to see Sophia encreased with his hope of finding her sentiments for him unchanged, and he regretted a thousand times his having suffered Mr. Herbert to go away without him.

CHAPTER XXV

Lets the reader into some circumstances
that help to display Sir Charles's conduct.

Mean time a card came from Mrs. Darnley and Harriot acquainting him that they were returned, and thanking him for the use of his servants and chariot. Sir Charles, eager to hear news of his Sophia, went immediately to wait on them; and scarce were the first compliments over, when he enquired for her with such apparent emotion, that Harriot, mortified to the last degree, resolved to be even with him, and said every thing that she thought would torment him, and prejudice her sister.[1]

She told him that Sophia was the most contented creature in the world; and that she was so charmed with her present way of life, and her new companions, that she seemed to have forgot all her old friends, and even her relations. "She is grown a meer country girl," said she, "is always wandering about in the fields and meadows, followed by a young rustic who has fallen in love with her. I rallied her a little upon her taste; but I found she could not bear it, and indeed he is extremely handsome, and she says, has had a genteel education."

Harriot was at once pleased and grieved at observing the effect these insinuations had on Sir Charles; his colour changed, he trembled, and fixing his eyes on the ground, he remained pensive and silent, while Harriot, notwithstanding her mother's insignificant frowns, proceeded in a malicious detail of little circumstances partly invented, and partly mistaken, which fixed the sharpest stings of jealousy in his heart.

If in dealing with cunning persons we were always to consider their ends, in order to interpret their speeches, much of their artifice would lose its effect; but Sir Charles had so contemptible an opinion of Harriot's understanding, that although he knew she was malicious, he never suspected her of being capable of laying schemes to gratify her malice; and did not suppose she was mistress of invention enough to form so plausible a tale as that she had told.

Impatient under those cruel doubts which now possessed him, he resolved to go, late as it was in the evening, to Mr. Lawson's house; and taking an abrupt leave of Mrs. Darnley and her daughter, he went home, and ordered his horses to be got ready. He scarce knew his own design by taking this journey at so improper a time; but in the extreme agitation of his mind, the first idea of relief that naturally presented itself was to see Sophia, who alone could destroy or confirm his fears; and this he eagerly pursued without any farther reflection.

The servant to whom he had sent his orders, made no haste to execute them, as conceiving it to be a most extravagant whim in

---

1 I.e., that would prejudice him against her sister.

his master to set out upon a journey so late, and in that manner. While he with studied delays protracted the time, hoping for some change in his resolutions, Sir Charles racked with impatience, counted moments for hours; message after message was dispatched to the groom. The horses at length were brought, and Sir Charles, with only one servant, galloped away, never stopping till he came to the place where Sophia resided.

It was now night, and the indecorum of making a visit at such a time in a family where he was a stranger, first striking his thoughts, he resolved to alight at an inn which he saw at a small distance, and there consider what it was best for him to do.[1]

A guest of his appearance soon engaged the attention of the host and his wife. They quitted two men with whom they had been talking, and, with a great deal of officious civility, attended upon Sir Charles, who desired to be shewn into a room. As he was following the good woman, who declared he should have the best in her house, the two persons before mentioned, bowed to him when he passed by them; the salute of the younger having a certain grace in it that drew his attention, he looked back on him, and at the sight of a very handsome face, and a person uncommonly genteel, his heart, by its throbbing emotions, immediately suggested to him, that this beautiful youth was the lover of his Sophia.

The jealousy which Harriot's insinuations had kindled in his heart, now raged with redoubled force; this rival, whom she had called a rustic, and whom he fondly hoped to find such, possessed the most attractive graces of form, and probably wanted neither wit nor politeness. Sophia's youth, her tenderness, her sensibility, wounded by his dissembled indifference, and the cruel capriciousness of his conduct, all disposed her to receive a new impression, and who so proper to touch her heart as this lovely youth, whose passion, as innocent as it was ardent and sincere, banished all doubt and suspicion, and left her whole soul open to the soft pleadings of gratitude and love?

While he was wholly absorbed in these tormenting reflections, and incapable of taking any resolution, the officious landlady entered his chamber to take his orders for supper.

---

1 Since travel in the eighteenth century was so slow, there were inns, pubs, alehouses, and taverns along the roads. These offered varying combinations of food and lodging. Most had separate rooms that were acceptable for members of the gentry such as Sir Charles.

Sir Charles, surprised to find it was so late, resolved to stay there all night, and after giving the good woman some directions, his restless curiosity impelled him to ask her several questions concerning the old man and the youth whom he had seen talking to her.

The hostess, who was as communicative as he could desire, told him, that the old man was one farmer Gibbons, of whom she had been buying a load of hay; that the young one was his son, and a great scholard.[1] "His aunt," pursued she, "breeds him up to be a gentleman; and she has a power of money, and designs to leave it all to him, much good may it do him, for he is as handsome a young man as one would desire to see. Some time ago it was all over our town that he was going to be married to the parson's youngest daughter, and she is a pretty creature, and *disarves*[2] him if he was more richer and handsomer than he is; but whatever is the matter, the old folks have changed their mind, and his aunt, they say, wants to make up a match between him and a fine London lady that boards at the parson's; but I'll never believe it till I see it, for she and the parson's daughter are great friends, they say, and it would not be a friendly part to rob the poor girl of her sweetheart. To say the truth, I believe there is some juggling[3] among them; but this I keep to myself, for I would not make mischief; therefore I never tell my thoughts to any body, but I wish the young folks well."

Sir Charles, who had listened to her with great emotion, dismissed her now, that he might be at liberty to reflect on what he had heard, which, although it did not lead him to a full discovery of the truth, yet it suggested thoughts which relieved him in some degree from those dreadful pangs of jealousy with which he had hitherto been tortured, and ballanced at least his fears and his hopes.

---

1   "Scholard" is simply a variant of scholar. By using this form, Lennox places the hostess in a long comic tradition, which includes Samuel Butler's satiric poem *Hudibras* (1663–80) and Peter Motteux's translation of *Don Quixote* (1700–03).

2   This version of "deserves" is probably a nod to Henry Fielding, who in *Shamela* (1741) has his sexually corrupt heroine speak of "vartue" rather than "virtue." Incidentally, Fielding also mentions a "scholard" in *Shamela*.

3   Trickery, deception.

CHAPTER XXVI

The Baronet's Jealousy accounted for: he leaves England.

His impatience to free himself from this state of perplexity and suspence, allowed him but little repose that night; he rose as soon as the day appeared, and it was with some difficulty that he prevailed upon himself to defer his visit till a seasonable hour; and then being informed that Mr. Lawson's house was scarce a mile distant, he left his servant and horses at the inn, and walked thither, amidst a thousand anxious thoughts, which made him dread as much as he wished for an interview, which was to decide his fate.

As he drew near the house, he perceived a young man sauntering about in an adjacent field, whose air and mien had a great resemblance of the youth whom he had seen in the inn. Sir Charles, eager to satisfy his doubts, followed him at a distance, and the youth turning again his wishing eyes towards the house, the baronet had a full view of his face.

At the sight of his young rival his heart throbbed as if it would leave his breast: he hastily retreated behind a hedge, determined to watch his motions; for he imagined, and with reason, that he came there to meet his mistress; and who that mistress was, whether Sophia, or the curate's daughter, was the distracting doubt, which he now expected to have satisfied.

He walked along by the side of the hedge, still keeping William in sight, who suddenly turning back, rather flew than ran to meet a woman who beckoned him. Sir Charles saw at once his Sophia, and the fatal sign, which planted a thousand daggers in his heart. Trembling and pale he leaned against a tree, which concealed him from view, and saw her advance towards his rival, saw her in earnest discourse with him; and, to compleat his distraction and despair, saw the happy youth throw himself at her feet, doubtless to thank her for the sacrifice she made to him of a richer lover.

Such was the inference he drew from this action; and now rage and indignation succeeding to grief, in these first transports, he was upon the point of discovering himself, and sacrificing the hated youth to his vengeance; but a moment's reflection shewed him the dishonour of a contest with so despicable a rival, and turned all his resentment against Sophia, who having quitted her supposed lover, took her way back again to the house. Sir Charles followed her with disordered haste, resolved to load her with reproaches for her inconstancy: then, unwilling to gratify her pride by such an acknowledgment of his weakness, he turned back, cursing love, women, and his own ill fate. In this temper he wandered about a long time; at last he again returned to the inn, where, after having given orders to have his horses got ready, he wrote that letter to Mr. Herbert, in which he so well disguised the anguish of his heart, that the good old man believed his breaking off the affair was the effect of his lightness and inconstancy only, though Sophia's quicker penetration easily discovered the latent jealousy that had dictated it.

Sir Charles ordered his servant to deliver the letter into Mr. Herbert's hands; then mounting his horse, he bid him follow him as soon as he had executed his commission. The young baronet, who retired to his country seat to conceal his melancholy, and fondly flattered himself that he should soon overcome that fatal passion which had been the source of so much disgust to him, found his mind so cruelly tortured with the remembrance of Sophia, that he reassumed his first design of going abroad, and unfortunately set out for Dover the day before Mr. Herbert's arrival.

The good old man being obliged to send Sophia this bad news, filled his letter with tender consolations, and wise and prudent counsels: he exorted her to bear this stroke of fortune with the dignity of patience which distinguishes the good and wise.

"The virtue of prosperity," said he, "is temperance, the virtue of adversity fortitude; it is this last which you are now called upon to exert, and which the innocence of your life may well inspire you with: for be assured, my dear child, that it is the greatest consolation under misfortunes to be conscious of having always meant well, and to be convinced that nothing but guilt deserves to be considered as a severe evil."

Sophia in her answer displayed a mind struggling against its own tenderness, offering up its disappointed hopes, its griefs, and desires, in pious sacrifice to the will of Providence, and seeking in religion all its consolation and support.

"Can a virtuous person," said she, "however oppressed by poverty, and in consequence neglected by the world, be said to want friends and comforters who can look into his own mind with modest approbation, and to whom recollection furnishes a source of joy? Every good action he has performed is a friend, every instance of pious resignation is a comforter, who cheer him with present peace, and support him with hopes of future happiness. Can he be said to be alone, and deprived of the pleasures of society, who converses with saints and angels? is he without distinction and reward whose life his almighty Creator approves?"

CHAPTER XXVII

Sophia meets with a new Subject of Affliction.

The loss of Sir Charles having clouded all Sophia's views of happiness, she earnestly intreated Mr. Herbert's permission to settle herself in that humble station to which Providence seemed to call her; and as she believed Mrs. Gibbons might be very useful to her upon this occasion, she resolved to apply to her as soon as she had his answer.

Notwithstanding all her endeavours to bear this shock of fate with patience, a fixed melancholy took possession of her mind, convinced that Sir Charles had loved her; and that, by an unfortunate concurrence of circumstances, he had been prevented from giving her the utmost proof of his affection; her tenderness no longer combatted by suspicions to his prejudice, gained new force every day, and all his actions now appeared to her in a favourable point of view: so true it is, that when a person is found less guilty than he is suspected, he is concluded more innocent than he really is.[1]

Mr. Herbert, after a long silence, at length acquainted her, that he was ill, and desired her not to leave Mr. Lawson's till she heard further from him.

The shortness of this billet, the trembling hand with which it appeared to be written, filled Sophia with the most dreadful apprehensions. Sir Charles was now forgot, and all her thoughts were taken up with the danger of her worthy friend: she determined to go to him; and although Mr. Lawson and his wife endeavoured to dissuade her from taking such a journey, and William, urged by Dolly, and his own eagerness to serve her, offered to go and bring her an exact account of the state of his health, yet her purpose remained unalterable.

"My dear benefactor is ill," said she, "and has none but strangers about him; it is fit that I should go and attend him; and if I must lose him," pursued she, bursting into tears, "it will be some comfort to me to reflect that I have done my duty."

She set out early the next morning in the stage-coach: Dolly wept at parting, and engaged her lover to attend Sophia to her

---

1   This maxim seems to come from *The History of the Rebellion and Civil Wars in England* by Edward Hyde, Earl of Clarendon (Oxford: Printed at the Theatre, 1702). Clarendon writes, "a man is no sooner found less Guilty than he is expected, but he is concluded more Innocent than he is" (8).

journey's end; that if Mr. Herbert should be worse than they apprehended, he might be near to assist and comfort her.

Sophia, when she saw him riding by the side of the coach, attempted to persuade him to return; but William, charmed to have an opportunity of expressing his zeal for her service, would not quit her; and her spirits being too weak to contest this point with him, she was obliged to suffer his attendance.

They reached the place where Mr. Herbert was, in the evening of the third day: he had taken lodgings at the house of a farmer, where he was attended with great tenderness and care.

Sophia appeared with so deep a concern upon her countenance, and enquired for him with such extreme emotion, that the good woman of the house concluding she was his daughter, thought it necessary before she answered her questions, to preach patience and submission to her, wisely observing, that we are all mortal, and that death spares nobody, from the squire to the ploughman.

She ran on in this manner till she perceived Sophia grow pale, and close her eyes: she had just time to prevent her from falling, and with William's assistance, placed her in a chair, where while she applied remedies to recover her from her swoon, the youth with tears in his eyes, asked her softly, how long Mr. Herbert had been dead.

"Dead!" repeated the farmer's wife, "who told you he was dead? no, no, it is not so bad as that neither."

William rejoiced to hear this, and as soon as Sophia shewed some signs of returning life, he greeted her with the welcome news. She cast a look full of doubt and anguish upon the countrywoman, who confirmed his report, and offered to go with her to the gentleman's room. Sophia instantly found her strength return; she followed her with trembling haste; and, lest her presence should surprise Mr. Herbert, she directed the good woman to tell him, that a friend of his was come to see him.

She heard him answer in a weak voice, but with some emotion, "It is my dear child, bring her to me."

Sophia immediately appeared, and throwing herself upon her knees at his bed-side, burst into tears, and was unable to speak.

The good old man holding one of her hands prest in his, tenderly blamed her for the trouble she had given herself in coming so far to visit him; but acknowledged at the same time, that this instance of her affection was extremely dear to him, and that her presence gave him inexpressible comfort.

Sophia entered immediately upon the office of a nurse to her benefactor, and performed all the duties of the most affectionate child to the best of parents.

Mr. Herbert employed the little remaining strength he had in endeavours to comfort her, and in pious exhortations. "Weep not for me, my dear child," would he say, "but rather rejoice that the innocence of my life has divested death of his terrors, and enabled me to meet him with calm resignation, and with humble hope. At this awful hour, how little would it avail me, that I had been rich, that I had been great and powerful? but what comforts do I not feel from an unreproving conscience? these comforts every one has it in his power to procure: live virtuous then, my dear Sophia, that you may die in peace: how small is the difference between the longest and the shortest life! if its pleasures be few, its miseries are so likewise; how little do they enjoy whom the world calls happy! how little do they suffer whom it pronounces wretched! one point of fleeting time past, and death reduces all to an equality. But the distinction between virtue and vice, and future happiness and misery are eternal."

CHAPTER XXVIII
The Character of Mrs. Howard.

Sophia had need of all the consolation she derived from her reflections on the virtue and piety of her friend, to enable her to bear the apprehensions of his approaching death with any degree of fortitude; but when she least expected it, his distemper took a favourable turn, and in a few days the most dangerous symptoms were removed.

The Bath waters being judged absolutely necessary for the entire re-establishment of his health, he resolved to go thither as soon as he had recovered strength enough to bear the journey.

Sophia at his earnest desire consented to return to Mr. Lawson's, and remain there till he came from Bath, but she would not quit him till he was able to take this journey; and by the sweetness of her conversation, her tender assiduity, and watchful care, contributed so much towards his recovery, that he was soon in a condition to travel with safety.

He accompanied her the first day's journey to Mr. Lawson's; and being met at the inn by this worthy friend and young William, he consigned his beloved charge to their care, and pursued his way to Bath.

Sophia was received with great joy by Mrs. Lawson and her daughters: Dolly hung a long time upon her neck in transports, and as soon as they were alone, informed her that Mrs. Gibbons and her mother were perfectly reconciled; that she had consented to her nephew's marriage, and even shewed an impatience to conclude it: "but I prevailed," said she, "to have the ceremony delayed till you, my dear friend, could be present; for I could not think of being happy, while you to whom I owe all, was afflicted."

Sophia embraced her tenderly, congratulated her upon her change of fortune, and gave many praises to her lover, to whom she acknowledged great obligations for his care and attention to her.

Dolly's cheeks glowed with pleasure while she heard her William commended by one whom she so much loved and revered.

The young lovers were married a few days afterwards; and Sophia, who had so earnestly endeavoured to bring about this union, and had suffered so much in her own interest by her solicitude concerning it, was one of those to whom it gave the most satisfaction.

Mean time Mr. Herbert continued indisposed at Bath, and Sophia uneasy, lest in this increase of his expences, her residence at Mr. Lawson's should lay him under some difficulties, resolved to ease him as soon as possible of the charge of her maintenance: she explained her situation to Mrs. Gibbons, and requested her assistance in procuring her a place.

Mrs. Gibbons expressed great tenderness and concern for her upon this occasion, and assured her she would employ all her interest in her service. She accordingly mentioned her with great praise to a widow lady of a very affluent fortune, who had established such a character for generosity and goodness, that she hoped, if she could be induced to take Sophia under her protection her fortune would be made.

Mrs. Howard, so was the lady called, no sooner heard that a young woman of merit, well born, and genteely educated was reduced to go to service for subsistence, than she exclaimed with great vehemence against the avarice and luxury of the rich and great, who either hoarded for their unthankful heirs, or lavished in expensive pleasures, those superfluous sums which ought to be applied to the relief of the indigent. "Oh that I had a fortune," cried she, "as large as my heart, there should not be one distressed person in the world! I must see this young lady, Mrs. Gibbons, and I must do something for her. You have obliged me infinitely by putting it in my power to gratify the unbounded benevolence of my heart upon a deserving object."

Mrs. Gibbons, when she related this conversation to Sophia, filled her with an extreme impatience to see the lady, not from any mean considerations of advantage to herself, but admiration of so excellent a character. She accompanied Mrs. Gibbons in a visit to her at her country seat, which was but a few miles distant from the village where they lived; and Mrs. Howard was so pleased with her at this first interview, that she gave her an invitation to spend the remainder of the summer with her, and this in so obliging a manner, that Sophia immediately complied, not thinking it necessary to wait till she had consulted Mr. Herbert upon this offer, as she was fully persuaded he could have no objections to her accepting it, Mrs. Howard being so considerable by her family and fortune, and so estimable by her character.

This lady, who had made an early discovery of Sophia's economical talents, set her to work immediately after her arrival; her task was to embroider a white sattin negligee, which she undertook with great readiness, pleased at having an opportunity of obliging a woman of so generous a disposition, and in some degree to requite her for her hospitality.

Mrs. Howard indeed always prevented those on whom she conferred favours, from incurring the guilt of ingratitude; for she took care to be fully repaid for any act of benevolence; and having a wonderful art in extracting advantage to herself from the necessities of others, she sometimes sought out the unfortunate with a solicitude that did great honour to her charity, which was sure to be its own reward. A few ostentatious benefactions had sufficiently established her character; and while her name appeared among subscribers to some fashionable charity,[1] who could suspect that her table was served with a parsimony which would have disgraced a much smaller fortune; that her rents from her indigent tenants were exacted with the most unrelenting rigor, and the naked and hungry sent sighing from her gate?

It has been well observed that what is called liberality is often no more than the vanity of giving, of which some persons are

---

1 Charities were often financed by taking collections from wealthy individuals, who were called subscribers. Any publications of the charity listed the subscribers, so Mrs. Howard's charitable contributions would have been on record for all to see.

fonder than of what they give.[1] But the vanity of giving publicly is most prevailing; and hence it happens, that those who are most celebrated for their charity, are in reality least sensible to the feelings of humanity: and the same persons from whom the most affecting representation of private distress could not force the least relief, have been among the first to send their contributions to any new foundation.

Sophia knew not how to reconcile many circumstances in Mrs. Howard's conduct with her general professions of benevolence and generosity; but that lady had been so used to disguise herself to others, that at last she did not know herself; and the warmth and vehemence with which she delivered her sentiments imposed almost as much upon herself as her hearers.

Sophia's amiable qualities however soon produced their usual effects, and inspired Mrs. Howard with as much friendship for her as so interested[2] a temper was capable of. She wished to see her fortune established, and was very desirous of serving her as far as she could, consistent with her prudent maxims which were to make other persons the source of those benefits, the merit of which she arrogated to herself.

Chance soon furnished her with an opportunity of exerting her talents in favour of Sophia, and of engaging, as she conceived, her eternal gratitude. A country lady of her acquaintance coming one day to visit her, with her son, a clownish ignorant youth, Mrs. Howard was encouraged by the frequent glances he gave Sophia, to form a scheme for marrying her to him; and in this she foresaw so many possible advantages to herself from Sophia's grateful disposition, that she pursued it with the most anxious solicitude.

CHAPTER XXIX
Mrs. Howard is taken in her own snare.

Mr. Barton, so was the young squire called, having conceived a liking for Sophia, repeated his visits frequently, emboldened by Mrs. Howard's civilities, who took every occasion of praising Sophia, and insinuating that he would be extremely happy in such a wife.

---

1 This maxim again comes from Rochefoucauld's *Moral Maxims* (1665): "What is call'd Liberality is seldom more than the Vanity of Giving; of which we are fonder than of what we give" (82n.).

2 Self-interested, selfish.

She sometimes left him alone with Sophia, in hopes that he would declare his passion to her: but the rustic, awed by the dignity of her person and manners, durst not even raise his eyes to look on her; so that Mrs. Howard, finding the affair did not advance so fast as she wished, rallied Sophia upon her ill-timed reserve, and hinted her views in her favour, which she considering as an effect of her friendship, listened with respect, and even gratitude, though her heart refused to concur in them.

This conversation passed in the presence of Mrs. Howard's only son, a youth about nineteen, who had come from the university to pass a few days with his mother. As soon as she quitted Sophia, he approached her, and, with a look of tenderness and concern, told her, "He was sorry to find his mother so zealous an advocate for Mr. Barton, who could not possibly deserve her."

"Nor can I possibly deserve him," replied Sophia with a smile; "he is too rich."

"Love only and merit can deserve you," resumed the young student, sighing, "and if love were merit, I know one who might—hope—"

He paused and hesitated, and Sophia, to whom the language of love in any mouth but Sir Charles's was odious, suddenly quitted him, to avoid the continuance of a discourse which she considered as mere unmeaning gallantry.

Mean time, her rustic lover not having courage enough to declare his passion to her, had recourse to the indulgence of his mother, who till that time had never refused any of his desires.

He told her that he never liked any young woman so well in his life as Mrs. Sophia Darnley; and that he was sure she would make a good wife, because Mrs. Howard had told him so, and encouraged him to break his mind to her, but he was ashamed: he declared he would marry no body else, and begged his mother to get her for him.

Mrs. Barton, full of rage against her neighbour, for thus endeavouring to ensnare her son into a marriage, as she conceived unworthy of him, resolved to go to her, and load her with reproaches. While her chariot was getting ready, she continued to question her son, and heard a great many particulars from him, which convinced her that his affections were more deeply engaged than she had imagined.

After ordering the young squire to be locked up till her return, she flew to Mrs. Howard, and, with the most violent transports of rage, upbraided her with the treacherous part she had acted, by seducing her son into a liking for a poor creature, who was dependent upon her charity, and whom she took this method to get rid of.

Mrs. Howard, who held Mrs. Barton in great contempt, on account of her ignorance, and valued herself extremely upon her philosophic command over her passions, listened with an affected calmness to all Mrs. Barton's invectives; and when she found she had railed herself out of breath, she began to declaim in a solemn accent against avarice, and that vile sordid disposition of parents, who, in the marriage of their children, preferred the dross of riches to the real treasures of wisdom and virtue. She very charitably lamented Mrs. Barton's want of discernment, and littleness of mind; and concluded that Miss Sophia's merit rendered her deserving of a husband even more considerable than Mr. Barton.

"Then marry her to your own son," replied Mrs. Barton, with a sneer; "no doubt but he will be more worthy of her."

"If my son should declare a passion for Miss Sophia," resumed Mrs. Howard, "it would soon be seen how far my sentiments are exalted above yours."

"I am glad to hear this," returned Mrs. Barton, "for I am very sure Mr. Howard is in love with this wonderful creature whom you praise so much; and since you are so willing to make her your daughter-in-law, I shall be under no fear of my son's marrying her."

Mrs. Howard, at this unexpected stroke, turned as pale as death, and, with a faultering voice, asked her, "What reason she had for supposing her son was in love with Miss Sophia?"

Mrs. Barton, who enjoyed her perplexity and confusion, suffered her to repeat her questions several times, and then maliciously referred her to the young gentleman himself, "Who," said she, "upon finding you so favourably disposed, will, I doubt not, be ready enough to own his inclinations."

Mrs. Howard was now so far humbled, that she condescended to intreat Mrs. Barton to tell her what she knew of this affair.

"All my information," said Mrs. Barton, "comes from my son, to whom Mr. Howard, considering him as his rival, declared his better right to the lady, as having first acquainted her with his passion."

At this intelligence Mrs. Howard's rage got so much the better of her prudence, that she uttered a thousand invectives against the innocent Sophia, which drew some severe sarcasms from Mrs. Barton who being now fully revenged, rose up to be gone; but Mrs. Howard, sensible that a quarrel upon this occasion might have consequences very unfavourable to her reputation, seized her hand, and led her half reluctant, again to her chair, where after she had soothed her into good humour, by some flattering expressions, which coming from one of her acknowledged understanding, had great weight. She told her with the most unblushing confidence, that she was now convinced she had been deceived in the character of the young woman on whom she had with her usual generosity conferred so many benefits. "I find to my inexpressible concern," pursued she, "that this modest, sensible, and virtuous young creature, as I once believed her, is in reality an artful hypocrite, whose only aim is to make her fortune, by ensnaring some unexperienced youth into a marriage. Let us join our endeavours then, my dear Mrs. Barton, to preserve our sons from this danger: this is a common cause, all mothers are concerned in it; we will shew the young dissembler in her proper colours, and prevent her imposing upon others as she has done upon us."

Mrs. Barton, who never carried her reflections very far, was so well pleased with Mrs. Howard's present behaviour, that she forgot all the past: these two ladies became on a sudden the best friends in the world, and this union was to be cemented with the ruin of Sophia's fame, such beginnings have certain female friendships, and such are the leagues in which the wicked join.

Mrs. Barton proposed to have her sent for into their presence, and after reproaching her severely, dismiss her with contempt; but the more politic Mrs. Howard, whose views were at once to destroy Sophia's reputation, and to secure her own, disapproved of this harsh treatment, as she called it, and charitably resolved to ruin her with all possible gentleness.

CHAPTER XXX
Sophia leaves Mrs. Howard.

Mrs. Howard accordingly wrote to Mrs. Gibbons, and acquainted her, that having discovered an intrigue carrying on between Sophia and her son, she thought it necessary to dismiss her immediately out of her family; but that the poor young creature might be exposed as little as possible to censure, she begged she would come herself to fetch her away, and deliver her to her friends, with a caution to watch her conduct carefully.

She recommended secrecy to her for Sophia's sake; and assured her that if it had not been for this discovery of her bad conduct, she had resolved to have provided for her handsomely.

Mrs. Gibbons, whom this letter threw into the utmost astonishment, immediately communicated the contents of it to Dolly and William, with whom she now lived.

Dolly burst into tears of grief and indignation, and earnestly intreated her to go immediately and take Miss Sophia out of a house where her merit was so little understood: but William, who looked farther into the consequences of this affair than either his wife or his aunt, believed it necessary for the justification of Sophia's honour, that Mr. Lawson should wait upon Mrs. Howard, and demand an explanation of those censures which she had cast upon a young lady confided to his care; rightly judging, that if malice was the source of her accusation, she would not dare to pursue it with a man of his character; and if it arose from the information of others, he would be able to detect the falshood of it.

These reasons prevailed with Mrs. Gibbons, who had been very desirous to shew her eloquence upon this occasion, and was resolved, she said, not to have spared Mrs. Howard for her *immature* conclusions.

William went immediately to his father-in-law, and acquainted him with what had happened. Mr. Lawson was grieved from the consideration of what Sophia's delicate sensibility would feel from such an attack upon her reputation; and this was the worst that he apprehended could happen from calumnies which the purity of her manners and the innocency of her life would be always a sufficient refutation of. A wise and virtuous person, he knew, was out of the reach of fortune, though not free from the malice of it. All attempts against such a one are, as the poet says, like the arrows of Xerxes; they may darken the day, but cannot stifle the sun.[1]

His impatience to take Sophia out of the hands of a woman whom he conceived to be either very malicious, or very imprudent, made him defer his visit no longer than till the afternoon.

When he sent in his name, Mrs. Howard, who had no suspicion of the occasion of his coming, ordered him to be shewn into a parlour, where she suffered him to wait near an hour before she admitted him to her presence; a country curate being in her

---

1 The "poet" here is Seneca. Once again, Lennox is quoting L'Estrange's translation titled *Seneca's Morals* (1678): "A Wise Man is out of the reach of Fortune, but not Free from the Malice of it; and all Attempts upon him are no more than *Xerxes* his Arrows; they may darken the Day, but they cannot Strike the Sun" (498).

opinion a person too insignificant to lay claim to any degree of consideration, and besides, this sort of neglect being affected by many persons of quality, to whom it certainly gives great importance and dignity, their imitators never lose any opportunity of exercising it.

Mr. Lawson was at last summoned to the lady's dressing-room, where he expected to have found Sophia, but was glad to see Mrs. Howard alone. She asked him with a little superciliousness, if he had any business with her; to which he replied, with a solemnity in his look and accent that surprised her, "That being a friend to miss Sophia Darnley, and the person to whose care she was confided by her relations, he thought it his duty to enquire what part of her conduct had given occasion for those unfavourable suspicions which were entertained of her.

"Mrs. Gibbons, madam," pursued he, "has communicated to me a letter which she has received from you, wherein there is a heavy charge against miss Sophia; a charge which none who know her can think it possible for her to deserve. There most certainly be some mistake here, madam; you have been misinformed, or appearances have deceived you, and in justice to you, as well as to one of the most virtuous and amiable young women in the world, I am resolved to trace the source of these calumnies, that her innocence may be fully cleared. I beg of you then, madam, let me know what foundation you have for believing that Miss Sophia—"

Mrs. Howard, whom this speech had thrown into great confusion, interrupted him here, to prevent his repeating those expressions in her letter, the meaning of which, though obvious, she durst not avow.

"I find," said she, "that you and Mrs. Gibbons have seen this affair in a worse light than I intended you should; my son has been foolish enough to entertain a liking for this girl, whom I took under my protection, with a view to provide for her handsomely, and she has been wise enough," pursued she, with an ironical smile, "to give him encouragement, I suppose; but with all her excellencies, I am not disposed to make her my daughter-in-law."

Mrs. Howard threw in this last softening expression, in hopes it would satisfy Mr. Lawson, and added, "that to prevent any thing happening, which might be disagreeable to her, she begged he would take Sophia home with him."

"Most willingly, madam," said he; "but since it seems to be your opinion, that this young gentlewoman has encouraged the clandestine addresses of your son, I think it will be proper to examine first into the truth of these suspicions, that you may not part with worse thoughts of her than she deserves."

Mrs. Howard being thus prest, and unwilling to enter into an explanation that would expose all her artifices, was forced to acknowledge that she had no other foundation for her fears than the passion her son had owned for her; and having made this unwilling concession, she left him with a countenance inflamed with stifled rage, saying she would send Sophia to him.

Accordingly she went into the room where she was at work, and told her, her friend the curate was waiting to carry her home. Observing her to look extremely surprised, "If you consider," said she, "what returns you have made me for the benefits I have conferred upon you, you will not think it strange that we should part in this manner."

"Bless me," cried Sophia, "what have I done to deserve such reproaches?"

"I cannot stay to talk to you now," said Mrs. Howard; "I have explained myself to Mr. Lawson; I am sorry to say, that I now can only wish you well."

She hurried out of the room when she had said this; and Sophia, in the utmost perplexity and concern, flew down stairs to Mr. Lawson, who was already at the gate waiting to help her into the chaise: she gave him her hand, asking him at the same time, with great emotion, "What Mrs. Howard accused her of?"

As soon as they drove away, Mr. Lawson related all that had past between that lady and him, which filled Sophia with new astonishment: she could not comprehend Mrs. Howard's motives for acting in the manner she had done with regard to her; all her conduct appeared to her highly extravagant and inconsistent; she asked Mr. Lawson a thousand questions, full of that simplicity which ever accompanies real goodness of heart.

He gave her some notion of the dangerous character of Mrs. Howard, and greatly blamed her for having so suddenly accepted her invitation, without first consulting Mr. Herbert. "It is a maxim," pursued he, "of one of the wisest of the antients, that in forming new connections of every sort, it is of great importance in what manner the first approaches are made, and by whose hands the avenues of friendship are laid open."[1]

Mr. Lawson, by this hint, gave Sophia to understand, that he did not think Mrs. Gibbons a proper person to introduce her into the world. She was now sensible that she had been too precipitate; but her motives were so generous, that Mr. Herbert, whom in a letter she acquainted with the whole affair, easily justified her in his own opinion, though he earnestly recommended it to her not to let her apprehensions of being burthensome to him draw her into new inconveniencies.

Mr. Lawson having, as he imagined, prevented Mrs. Howard from making any future attack upon Sophia's reputation, by obliging her to acknowledge her innocence, was surprised to hear wherever he went, of the calumnies she invented against her.

Nothing is more common than for persons to hate with extreme inveteracy those whom they have injured; and although Mrs. Howard was convinced, that Sophia would not admit a visit from her son, (who now openly avowed his passion for her;) that she refused to receive his letters, and shunned every place where she thought it possible to meet him; yet pretending to be apprehensive that the youth would be drawn into a clandestine marriage,[2] she sent him away precipitately upon his travels, and this gave a colour to new invectives against Sophia, who trusting only to her innocence for her justification, had the satisfaction to find that innocence fully acknowledged in the esteem and respect

---

1 Cicero (106–43 BCE), famous Roman author, lawyer, and politician. In a letter to Marcus Junius Brutus (85– 42 BCE), Cicero writes, "But in forming new connections of every sort, it is of much importance in what manner the first approaches are made, and by whose hands the avenues of friendship (if I may so express myself) are laid open" (*The Letters of Marcus Tullius Cicero to Several of his Friends: with Remarks by William Melmoth*, 3 vols. [London: Dodsley, 1753], 2:329.

2 In the 1740s, as many as 15–20 per cent of all marriages were clandestine, which allowed weddings to go forward without parental consent and without social repercussions if there was a large class difference between the bride and groom. Also, poorer couples could often simply not afford the expense of an open wedding. In 1753, clandestine marriages were outlawed by the Marriage Act of Lord Chancellor Hardwicke, and they did subsequently constitute a lower percentage of all marriages. However, clandestine marriages continued to occur because couples found a loophole, absconding to the southern-most point in Scotland, Gretna Green, to get married there—since the Marriage Act only covered England.

with which she was treated by all the persons of fashion in the neighbourhood.

CHAPTER XXXI

Sophia returns to Town, and hears news that reduces her to Despair.

Mr. Herbert, who in every new trial to which Sophia was exposed, found greater cause for admiration of her character, praised the gentleness and forgiving spirit which she discovered upon this occasion; but Mrs. Gibbons was not wholly satisfied with her conduct, "You ought to *discriminate* upon Mrs. Howard," said she, "and tell the world how desirous she was to have you married to her friend's son, though she makes such a clutter about her own: indeed you want spirit, miss Sophia," added the old lady, with a little contempt.

"I am not of your opinion, madam," replied Sophia; "for in taking revenge upon our enemies, we are only even with them; in passing over their malice we are superior."

"Well, well," interrupted Mrs. Gibbons, "I have no notion of such *superiousness*: I always resent injuries, and Mrs. Howard shall feel my resentment for her malice to you. I have not returned her last visit yet, and perhaps I may not this month; this is pretty severe I think."

Sophia, composing her countenance as well as she could, thanked Mrs. Gibbons for this instance of her friendship to her; but she had no opportunity to observe whether she kept her word, for she was summoned to town by a letter from her mother, which gave her a melancholy account of her affairs.

Mrs. Darnley acquainted her that the gentleman who paid her the annuity which Sir Charles had stipulated for her when he procured him her late husband's place, was dead. She desired her to come immediately to town to assist her under her misfortunes; and added in a postscript, as if reluctantly, that Harriot had left her, and was not so dutiful as she could wish.

Sophia read this letter with tears; and, impatient to comfort her afflicted mother, she instantly prepared for her little journey.

All Mr. Lawson's family parted from her with great regret; but Dolly's affliction was extreme, and Sophia amidst so many greater causes of sorrow, felt a new pang when she took leave of her tender and innocent friend.

To spare Mr. Lawson the trouble of conducting her to town, she accepted a place in the coach of a lady with whom she had lately become acquainted, and who professed a particular esteem for her.

On her arrival at her mother's house, she found only a servant there, who informed her that her mistress had taken lodgings at Kensington[1] for the air, having been indisposed for some weeks past.

Sophia ordered her to get a hackney coach to the door, and was hurrying away without daring to enquire for her sister, when the maid told her miss Darnley desired to see her before she went to Kensington.

"Where is my sister?" said Sophia, with a faultering accent.

The answer she received was a stroke of fortune more cruel than any she had yet experienced: her sister, she found, lived in the house which Sir Charles had once offered to her.

Trembling and pale she ordered the coachman to drive thither, and drawing up the windows, relieved her labouring heart with a shower of tears.

CHAPTER XXXII
Which leaves Sophia in her former Perplexity.

The first thought that struck the amazed Sophia was, that Sir Charles, either following the motions of his natural inconstancy, or in revenge of her supposed contempt of him, had married Harriot. Certain that she had now lost for ever this lover, who with all his real or imputed faults, she had never been able to banish from her heart, she resigned herself up to the sharpest agonies of despair, and had already arrived at her sister's house before she was able to stop the course of her tears.

A servant in the livery of her own family[2] opened the door. This circumstance surprised Sophia, who pulling her hat over her eyes to conceal her disorder, asked him, with some hesitation, if his mistress was at home.

---

1 Kensington was a village east of London that is a part of London today. The air would have been better there because the town had fewer people and less industry than London.

2 Livery was a kind of uniform that masters provided for their servants. It conferred some status upon those servants and made them identifiable, since masters chose family colors or put family coats of arms on the livery.

The fellow replied, he believed she was, and opening the coach-door, shewed her into a parlour, telling her, with a smart air, that he would enquire of his lady's woman whether she was visible[1] yet or no.

Sophia having summoned all her fortitude to enable her to go through this severe trial with dignity, had time enough to recollect and compose herself before any one appeared; and now several circumstances rushed upon her memory which, in the first transports of her astonishment and grief, had escaped her attention.

Mrs. Darnley, in her letter, had not mentioned Harriot's marriage, but barely said she had left her. The servant who delivered her message called her miss Darnley; and though she lived in a house that belonged to Sir Charles, yet it was scarcely suitable to the quality of his wife.[2]

A few moments reflection upon these appearances made the generous Sophia change the object of her concern. The misfortune for which she had grieved so much, seemed light, compared with that she apprehended: she wept no longer for the inconstancy of her lover; she trembled for the honour of her sister; and her greatest fear now was, that Sir Charles was not married.

While she was absorbed in these melancholy thoughts, Harriot's maid entered the room, who after glancing over Sophia with a supercilious eye, (for she was very simply drest,) asked her, "If she had any business with her lady."

"Tell her," replied Sophia, "that her sister is here."

The girl blushed, courtesied, and flew to acquaint her mistress; and Sophia was instantly desired to walk up stairs.

She found Harriot in her dressing room, in an elegant dishabille,[3] having just finished her morning's work, which appeared in a suit of ribbons made up with great taste.

As soon as she saw Sophia, she rose from her chair, and saluted her with affected dignity; but at the same time with an air of embarrassment that encreased every moment: so that being unable to bear the sweet but penetrating looks of her sister, she resumed her work, altering and unripping, without any apparent design, yet affecting to be extremely busy, and to shew how perfectly she was at ease, talked of the most trifling matters imagi-

---

1   Presentable, available for visits.
2   I.e., the quality of the house was fine, but not good enough for the wife of a member of the gentry like Sir Charles.
3   Loose dress worn about the house in private or with family.

nable, while Sophia gazed on her in silent anguish, anxious to know the truth of her situation, yet dreading to have it explained. At length she told her that she was going to Kensington to her mother, and desired to know if she had any message to send to her.

Harriot suddenly interrupting her, as if she feared some further questions, began to exclaim against her mother's unreasonable temper, saying, that she had offended her violently only because she had it not in her power to comply with some very extravagant expectations which she had formed.

"Sister," said Sophia, "I am wholly ignorant of your affairs; I know not what cause of discontent you have given my mother, but I see there is a great alteration in your condition of life, and I hope—"

"What do you hope, pray Miss?" interrupted Harriot, reddening: "I suppose I am to have some of your satirical flings; your temper is not altered I find."

"Dear Harriot," resumed Sophia, with tears in her eyes (this causeless anger confirming her suspicions) "why do you reproach me with being satirical? is it a crime to be anxious for your happiness?"

"I wish you would not trouble yourself about me," replied Harriot, "I know best what will make me happy; you should not pretend to instruct your elders, miss Sophy; I am older than you; you know, you have often upbraided me with that."

"Sister," said Sophia calmly, "you desired to see me, have you any thing to say to me?"

"I know," answered Harriot, "that I shall meet with ungrateful returns for my kindness; nevertheless I shall act like a sister towards you, and it was to tell you so that I wished to see you: I very much doubt whether, if you were in prosperity, you would do the same by me."

"Have I behaved so ill in adversity then," said Sophia, "that you form this hard judgment of me, Harriot?"

"Pray don't upbraid me with your behaviour, miss," said Harriot; "other people may have behaved as well as you, though they are not prudes."

"You say you are in prosperity, sister," said Sophia, "but perhaps you and I have different notions of prosperity: let me know the truth of your situation, and if I find you happy according to my notions of happiness, you will soon be convinced that I can take a sister's share in it."

"I am not obliged to give an account of my conduct to you," replied Harriot, who had listened to this speech with great emotion; "and I must tell you, sister Sophia, that if you go on taking this liberty of questioning and censuring me, I shall not care how seldom I see you. As to my mother, I know that it is my duty to do every thing for her that is in my power; and this I have offered to do already."

Saying this, she rang the bell, and her maid appearing, she gave her some orders which necessarily required her attendance in the room; so that Sophia, finding she could have no further discourse with her sister, rose up and took leave of her with an aching heart. Her griefs all aggravated by the apprehension of her sister's dishonour, and the hatred which she felt for Sir Charles, as her seducer, struggling with a tender remembrance, her gentle bosom was torn with conflicting passions, and she proved but too well the truth of that maxim, That philosophy easily triumphs over past and future evils, but the *present* triumph over her.[1]

CHAPTER XXXIII
Contains an interesting Discovery.

Mrs. Darnley received her daughter with unusual tenderness; she felt how much she stood in need of her filial care; and her behaviour was dictated by that interested kindness which only gives in expectation of receiving back doublefold.

Sophia saw her pale and emaciated, and was greatly affected with the sight: she would not mention her sister, for fear of discomposing her; but Mrs. Darnley soon introduced the subject that was most in her thoughts, and exclaimed against Harriot's undutifulness and want of affection with the most violent transports of passion.

"I have been the best of mothers to her," said she, melting into tears; "I have always indulged her in all her wishes, and impaired my fortune to support her extravagancies, and how has she returned this kindness! Would you think it, my dear Sophy, though she is in affluent circumstances, and I, by the loss of my annuity, am plunged into all my former distresses, she has refused to pay those debts which I contracted during the time she lived with me; and thinks it sufficient to invite me to reside in her house, where, no doubt, I should feel my dependence severely."

---

1 Rochefoucauld's *Moral Maxims* (1665): "Philosophy easily triumphs over past and future Ills; but the *present* triumph over her" (76).

"Sir Charles," said Sophia sighing, "does not act with his usual generosity; if he has married my sister, why does he suffer you to be in distress?"

"Married your sister!" repeated Mrs. Darnley, in astonishment.

"Ah, madam," resumed Sophia, "is she not married then to Sir Charles?"

"Why, is it possible that you can wish him to be married to Harriot?" said Mrs. Darnley.

"Alas!" cried Sophia, "ought I not to wish it, when I see her in his house?"

"Oh," resumed Mrs. Darnley, "I perceive your mistake; but that house is not Sir Charles's now; Lord L— bought it of him, with the furniture, some time ago; it might have been yours, and without any offence to your virtue too, yet you thought fit to refuse it: but I will not pretend to reprove one so much wiser than myself—"

"Well, madam," interrupted Sophia eagerly, "then it is not to Sir Charles that my sister is married, to whom is she married?"

"You have seen her, have you not?" said Mrs. Darnley, looking a little confused.

"I have indeed seen her," said Sophia, "but she did not explain her situation to me."

"And do you imagine," resumed Mrs. Darnley, peevishly, "that she would be less reserved with her mother? and if she was afraid of telling you the truth, is it likely she would own it to me?"

"Then I fear it is bad indeed with Harriot," cried Sophia, in a melancholy accent, "since she has so much to conceal from a mother and a sister."

"You were always censorious, Sophy," said Mrs. Darnley, with some passion; "for my part, I am resolved to think the best. If Lord L— is married privately to your sister, her character will one day be cleared to the world, and she thinks no prudent person can blame her, for chusing to bear for a time a few undeserved censures, rather than to struggle with poverty and contempt."

Sophia, now convinced of Harriot's unhappy conduct, burst into tears. Mrs. Darnley, after looking at her in silence a moment, said, with some confusion; "Then you do not believe your sister is married, Sophy?"

"Ah, madam," replied Sophia, "you do not say that you know she is, and whatever reasons there might be for concealing her marriage from the world, certainly there are none for hiding it from you.—In vain," added she, with still greater emotion, "would your parental tenderness seek to deceive yourself."

"Reproach me no more with my tenderness for your sister," interrupted Mrs. Darnley, angrily; "I am too much affected with her ingratitude already."

"I am sorry she is ungrateful," said Sophia; "but, oh! my dear mamma, it is not fit you should accept of her assistance."

"I hope," said Mrs. Darnley, casting down her eyes, "that I know what to do as well as my daughter.—But Sophy," added she, after a little pause, "I am sorry to tell you, if you do not know it already, that if you have still any thought of Sir Charles, you deceive yourself; I am very well informed, that a match has been proposed to him, and he has given so favourable an answer that it is expected the marriage will be concluded, as soon as he comes from Paris: I heard it all from one of the young lady's relations."

This was a severe stroke to poor Sophia, who had just begun to breathe again, after the anguish she had suffered, in the belief that Sir Charles had forsaken her for her sister, and added perfidy and baseness to his inconstancy.

Mrs. Darnley, who saw her grow pale, and her eyes swimming in tears, while she struggled to conceal her emotions, could not help being affected with her distress, and endeavoured to console her.

Sophia, more softened by this tenderness, suffered her tears to flow a few moments unrestrained; then suddenly wiping her charming eyes, "Pardon this weakness, madam," said she, "this indeed is not a time to weep for myself, your sorrows claim all my tears."

"Aye, I have sorrows enough, Heaven knows," said Mrs. Darnley, "my debts unpaid, my annuity gone, what have I to trust to?"

"Providence," interrupted Sophia, "your piety and my industry. Alas! my dear mamma, your greatest affliction is not the loss of your annuity, or the debts with which you are encumbered, it is my sister's unhappy fall from virtue. That parent," pursued she, "who sees a beloved child become a prey to licentious passions, who sees her publicly incur shame and reproach, expelled the society of the good and virtuous, and lead a life of dishonour embittered with the contempt of the world, and the secret upbraidings of her own conscience; that parent can best judge of your anguish now: I have only a sister's feelings for this misfortune! but these feelings are strong enough to make me very unhappy."

Mrs. Darnley appeared so much moved with this discourse, that Sophia pursued it, till she brought her mother to declare, that she would rather suffer all the inconveniencies of poverty, than give a sanction to Harriot's guilt, by partaking of its reward.

Sophia, to relieve her anxiety, laid down a plan for their future subsistence, and proved to her, that by her skill in several little useful arts, it would be easy for her to supply her with all the necessaries of life. "We will first," said she, "pay your debts."

"How is that to be done?" said Mrs. Darnley hastily.

"The furniture of your house," said Sophia, "the plate, and other pieces of finery, which Sir Charles Stanley presented to you, will, if converted into money, not only pay your debts, but provide a little fund for present expences, and a reserve for future exigencies; mean while, my industry and care will, I hope, keep want far from you. I have friends, who will find employment for my little talents; and if I can but make your life easy and comfortable, I shall think myself happy."

Mrs. Darnley, with tears in her eyes, embraced her daughter, bid her dispose of every thing as she pleased, and assured her she would endeavour to bear her new condition of life with patience and resignation.

Sophia immediately wrote to a gentleman of the law, who had been an intimate friend of her father's; and he undertook to manage their little affairs in town. A few days afterwards he brought them a hundred pounds, which was all that remained from the sale, after every demand upon Mrs. Darnley was paid.

She read over the accounts with great emotion, bitterly regretting every trinket she had parted with, and told Sophia, that it was absolutely necessary they should settle in some village near town, for she could not bear the thoughts of exposing her poverty, to her acquaintance, and of being seen in a worse condition than formerly.

CHAPTER XXXIV

Sophia continues to act romanticly,
and Harriot like a Woman who knows the World.

Sophia, who thought her mother's declining health a better reason for not residing in London, hired in an adjacent village, at a very small rent, a little house, or rather cottage, so neat, and situated so happily, that an imagination lively as hers was, and a little romantick, could not fail of being charmed with it. To this place she removed her books, and being provided by her friend Dolly with an innocent country girl for a servant, she conducted her mother to her rural abode, and had the satisfaction to find her pleased with it, novelty having always charms for her, and here for a few days, it supplied the place of those other gratifications to which she had been accustomed.

In the midst of these cares, Sophia did not forget her unhappy sister: she wrote several letters to her, in which she employed all the power of virtuous eloquence to bring her to a sense of her errors, but in vain.

Harriot did not deign to answer her, but in a letter to her mother, she complained of the injurious treatment she received from Sophia, and earnestly intreated her to leave her sister, and reside with her.

Although Mrs. Darnley refused this offer with seeming steadiness, yet her discontent was but too apparent. A life of retirement, which often obliged her to seek in herself, those resources against languor and melancholy, which she used to find in the dissipations of the town, could not be grateful to one who had never accustomed herself to reflection, whose mind was filled with trifles, and its whole stock of ideas derived from dress, cards, and every other fashionable folly.

To be capable of enjoying a rural life, there is something more necessary than a good understanding: innocence and purity of manners must contribute to give a relish to pleasures, which are founded in reason, virtue, and piety.

Hence it was, that Sophia, in the bloom of youth, found happiness in the solitude of a village, while her mother, in a declining age, panted after the vanities of the town.

In vain did Mr. Herbert fill the letters he wrote to Mrs. Darnley, with maxims of morality and pious admonitions; he experienced here the truth of that observation, that it is a work of great difficulty to dispossess vice from a heart, where long possession seems to plead prescription.[1]

Sophia, who knew her mother's taste for living at ease, that she might be able to gratify it, applied herself diligently to her work, which was a piece of embroidery, that had been bespoke by a benevolent lady, in order to give her present employment; and, by

---

1 South's *Twelve Sermons* (1694): "And it will be found a Work of no small difficulty to dispossess and throw out a Vice from that Heart, where long Possession begins to plead Prescription" (311).

exhibiting it as a proof of her ingenuity, to procure her more. She likewise exercised her invention in drawing little designs for fan-mounts;[1] and always chose such subjects as conveyed some moral lesson to the mind, while they pleased the imagination.

Some of these drawings were disposed of, by the lady her friend, so advantageously, that Sophia was encouraged to pursue her labour; and Mrs. Darnley, flattered by the prospect of more easy circumstances, began to enlarge her scheme of expence, made little excursions about the country in a post-chaise, talked of hiring a better house, and of passing two months at least in London during the winter.

Mean time Harriot became more earnest in solicitations to her mother, to come and live with her; her situation began to be so generally suspected, that she was in danger of being wholly neglected.[2]

She wrote to her in a strain of tenderness and duty, that revived all the ill-judging parent's affection, who invited her to make her a visit in her little retreat, and promised her a favourable reception even from Sophia herself.

Sophia was indeed far from opposing this visit; she was rather desirous of drawing her sister thither frequently, with a hope that her example and arguments might one day influence her to change her conduct.

Harriot received this invitation with joy; for such was the depravity of her mind, that she exulted in having an opportunity of displaying the grandeur of her dress, and equipage to her sister; to her who had made virtuous poverty her choice, and shewn that she despised riches, when they were to be purchased by guilt. *The pride of human nature* (says an eminent writer) *takes its rise from its corruption, as worms are produced by putrefaction.*[3]

---

1 Frame on which a fan is mounted.
2 Once it became known that a woman was a kept mistress, no other fashionable or respectable female would interact with her socially.
3 Probably adapted from John Flavel's *The Method of Grace* (London: Printed for M. White, 1681): "As worms in the body are bred of the putrefaction there, so the worm of conscience is bred of the moral putrefaction or corruption that is in our natures and conversations" (523). Flavel (1628?–91) was a Presbyterian minister who was ejected from his parish for his nonconformist views, but who continued to preach independently. *The Method of Grace*, however, was not reprinted after 1699, so it is unclear if Lennox could have read the sermon.

The wretched fallen Harriot was proud! the diamonds that glittered in her hair, the gilt chariot, and the luxurious table; these monuments of her disgrace contributed to keep up the insolence of a woman, who by the loss of her honour was lower than the meanest of her servants, who could boast of an uncorrupted virtue.

CHAPTER XXXV
Harriot visits her mother in her Cottage.

Sophia was busily employed upon her embroidery, when Harriot, from her gay chariot, alighted at her door; she entered that humble abode of innocence and industry, in a kind of triumph, and accosted her sister with a haughty expression of superiority in her looks and air, as if she expected the splendor of her appearance should strike her with awe.

Sophia received her with the modest dignity of conscious virtue; and Harriot, tho' incapable of much reflection, yet soon perceived the miserable figure she made, in the presence of such a character, and stood silent and abashed, while Sophia contemplated her finery with an eye of pity and of anguish.

Harriot, at length recovering herself, asked for her mother, who that moment entered the room. The sight of her daughter's equipage, had thrown her into an agreeable flutter of spirits, and she readily pardoned the fine lady, all the faults of the ungrateful child.

Harriot, emboldened by so kind a reception, proposed to her to accompany her to town, promising to make her abode with her agreeable, by every instance of duty and affection.

Mrs. Darnley blushed, and was silent. Sophia fixed her eyes upon her mother, anxious and impatient for her answer; she cast a timid glance at Sophia: she read in her speaking eyes her sentiments of this proposal; and turning to Harriot, she told her faintly, that not being satisfied with her conduct, it would be very improper for her to countenance it, by residing with her.

Harriot burst into tears, and exclaimed against her sister's malice, who, she said, acted like her most cruel enemy, and sought to ruin her character, by estranging herself from her company, and preventing her mother from taking notice of her.

Sophia, with great gentleness, proved to her, that the loss of her reputation was the necessary consequence of her living in a manner unsuitable to her circumstances; that her mother and her, by complying with her request, could not preserve her from censure, but would incur it themselves.

"You call me cruel, Harriot," said she, "for estranging myself from your company; but consider a little, whether it is not you that are both cruel and unjust. Why would you deprive me of the only reward the world bestows on me, for a life of voluntary poverty; you have exchanged a good name for dress and equipage; and I, to preserve one, subject myself to labour and indigence: you enjoy your purchase; but should I lose mine, were I to have that complaisance for you which you require. Leave me my reputation then, since it is the sole recompence of those hardships to which I willingly submit; and if you wish to recover yours, be contented to be poor like me."

Sophia, finding her sister listened to her, tho' it was sullenly, and with down-cast eyes, expatiated in a tender manner upon the errors of her conduct, and the fatal consequences that were likely to follow.

Harriot at length interrupted her, with a pert air, and said, "She would not be taught her duty by her younger sister;" then turning to her mother, "I hope, madam," said she, "my sister will not have so much power with you, as to make you forbid my coming here."

She put her handkerchief to her eyes, as she said this; to which Mrs. Darnley replied, with great vehemence, "That no person on earth should ever prevail upon her to cast off her child."

Sophia was silent, and observing that her presence seemed to lay them under some restraint, she rose up, to retire to her work, telling her sister, as she passed by her "That far from hindering her visits, she would rather encourage her to repeat them often, that she might be convinced it was possible, to be happy in a cottage."

Harriot laughed, and muttered the words romantick and affectation, which Sophia took no notice of, but left her at liberty to converse freely with her mother.

Mrs. Darnley talked to her at first in a chiding strain, and affected to assume the authority of a parent; but, a slave to her appetites, she could not resist any opportunity of gratifying them; and Harriot found it no difficult matter to force a present upon her, to supply those expences which her extravagance, and not her wants, made necessary.

Harriot now came often to the village, and gave it out, that she was upon the best terms imaginable with her mother and sister, not doubting but the world would cease to suspect her, since Sophia approved her conduct.

The frequency and the length of her visits made Sophia entertain hopes of her reformation, since the time she spent with her mother, was taken from that dangerous and immoral dissipation, which forms the circle of what is called a gay life. For it is with our manners as with our health; the abatement of vice is a degree of virtue, the abatement of disease is a degree of health.[1]

Mr. Herbert being perfectly recovered, filled Sophia with extreme joy, by the account he sent her of it, and of his resolution to come and live near her.

While she impatiently expected his arrival, and sent many a longing look towards the road, near which her little cottage was situated, she one day saw a gentleman ride by full speed, who in his person and air had a great resemblance to Sir Charles Stanley. Her heart, by its throbbing emotion, seemed to acknowledge its conqueror; for poor Sophia was still in love: she loved, though she despaired of ever being happy; and by thus persisting in a hopeless passion, contradicted that maxim, that love, like fire, cannot subsist without continual motion, and ceases to be as soon as it ceases to hope or fear.[2]

Sophia, not able to remove her eyes from the place where she fancied she had seen Sir Charles, continued to look fixedly towards the road, and was beginning to believe she had been mistaken, when a servant in Sir Charles's livery rode by also, and put it out of doubt that she had really seen the master.

This unexpected incident awakened a thousand tender melancholy ideas in her mind; and finding herself too much softened, she had recourse again to her work, to divert her imagination from an object, she had vainly endeavoured to forget.

CHAPTER XXXVI
Sir Charles appears again upon the Scene.

Sophia was not deceived when she imagined she had seen Sir Charles; it was really he who had rode by her window, and it was her little abode he was in search of, though in his extream eagerness he had overlooked it.

---

1   L'Estrange's *Seneca's Morals* (1678): "It is with our Manners, as with our Healths; 'tis a Degree of Virtue, the Abatement of Vice; as it is a Degree of Health, the Abatement of a Fit" (468).

2   Rochefoucauld's *Moral Maxims* (1665): "Love, like Fire, can't subsist without continual Motion; and ceases to exist, as soon as it ceases to hope or fear" (85).

He had left England with a hope that change of scene, and a variety of new objects, would efface the idea of Sophia from his heart, and restore him to his former tranquility; but amidst all the delights of Paris he found himself opprest with languor: no amusements could entertain him, no conversation engage his attention; disgusted with every thing he saw and heard, peevish, discontented, and weary of the world, he avoided all company, and had recourse to books for relief; but Sophia was too much in his thoughts to render study either instructive or amusing.[1] He past whole days in solitude, feeding his melancholy with the reflection of a thousand past circumstances which served to soften his mind, and make him feel his loss more sensibly.

When he reflected on her exalted virtues, her wit, her elegance, the attractive graces of her person, and the irresistable sweetness of her manners, he lamented his hard fate that had put such a treasure out of his reach; but when his conscience told him that it had once been in his power to have become possessor of this treasure, that he had trifled with that innocent affection till he had alienated it from himself to another object; his anguish became insupportable, and he sought to relieve it by rousing his indignation against her, for her preference of so unworthy a rival.

He called to mind her interview with this happy rival in the field, and concluded he was far more favoured by her than himself had ever been, since her discourse to him had produced so tender and passionate an expression of acknowledgment as that he had beheld.

These circumstances, which his imagination dwelt upon in order to lessen his regret, added to it all the stings of jealousy; so that, almost frantic with rage and grief, he was a hundred times upon the point of committing some desperate action.

A violent fever was the consequence of these transports, which, after confining him a long time to his bed, left his body in a weak and languishing condition, and his mind sunk in an habitual melancholy.

His physicians recommended to him the air of Montpelier,[2] and he was preparing to set out for that place when he happened to meet with a gentleman who made him alter his resolution.

---

1 Lennox alludes to the Horatian maxim that literature should "please. and instruct."

2 According to the first edition of the *Encyclopædia Britannica*, 3 vols. (Edinburgh: Bell and Macfarquhar, 1771), Montpellier (as it is usually spelled today), France was "a place famous for its delightful situation, and its healthy serene air" (3:270).

This person had been his governor,[1] and now attended Mr. Howard in the same quality.

Sir Charles, who had a slight acquaintance with Mrs. Howard, was prevailed upon, notwithstanding his aversion to company, to receive a visit from her son: he invited the young gentleman to dine with him, and he having not yet forgot the lovely Sophia, drank her health after dinner by the name of miss Darnley.

Sir Charles, who could not hear that name without a visible emotion, told him he knew two ladies so called, and asked whether it was the eldest or the youngest sister that he meant?

Mr. Howard replied, "That he was ignorant till then that miss Darnley had a sister."

"Yes she has a sister," said his governor, "who is much handsomer than herself, and for whom a youthful passion would be thought perhaps more excusable."

The young gentleman, who knew his governor talked in that contemptuous manner of Sophia in compliance with his mother's humour, in revenge avowed his admiration of her in the most passionate terms, and forgetting that Sir Charles had said he was acquainted with her, described her excellencies with all the enthusiasm of a lover.

Sir Charles listened in silence; and when the other had done speaking told him, with an air of forced gaity, that it was easy to see he was very much in love.

This, indeed, was his real opinion; nevertheless, he felt no emotions of jealousy or resentment against a rival whom he believed as unhappy as himself; he asked him with a seeming carelessness if miss Sophia was not to be married to the son of a rich farmer in the village where she lived? and waited his answer with an agitation of mind which appeared so plainly in the frequent changes of his colour, that Mr. Howard must have observed it, had not the question given him almost as much concern.

After a short pause he replied, "That he never heard she was going to be married;" but, added he, sighing, "I remember I have seen a very handsome young man at Mr. Lawson's, who perhaps—"

"Aye, aye," interrupted his governor, smiling, "he was the favoured lover no doubt, you have nothing to do but to forget her as soon as you can."

---

1 Tutor, companion.

The youth sat pensive and silent for some time, then suddenly rising, took leave of Sir Charles and went away; his governor prepared to follow him, but the baronet, anxious to hear more of Sophia, detained him to ask several questions concerning her acquaintance with Mr. Howard.

CHAPTER XXXVII
Gives the reader some necessary information.

Sir Charles found his old friend had lost no part of his former candor and sincerity: though by the trust reposed in him he was obliged to discountenance as much as possible the passion of his pupil for a young woman so much his inferior in rank and fortune; yet having seen and conversed with Sophia, he did justice to her extraordinary merit, and acknowledged that Mrs. Howard had treated her harshly.

He related to Sir Charles in what manner Mrs. Howard had invited her to her house, and the suspicions she entertained of Sophia's encouraging her son's passion, and design to ensnare him into a clandestine marriage. "Suspicions," added he, "which her subsequent behaviour entirely destroyed, for the youth was rash enough to avow his passion openly, and sollicited her by frequent letters and messages to grant him an interview, which she absolutely refused, and this conduct did her honour and procured her great esteem; yet it is very likely that her affections are otherwise engaged, and that she has some difficulties to encounter, for she looks thoughtful and melancholy, and affects retirement more than persons of her age generally do."

Sir Charles was thrown into so profound a reverie by this account of Sophia, that he heard not a word of what his friend afterwards said which had no relation to this interesting subject, and scarce perceived when he went away.

After reflecting a long time with mingled grief, resentment, and compassion, upon her melancholy, which he supposed was occasioned by some disappointment in the affair of her marriage with the young farmer, and which probably her want of fortune was the cause of, he suddenly formed the generous design of removing this obstacle to her union with the person whom she preferred to him, and, by making her happy, entitle himself to her esteem, since he had unfortunately lost her heart.

The novelty of this resolution and its extraordinary generosity, filled him with so many self-flattering ideas, as suspended for a while his jealousy and his grief.

Instead of going to Montpelier he set out immediately for England, and during his journey was continually applauding himself for the uncommon disinterestedness of his conduct.

Nothing is more certain, than that the motives even of our best actions will not always bear examination; we deceive ourselves first, and our vanity is too much interested in the deception, to make us wish to detect it. Sir Charles either did not or would not perceive the latent hope that lurked within his bosom, and which, perhaps, suggested the designs he had formed.

How must such an instance of generous passion, thought he, affect a mind so delicately sensible as Sophia's! she who had once loved him, and what was more than probable had not yet entirely forgot him.

He never asked himself, why his imagination dwelt upon these pleasing images? why he prosecuted his journey with such eager haste, as if the purport of it was to receive, not to resign for ever the woman he so passionately loved?

When he arrived at his own house scarce would he allow himself a few minutes rest after his fatiguing journey: he hastened to Mr. Herbert's lodgings, to prevail upon him to justify by his concurrence the designs he had formed in favour of Sophia.

Mean time the secret and powerful impulse by which he was actuated, kept his mind in a continual tumult. He hoped, he feared, he wished: he was all anxious expectation, all trembling doubt; he heard with grief that Mr. Herbert was at Bath; for now he knew not how to get access to Sophia, who being ignorant of his intentions, and offended by his behaviour, might possibly refuse to see him.

He went to the house where Mrs. Darnley lived when he left England; he was surprised to see it shut up. This incident perplexed him more, and rendered him more impatient.

He returned to his house, passed a restless night, and early in the morning ordering his horses to be saddled, set out immediately for Mr. Lawson's; where he arrived before he had resolved how to introduce himself, or who he should enquire for.

However, upon the appearance of a servant at the door, he asked for Mr. Herbert; which Mr. Lawson hearing, came out himself, and, though he did not know Sir Charles, politely requested him to alight, telling him, he had just received a letter from Mr. Herbert, which acquainted him that he was perfectly recovered, and that he was on the way to London.

CHAPTER XXXVIII
Sir Charles has an interview with Mr. Lawson.

Sir Charles accepted Mr. Lawson's invitation, and alighting, followed him into a parlour, but in such perturbation of mind that he scarce knew what he did. The good curate, surprised at the pensiveness and silence of his guest, knew not what to say to him, or how to entertain him: he gave him an account of Mr. Herbert's illness, which seemed to engage his attention very little; but happening to mention Sophia in the course of his relation, the young baronet started as from a dream, and turned his eyes upon him with a look of eagerness and anxiety, but said not a word.

Mr. Lawson paused, as expecting he was going to ask him a question, which Sir Charles perceiving, said with some confusion, "I beg your pardon, Sir, you mentioned miss Sophia, I have the honour to know her, pray how does she do?"

"I hope she is well, Sir," replied Mr. Lawson, "I have not seen her a long time."

"Then she does not reside with you now," said Sir Charles, with a countenance as pale as death, dreading to hear something still more fatal.

As Mr. Lawson was going to answer him, William, not knowing his father-in-law had company, entered the room abruptly; but seeing the baronet, he bowed, apologized for his intrusion, and instantly retired.

The various emotions with which this sudden and unexpected sight of his rival filled the breast of Sir Charles, caused such a wildness in his looks, that Mr. Lawson, in great astonishment and perplexity asked him if he was taken ill?

Sir Charles endeavouring to compose himself, replied, "That he was very well," but in a faultering accent asked, who the young gentleman was that had just left the room.

Mr. Lawson told him he was his son-in-law.

"Your son-in-law!" cried Sir Charles, eagerly, "what! married to your daughter! is it possible?"

Mr. Lawson knew enough of Sophia's story to make him comprehend now who this young gentleman was, who discovered so extraordinary a concern upon this occasion: and, charmed to have an opportunity of doing her service by removing those suspicions which he had been told had produced so fatal a reverse in her fortune, he gave the baronet a circumstantial account of his daughter's marriage: sensible that he was too much interested in this detail to make him think it impertinent, he introduced it no otherways than by declaring himself under the greatest obligation to miss Sophia, who having honoured his daughter with her friendship, had been the chief instrument of her present happiness.

While the good curate related all the circumstances of an affair which had had such melancholy consequences, the baronet listened to him with an attention still as the grave; his eyes were fixed upon his with a look of the most eager anxiety, and he scarce suffered himself to breathe for fear of losing any of his words.

In proportion as his doubts were removed, his countenance expressed more satisfaction, and when, upon his reflecting on all that he had heard, it appeared plainly that the fatal meeting which had caused him so much anguish, was the effect of Sophia's solicitude to serve her friend, and that the passionate action of the youth was an acknowledgment of gratitude, not an expression of love, he was not able to conceal the excess of his joy; but, rising up in a sudden transport, he took the curate's hand, and pressing it eagerly, "You know not," said he, "Mr. Lawson, how happy you have made me! but where is miss Sophia, is she gone to Bath with her good friend Mr. Herbert?"

"No, Sir," replied Mr. Lawson; "she lives with her mother. You know, I suppose, that Mrs. Darnley has lost her annuity by the death of the gentleman upon whom it was charged."

"I never heard it till now," said the baronet, whose tenderness was alarmed for his Sophia; "tell me I beg you what is her present situation."

"Her eldest daughter has left her," said Mr. Lawson, "and she has retired with miss Sophia to a village about five miles from hence, in the road to London, where that excellent young lady supports her mother and herself by the labour of her hands."

"Angelick creature!" exclaimed Sir Charles, with his eyes swimming in tears. Then, after a little pause, he desired a direction to the place where Mrs. Darnley lived, and took a kind leave of Mr. Lawson, telling him he hoped soon to visit him again.

Sir Charles, although he galloped as fast as it was possible, found his horse went too slow for his impatience; so eager was he to see Sophia, and gain her pardon for the unreasonable conduct which his jealousy and rage had made him guilty of.

The account Mr. Lawson had given him of the part she had taken in his daughter's marriage with the youth whom he had considered as his rival, not only removed the torturing pangs of jealousy, which he had so long felt, but made him view several circumstances in Sophia's behaviour in a light favourable to his own ardent wishes.

He fondly fancied that the melancholy in which he had heard she was plunged, was occasioned by a tender remembrance of him; and that the hope of still being his, might have been the chief cause of her rejecting the addresses of Mr. Howard.

How different were these ideas from the gloomy ones which had hitherto perplexed his mind! he seemed like a man waked from a frightful dream of despair and death, to a certainty of life and joy.

Amidst these transporting reveries he had passed by Sophia's house, without perceiving it to be the same he had been directed to; and when he had reached the end of the village, he looked about for it in vain, and saw no one of whom he could enquire for it but an old woman, who was sitting under a tree near the road, making up a nosegay[1] of some flowers, such as the late season produced.

He stopped his horse, and asked her if she knew where Mrs. Darnley lived? At the mention of that name she rose hastily as her feebleness would permit her, and told him, she knew the house very well; and, if he pleased, would go and shew it him. "I am making up this nosegay for the sweet young gentlewoman her daughter," said the old woman: "I carry her flowers every day; heaven bless her, she is my only support. There is a great many fine folks here-abouts, from whom I could never get any relief; but since she came hither I have wanted for nothing. Pray let me shew you her house; old and weak as I am, I would walk ten miles to do her service."

Sir Charles, alighting from his horse, ordered his servant to lead it to the nearest public house, and wait for him there; he told the old woman, he would accept of her offer, and walk along with her. Then taking two guineas out of his pocket, he gave them to her, in reward, he said, for the gratitude she expressed for her young benefactress.

The good woman received his bounty with a transport of surprise and joy, and pleasingly repaid him by talking of his beloved Sophia; of whom she related many instances of tenderness and charity towards the poor of the village, and filled him with admiration of that true benevolence, which even in the midst of indigence, could administer to the greater wants of her fellow creatures.

---

1 Bouquet.

CHAPTER XXXIX
Sophia receives an unexpected Visit.

When they came within sight of Sophia's little cottage, the old woman, pointing to it, told him, Mrs. Darnley and her daughter lived there: upon which the baronet, dismissing her, walked up to it with disordered haste. A row of wooden pales[1] led to a small grass-plat[2] before the door.

As he approached, he saw Sophia sitting at a window at work. He stopped to gaze upon her; she appeared to him more lovely, more engaging than ever. He wished, yet dreaded her looking up, lest her first thoughts upon seeing him being unfavourable, she should resolve to refuse his visit. He went forwards with a beating heart, and cautiously opening the little gate, reached the door of this humble habitation unheard and unseen by Sophia: the door flew open at his touch; poverty has no need of bolts and bars, and every good angel is the guard of innocence and virtue.

The noise he made in entering, and the sound of her name, pronounced in a tender accent, made Sophia hastily raise her head. At sight of Sir Charles, she started from her chair, her work fell from her trembling hands, she looked at him in silent astonishment, unable, and perhaps unwilling to avoid him.

The baronet, whose heart laboured with the strongest emotions of tenderness, anxiety, hope, and fear, had not power to utter a word; and while her surprise kept her motionless, threw himself at her feet, and taking one of her hands, pressed it respectfully to his lips, tears at the same time falling from his eyes.

Sophia, whose gentle mind was sensibly affected with this action, and the paleness and languor which appeared in his countenance, found it impossible to treat him with that severity which his capricious conduct seemed to demand of her; nevertheless, she drew away her hand, which he yielded with reluctant submission.

"I hoped," said she, in an accent that expressed more softness and grief than anger or disdain, "that I should be spared any farther insults of this sort from you; those I have already suffered have sufficiently punished me for my weak credulity."

Sir Charles, when she began to speak, rose up; but continued

---

1 Slat of a fence.
2 Small area of turf, sometimes with ornamental flowers.

gazing on her with the most passionate tenderness, while every word she uttered seemed to pierce his heart.

"I will not," pursued Sophia, gathering firmness as she spoke, "ask you, why you have intruded upon me thus unexpectedly? or why you assume a behaviour so little of a-piece with your past actions? I only beg you to believe, that I am not again to be deceived; and although I am persuaded my good opinion is of no consequence to you, yet I will tell you, that if it is possible to regain it, it will be by never more importuning me with visits, which my situation in life makes it very improper for me to admit of."

Sophia, when she had said this, went out of the room, without casting a look back upon Sir Charles, who followed her in great disorder, conjuring her only to hear what he had to say.

As she was passing to her own chamber, she was met by her mother, who seeing Sir Charles, was filled with surprise and joy; and perceiving that Sophia was avoiding him, cried to her with an angry accent, "Where are you going? what is the meaning of this rudeness?"

Sophia, without answering her, retired to her own room, not without great perturbation of mind; for there was something in the baronet's looks and words that seemed to merit a hearing at least; but she dreaded the weakness of her own heart, and was fully persuaded that any condescension on her side would give him too great an advantage over her.

Mrs. Darnley, finding any endeavours to retain her were fruitless, advanced towards Sir Charles with great obsequiousness, congratulated him upon his return, and thanked him for the honour he did her in visiting her in her poor little habitation.

Sir Charles saluted her respectfully, and took a seat. "There is a sad alteration, Sir," said she, "in my poor affairs since I saw you last. I never thought to have received you in such a hovel! You have heard, I suppose, of my misfortune?"

Sir Charles, who was in great confusion of thought, and had scarce heard a word she said, replied carelessly, "Yes, madam, I am sorry for it."

The coldness of this answer cast a damp upon those hopes which she had eagerly admitted upon seeing him again; and, impatient to be relieved from her tormenting anxiety on account of this unexpected visit, she asked him abruptly, "whether she might wish him joy, for she heard," she said, "that he was going to be married."

Sir Charles, rouzed by this question, replied hastily, "Who

could have told you any thing so unlikely? Married! no, madam, there never was any foundation for such a report."

"Indeed I believe so," said Mrs. Darnley, almost breathless with joy to find him deny it so earnestly. "To be sure people are very envious and ill-natured, and those who told me, no doubt, designed to do you an ill office."

"And they have succeeded," said Sir Charles, sighing, "if they have been able to persuade miss Sophia, that after having aspired to the possession of her, I could descend to love any other woman. I came to implore her pardon, madam," pursued he, "for all the extravagancies of my past conduct, and for that unreasonable jealousy which was the source of them, could I have been so happy to have prevailed upon her to have heard me."

"What!" interrupted Mrs. Darnley eagerly, "and was my daughter so rude as to leave you without hearing what you had to say. I protest I am ashamed of her behaviour; but I hope you will be so good to excuse it, Sir; I will insist upon her coming in again."

"No, madam," said Sir Charles, holding her, for she was hurrying away, "miss Sophia must not be constrained:[1] I cannot bear that."

Mrs. Darnley unwillingly resumed her seat, and inly fretting at her daughter's obstinacy, trembled for the event of this visit.

Sir Charles, after a silence of some minutes, suddenly rose up, and took his leave. Mrs. Darnley, in great anxiety, followed him to the door, and said she hoped to see him again. He answered only by a low bow, and walked away full of doubt and perplexity.

Sophia's steadiness in refusing to hear him, banished all those flattering ideas of her tenderness for him, which he had so eagerly admitted; for he concluded that if her heart had not been steeled by indifference, she would, notwithstanding her just reasons for resentment, have been rejoiced to give him an opportunity of justifying himself.

He had reached the house where his servant was attending with the horses, without having determined what to do. To return to town without seeing Sophia again, and being assured of a reconciliation, was misery which he could not support; and he dreaded making a new attempt to see her, lest he should receive more proofs of her insensibility and disdain.

---

1 I.e., forced to do something.

In this perplexity the sight of Mr. Herbert alighting from a stage-coach, was a relief as great as it was unexpected; and in the sudden joy he felt at meeting with a man whose interposition could be so useful to him, he forgot that his former behaviour must necessarily have given rise to strong prejudices against him, and ran up to embrace the good old man with extreme cordiality.

CHAPTER XL
In which the History begins to grow dull.

Mr. Herbert was surprised at this meeting, and repaid the civilities of the young baronet with some coldness: upon which Sir Charles, in some confusion, desired to have a few moments conversation with him.

They walked together down a meadow; and Sir Charles, having with a candor and sincerity becoming the rectitude of his intentions, related all those circumstances which had concurred to excite his jealousy, and with that powerful eloquence which passion inspires, expatiated upon the motives of his conduct, a conduct which he acknowledged laid him open to the most unfavourable suspicions; Mr. Herbert, convinced of his sincerity, and full of compassion for the uneasiness which his mistaken jealousy had caused him, undertook to make his peace with Sophia, and assured him he would very shortly wait upon him in town.

This would not satisfy the anxious lover; he declared he would not leave the place till he was assured of his pardon; and Mr. Herbert, who certainly was not displeased with his obstinacy, could with difficulty persuade him to wait only till the next day for an account of his success.

Sir Charles unwillingly took the road to London, and Mr. Herbert hastened to congratulate his beloved charge upon the agreeable prospect that was once more opening for her.

Mrs. Darnley had, during this interval, been employed in reproaching poor Sophia for her behaviour to Sir Charles. In the vexation of her heart, she exclaimed in the severest terms against her pride and obstinacy; she told her, she might be assured Sir Charles would never attempt to see her again; that it was plain he was disgusted with her bad temper.

She burst into a passion of tears, while she enumerated the glorious advantages of that rank and fortune, which, she said,

Sophia had thrown from her; and among many motives which she urged, ought to have determined her to act otherwise, that of being able to out-shine her sister was one.

Sophia answered only by sighs: she herself was not absolutely satisfied with the unrelenting severity with which she had treated Sir Charles. The more she reflected upon his behaviour, the more she condemned herself for not hearing what he had to offer in his own defence.

She had once thought it probable that he had been deceived by the report that was spread through Mrs. Gibbons's folly, of her encouraging the addresses of her nephew, and his extravagant conduct might be occasioned by jealousy: a fault which a woman is always disposed to pardon in a lover. While she revolved these thoughts in her mind, Mrs. Darnley perceived her uneasiness, and added to it by new reproaches.

Mr. Herbert's arrival put an end to this tormenting scene. Sophia first heard his voice, and flew to receive him; Mrs. Darnley followed, and seeing her bathed in tears, while the good old man saluted her with the tenderness of a parent, she told him, with an air half serious, half gay, that her daughter loved him so well, she had no affection for any one else. She then entered abruptly upon the affair of Sir Charles, though she hardly expected Mr. Herbert would join with her in condemning Sophia.

He pleasingly surprised her by saying, that Sophia was to blame; and that he came prepared to chide her for her petulance and obstinacy.

Mr. Herbert, who saw a sweet impatience in Sophia's looks, explained himself immediately, and told her he had met Sir Charles; who had fully removed all the suspicions his strange conduct had occasioned, and convinced him, that he deserved more pity than censure.

"No doubt," pursued he, looking on Sophia with a smile, "you will be surprised to hear, young lady, that Sir Charles was witness to the interview you had in the meadow behind Mr. Lawson's house, with a certain handsome youth, whom he had heard was his rival, and a favoured rival too. What were his thoughts, do you imagine, when he saw this handsome youth throw himself at your feet, and kiss your hand?"

Mrs. Darnley now looked at her daughter in great astonishment; and Sophia, who yet did not recollect the circumstance of her meeting William, was so perplexed, she knew not what to say.

Mr. Herbert enjoyed her innocent confusion for a few moments, and then repeated all that Sir Charles had told him, of his jealousy and rage; his vain attempts to banish her from his remembrance; the resolution he had formed after his conversation with Mr. Howard concerning her; and how happily he had been undeceived at Mr. Lawson's, where he found his supposed rival was the husband of her friend.

"Well," interrupted Mrs. Darnley, with great vehemence, "I hope you are satisfied now, Sophia! I hope you will treat Sir Charles with more civility if he comes again.—Mr. Herbert, I beg you will exert your power over her upon this occasion—I think there is no doubt of Sir Charles's honourable intentions."

Thus she ran on, while Sophia, who had listened to Mr. Herbert's relation with the softest emotions of pity, tenderness, and joy, continued silent with her eyes fixed upon the ground.

Mr. Herbert, willing to spare her delicacy, told Mrs. Darnley, that relying upon Sophia's good sense and prudence, he had ventured to assure Sir Charles of a more favourable reception, when her prejudices were removed.

"He will come to-morrow, my child," pursued he, "to implore your pardon for all the errors of his past conduct, and to offer you his hand. I am persuaded you will act properly upon this occasion; and in a marriage so far beyond your hopes and expectations, acknowledge the hand of Providence, which thinks fit to reward you, even in this world, for your steady adherence to virtue."

Sophia bowed and blushed; her mother, in a rapture, embraced and wished her joy.

Mr. Herbert now endeavoured to change the conversation to subjects more indifferent; but Mrs. Darnley, ever thoughtless and unseasonable, could talk of nothing but Sir Charles, and the grandeur which awaited her daughter.

All night her fancy ran upon gilt equipages, rich jewels, magnificent houses, and a train of servants; and she was by much too happy to taste any repose.

Sophia enjoyed the change of her fortune with much more rational delight; and among all the sentiments that arose in her mind upon this occasion, that of gratitude to heaven was the most frequent and the most lively.

CHAPTER XLI
The History concluded.

Mr. Herbert, who had accepted a lodging in Sophia's cottage, went to Sir Charles the next day, according to his promise. He found him waiting for him full of anxious impatience; and hearing from the good old man, that Sophia was disposed to receive him favourably, he embraced him in a transport of joy; and his chariot being already ordered, they drove immediately to the village.

Mrs. Darnley welcomed the baronet with a profusion of civilities. Sophia's behaviour was full of dignity, mingled with that softness peculiar to her character.

Sir Charles, after a long conversation with her, obtained her leave to demand her of her mother, to whom he shewed the writings, which were already all drawn;[1] and by which Sophia had a jointure and pin-money, equal to the settlements that had been made upon Lady Stanley.

He now ventured to intreat that a short day might be fixed for their marriage. It was with great difficulty, that Sophia was prevailed upon to consent; but her mother's impetuosity carried all before it, and Mr. Herbert himself supported the young baronet's request.

The ceremony was performed by Mr. Lawson in his own parish-church: after which he and his amiable family accompanied the new wedded pair to their country-seat, where they passed several days with them.

Mr. Herbert having previously acquainted Sir Charles with Harriot's situation, the baronet, tho' he detested her character, and declared he never could pardon her for the miseries she had caused him; yet was desirous to have her decently settled, and promised to give her a thousand pounds with her in marriage, if a reputable match could be found for her: he even put notes for that sum into Mr. Herbert's hands, and earnestly recommended it to him, to take the affair under his management.

Harriot, during the time she lived with her mother, had been courted by a young tradesman in tolerable circumstances; and although she thought it great insolence for a person in business to pretend[2] to her, yet, actuated by a true spirit of coquetry, while she despised the lover, she took pleasure in his addresses.

This young man still retained some tenderness for her, and allured by the prospect of a fortune, was willing, notwithstanding any faults in her conduct, to make her his wife.

Mrs. Darnley proposed him to her, and Mr. Herbert enforced her advice with all the good sense he was master of. But Harriot

1 I.e., the marriage contract, which was written up already.
2 Aspire.

received the proposal with the utmost disdain; insisted that she was married as well as her sister; that her rank in life was superior to hers; and added, by way of threat, that her appearance should be so likewise.

The extraordinary efforts she made to support this boast engaged lord L. in expences that entirely alienated his affections from her, disgusted as he long had been with her insolence and folly.

His relations concluded a match for him with a young lady of suitable rank and fortune; and, after making a small settlement on Harriot, he took leave of her for ever.

The vexation she felt from this incident, threw her into a distemper very fatal to beauty. The yellow jaundice made such ravage in her face,[1] that scarce any of those charms on which she had valued herself so much, remained. All her anxious hours were now employed in repairing her complexion, and in vain endeavours to restore lustre to those eyes, sunk in hollowness, and tinctured with the hue of her distemper.

Although thus altered, the report of the fortune she was likely to have made her be thought a prize worthy the ambition of a young officer, who had quitted the business of a peruke maker,[2] in which he was bred, for an ensign's commission, which made him a gentleman at once.

He offered himself to Harriot with that assurance of success, which the gaiety of his appearance, and his title of captain, gave him reason to expect, with a lady of her turn of mind.

Harriot, charmed with so important a conquest, soon consented to give him her hand; and Sir Charles Stanley, finding his character not exceptionable, gave her the fortune he had promised, to which Sophia generously added a thousand pounds more. The baronet procured her husband a better commission; but designedly in one of the colonies, whither he insisted upon his wife's accompanying him.

Harriot, in despair at being obliged to quit the delights of London, soon began to hate her husband heartily, and he, entering into her disposition and character, lost all esteem and tenderness for her. Her behaviour justified the rigid confinement he kept her in; and while she suffered all the restraint of jealousy, she was at the same time mortified with the knowledge that pride and not love was the source of it.

---

1 Yellow fever results in jaundice (a yellowing of the skin) and sometimes has the long-term effect of disfiguring the face.
2 Wig maker.

Mrs. Darnley lived not long after the departure of her favourite daughter; for so Harriot always continued to be.

Sophia attended her mother during her long illness with the must duteous care, and had the satisfaction to be assured by Mr. Lawson, who assisted her in her preparation for death, that her attachment to the world, which the affluent circumstances to which she was raised but too much increased, had at length given way to more pious sentiments; and she died with the resignation of a christian.

The ill conduct of her sister, and the death of her mother, proved at first some interruption to Sophia's happiness; but these domestic storms blown over, she began to taste the good fortune which heaven had bestowed on her: her chief enjoyment of it was to share it with others; and Sir Charles, who adored her, put it amply in her power to indulge the benevolence of her disposition.

He took upon himself the care of rewarding her friends; he presented Mr. Lawson to a very considerable living: he procured Dolly's husband a genteel and lucrative employment; and married her sister to a relation of his own.

Mr. Herbert, who was above receiving any other gratification from Sir Charles than the entire friendship which he ever preserved for him, had the satisfaction to spend most part of his time with his beloved daughter, as he used tenderly to call Sophia, and to behold her as happy as the condition of mortality admits of.

Sir Charles's tenderness for her seemed to increase every day; and when Mr. Herbert some years after this marriage took occasion to compliment him upon the delicacy, the ardor, and the constancy of his affection, he replied, "You attribute to me a virtue, which, in this case, I cannot be said to possess; had my passion for my Sophia been founded only on the charms of her person, I might probably ere now have become a mere fashionable husband;[1] but her virtue and wit supply her with graces ever varied, and ever new. Thus the steadiness of my affection for her," pursued he, smiling, "is but a constant inconstancy, which attaches me successively to one or other of those shining qualities, of which her charming mind is an inexhaustible source."

FINIS

---

1 I.e., a husband in name only.

Appendix A: Textual Variants

[This section collects a few significant variations between the initial periodical publication of "The History of Harriot and Sophia" in *The Lady's Museum* (1760–61) and the subsequent publication of the novel as *Sophia* by James Fletcher (1762). The most significant difference is given in two blocks for easier comparison. The list of variants that follows first gives *The Lady's Museum* version (concluded with a square parenthesis) and then the *Sophia* version (followed by the page number in the present volume). The table at the end of this Appendix compares the breakdown of the installments in "The History of Harriot and Sophia" to chapter division in *Sophia*.]

1. Two Versions of the Introductions of Harriot and Sophia

a. Version in "The History of Harriot and Sophia":
Sophia she affected to despise, because she wanted in an equal degree those personal attractions, which in her opinion constituted the whole of female perfection. Meer common judges however allowed her person to be agreeable; people of discernment and taste pronounced her something more. The striking sensibility of her countenance, the soft elegance of her shape and motion, a melodious voice in speaking, whose varied accents enforced the sensible things she always said, were beauties not capable of striking vulgar minds, and which were sure to be eclipsed by the dazzling lustre of her sister's complexion, and the fire of two bright eyes, whose motions were as quick and unsettled as her thoughts.

b. Version in Sophia:
Sophia she affected to despise, because she wanted in an equal degree those personal attractions, which in her opinion constituted the whole of female perfection. Mere common judges, however, allowed her person to be agreeable; people of discernment and taste pronounced her something more. There was diffused throughout the whole person of Sophia a certain secret charm, a natural grace which cannot be defined; she was not indeed so beautiful as her sister, but she was more attractive; her complexion was not so fair as Harriot's, nor her features so

regular, but together they were full of charms: her eyes were particularly fine, large, and full of fire, but that fire tempered with a tenderness so bewitching, as insensibly made its way to the heart. Harriot had beauty, but Sophia had something more; she had graces.

One of the most beautiful fictions of Homer, says the celebrated *Montesquieu*, is that of the girdle which gave Venus the power of pleasing. Nothing is more proper to give us an idea of the magick and force of the graces, which seem to be given to a person by some invisible power, and are distinguished from beauty itself.

Harriot's charms produced at the first sight all the effect they were capable of; a second look of Sophia was more dangerous than the first, for grace is seldomer found in the face than the manners; and, as our manner is formed every moment, a new surprise is perpetually creating. A woman can be beautiful but one way, she can be graceful a thousand.

Harriot was formed to be the admiration of the many; Sophia the passion of the few, the sweet sensibility of her countenance, the powerful expression of her eyes, the soft elegance of her shape and motion, a melodious voice, whose varied accents enforced the sensible things she always said, were beauties not capable of striking vulgar minds; and which were sure to be eclipsed by the dazling lustre of her sister's complexion, and the fire of two bright eyes, whose looks were as quick and unsettled as her thoughts.

2. Variants between "The History of Harriot and Sophia" and *Sophia*

loved her much] loved her with any great degree of affection (59)
with the uncommon sensibility of her] with that inexplicable charm in her (62)
the encroachments] the secret encroachments (67)
taken so little pains] taken no pains (77)
Mr. Herbert] The old gentleman (91)
to board] to place (92)
the place] the village (92)
her child] her daughter (92)
"Sister, said Sophia, no woman] "You might also have read, sister," said Sophia, "that no woman (96)

elegance of her address] elegance of her person and address (99)

food for tender melancholy.] food for tender melancholy, and the soft reveries of imagination. (100)

lost that care] lost that awe (101)

the tender things] the fine things (109)

"By no means] "Oh! I must not admit of that by any means (118)

Mr. Gibbons] farmer Gibbons (123)

to insinuate herself into her favour] to recover her favour (129)

and he flew] and he eagerly flew (141)

said the youth smiling] said the youth (142)

providence] Providence (145)

disculpate] discapitulate (147)

the virtues and the graces] the Virtues and the Graces (150f.)

significant frowns] insignificant frowns (153)

the two men with whom she had been talking] the two persons before mentioned (154)

Nothing is more certain than that] It has been well observed that (162)

She wrote] Mrs. Howard accordingly wrote (166)

impaired my circumstances] impaired my fortune (175)

fifty pounds] a hundred pounds (178)

forced gravity] forced gaity (185)

He returned to his house, ordered his horses] He returned to his house, passed a restless night, and early in the morning ordering his horses (187)

was at a loss what to say to him] knew not what to say to him (188)

more and more joy] more satisfaction (189)

turn her head] raise her head (191)

said to her] cried to her (192)

no tenderness] no affection (195)

Sophia's behaviour was full of dignity and soft reserve.] Sophia's behavior was full of dignity, mingled with that softness peculiar to her character. (197)

when Mr. Herbert once took occasion] when Mr. Herbert some years after this marriage took occasion (199)

3. Table Comparing Breakdowns into Installments and Chapters

Installment in "The History of Harriot and Sophia"	Chapters in *Sophia*
1	1–4
2	5–6
3	7–8
4	9–11
5	12–14
6	15–17
7	18–21
8	22–26
9	27–31
10	32–35
11	36–41

Appendix B: Lennox's Life

1. "MRS. LENNOX," *The British Magazine and Review* 3 (July 1783): 8–11

[This biographical sketch was repeated in the *Edinburgh Weekly Magazine* on 9 October 1783. Since Lennox was still alive, and since these magazines were publishing poems allegedly written by Lennox's son George Louis at the same time, we can speculate that Lennox may have been involved in (or at least knew about) this article, which most likely presents a fairly truthful account— or at least represents what Lennox wanted the public to believe about her life. In the eighteenth century, Lennox was often spelled "Lenox." Here and throughout this edition, the spelling has been standardized as "Lennox."]

The great Bishop Warburton, in a letter written about twenty years since, to Mr. Millar, the bookseller of the lady with whose memoirs we are now enabled to gratify our reader, and full of eulogiums on her very great abilities, has the following significant phrase— "Nothing is more public than her writings, nothing more concealed than her person."[1] As this observation still maintains great part of its original force, we have met with no small difficulty in obtaining that genuine and satisfactory information, without which we are resolved nothing shall induce us to undertake the delineation of any character, however popular, and of course however greedily sought after by those superficial readers who are indifferent as to the facts, provided they receive a temporary gratification of their curiosity. We write, it is true, for the amusement of our readers, but their information is our primary object: about the former we are solicitous, but we are determined as to the latter.

Mrs. Charlotte Lennox is the daughter of Colonel James Ramsay, who was lineally descended from the noble and ancient house of Dalhousie in Scotland. Colonel Ramsay's father, besides the command of a troop of horse, enjoyed a very honourable post in Ireland; and his mother, whose maiden name was Lumley, was of the Scarborough family. His father died young, leaving three sons; the eldest of whom was Chaplain General and Judge Advo-

---

1   William Warburton (1698–1779), Bishop of Gloucester: the quotation, if it is indeed one, has not been traced.

cate of the Fleet, in the reign of King William;[1] the second was captain of a man of war; and the youngest, the father of Mrs. Lennox, commanded a company at the siege of Gibraltar in the year 1731. In this truly good man were united the brave soldier, the sincere Christian, and the true gentleman: beloved and revered while living, his memory is still dear to many persons of high rank and distinguished worth! After the siege, Colonel Ramsay sent for his lady; their family, which then consisted only of a son and daughter, being left in England for their education. Mrs. Ramsay was sister to the Reverend Dr. Tisdale of Ireland, the friend and companion of the celebrated Dean Swift, who has mentioned him with much respect and kindness in several of his Letters.[2] In Gibraltar, she had three children, two of whom died; and the youngest, the subject of these memoirs, was still an infant, when the regiment in which her father served being reduced, he came over to England, where he procured a lieutenancy in the guards, and some time after obtained the rank of colonel, on being appointed to the command of a company. In this station he continued several years; but finding it difficult to support the appearance which his situation required, and at the same time make a proper provision for his children, (though the son was already provided for by a genteel legacy from his uncle) he accepted an advantageous post at New York, where he was second in military command to the governor. And here, if he had lived a few years, he might have left his family in the circumstances he so ardently wished; but, unfortunately, this worthy parent died in less than two years after his departure from England.[3]

Mrs. Ramsay, who was a most affectionate wife, could by no means be prevailed on to quit the melancholy spot where the ashes of her husband were deposited: but her sister, Mrs.

---

1 The Dutch Protestant prince William of Orange (1650–1702) was called to England during the Glorious Revolution of 1688–89 to replace his Catholic father-in-law King James II, who had fled Britain. William reigned as William III with his wife Mary 1689–94 and after her death until 1702.

2 Anglo-Irish author Jonathan Swift (1667–1745) is best known today for his satire "A Modest Proposal" (1729) and for his novel *Gulliver's Travels* (1726). Swift and the Irish clergyman William Tisdall (1669–1735) were friends from the mid-1690s until they had a falling out over a woman in 1704.

3 James Ramsay died on 10 March 1742 (Séjourné 132).

Lucking, of Messing Hall, the widow of a gentleman of an honourable family and good fortune in Essex, earnestly requesting to have the care of Miss Charlotte, then about fourteen; she was sent over accompanied by a female relation.

The first news the young lady heard, on her arrival in England, was the death of her aunt. The only son of that lady, who was heir to a title and large estate, having met with a fatal accident, the unhappy mother, on receiving the melancholy intelligence, immediately lost her senses, and soon after her life.

The friends of Miss Charlotte were now preparing to send her back to America, as soon as a proper opportunity should occur: in the mean time, some of her little compositions being handed about, they drew upon her the notice of several persons of distinction.

Lady Isabella Finch, in particular, first Lady of the Bedchamber to the Princess Amelia,[1] took Miss Charlotte under her protection; declaring her intention of placing the young lady about the person of that princess as soon as she was a little older, being then under fifteen.

Miss Charlotte was now constantly with her ladyship, or the late Dowager Marchioness of Rockingham, sister of Lady Isabella: and she was actually preparing to go with the marchioness into the country, when this connection was dissolved by her marriage with Mr. Lennox; a young gentleman of good family, and genteel education, but whose fortune, like that of the object of his regards, consisted wholly in hopes and expectations.[2]

In this situation, they must, unquestionably, soon have been reduced to great difficulties, if a friend of the young lady had not fortunately reminded her of the possibility of making some substantial advantages of that genius with which Heaven had so liberally blessed her. A bookseller was accordingly found, who agreed

---

1   Isabella Finch (1700–71) was maid of honor to Princess Amelia, sister of George II. Through an inheritance, she became financially independent, allowing her to pursue her own and her friends' interests at Court, which she managed with great success. Her sister Mary (1701–61) was married to Thomas Watson Wentworth, first Marquess of Rockingham.

2   This is the only existing account we have that suggests that Lennox's husband Alexander came from a "good family." When Lennox married her husband, he was working for a printer; he became Deputy King's Waiter in the custom's office after Charlotte declined a position for herself. Later in life, Lennox and her husband had separate residences.

to purchase her first novel: this was Harriet Stewart, published in December 1750,[1] which met with a very favourable reception.

Thus encouraged to proceed, our fair author went earnestly to work; and, in the beginning of 1752, published the Female Quixote, which at once put the indelible seal on her literary reputation. The celebrity of this work is so great, that the first impression went off in a few weeks; and one of the most distinguished writers the world ever saw, with a candour and generosity which add lustre to his character, has acknowledged, in the Covent Garden Journal of the 24th of March 1752, that in many instances this copy of Cervantes even excels the great original. "It is, indeed," says Mr. Fielding, "a work of true humour, and cannot fail of giving a rational, as well as very pleasing amusement, to a sensible reader, who will at once be instructed and highly diverted."[2]

After the Female Quixote, Mrs. Lennox produced her Shakespeare Illustrated, in 3 vols. A Translation of the Life of Madame de Maintenon, in 5 vols. and The Countess of Berci, an Heroic Romance, taken from the French, in 2 vols.

She next undertook a Translation of the Duke of Sully's Memoirs, in 3 vols. quarto,[3] which was published in the year 1756. This celebrated work was dedicated to the late Duke of Newcastle, who received it with every mark of respect and consideration; not only making Mrs. Lennox a most liberal present, but kindly observing that her birth and merit entitled her to Royal notice, declared that he would recommend her to the king as a person who well deserved a pension. This, however, Mrs. Lennox very politely declined, in favour of her husband; for whom she solicited a place, which the duke promised to procure him the first opportunity.[4]

The constitution of Mrs. Lennox, which was never very strong, became now considerably impaired by her early and con-

---

1 See introduction p. 16.

2 This quotation comes from Henry Fielding's review of *The Female Quixote* in his *Covent-Garden Journal* #24 (March 24, 1752), where he argues that Lennox's work is actually superior to Cervantes' original. See Fielding, *Covent-Garden Journal* 158-61.

3 "Quarto" describes the size of a book (about 10x8 inches) and specifically denotes the number of pages created out of one sheet of paper (4).

4 Alexander Lennox became Deputy King's Waiter in the customs office some time between 1760 and 1765 through the patronage of the Duke of Newcastle; he remained in this position until around 1782.

tinual application to her pen; but the duke's promise not immediately taking effect, she was obliged to engage in a new and laborious work, the Translation of Father Brumoy's Greek Theatre, in 3 vols. quarto. The late Earl of Corke and Orrery, and some other eminent persons, favoured her with translations of several pieces in this work,[1] which are pointed out and acknowledged in an advertisement prefixed; and that bright star of literature, Dr. Samuel Johnson, suffered his great name to appear to a translation[2] of one of the articles. This work was dedicated to his present Majesty, then Prince of Wales, who had before honoured Mrs. Lennox with his notice; and who, in consequence of the generous representations of the Earl of Bute, made her a munificent present.[3] To the earl's amiable lady she has likewise been often heard to acknowledge herself most highly obliged.[4]

Mrs. Lennox, after this, wrote Henrietta, a novel, in two volumes, which was given to the public in 1758.

The Ladies Museum, published monthly, then came out under Mrs. Lennox's name; to which her friends largely contributed, whose favours are all separately acknowledged. In this work Mrs. Lennox's novel of Harriet and Sophia first appeared, which has since been reprinted under the title of Sophia.

Mrs. Lennox dedicated the second edition of Henrietta to the Dutchess of Newcastle, who had always honoured her with her friendship and esteem.[5] Her Grace procured the long promised

1 John Boyle, fifth Earl of Cork, fifth Earl of Orrery, and second Baron Marston (1707–62), was descended from a noble family and was a Member of Parliament. He is remembered mostly for his literary work, particularly his *Remarks on the Life and Writings of Dr. Jonathan Swift* (1751). The other "eminent persons" who assisted with the *Greek Theatre* were Dr. Gregory Sharpe, Dr. James Grainger, John Borryau, and an unidentified "young gentleman" (Small 218).

2 I.e., appear attached to a translation.

3 Each male heir first in line to the British throne receives the title "Prince of Wales." So in 1759, when *The Greek Theatre of Father Brumoy* was published, the future George III, who ascended the throne in 1760, was Prince of Wales. No records exist of a "munificent present" he gave Lennox.

4 John Stuart, third Earl of Bute (1713–92), a well-known patron of the arts, was Prime Minister 1762–63 and was close to the Prince of Wales. Bute's wife was Mary Stuart, Countess of Bute (1718–94). A letter from the Countess of Bute to Lennox from 1775 still exists (Isles 176–77).

5 Lady Henrietta (Harriet) Godolphin, Duchess of Newcastle (d.1776), was married to one of the most influential politicians of the eighteenth century. She was interested in painting and music and patronized artists across various genres.

place for Mr. Lennox; and, some years after, did Mrs. Lennox the honour of standing godmother to her daughter.

After this period we do not find any work published by Mrs. Lennox, except Eliza, a novel, in two small volumes; and the Life of Madame de la Valliere, with a translation of her Devotions, in a single volume.

. Mrs. Lennox's dramatic pieces are, the Sister, a comedy; Old City Manners, a comedy, altered from Ben Johnson; and Philander, a dramatic pastoral. She also published a small volume of Poems very early in life, of which we have never been able to procure a copy: but if we may judge from the single specimen we have seen, (the Art of Coquetry, in Mr. Harrison's Collection, Vol. IV, p. 303)[1] as well as from the several distinguished friends these juvenile productions appear to have obtained her, they certainly possess very extraordinary merit.

The character of this lady cannot be better illustrated, than by the observations of two great men: that of the late Bishop of Gloucester, mentioned in the beginning of these memoirs; and a remark of the universally celebrated Dr. Johnson, who observes, in his pointed way, that "Mrs. Lennox writes as well as if she could do nothing else, and does every thing else as well as if she could not write."[2]

After the eulogiums of these elevated characters, it might appear as presumptuous, as it is certainly unnecessary, for us to add that testimony which we should proudly contribute to the distinguished merits of this sprightly, humorous, satirical, and sensible writer; whose novelty and genius as an original author, and whose elegance and fidelity as a translator, have not often been exceeded.

It is with real pain we feel ourselves obliged to add, that this lady's ill state of health forbids us to expect many future productions from her elegant pen; though we have, at the same time, some reason to hope, that she will yet favour the world with at least one or two other performances which she has long had in contemplation.[3]

Mrs. Lennox has had three children: two sons, and a daughter.

---

1 Lennox's poem "The Art of Coquetry," originally published in her *Poems on Several Occasions* (London: Paterson, 1747), was reprinted many times in the eighteenth century.
2 Quotation not traced.
3 The only work of Lennox's that appeared after the publication of this biographical notice was her last novel *Euphemia* (London: Cadell and Evans, 1790).

Miss Harriet, now about sixteen, is the eldest. One of the sons died in infancy; and the other is that most astonishing proof of early and extraordinary genius, Master George Lewis Lennox, who is not yet twelve years of age, and whose elegant productions enrich the poetical department of our last and present numbers. The number of poems, on various subjects, this young gentleman has written, is truly surprising:* nor is the uncommon genius of this extraordinary youth by any means confined to versification; his familiar letters to his friends are pregnant with good sense, as well as remarkably accurate; and he has actually completed at least one dramatic piece, which is far from being ill conducted, and contains some lively strokes of genuine wit, superior to what we can discover in some of the entertainments lately produced at our Theatres Royal.

2. Obituary, *The Gentleman's Magazine* (January 1804): 89–90

[The length and detail of this obituary demonstrate that Lennox was well known at the time of her death, in spite of her advanced age and the fact that she had not published a book in over a decade. The obituary particularly stresses the financial support Lennox received in her old age from the Royal Literary Fund.]

Aged 84,[1] Mrs. Charlotte Lennox, a lady of considerable genius, and who has long been distinguished for her literary merit. She may boast the honour of having been the *protegée* of Dr. Samuel Johnson, and the friend of Mrs. Yates.[2] She published, so early as 1752, "The Female Quixote," and "Memoirs of Harriet Stuart." In the former of these novels, the character of Arabella is the

---

* These productions, which are now collecting, and preparing for the press, by Master Lennox, will in a short time be published together, by subscription, for the young gentleman's emolument. [Note in the original. George Louis Lennox published a number of poems, mostly in the *British Magazine and Review* and in the *Edinburgh Weekly Magazine*, in 1783–84. They were never published, however, in a separate volume.]

---

1 The anonymous author of this obituary was laboring under the mistaken assumption that Lennox was born around 1720 (see Carlile 390–92).
2 Mary Ann Yates (1728–87) was one of the premier British tragic actors of the second half of the eighteenth century.

counterpart of Don Quixote; and the work was very favourably received. In the following year she published "Shakspeare Illustrated," in two volumes, 12mo;[1] to which she soon afterwards added a third. This work consists of the novels and histories on which the Plays of Shakspeare [sic] are founded, collected and translated from the original authors; to which are added critical notes, intended to prove that Shakspeare has generally spoilt every story on which his Plays are founded, by torturing them into low contrivances, absurd intrigues, and improbable incidents. In 1756 Mrs. Lennox published "The Memoirs of the Countess of Berci, taken from the French," 2 vols. 12mo; and "Sully's Memoirs," translated, 3 vols. 4to; which have since been frequently reprinted in octavo, and are executed with great ability. In 1758 she produced "Philander, a Dramatic Pastoral," and "Henrietta," a novel of considerable merit, 2 vols. 12mo; and, in 1760, with the assistance of the Earl of Cork and Orrery and Dr. Samuel Johnson, she published a translation of "Father Brumoy's Greek Theatre," 3 vols. 4to; the merit of which varies very materially in different parts of the work. Two years after, she published "Sophia, a Novel," 2 vols. 12mo, which is inferior to her earlier performances; and then, after an interval of seven years, she brought out, at Covent-garden theatre, "The Sisters, a Comedy," taken from her novel of "Henrietta," which was condemned on the first night of its appearance.[2] In 1773 she furnished Drury-lane theatre with a comedy, intituled, "Old City Manners;" and has only written, we believe, since that time, "Euphemia, a Novel, 1790," 4 vols. 12mo; a performance which by no means deviates from the line of credit which she has always traced. Her father was a field-officer, lieutenant-governor of New York, who sent her over at 15 to a wealthy aunt, who desired to have her, but who, unfortunately, on the arrival of her niece, was out of her senses, and never recovered them; immediately after which, the father died, and the daughter from that time supported herself by her literary talents, which she always employed usefully. Her latter days have been clouded by

---

1   "12mo" or duodecimo means that the sheet of paper was folded four times, producing twelve pages of about 7x5 inches.
2   A large group attended the premiere of Lennox's *The Sister* with the express purpose of disrupting the performance (a not uncommon practice at the time). When they threatened to continue their interruptions, the theater withdrew the play. The reason for the disruptions is not known, although it may have been that readers were upset with Lennox's treatment of Shakespeare in her *Shakespear Illustrated*.

penury and sickness; calamities at her advanced period of life peculiarly distressing. These, however, were in a considerable degree alleviated by the kindness of some friends, who revered alike her literary and her moral character. Among these it would be unjust not to mention the names of the Right Honourable George Rose, and the Rev. William Beloe.[1] But the most effectual balm to her wounded spirit arose from the assistance she for a considerable time has received from the managers of that truly-useful and highly-important institution, *The Literary Fund*; by whose timely aid her only son was, a few years since, enabled to fit himself out for an employment in the American States; and by whose bounty the means of decent subsistence have, for the last twelvemonth, been afforded to the mother.

3. Obituary, *The European Magazine* 45.2 (February 1804): 158

[The notice in the *European Magazine* is short, but still the longest of the 66 obituaries in this issue of the journal.]

Jan. 4, 1804. Mrs. Charlotte Lennox, aged 84, authoress of the Female Quixote, 2 vols. 1752; Harriet Stuart, 2 vols; Memoirs of the Countess of Berci, 2 vols. 1756; Henrietta, 2 vols. 1758; Sophia, 2 vols. 1760; Euphemia, 4 vols. 1790; a translation of Brumoy's Greek Theatre and Sully's Memoirs; and some dramatic pieces. Her maiden name was Ramsay, and she was a native of New York. The latter part of her life was spent in a state of poverty, her chief support being from the Literary Fund.

4. "Memoir of Mrs. Lennox," *The Lady's Monthly Museum*, n.s.14.6 (June 1813): 313–15

[This anonymous biographical sketch was written less than a decade after Lennox's death, so it is possible that the author had

---

1   George Rose (1744–1818), called "the Right Honourable" as a Member of Parliament for Christchurch, was interested in poor relief, but his direct connection to Lennox is unknown. William Beloe (1758–1817) was a man of letters who is best known today for his multi-volume memoirs *Anecdotes of Literature and Scarce Books* (1806–12) and *The Sexagenarian, or, Recollections of a Literary Life* (1817). As a member of the Royal Literary Fund (a charity for indigent authors), he was instrumental in securing financial aid for Lennox.

known her. Several passages are lifted from previous biographical notices or obituaries.

This lady, who was much distinguished in the literary world for her extraordinary merit, had the honour of being the *protegée* of Dr. Johnson. Her maiden name was Charlotte Ramsay. Her father, a field-officer, and lieutenant-governor of New York (where she was born),[1] sent her to England at the age of fifteen, to a wealthy aunt, who, unfortunately, upon her arrival, had lost her senses, which she never recovered. Soon after this distressing occurrence, her father died, and Miss Ramsay from that time supported herself solely by her literary talents. She was married at a very early age to Mr. Lennox, a gentleman in a public office;[2] and, in the year 1752, published two very excellent novels, "The Female Quixote," and "The Memoirs of Harriet Stuart." It was soon after the publication of the former work that she was introduced to Dr. Johnson, as a young lady of considerable genius; but nothing could exceed the astonishment of Mrs. Lennox, at the odd manner in which she was received. The doctor took her on his *knee*, as if a *mere child*; after which he *carried her in his arms*, to shew her his library; and, as if resolved to be uniform in his conduct, sent his servant to a pastry-cook, to purchase some cakes for the young lady. Mrs. Lennox found herself greatly embarrassed; but a respect for his character stifled even the idea of resentment, and she preserved an intimacy with him till near the period of his decease.[3]

Her novel of "The Female Quixote" was favourably received. In the following year she published, "Shakspeare illustrated," in two volumes 12mo. to which she soon afterwards added a third. This work consists of the novels and histories on which the plays of Shakspeare are founded, collected

---

1 Actually, Lennox was probably born in Gibraltar (Carlile 390–92).
2 The writer here is chronologically confused: Alexander Lennox did not get his position in "public office" until later, some time between 1760 and 1765.
3 This passage is lifted almost verbatim from the "Anecdote of a Literary Lady" in John Adams's *A Second Volume of Anecdotes, Bon-Mots, and Characteristic Traits* (London: Kearsley, 1792), 120–21.

and translated from the original authors; to which are added many critical notes, tending to prove (what the admirers of our immortal bard will never admit), that Shakspeare has disfigured the stories in dramatizing them, by low contrivances, absurd intrigues, and improbable incidents. In 1756, Mrs. Lennox published the "Memoirs of the Countess of Berci," taken from the French, in two volumes 12mo. and "Sully's Memoirs," translated also from that language, in three volumes 4to. which being executed with much ability, has been frequently reprinted. In 1758, she produced "Henrietta," a novel of some repute, in two volumes 12mo. and in 1760, with the assistance of the Earl of Cork and Orrery, and Dr. Johnson, she published a translation of "Father Brumoy's Greek Theatre," in three volumes 4to. the merit of which varies very materially in different parts of the work. Two years after, she published "Sophia," a novel, in two volumes 12mo. which is inferior to her earlier performances. To these she afterwards added "Euphemia," a novel, 1790, in four volumes 12mo. Her success in the dramatic line was not equal to that which she experienced in general literature and romance. In 1757, she produced "Philander," a pastoral drama, taken from the *Pastor Fido* of Guarini,[1] but not adapted for the stage. The catastrophe of this performance[2] would have been more interesting, had it been formed on the Italian poet: it would at least have rendered unnecessary the introduction of a personage, whose appearance ought seldom or never to be tolerated, except in masques, and allegorical pieces; we mean a deity in his own person.[3] In 1769, she brought forward "The Sister," a Comedy, taken from her own novel of "Henrietta." "Though it was treated severely," says a late able critic, "and performed but one night, at Covent-garden Theatre, it is written," he observes,

---

1 In the dedication to *Philander* (London: Millar, 1758), Lennox acknowledges that "the first hint [for her play] was taken from the PASTOR FIDO" (vi). Battista Guarini's *Il pastor fido* (The Faithful Shepherd [1589]) was one of the most popular pastoral dramas throughout Europe in the seventeenth and eighteenth centuries.
2 I.e., the climax of the plot.
3 The author here objects to Apollo appearing in person as a *deus ex machina* at the end of Lennox's play.

"with a considerable degree of good sense and elegance."[1] Dr. Goldsmith's Epilogue to it is perhaps one of the best that has appeared in the course of the last fifty years. Her last dramatic piece was "Old City Manners," a comedy, acted at Drury-lane, 8vo.[2] 1775, altered from "Eastward Hoe," by Ben Jonson, and others; from which, it is said, Hogarth took the plan of his series of prints, called "The Industrious and Idle Apprentices."[3] Mrs. Lennox's alteration was favourably received. The patronage she received from writers of established celebrity, combined with the encouragement she met with from a discerning public, ought to have secured her a decent competence;[4] but this, from some cause or other, was not the case. The latter part of her life was clouded by sickness and penury, and her chief support was derived from the Literary Fund. Mrs. Lennox died on the 4th of January, 1804, at the advanced age of eighty-four.

---

1 The quoted assessment comes from the new edition of the *Biographica Dramatica, or, A Companion to the Playhouse* (London: Rivington et al., 1783) of David Erskine Baker (1730–67): "This comedy was taken from the authoress's own novel, intituled *Henrietta*. Though it was treated severely, and performed but one night at Covent-Garden, it is written with a considerable degree of good sense and elegance. Dr. Goldsmith's Epilogue to it is, perhaps, the best that has appeared in the course of the last thirty years" (364). Since Baker was long dead by the time the new edition came out (the first edition appeared in 1764), it is unclear who exactly the "late able critic" is.

2 "8vo" (sometimes "8mo") designates the paper size octavo.

3 This is confusing: Hogarth (perhaps) got his inspiration from *Eastward Ho!* by George Chapman, Ben Jonson, and John Marston, not from Lennox's adaptation of their play.

4 I.e., decent financial compensation.

Appendix C: Reviews of Sophia

[The range of reviews of *Sophia* is fairly typical for a novel by an established female writer—from the four words in the *British Magazine* to the extensive plot summary in the *London Magazine* (May 1762, pp. 273–75), which is not included here because that is all it offers. The most remarkable item is the advertisement by James Hoey, junior, the publisher of the pirated Dublin edition of the novel. I have not been able to find the original publication of the letter in the *Public Ledger*, but there is no reason to doubt its existence. The letter would have been placed by James Fletcher, the publisher of a London version of *Sophia*, and it is interesting that the publisher of a pirated edition based on the earlier text advertises with a letter about a later, corrected, legitimate edition. James Hoey may also have pirated the entire *Lady's Museum*, since he advertised in 1763 for *The Ladies Friend, Being a Museum for the Fair-Sex, or Cabinet of Polite Literature and Rational Amusement for Ladies*, by Euphrosine, in two volumes, and claimed that three quarters of the text were Lennox's novel *Sophia*. However, no copies of this work (if it was ever published) seem to have survived. Hoey also published an abridgement of *Sophia* in his newspaper, the *Dublin Mercury*, between February 23 and July 6, 1769, and he released "The History of the Count de Comminge" from *The Lady's Museum* as a separate book titled *The History of the Marquiss of Lussan and Isabella* (Dublin: Hoey, 1764).]

1. *The Critical Review* (May 1762): 434–35

In this little history is exemplified the triumph of wit and virtue over beauty, with that delicacy peculiar to all the novels of the ingenious Mrs. Lennox. The lesson is instructive, the story interesting, the language chaste, the reflections natural, and the general moral such as we must recommend to the attention of all our female readers. It is commonly asserted, that women are sooner corrupted by the vicious of their own sex, than of ours; we have before us an instance, which evinces they are more agreeably instructed. A woman only can enter justly into all the scruples and refinements of female manners.

2. *The Library* (May 1762): 262

Such of our readers as are fond of novels, will receive ample gratification from two which the last month has produced. The first is Sir Launcelot Greaves, by Dr. Smollet, whose excellent talent at this species of writing hath been fully experienced in some former works, and particularly in his Roderick Random.[1] [...]

The other novel is Sophia, by the justly celebrated Mrs. Lennox: it is an agreeable love-tale, composed with great purity of sentiment and stile. The characters, though not numerous, are well executed, and the contrast between the two sisters, while it is finely kept up, is very instructive and useful.

3. *The British Magazine, or, Monthly Repository for Gentlemen & Ladies* (June 1762): 324

Ingenious, delicate, and interesting.

4. *The Gentleman's Magazine* (June 1762): 295

It would, perhaps, be a sufficient recommendation of this work to say, that it is written by Mrs Charlotte Lennox, the celebrated authoress of the Female Quixote; it is, however, but justice to add, that this novel is natural, elegant, and interesting; that it contains many observations which shew a perfect knowledge of the human heart, and a delicate sense of sublime virtue: To retail the story would be to injure the writer, in whose words alone it ought to be read, and at the same time to preclude a pleasure which we wish all our readers to partake, and which can only be found in the work itself.

5. *The Monthly Review* (July 1762): 73–74

It is a common error, with such adventurers as meet with any degree of success, either in brandishing the goose-quill or the truncheon, to push their good luck too far, and risk a reverse of fortune by keeping the field too long. Next to the difficulty of

---

1 Many critics consider Tobias Smollett's *Sir Launcelot Greaves* to be the first serial novel in English literature—see introduction p. 32. Smollett's first novel *Roderick Random*, which is remarkable for its depiction of life in the eighteenth-century British navy, was published in 1748.

making an honourable retreat, after a battle lost, is that of knowing how far to pursue the good fortune of conquest, and when to retire securely, to enjoy the spoils of victory. The petty acquisition, that might do honour to a novice in literature or in arms, would rather diminish than increase the reputation of a veteran practised in great atchievements, and repeatedly crowned with laurels. Hence it is expected of a writer, who hath acquired any portion of literary fame, that every new work he produces should be superior to the last; and if it prove otherwise, it detracts from his general character, by just so much as its merit falls short of expectation. The current of a living Author's reputation is thus ever on the ebb and flow. To this, it may be added, that even novelty in the author, as well in the performance, is, in this novelty-loving age, become requisite to make a work of entertainment compleatly *taking*. However new the design, incidents, or model of the composition, yet, if the author hath been long known, the pre-conceived notion of the style and manner, gives the whole an old-fashioned air, and it is not *quite a new thing*, at least with the ladies; for whose use and amusement works of this kind are chiefly calculated. The disposition of the public may be imagined, in this respect, like that of a froward child, equally capricious and unaccountable. But, so it is. Mrs. Lennox, therefore, should not be disappointed if her *Sophia* does not meet with so warm a reception as the *female Quixote, Henrietta,* and some other of her pieces, have been honoured with. Indeed, we must confess, that this performance, consisting of a love-story, not uninteresting in point of incident, nor inelegantly written, wants, nevertheless, much of that spirit and variety which this species of composition peculiarly requires, and which are more conspicuous in some of her former works.

6. Books printed by and for James Hoey, junior (12-page advertisement from 1763)

ARTICLE III

The History of SOPHIA: By the celebrated Mrs. LENNOX, author of the FEMALE QUIXOTE, HENRIETTA, &c.—*Price bound in calf and lettered, 2s. 2d: sewed 1s. 7½d.*

Concerning which the following letter has appeared in the PUBLIC LEDGER, a London literary paper.—

"Among the number of Novels lately published, I must confess I am not a little pleased with one adorned with the name of a lady, who, without any hyperbole, may by stiled, *The glory of the female sex, and an honour to the British nation.* HARRIOT STEWART, the FEMALE QUIXOTE, HENRIETTA, &c. are lasting monuments of her fine taste and superior genius as an original writer; and the elegant English dress she has given to SULLY's *Memoirs*, (which on various occasions, I have quoted and applied, to the satisfaction of the public) and BRUMOY's *Greek Theatre*, now published in three volumes quarto, sufficiently evince her thorough knowledge of the languages, and her abilities as a translator. Most of her original pieces have also obtained the approbation of foreigners, and have been translated into French and other languages.[1] I hope this circumstance alone will procure *The History of* SOPHIA DARNLEY,[2] what the intrinsic merit of the work itself deserves, a favourable reception from the public. Mrs. LENNOX has forfeited no part of her reputation by this publication, which I warmly recommend as one of the best and most pleasing novels that has appeared for some years. The story is quite new, uniform and interesting; the characters are natural and properly supported; the stile equal, easy, and well kept up, sinking no where below the level of genteel life, a compliment which cannot be paid to one of the most celebrated novel writers we have.

PROBUS."[3]

---

1   A German translation of Lennox's *The Female Quixote* was published in 1754, and two French translations of *Henrietta* appeared in 1760.
2   Hoey uses a title that never appeared in print.
3   Latin for morally upright or virtuous.

Appendix D: Selections from The Lady's Museum

1. *The Lady's Museum* 1 (March 1760): 1–80

[The first issue of *The Lady's Museum* helps to establish the context of the first installment of *Sophia*, titled "The History of Harriot and Sophia." For this reason, it is included here in its entirety. The contents include the following: the introduction; an essay by the authorial persona (the "Trifler"); the first installment of the text "Of the Studies Proper for Women";[1] the first installment of "The History of Harriot and Sophia"; a song set to music by James Oswald (1710–69) from Lennox's dramatic pastoral *Philander*; four poems (presumably by Lennox); and the first installment of "The History of the Dutchess of Beaufort." The issue included three illustrations (a frontispiece, the illustration for *Sophia*, and a portrait of the Duchess of Beaufort) as well as a plate of the music for the song from *Philander*.]

THE
LADY's MUSEUM

As I do not set out with great promises to the public of the wit, humour, and morality, which this pamphlet is to contain, so I expect no reproaches to fall on me, if I should happen to fail in any, or all of these articles.

My readers may depend upon it, I will always be as witty as I can, as humorous as I can, as moral as I can, and upon the whole as entertaining as I can. However, as I have but too much reason to distrust my own powers of pleasing, I shall usher in my pamphlet with the performance of a lady, who possibly would never have suffered it to appear in print, if this opportunity had not offered.[2]

---

1   This is chapter 2 of *L'Ami des femmes ou La Morale du sexe* by Pierre Joseph de Villemert, published in French in 1758 and translated anonymously—by someone other than Lennox—into English in 1766 as *The Ladies Friend*.

2   There is no reason to suspect that the following piece by "The Trifler" is not by Lennox. In the eighteenth century, authors frequently pretended merely to be editors in order to increase the authority of the texts they presented.

If her sprightly paper meets encouragement enough to dispel the diffidence natural to a young writer, she will be prevailed upon, I hope, to continue it in this Museum; I shall therefore, without any farther preface, present it to my readers.

The TRIFLER
[NUMBER I]

Cast your eyes upon paper, madam; there you may look innocently, said a polite old gentleman of my acquaintance to me, one day, in the words of a wit to a fine lady. A compliment is no unpleasing way of conveying advice to a young woman, and when that advice may be so construed, as to become perfectly agreeable to her own inclinations, it is certain to be well received, and quickly complied with. It is indeed very clear to me, that my friend in this borrowed admonition recommended reading to eyes which he probably thought were too intent upon pleasing; but I, with a small deviation from the sense, applied it, to what is I freely own my predominant passion; and therefore resolved to write, still pursuing the same darling end, though by different means.

So frankly to acknowledge the desire of pleasing to be my predominant passion, is in other words, to confess myself, one of that ridiculous species of beings, called a coquet.——This will be said by some, and thought by others, for all do not say what they think on such occasions.

Yet to that laudable principle, in women mistaken for coquetry, we owe the thunder of eloquence in the senate, as well as the glitter of dress in the drawing-room. An animated speech, and a well-chosen silk, are equally the effects of a desire to please, both in the patriot and the beauty: and if the one is ever observed to be silent, and the other without ornaments, it is because he is persuaded, that silence is most expressive; and she, that negligence is most becoming.

But for this active principle, the statesman would be no politician, and the general no warrior. The desire of fame, or the desire of pleasing, which, in my opinion, are synonimous terms, produces application in one and courage in the other. It is the poet's inspiration, the patriot's zeal, the courtier's loyalty, and the orator's eloquence. All are coquets, if that be coquetry, and those grave personages and the fine lady are alike liable to be charged with it.

But it will be objected, that the distinguishing characteristic of a coquet is to use her powers of pleasing to the ungenerous purpose of giving pain; the same may be said of each of the others. All human excellence, as well as human happiness, is comparative. We are admired but in proportion as we excel others, and whoever excels is sure to give pain, to his inferiors in merit, either from envy or emulation; passions which produce sensations nearly alike, although their consequences are very different.

I hope I have now fully proved, that I, tho' a woman, young, single, gay, and ambitious of pleasing, deserve not the odious appellation of coquet; I say, I hope, I have proved it, for I am but eighteen, and not used to be contradicted in argument.

If seldom your opinions err;
Your eyes are always in the right,

says the gallant Prior.[1] Hence it follows that we always triumph in a dispute, though I cannot help allowing, that we often triumph without victory.

Universally as I could wish to please in this paper, yet I shall be contented, if it finds only a favourable acceptance with my own sex, to whose amusement it is chiefly designed to contribute.

To introduce it to them under the denomination of a trifle may be thought an affront to their understandings. But in the choice of my title, I remembered the fable of the mountain that brought forth a mouse.[2] That I have promised little is my security from censure; if I give more it will be my best claim to praise. I should indeed have thought some apology necessary for an undertaking

---

1 Matthew Prior (1664–1721) was one of the most successful Restoration and early eighteenth-century poets. The poem quoted here is entitled "To a Lady: She Refusing to Continue a Dispute with Me, and Leaving Me in the Argument: An Ode," *Poems on Several Occasions* (London: Tonson, 1709).

2 An allusion to the moral of Aesop's fable, "A Mountain in Labour." In the edition of *Æsop's Fables* (London: Rivington: 1740) that Lennox probably used, the story reads as follows:

> A Rumour went that the Mountain was in Labour, and all the Neighbourhood got together to see what a monstrous Issue so great a Mother would bring forth; when, behold! of a sudden, out run [*sic*] a ridiculous Mouse.

MORAL

Nothing so much exposes Man to Ridicule, as when, by vain Blusters, he raises Expectation of all around him, and falls short in his Performance.

of this kind, had I not been persuaded, it was a mighty easy one, from its being so frequently attempted, and by persons too of my own sex.

The subjects I propose to treat of will be such as reading and observation shall furnish me with; for, with a strong passion for intellectual pleasures, I have likewise a taste for many of the fashionable amusements, and in the disposition of my time, I have contrived to gratify both these inclinations; one I thought too laudable to be restrained, the other I found too pleasing to be wholly subdued.

I am already aware that I have talked too much of myself: it is indeed a subject one cannot easily quit, and perhaps I am not sorry, that in introductory papers of this sort, the writers have generally given some account of themselves.[1] Every one knows that long custom has the force of a law; and, in obedience to this, I shall fill up my first paper with a short history of myself.[2]

I am the daughter of a gentleman remarkable only in this, that during the course of a pretty long life, he never lost a friend, or made an enemy. From which singular circumstance I leave the reader to collect his character. My mother was generally allowed to be a well bred-woman, and an excellent economist. In her youth she was extremely indulged by her parents, who, on account of a slight disorder in her eyes, would not suffer her to use a needle, or look into a book, except on Sundays or holidays, when she was permitted to read two or three verses of a chapter in the Bible.

My mother therefore grew up, not only without any taste, but with a high contempt for reading; and those of her female acquaintance who had made any proficiency that way were sure to be distinguished by her, with the opprobrious term of being *book-learned*, which my mother always pronounced with a look and accent of ineffable scorn.

My sister, who is a year younger than myself, so entirely engrossed her affection, that I was wholly neglected by her. My fondness for reading, which I discovered very early, encreased her dislike of me. As she seldom chose to have me in her sight, I had opportunities sufficient to indulge myself in this favourite amuse-

---

1 Eighteenth-century periodicals often began with an introduction of the narrative persona (see introduction p. 39). For instance, in its first issue, Addison and Steele's *Spectator* introduces Mr. Spectator.

2 There is no evidence that the following "biography" in any way relates to Lennox's life.

ment, for I had taken possession of all the books my brother left behind him, when he went to the university; but having great sensibility of soul, I was so affected with my mother's partial fondness for my sister, and neglect of me, that young as I then was, I often past whole nights in tears, lamenting my misfortune.

But his sensibility entirely ruined me with my mother; for, being one day excessively shocked at some new instance of her partiality, I went up sobbing to the nursery, and had recourse to a book for my relief. It happened to be Æsop's Fables: I opened it at the following one, which striking my imagination, then full of the preference given by my mother to my sister, I followed a sudden impulse, and sent it to my mother, desiring she would be pleased to read it; for I did not doubt but she would make a proper application of it.

"An ape had twins: she doated upon one of them, and did not much care for the other. She took a sudden fright one day, and in a hurry whips up her darling under her arm, and took no heed of the other, which therefore leaped astride upon her shoulders. In this haste down she comes, and beats out her favourite's brains upon a stone, while that which she had on her back came off safe and sound."[1]

My mother, surprised at the novelty of the request, read the fable, and immediately afterwards came up to the nursery in great wrath, and corrected me severely, for calling her an *ape*, prophetically declaring that a girl who at nine years old could be so wicked, as to compare her mother to an *ape*, would never come to good.

Every one who came to the house was told the horrid crime I had been guilty of, the servants held me in the utmost detestation for comparing my mother to an *ape*, never mentioning it, without lifted up hands and eyes, in abhorrence of such early undutifulness.

My father, who had loved me with great tenderness, was dead when this incident happened; and the most effectual way of paying court to my mamma being to caress my sister, and take no notice of me, I met with very few friends, either at home or abroad.

In this state of humiliation and disgrace my brother found me, at his return from the university. When my sister and I were presented to him, my mother did not fail to relate the crime for

---

1   From *Æsop's Fables* (London: Rivington, 1740), 146; see introduction p. 40.

which I had suffered so much, shewing him the book, which she had kept carefully ever after, with the leaf doubled down, at the fatal fable, declaring she thought herself very unhappy in having given birth to a child who was likely to prove so great an affliction to her; "for may not every thing that is bad," said she, "be expected from a girl who at her years could compare her mother to an *ape?*"

My brother read the fable, and my mother leaving the room to give some necessary orders, he ran eagerly to me, snatched me up in his arms, and gave me a hundred kisses. My little heart was so sensibly affected with a tenderness to which I had not been accustomed, that I burst into tears.

My mother after her return found me sobbing, with the violence of my emotions, and did not doubt but my brother had been chiding me. He told her gravely, that since I was so fond of reading, he would regulate my studies himself, and take care I should read no books which might teach me to be undutiful.

To this dear brother I owe the advantage of a right education, which I had like to have missed. After my mother's death he took me entirely under his own care. My sister chose to reside with an aunt, whose heir she expects to be; and while she is a slave to the caprices of an old woman, I have the pleasure of being the mistress of a well-ordered family, for I keep my brother's house; and by endeavouring to make him an useful as well as agreeable companion, enjoy the sweet satisfaction of shewing every day my gratitude for obligations it can never be in my power to return.

OF THE
STUDIES proper for WOMEN

Translated from the French

To prohibit women entirely from learning is treating them with the same indignity that Mahomet did, who, to render them voluptuous, denied them souls;[1] and indeed the greatest part of women act as if they had really adopted a tenet so injurious to the sex, and appear to set no value upon that lively imagination, that sprightly wit which makes them more admired than beauty itself.

---

1   This reference to the Muslim prophet Mohammed reflects a widely held eighteenth-century prejudice.

When we consider the happy talents which women in general possess, and how successfully some have cultivated them, we cannot without indignation observe the little esteem they have for the endowments of their minds which it is so easy for them to improve. They are, as Montaigne[1] says, flowers of quick growth, and by the delicacy of their conception, catch readily and without trouble the relation of things to each other. It is a melancholy consideration that the most precious gifts of nature should be stifled, or obscured by a shameful neglect.

The charms of their persons, how powerful soever, may attract, but cannot fix us; something more than beauty is necessary to rivet the lover's chain. By often beholding a beautiful face, the impression it first made on us soon wears away. When the woman whose person we admire is incapable of pleasing us by her conversation, languor and satiety, soon triumph over the taste we had for her charms: hence arises the inconstancy with which we are so often reproached; it is that barrenness of ideas which we find in women that renders men unfaithful.

The ladies may judge of the difference there is among them, by that which they themselves make between a fool who teases them with his impertinence, and a man of letters who entertains them agreeably; a very little labour would equal them to the last, and perhaps give them the advantage. This is a kind of victory which we wish to yield them. We would, without envy, see them dividing with us a good, whose value is always greater than the labour by which it is acquired.

The more they shall enlarge their notions, the more subjects of conversation will be found between them and us, and the more sprightly and affecting will that conversation be. How many delicate sentiments, how many nice sensibilities are lost by not being communicable, and in which we should feel an increase of satisfaction could we meet with women disposed to taste them!

But what are the studies to which women may with propriety apply themselves? This question I take upon myself to answer; and I intreat the ladies to pardon me, if among the sciences which exercise the wonderful activity of the human mind, I pronounce that only some are fit to be cultivated by them. I would particularly recommend to them to avoid all abstract learning,

---

1 The French writer Michel de Montaigne (1533–92) pretty much invented the modern genre of the essay with his *Essais* (1580–95). His works were frequently quoted in eighteenth-century Britain.

all thorny researches, which may blunt the finer edge of their wit, and change the delicacy in which they excel into pedantic coarseness.

If their sex has produced Daciers* and Chatelets,† these are examples rarely found, and fitter to be admired than imitated: for who would wish to see assemblies made up of doctors in petticoats, who will regale us with Greek and the systems of Leibnitz.[1] The learning proper for women is such as best suits the soft elegance of their form, such as may add to their natural beauties, and qualify them for the several duties of life. There is nothing more disgustful than those female theologians, who, adopting all the animosity of the party they have thought fit to join, assemble ridiculous synods in their houses, and form extravagant sects. A Bourignon,‡ a virgin

---

* Anne le Fevre, wife of monsieur Dacier. She translated Florus, Terence, and Homer, and added very learned notes of her own. [Lennox's note. Anne Dacier née Lefèvre (1651–1720) was a translator and editor who became famous by intervening in the Battle of the Ancients and Moderns, the fight over whether contemporary writers could ever replicate the achievements of antiquity. Dacier believed that the writings of the ancients could never be surpassed.]

† Gabriella Emilia de Bréteuil, marchioness du Châtelet. She explained Leibnitz, translated Newton, and commented upon him. We have philosophical institutions of hers, which prove the force of her wonderful genius to all who have learning enough to render them capable of judging it. [Lennox's note. Gabrielle Emilie le Tonnelier de Bréteuil de Châtelet (1706–49) was married to the Marquis du Châtelet, but she had affairs with several men, including Voltaire. In spite of an unofficial ban against women, she became a member of several intellectual circles in eighteenth-century France.]

‡ Antoinette Bourignon, a celebrated visionary, who purchased the island of Nordstrand, to establish a sect of mysticks there. She composed nineteen large volumes, and wasted a very considerable fortune by her attempts to propagate her extravagant dreams. [Lennox's note. Antoinette Bourignon (1616–80) was a Flemish Christian quietist mystic who opposed organized religion and advocated withdrawal from the world.]

---

1 Gottfried Wilhelm Leibniz (1646–1716) was a German mathematician and philosopher. The text could be referring to how difficult his metaphysics or his differential calculus were.

of Venice,* a madame Guyon,† are characters more detestable than libertines, like Ninon.‡

It is in such parts of learning only as afford the highest improvement that we invite women to share with us. All that may awaken curiosity, and lend graces to the imagination, suits them still better than us. This is a vast field where we may together exercise the mind; and here they may even excel us without mortifying our pride.

History and natural philosophy are alone sufficient to furnish women with an agreeable kind of study. The latter, in a series of useful observations and interesting experiments, offers a spectacle well worthy the consideration of a reasonable being. But in vain does nature present her miracles to the generality of women, who have no attention but to trifles: she is dumb to those who know not how to interrogate her.

Yet surely it requires but a small degree of attention to be struck with that wonderful harmony which reigns throughout the universe, and to be ambitious of investigating its secret springs. This is a large volume which is open to all; here a pair of beautiful eyes may employ themselves without being fatigued. This amiable study will banish languor from the sober amusements of the country, and repair that waste of intellect which is caused by the dissipations of the town. Women cannot be too much excited to raise their eyes to objects like these, which they but too often debase to such as are unworthy of them.

The sex is more capable of attention than we imagine: what they chiefly want is a well directed application. There is scarcely a young girl who has not read with eagerness a great number of

---

*   The virgin of Venice, an old woman, who, supported by Postel, called herself the Messiah of women. [Lennox's note. Guillaume Postel was the first French person to read the Kabala. In 1549, he claimed to recognize God in a 50-year-old Venetian woman, Madre Zuana.]

†   Madame Guyon, a lady of great beauty and fortune, who in the reign of Louis XIV. preached the doctrine of pure love, and renewed the extravagancies of quietism. [Lennox's note. Jeanne-Marie Bouvier de la Motte-Guyon (1648–1717) was a Christian mystic who expressed her faith in her autobiography. Her most famous pupil was Fénelon (see p. 246).]

‡   Ninon Leclos, a woman of gallantry in the last age. [Lennox's note. Ninon de Lenclos (1615–1705) went through a series of famous lovers in the first part of her life and was a leader of Paris fashion and culture in the second.]

idle romances, and puerile tales, sufficient to corrupt her imagination and cloud her understanding. If she had devoted the same time to the study of history, she would in those varied scenes which the world offers to view, have found facts more interesting, and instruction which only truth can give.

Those striking pictures, that are displayed in the annals of the human race, are highly proper to direct the judgment, and form the heart. Women have at all times had so great a share in events, and have acted so many different parts, that they may with reason consider our archives as their own: nay, there are many of them who have written memoirs of the several events of which they had been eye-witnesses. Mademoiselle de Montpensier, Madame de Némours, Madame de Motteville, are of this number. Christina de Pisan, daughter to the astronomer, patronised by the Emperor Charles the fifth, has given us the life of that prince; and long before her, the princess Anna Comnenus wrote the history of her own times.[1] We call upon the ladies to assert their rights, and from the study of history to extract useful lessons for the conduct of life.

This study, alike pleasing and instructive, will naturally lead to that of the fine arts, which it is fit the ladies should have a less superficial knowledge of. The arts are in themselves too amiable to need any recommendation to the sex: all the objects they offer to their view have some analogy with women, and are like them adorned with the brightest colours. The mind is agreeably soothed by those images which poetry, painting, and musick trace out to it, especially if they are found to agree with purity of manners. It was these three charming arts, which, in the last reign, rendered Mademoiselle Chéron so celebrated; a lady in

---

1   Anne-Marie Louise d'Orleans, Duchess of Montpensier (1627–93), was involved in the civil war that raged in France 1648–52 and documented her experiences in her *Mémoires* (published posthumously in 1729). Marie d'Orleans-Longueville, Duchess of Nemours (1625–1707), detailed the same civil war in her own *Mémoires* (1709). Françoise Bertaut de Motteville (c.1621–89) was a companion of Louis XIII's wife Anne of Austria. De Motteville's *Mémoires* chronicle Anne's life. Christine de Pisan (1364–1430), arguably the first professional female author, wrote over 40 works, including a biography of the French King. Today, she is better known for her feminist *The Book of the City of Ladies*. Anna Comnena (1083–1153) was the daughter of the Byzantine emperor Alexius I Comnenus and documented his reign in the *Alexiad*.

whom the talents of Sappho, of M——, and of Rosalba were united.[1]

To familiarize ourselves with the arts is in some degree to create a new sense. So agreeably have they imitated nature, nay, so often have they embellished it, that whoever cultivates them, will in them always find a fruitful source of new pleasures. We ought to provide against the encroachments of languor and weariness by this addition to our natural riches; and surely when we may so easily transfer to ourselves the possession of that multitude of pleasing ideas which they have created, it would be the highest stupidity to neglect such an advantage.

There is no reason to fear that the ladies, by applying themselves to these studies, will throw a shade over the natural graces of their wit. No; on the contrary, those graces will be placed in a more conspicuous point of view: what can equal the pleasure we receive from the conversation of a woman who is more solicitous to adorn her mind than her person? In the company of such women there can be no satiety; every thing becomes interesting, and has a secret charm which only they can give. The delightful art of saying the most ingenious things with a graceful simplicity is peculiar to them: it is they who call forth the powers of wit in men, and communicate to them that easy elegance which is never to be acquired in the closet.

But what preservative is there against weariness and disgust in the society of women of weak and unimproved understanding? In vain do they endeavour to fill the void of their conversation with insipid gaiety: they soon exhaust the barren funds of fashionable trifles, the news of the day, and hackneyed compliments; they are at length obliged to have recourse to scandal, and it is well if they stop there: a commerce in which there is nothing solid must be either mean or criminal.

There is but one way to make it more varied and more interesting. If ladies of the first rank would condescend to form their taste upon our best authors, and collect ideas from their useful

---

1 Elisabeth Sophie Chéron (1648–1711) was a successful French portrait painter who became a member of the Academie Royal in 1672. She was also a musician and a poet. According to Villemert, she combined the talents of the ancient Greek lyric poet Sappho and the Venetian painter Rosalba Carriera (1675–1757). I have been unable to identify "M—" with any certainty, but the reference may be to Madame de Maintenon, who founded the convent school Maison Royale St-Louis de Saint-Cyr, where music was regularly performed, and whose memoirs Lennox translated.

writings, conversation would take another cast: their acknowledged merit would banish that swarm of noisy impertinents who
flutter about them, and who endeavour to render them as contemptible as themselves: men of sense and learning would then
frequent their assemblies, and form a circle more worthy of the
name of *good company*.

In this new circle gaiety would not be banished, but refined by
delicacy and wit. Merit is not austere in its nature; there is a calm
and uniform chearfulness that runs through the conversation of
persons of real understanding, which is far preferable to the noisy
mirth of ignorance and folly. Those societies formed by the Sevi-
gnes, the Fayetts, the Sablières, with the Vivonnes, the La Fares,
and Rochefoucaults, were surely more pleasing than the assemblies of our days.[1] Among them learning was not pedantic, nor
wisdom severe; and subjects of the highest importance were
treated with all the sprightliness of wit.

The ladies must allow me once more to repeat to them that
the only means of charming, and of charming long, is to
improve their minds; good sense gives beauties which are not
subject to fade like the lillies and roses of their cheeks, but will
prolong the power of an agreeable woman to the autumn of her
life.[*] If the sex would not have their influence confined to the
short triumph of a day, they must endeavour to improve their
natural talents by study, and the conversation of men of letters.
Neglect will not then steal upon them in proportion as their
bloom decays; but they will unite in themselves all the advantages of both sexes.

---

[*] It was by her wit that the Dutchess of Valentinois charmed three succes-
sive monarchs, and preserved her influence to an extreme old age. It
was to their wit that Madame de Vérac, Madam Tencin, and several
other ladies owed their power of charming when their youth was fled.
The graces of a fine understanding, improved by study, never grow old.
[Lennox's note. The first reference is probably to Diane de Poitiers,
Duchess of Valentinois.(1499–1566), mistress of the French King Henry
II. Claudine-Alexandrine Guérin de Tencin (1682–1749) was one of the
most influential women of her time in the areas of culture and politics. I
have been unable to identify Madame de Vérac.]

---

1 All of these names refer to women who held "salons," i.e., intellectual
gatherings, in seventeenth-century France.

We live no longer in an age when prejudice condemned women as well as the nobility, to a shameful ignorance. The ridicule with which pedantry was treated had so much discredited every kind of knowledge, that there were many ladies who thought it graceful to murder the words of their native language; but some were still found, who, shaking off the yoke of fashion, ventured to think justly, and speak with propriety; and even at this time there are a small number who are not ashamed of being more learned than the idle man of fashion, and the fluttering courtier.

THE
HISTORY
OF
HARRIOT AND SOPHIA

[The first installment of *Sophia* in its periodical publication covers the first four chapters of the novel version. There are no chapter breaks in this version.]

A SONG, in PHILANDER
A Dramatic Pastoral
Set by Mr. OSWALD

[The first stanza is not printed separately, but given in the score of the music. See Figure 4.]

II.
For oh! in vain the sigh's represt
That struggling heaves her anxious breast.
In vain the falling tear's with-held,
The conscious wish in vain repell'd.

III
Her faded cheeks, and air forlorn,
Coarse jests invite, and cruel scorn.
To hopeless love she falls a prey,
And wastes in silent grief away.

A SONG, in PHILANDER.

A Dramatic Paſtoral.

Set by Mr. OSWALD.

Think what the hapleſs virgin proves, who loves in vain, yet fondly loves; While modeſty and female pride, The ſlighted paſſion ſeek to hide.

II.

For oh! in vain the ſigh's repreſt
That ſtruggling heaves her anxious breaſt.
In vain the falling tear's with-held,
The conſcious wiſh in vain repell'd.

III.

Her faded cheeks, and air forlorn,
Coarſe jeſts invite, and cruel ſcorn.
To hopeleſs love ſhe falls a prey,
And waſtes in ſilent grief away.

On

Figure 4: Score (melody, text of first stanza, bass line) for "A Song" from the first act of Lennox's dramatic pastoral *Philander*, music by James Oswald (1710-69). *Philander* was never produced on stage. © British Library Board. All Rights Reserved (C.175.n.15)

On reading a POEM *written by a Lady of Quality.*

I

Afraid to be pleas'd, and with envy half fir'd,
Still wishing to blame, while by force I admir'd,

New beauties appearing as farther I read,
At last in a rage to Apollo[1] I said:

II

Oh thou whom the lean tribe of authors adore!
And proud of thy gifts, are content to be poor;
Say, why must a peeress thus put in her claim,
For the poet's poor airy inheritance, fame?

III

Needs that brow which a coronet circles be bound
With the wreath that your glorious starv'd fav'rites have crown'd.
Why should she who at ease in gilt chariots may ride,
Our tir'd Pegasus[2] mount, and so skilfully guide?

IV

With Gallia's[3] rich vintage, her thirst she may slake,
Then why such large draughts from our Helicon take?
And blest here with corn-fields, and meadows, and pastures,
Has she need of grants in the realm of Parnassus?[4]

V

Thus I: nor to answer Apollo disdain'd,
My Stella[5] from fortune those trifles obtain'd;
In wit I decreed her supremely to shine,
When were titles and riches suppos'd gifts of mine?
But your clamours to stop, and your anger to tame,
She shall smile on your works, and her praise shall be fame.

An ODE

I

How long from they inchanting sway

---

1 Apollo was the Greek god of music and poetry (among other things).
2 In Greek mythology, Pegasus was a winged horse. Pegasus is also a
  symbol of poetic inspiration.
3 "Gallia" is the Latin name for France—the peeress can drink expensive
  French wine.
4 Mount Helicon, part of the Parnassus mountain range, was supposedly
  a favorite residence of the Muses. There are many springs and brooks on
  Mount Helicon
5 Here, Stella is an elaborate name for the poetess.

Shall I my freedom, Love, maintain!
The young, the beauteous, and the gay
    Still spread the pleasing snare in vain.

II

The study'd air, the borrow'd grace,
    All affectation's numerous wiles,
Send blunted darts from ev'ry face,
    Conceal'd in blushes, sighs, and smiles.

III

For these my heart feels no alarms,
    Whose honest wish is but to prove
The genuine force of artless charms,
    The soft simplicity of love.

IV

The heaving bosom's fall and rise,
    Compassion only should display.
The glance that can my soul surprise
    To wit must owe the pointed ray.

V

The smile that would my soul inflame,
    Good nature only must bestow.
Sweet modesty, ingen'ous shame,
    Must give the kindling cheek to glow.

VI

Mere outward charms the mind delude
    To own a short compulsive reign,
By wit, and virtue when subdu'd,
    She forges for herself her chain.

To DEATH. An irregular ODE.

I

Oh death, thou gentle end of human pain,
    Why is thy stroke so long delay'd?
Why to a wretch, who breathes but to complain,
    Dost thou refuse thy welcome aid?
Still wilt thou fly the plaintive voice of woe,

And where thou'rt dreaded, only aim the blow.

II

Oh leave, fantastick tyrant, leave,
  The young, the gay, the happy, and the free:
On them bestow a short reprieve,
  And bend thy fatal shafts at me.
The beauteous bride, or blooming heir,
Let thy resistless power spare,
And aim at this grief-wounded heart
That springs half way to meet the welcome dart.

III

Still must I view with streaming eyes,
Another, and another morn arise;
Are my days length'ned to prolong my pain?
Do grief and sickness waste this frame in vain?
A finish'd wretch e'er youth has ceas'd to bloom,
By early sorrow ripen'd for the tomb.

[The last item in the first issue of *The Lady's Museum*, the first of two installments of "The History of the Duchess of Beaufort," is not reprinted here.]

2. "Philosophy for the Ladies," *The Lady's Museum* 2 (April 1760): 129–33

[This essay refers back to "Of the Studies Proper for Women," but does not seem to come from Villemert's book. This piece appears to have been written by Lennox herself. Here, she encourages women to pursue knowledge, particularly philosophy, as mind-opening and enjoyable. She ends the text with a grand overview of the knowledge she intends to introduce, a promise she mostly keeps over the next ten installments of *The Lady's Museum*.]

In the enumeration of those studies which the fair sex may properly be permitted to employ some part of their time in an application to, given in our last Number, it may be remembered that history and natural philosophy stood foremost in the list. Curiosity is one of the most prevalent, and, when properly applied, one of the most amiable, passions of the human mind; nor can it in any way find a more rational scope for exertion, than in the recollection of historical facts, and a curious inquisition into the wonders of creation. To this application of that passion the female part of the world are unquestionably most happily adapted. Undisturbed by the more intricate affairs of business; unburthened with the load of political entanglements; with the anxiety of commercial negotiations; or the suspense and anguish which attend on the pursuit of fame or fortune, the memories of the fair are left vacant to receive and to retain the regular connection of a train of events, to register them in that order which fancy may point out as most pleasing, and to form deductions from them such as may render their lives more agreeable to themselves, and more serviceable to every one about them. Their more exalted faculties, not being tied down by wearisome attention to mathematical investigations, metaphysical chimeras, or abstruse scholastic learning, are more at liberty to observe with care, see with perspicuity, and judge without prejudice, concerning the amazing world of wonders round them than those of men, who, very frequently by attempting to arrive at *every* kind of knowledge, find themselves stopped short in their career by the limited period of life, before they can properly be said to have reached *any*.

To gratify and furnish food for this laudable curiosity, therefore, in both these branches of knowledge, shall be one of our principal aims in the prosecution of this work; yet as amusement no less than instruction will ever constitute one of the main columns of our edifice, and that our wish is to render the ladies though learned not pedantic, conversable rather than scientific, we shall avoid entering into any of those minutiæ, or diving into those depths of literature, which may make their study dry to themselves, or occasion its becoming tiresome to others.

If therefore we treat of philosophy, it shall be polished from the rust of theoretical erudition, and adorned with all those advantages which a connexion with the polite arts and sciences can throw upon it. If of history, a pleasing relation of the most interesting facts shall be endeavoured at, the movement of the grand machine of government shall indeed be set before our readers, and the influence of each apparent wheel be rendered visible: but we shall think it unnecessary to look into every secret spring whereby these wheels are actuated; and shall dispense with entering into the never to be discovered causes of the rise and fall of nations now no more, to make room for the more useful knowledge of those movements of the human heart on which depend the happiness or ruin of individuals. If geography should form, as we propose it shall, one portion of each number, it will not be with us the meer description of large tracts of land, where woods and plains, mountains and valleys, rivers and sandy deserts occur alike in all; but only a detail in every country of those things which are peculiar to itself: a picture not of the face of the earth, of sea and air, in different latitudes and longitudes, but a more varied prospect of human nature diversified by different laws, by different constitutions, and different ideas.

Thus much will be sufficient to premise in regard to the matter of our researches on these kind of subjects, in order to obviate the horrid idea which the word philosophy might perhaps otherwise impress on the minds of our female readers, who might from that term expect to find a work intended and calculated chiefly for their amusement and instruction, loaded with dry and abstruse investigations, which some of them might not have the time, or others even want attention, to examine with the application necessary to become mistresses of them; and which if they were attained would stand a chance of more than ten to one of exciting the outcry of the world against them.

As to the method we intend to pursue, however, something, though not much, will be necessary to add. Which will be only to observe that no regular course of philosophy, no long train of historical events, nor any close confinement to one branch of geographical knowledge, shall be aimed at in our essays on these subjects. Variety is the soul of study, as well as the pleasure of life; and a thousand useful pieces of knowledge steal into the vacancies of our mind when detached, which would never find their way thither if they were entangled with each other, or mingled in the grand mass of philosophical enquiries.

Learning, in short, is the old man's bundle of rods: when bound up in the cluster, it is almost impossible to overcome, yet every single twig may easily be mastered. In short, we see not the labour we have to go through, when it is presented to us in minute portions; yet still it answers the end proposed,

Small sands that mountain, moments make the year.[1]

We accumulate knowledge by golden grains, and find ourselves possessed of an ample treasure before we are even aware that we

---

1 Edward Young (1683–1765), *The Love of Fame, the Universal Passion*, Satire VI (205–08) reads:
   Think nought a trifle, though it small appear:
   Small sands the mountain, moments make the year,
   And trifles life. Your care to trifles give;
   Or you may die before you truly live. (Young I.394)

have attained the necessary store for our passing easily through life.

To render this accumulation therefore thus easy, we shall fix ourselves to no peculiar order, but make variety our aim; transport our reader by turns through all the regions of earth, air, and ocean, and to different climates, with expedition beyond the power of a magician's wand. No bars of time, of place, or distance, or even impossibility itself, shall stop our progress. One Number of our work perhaps shall leave us admiring the stupendous fabric of the immense extended universe; the next shall find us aiding our limited sight by help of glasses in observations on a world of unknown beings contained within a drop of fluid, or forests waving in the narrow circuit of a small piece of moss. To-day we shall converse with almost our cotemporaries, enquire their actions, and censure or applaud them as we please; to-morrow shall introduce us to an intercourse with the great founders of long abolished empires. One page shall teach the manners used by nations where splendour and magnificence surpass even the most volatile imagination; the next point out the various artifices which want, the parent of inventive labour, instructs the poor unhappy savage to make use of for the supply of those necessities which barren wilds and mountains desolate deny the fuller solace of. In short, every thing curious, every thing instructive, every thing entertaining, shall be carefully sought out, and offered to the view, without distinction or respect to order; still leaving to the mind of every reader to range and form them into systems according to his pleasure.

3. "To the Author of the Lady's Museum," *The Lady's Museum* 3 (May 1760): 182–89

[This "letter" to the editor of *The Lady's Museum* investigates the relationship between wealth and happiness, arguing that women should not pursue rich husbands but strive for virtue instead. The author "W.M." is not necessarily a real person; it was common practice for authors of periodicals in the eighteenth century to place similar "letters" written by themselves in their journals.]

MADAM,

As I apprehend the object of this publication is no less the moral than the literary improvement of your sex, permit me, through the channel of this useful work, to point out to your fair readers the fatal consequences of an opinion too generally received among them.

The opinion I could wish to see corrected is, that grandeur and happiness signify one and the same thing. How far the same wrong notion prevails among men, is not my present purpose to examine; but I will venture to affirm, that in the system of female logic, grandeur and happiness are convertible[1] terms. It is not surprising that this notion should be extremely prevalent, when we consider, that the whole system of female education tends to promote and extend it. Whence it is, that many misses are instructed in accomplishments evidently above their rank, but in order to obtain a station in life to which they could not reasonably aspire.

In truth, it is more the vanity of being thought to possess such accomplishments than any pleasure arising from those attainments, that is the inducement to pursue them. I have been assured by the parents of many young ladies, that their daughters were perfect mistresses of French, musick, &c. when upon better acquaintance, I plainly perceived, they had been at much expence only to say they had been learners.

I would not be thought to mean, that the polite accomplishments are not very useful and becoming to persons of a certain rank and character; but I would observe, that the promiscuous aim of all ranks of females, to acquire those elegant distinctions, evidently proves my first principle, namely, that an appetite for vanity and splendor pervades the whole system of modern education.

The polite attainments too frequently give young ladies of middling station[2] an unhappy propensity to dissipation and pleasure, and indispose them to the ordinary and necessary occupations of life. It may be useful to consider what probability there is, that an appetite for distinction may be gratified, and then examine what superior happiness such envied distinctions necessarily confer.

I shall take it for granted, that a good establishment in marriage is the object of most women's wishes. It has been computed that nineteen marriages in twenty, among persons of liberal condition, are concluded upon no great inequality of circumstances. It is plain then, that a lady who flatters herself, that she shall marry above her rank, runs no less a risk than twenty to one of a disappointment. In fact this is unavoidable; for persons of rank and opulence are not very numerous, and frequently intermarry with each other: yet upon so slender a

---

1 I.e., synonymous.
2 I.e., from the commercial and professional middle classes.

prospect has many a poor lady tired both herself and the public with a repetition of her countenance for many years past at every place of amusement.

To these dazzling and delusive hopes are ease and content-ment often sacrificed, from a mistaken opinion that grandeur and happiness are inseparable; or rather, that the latter was not possible without the former: hence anxious days and sleepless nights, not to mention that virtue is much endangered by pursuits giddy and fantastical. After years of vain expectation the point in view is at a greater distance than ever, to obtain which dancing-masters and milliners have assisted in vain. If it be said, that we hear sometimes of ladies, who from private stations have rose to great rank and riches, I answer, that particular exceptions conclude nothing against the general observation, that unreasonable expectation must almost always be disappointed.[1]

Instances of surprising good fortune happen in all pursuits, and seeming accident will have its share in the happy events of matrimony, as well as in most others. But if young people inflame their imaginations with extraordinary occurrences, and soar upon the waxen wings of expectation to regions of imaginary bliss, they will quickly find, like Icarus, misfortune interrupting the dream of vanity, and may possibly pay almost as dear for the experiment.[2]

With respect to the blessings of Providence, we rather lament the absence of things perhaps not necessary, than make a proper use of those we have. It sufficiently appears, that a passion for grandeur is not likely to be gratified; and that such wishes must, in the nature of things, much oftener miscarry than succeed.

But for once let us suppose the point obtained, and examine what happiness is annexed to that envied condition. Providence, for the wisest reasons, has made a great difference in the external circumstances of his creatures, but not in their happiness. In fact, the greatest blessings of life are proposed in common to us all. Health and an approving conscience are the grand satisfactions of our being, as sin and pain are almost the only evils: nor can we cease to adore that goodness who has made the best things in life attainable by all conditions, without a possibility of interfering with each other. In these two grand articles, it appears, that

1 The harangue on women marrying above their station may be a dig at Samuel Richardson's novel *Pamela* (1740), where the eponymous heroine marries her master, Mr. B—.

2 In Greek mythology, Icarus tried to flee his prison with wings held together with wax, but crashed when he flew too close to the sun.

persons of wealth and station have no advantage over more moderate conditions. The former are more exposed to temptations, and a full tide of prosperity has been always reckoned dangerous to virtue.

Besides, those who have large possessions and connexions are much broader marks for misfortune than others. Socrates accounted those happiest who had fewest wants, as the happiest of all beings is he who wants nothing.[1] The more our wants are enlarged, and our appetites indulged, they become more ungovernable, and exceed our powers of satisfying them. Such persons are exposed to perpetual disappointment, as it is much easier to imagine than obtain.

How many persons may we not presume, who are shining themselves, and shone on by fortune, that are inwardly miserable, and sick of life? Wealth and station may indeed procure a great variety of sensual gratifications, out of reach of humbler fortunes: but of what nature are such pleasures? fleeting and dissatisfactory in the confession of all.

Let us reflect a little on the most exalted pleasures our nature is capable of. We shall find them attainable by private stations, and from some of the best of them the very lowest conditions not excluded. Even those who are condemned to the drudgery of manual labour may, and do often enjoy a healthful body and a tranquil mind. Though they are in a great measure excluded from intellectual enjoyments, yet even this view of their condition is not without its compensations. It will not be denied, that our best enjoyments here below arise from temperance, moderate desires, easy reflexions, and a consciousness of knowledge and virtue. I would ask my fair countrywomen, whether high rank and great riches are necessary to these attainments? The purest and most substantial pleasures are certainly those arising from religion and virtue; the pleasures of knowledge, and of friendship: which are attainable by the middling, if not all classes of life, depend much upon ourselves, and are little subject to accident or diminution. So far from being the constant companions of rank and riches, that perhaps they are seldomer found among persons of elevated stations than most others. It were easy to assign the reasons; as

---

1 According to Diogenes Laertius (flourished in the third century CE) in his *Lives of the Ancient Philosophers* (London: Nicholson and Newborough, 1702), Greek philosopher Socrates said, "To stand in need of the fewest things, is the nearest degree to Divine Nature, which wants nothing" (80).

the necessaries of life are not difficult to obtain, so neither are its best comforts. A person must have reflected indeed to very little purpose who is not sensible, that the prospect of the divine favour in another life, is the grand foundation of contentment in this imperfect and probationary state.

It will be said, that a competency of the good things of life, is necessary to our happiness, and truly desirable. Most undoubtedly it is: but the misfortune is, our ideas of a competency are not taken from nature, or even from our proper station and character, but from our imaginations and wrong habits; and what is yet more preposterous, from our comparisons with others.

A competency is not to be defined, because it varies according to the station and necessities of individuals. To use a familiar comparison—Suppose a person undertakes a journey into a remote country, and has sufficient to defray his necessary expences, may he not enjoy the true pleasures of the scene equally with him who travels the same journey, attended with all the parade of equipage, and encumbered with a superfluity of wealth? May not as successful a voyage be made in a small, convenient bark, as in a galley no less splendid than Cleopatra's?[1]

Let nothing here advanced be supposed to mean, that wealth and station incapacitate their possessors from enjoying the truest happiness of their nature. Among other advantages in common with their fellow-creatures, they eminently enjoy the godlike power of doing good to others. It is the exercise of that power that gives rank and riches their true dignity, and is the constant employment of him who is the source of all excellence. But let not people mistake that which may be made the means of happiness for the necessary and never failing cause of it; nor repine at the want of those distinctions in the possession of which there occur so many examples extremely miserable.

I cannot conclude this letter without observing, that an appetite for grandeur very fatally predominates at a crisis in life, wherein, of all others, it behoves us to act with the truest wisdom: I mean at the time of marriage. Matches are now deemed good or bad, not from the qualities, but the external circumstances of the parties. The opinion of Themistocles, like many other old

---

1 In the eighteenth century, Egyptian queen Cleopatra was notorious for her ostentatious displays of wealth.

opinions, is quite exploded, who declared, "That he would rather marry his daughter to a man without an estate, than to an estate without a man."[1]

The candidates for the ladies' affections, or more properly their fortunes, undergo the most exact scrutiny into their estates, expectations, and alliances; nor is any enquiry omitted, but into their sense and morals. If your fair readers please to extend this charge to their admirers, they have my consent, only remembering, that folly on one side, never excuses it on another; and that they are most likely to be greater sufferers by an ill choice, as their condition is more dependent.

It is agreed on all sides, that the sure supports of conjugal felicity are the unreserved friendship and mutual esteem of the parties: now it is an axiom, that friendship cannot exist but between virtuous minds; and surely no dreams of a lunatic were ever more visionary, than to suppose there can be any abiding pleasure without virtue, since in our system of being there is nothing durable but the consequences of it.

Many a thoughtless female, who despised all considerations but rank and riches, serves only to exhibit a wretched spectacle of their insufficiency. I doubt not but this essay may fall into the hands of some of your fair readers, who have dragged out an insipid length of days, doating about vain and perishable distinctions, and have sunk into utter contempt and oblivion, who, by a better conduct, might have enjoyed happy and comfortable establishments.

Let those whose cases are retrievable, consider that elevation must ever be the lot of very few; nor when it is attained does it invariably produce happiness. The truest satisfactions in life are not necessarily connected with great estates or coronets, but are to be found among persons of all conditions, whose lives are governed by sense and virtue. Of one thing they may be infallibly certain, that a life conducted by vanity cannot fail to end in misery.

> I am, Madam,
> Your very Humble Servant,

---

1 This quotation from Plutarch's *Lives* is translated slightly differently in various eighteenth-century versions. For instance, in *Plutarch's Lives, in Six Volumes: Translated from the Greek* (London: Tonson, 1758), the text reads, "Of two [neighbors] who made love to his daughter he preferred the virtuous before the rich, saying, *he desired a man without riches, rather than riches without a man.* These things I have mentioned as specimens of his wit and pleasantry" (I 305).

4. "Of the Importance of the Education of Daughters," The Lady's Museum 4 (June 1760): 294–97

[This selection is a version of the first chapter of *Instructions for the Education of a Daughter* (1687)—the rest of the text was printed in subsequent installments in *The Lady's Museum*. The *Instructions*, by François de Salignac de La Mothe-Fénelon (1651-1715), a French cleric, man of letters, and educational reformer, were first translated into English in 1707 and went through at least seven editions in London, Dublin, Glasgow, and Edinburgh by 1753. However, it seems that Lennox did her own translation of the French text or at least adapted the available one. While Fénelon certainly believes in the essentialist notion that women are fundamentally less intellectually capable than men, the *Instructions* are still critical of differences of the educational practices of the time between men and women. Fénelon believes that since women raise children, who are so important to a society's future, they too need decent education.]

Nothing is more neglected than the education of daughters; custom, and the caprice of mothers, are for the most part absolutely decisive on that point. It is taken for granted, that a very little instruction is sufficient for the sex; whereas, the education of sons is looked upon as of principal concern to the public; and although there is scarce less mismanagement in this than in bringing up daughters, nevertheless people are fully persuaded that no small degree of discernment is requisite to insure success. How many masters do we see? how many colleges? what expence for impressions of books, for researches into the sciences, methods of learning languages, and choice of professors?

All these grand preparations have frequently more shew than solidity; however, they indicate the high notion people have of the education of boys. As for girls, say they, what necessity is there for them to be scholars; curiosity makes them vain and conceited; it is sufficient they learn in time how to govern their families, and submit to their husbands without debate: and here they are ready to produce a number of known instances of women grown ridiculous by pretence to scholarship; after this they think themselves justified in blindly abandoning girls to the management of ignorant and indiscreet mothers: it is true we ought to be very cautious of making pedantick ladies. Women, for the most part, have less strength of understanding than men, but more curiosity;

wherefore it is not proper to engage them in studies likely to disturb their heads. It is not for them to govern the state, direct the operations of war, or to interfere in the administration of religious affairs. Thus they may stand excused from those extensive articles of knowledge relative to politics, the art military, jurisprudence, theology: even the far greater part of the mechanic arts are not suitable to them. They are formed for gentler occupations: their bodies, as their understanding, are less vigorous, less robust than those of men; but nature, in compensation, has appropriated to them industry, neatness, and economy, and hence arises their taste for the calm duties of domestic life—But what are we to conclude from the natural weakness of women? the weaker they are, of the greater moment it is to give them strength. Have they not duties to fulfil, nay, duties on which the life of society depends? Is it not by them that families are ruined or upheld? they, who have the regulation of the whole train of domestic affairs, who have a general influence upon manners, and by consequence the sway in what most nearly affects all mankind.

A woman of judgment, application, and real piety, is the soul of a whole great family: she inspires that order, that prudence, and purity of manners which secure happiness here and hereafter. It is not in the power of men, tho' vested with all public authority, by their deliberations, to make any establishments effectually good, unless women are aiding in the execution.

The world is not a phantome: it is an assemblage of families; and who can adjust the government of them with more exactness than the women? They, besides their natural authority, and assiduity in their houses, have the further advantage of being born careful, minutely attentive, industrious, insinuating, and persuasive.

As for mankind, where else must they look for the comforts of life, if marriage, that closest of all alliances, shall be converted into bitterness? and children, who in their turn will be called mankind, what will become of them, if spoiled by their mothers from infancy.

Observe the parts women have to act, they are not of less moment than those of men; inasmuch as they have a house to regulate, a husband to make happy, children to bring up well; add that public virtue is no less necessary for the women than for the men. Without insisting on the good or evil import they may be of to the world, they are half of the human species redeemed by the blood of Jesus Christ, and destined to life eternal. Finally, to omit the good influence of women well brought up, let us consider the evils they are productive of, in defect of an education inspiring them with virtue. It is certain this defect in them is more mischievous than in men, because the irregularities of men frequently proceed from the bad education they have imbibed from their mothers, and from those passions other women have inspired them with in their riper years. What intrigues does history present to our view? What subversion of laws and morals? What bloody wars, innovations of religion, revolutions of state? all caused by the vices of women. These are proofs of the importance of a good education for girls. Let us consider the means.

Appendix E: Sentimentalism and Moral Philosophy

[The first three texts here present aspects of moral philosophy, the ideas that influenced sentimentalism throughout the eighteenth century. The final two are excerpts by authors writing towards the end of the century who had become critical of the sentimental novel.]

1. **From Anthony Ashley Cooper, Earl of Shaftesbury, "An Inquiry Concerning Virtue and Merit,"** *Characteristicks of Men, Manners, Opinions, Times.* **3 vols. (London: Darby, 1711) 2:28–31**

[In this monumental work, Shaftesbury (1671–1713) asserts the equivalence of self-interest and public interest. He describes a "moral sense" that he believes is innate to all humans, distinguishing them from animals. This moral sense allows humans to make unbiased judgements, in other words to separate their judgements from calculations of benefit and loss for themselves.]

In a Creature capable of forming general Notions of Things, not only the outward Beings which offer themselves to the Sense, are the Objects of Affection; but the very *Actions* themselves, and the *Affections* of Pity, Kindness, Gratitude, and the Contrarys, being brought into the Mind by Reflection, become Objects. So that, by means of this reflected Sense, there arises another kind of Affection towards those very Affections themselves, which have been already felt, and are now become the Subject of a new Liking or Dislike.

The Case is the same here, as in the ordinary *Bodys*, or common Subjects of Sense. The Shapes, Motions, Colours, and Proportions of these being presented to our Eye; there necessarily results a Beauty or Deformity, according to the different Measure, Arrangement and Disposition of their several Parts. So in *Behaviour* and *Actions*, when presented to our Understanding, there must be found, of necessity, an apparent Difference, according to the Regularity or Irregularity of the Subjects.

The Mind, which is Spectator or Auditor of *other Minds*, cannot be without its *Eye* or *Ear*; so as to discern Proportion, distinguish Sound, and scan each Sentiment or Thought that comes before it. It can let nothing escape its Censure. It feels the Soft, and Harsh, the Agreeable, and Disagreeable, in the Affections; and finds a *Foul* and *Fair*, a *Harmonious*, and a *Dissonant*, as really and truly here, as in the outward Forms or Representations of sensible Things.

As in the sensible kind, the Species or Images of Bodys, Colours, and Sounds, are perpetually moving before our Eyes, and acting on our Senses, even in Sleep, and when the real Objects themselves are absent; so in the moral and intellectual kind, the Forms and Images of Things are no less active and incumbent on the Mind.

In these vagrant Characters or Pictures of Manners, which the Mind of necessity figures to it-self, and carries still about with it, the Heart cannot possibly remain neutral; but constantly takes part one way or other. However false or corrupt it be within it-self, it finds the Difference, as to Beauty, and Comeliness, between one *Heart* and another, one *Turn of Affection*, one *Behaviour*, one *Sentiment* and another; and accordingly, in all disinterested Cases, must approve in some measure of what is natural and honest, and disapprove what is dishonest and corrupt.

Thus the several Motions, Inclinations, Passions, Dispositions, and consequent Carriage and Behaviour of Creatures in the various Parts of Life, being in several Views or Perspectives represented to the Mind, which readily discerns the Good and Ill towards the Species or Publick; there arise a new Trial or Exercise of the Heart: which must either rightly and soundly affect what is just and right, and disaffect what is contrary; or, corruptly affect what is ill, and disaffect what is worthy and good.

And in this Case alone it is that we call any Creature *Worthy* or *Virtuous*, when it can have the Notion of a publick Interest, and can attain the Speculation or Science of what is morally good or ill, admirable or blameable, right or wrong. For tho we may vulgarly call an ill Horse *vitious*; yet we never say of a good-one, nor of any mere Beast, Idiot, or Changeling, tho ever so good-natur'd, that he is *worthy* or *virtuous*.

So that if a Creature be generous, kind, constant, compassionate; yet if he cannot reflect on what he himself does, or sees others do, so as to take notice of what is *worthy* or *honest*; and make that Notice or Conception of *Worth* and *Honesty* to be an Object of his Affection, he has not the Character of being *virtuous*: for thus, and no otherwise, he is capable of having a *Sense of Right or Wrong*; a Sentiment or Judgment of what is done thro just, equal, and good Affection, or the contrary.

2. From David Hume, "Moral Distinctions Deriv'd from a Moral Sense," *A Treatise of Human Nature*, 3 vols. (London: Noon and Longman, 1739–40) 3:26–30

[In the *Treatise of Human Nature*, Hume (1711–76) applies the principles of scientific investigation to an examination of morals. Hume is an "empiricist": he does not think that humans are born with innate principles, but argues instead that they acquire all their ideas and impressions through sensory experience. Nevertheless, Hume argues that it is possible to arrive at rigorous morals through a process of reasoning. In the present excerpt, literature functions as an important example in his argument.]

Thus the course of the argument leads us to conclude, that since vice and virtue are not discoverable merely by reason, or the comparison of ideas, it must be by means of some impression or sentiment they occasion, that we are able to mark the difference betwixt them. Our decisions concerning moral rectitude and depravity are evidently perceptions; and as all perceptions are either impressions or ideas, the exclusion of the one is a convincing argument for the other. Morality, therefore, is more properly felt than judg'd of; tho' this feeling or sentiment is commonly so soft and gentle, that we are apt to confound it with an idea, according to our common custom of taking all things for the same, which have any near resemblance to each other.

The next question is, Of what nature are these impressions, and after what manner do they operate upon us? Here we cannot remain long in suspense, but must pronounce the impression arising from virtue, to be agreeable, and that proceding from vice to be uneasy. Every moment's experience must convince us of this. There is no spectacle so fair and beautiful as a noble and generous action; nor any which gives us more abhorrence than one that is cruel and treacherous. No enjoyment equals the satisfaction we receive from the company of those we love and esteem; as the greatest of all punishments is to be oblig'd to pass our lives with those we hate or contemn. A very play or romance may afford us instances of this pleasure, which virtue conveys to us; and pain, which arises from vice.

Now since the distinguishing impressions, by which moral good or evil is known, are nothing but *particular* pains or pleasures; it follows, that in all enquiries concerning these moral distinctions, it will be sufficient to shew the principles, which make us feel a satisfaction or uneasiness from the survey of any character, in order to satisfy us why the character is laudable or blameable. An action, or sentiment, or character is virtuous or vicious; why? because its view causes a pleasure or uneasiness of a particular kind. In giving a reason, therefore, for the pleasure or uneasiness, we sufficiently explain the vice or virtue. To have the sense of virtue, is nothing but to *feel* a satisfaction of a particular kind from the contemplation of a character. The very *feeling* constitutes our praise or admiration. We go no farther; nor do we enquire into the cause of the satisfaction. We do not infer a character to be virtuous, because it pleases: But in feeling that it pleases after such a particular manner, we in effect feel that it is virtuous. The case is the same as in our judgments concerning all kinds of beauty, and tastes, and sensations. Our approbation is imply'd in the immediate pleasure they convey to us.

I have objected to the system, which establishes eternal rational measures of right and wrong, that 'tis impossible to shew, in the actions of reasonable creatures, any relations, which are not found in external objects; and therefore, if morality always attended these relations, 'twere possible for inanimate matter to become virtuous or vicious. Now it may, in like manner, be objected to the present system, that if virtue and vice be determin'd by pleasure and pain, these qualities must, in every case, arise from the sensations; and consequently any object, whether animate or inanimate, rational or irrational, might become morally good or evil, provided it can excite a satisfaction or uneasiness. But tho' this objection seems to be the very same, it has by no means the same force, in the one case as in the other. For, *first*, 'tis evident, that under the term *pleasure*, we comprehend sensations, which are very different from each other, and which have only such a distant resemblance, as is requisite to make them be express'd by the same abstract term. A good composition of music and a bottle of good wine equally produce pleasure; and what is more, their goodness is determin'd merely by the pleasure. But shall we say upon that account, that the wine is harmonious, or the music of a good flavour? In like manner an inanimate object, and the character or sentiments of any person may, both of them, give satisfaction; but as the satisfaction is different, this keeps our sentiments concerning them from being confounded, and makes us ascribe virtue to the one, and not to the other. Nor is every sentiment of pleasure or pain, which arises from characters and actions, of that *peculiar* kind, which makes us praise or condemn. The good qualities of an enemy are hurtful to us; but may still command our esteem and respect. 'Tis only when a character is considered in general, without reference to our particular interest, that it causes such a feeling or sentiment, as denominates it morally good or evil. 'Tis true, those sentiments, from interest and morals, are apt to be confounded, and naturally run into one another. It seldom happens, that we do not think an enemy vicious, and can distinguish betwixt his opposition to our interest and real villainy or baseness. But this hinders not, but that the sentiments are, in themselves, distinct; and a man of temper and judgment may preserve himself from these illusions. In like manner, tho' 'tis certain a musical voice is nothing but one that naturally gives a *particular* kind of pleasure; yet 'tis difficult for a man to be sensible, that the voice of an enemy is agreeable, or to allow it to be musical. But a person of a fine ear, who has the command of himself, can separate these feelings, and give praise to what deserves it.

3. From Adam Smith, "Of Sympathy," *The Theory of Moral Sentiments* (London: Millar, 1759). 1–3

[In *The Theory of Moral Sentiments*, Smith (1723–90) argues that human egotism is tempered by sympathy. This sympathy (or identification), he contends, is the basis for all systems of morality.]

How selfish soever man may be supposed, there are evidently some principles in his nature, which interest him in the fortune of others, and render their happiness necessary to him, though he derives nothing from it except the pleasure of seeing it. Of this kind is pity or compassion, the emotion which we feel for the misery of others, when we either see it, or are made to conceive it in a very lively manner. That we often derive sorrow from the sorrow of others is too obvious to require any instances to prove it; for this sentiment, like all the other original passions of human nature, is by no means confined to the virtuous and humane, though they perhaps may feel it with the most exquisite sensibility. The greatest ruffian, the most hardened violator of the laws of society, is not altogether without it.

As we have no immediate experience of what other men feel, we can form no idea of the manner in which they are affected, but by conceiving what we ourselves should feel in the like situation. Though our brother is upon the rack, as long as we are at our ease, our senses will never inform us of what he suffers. They never did and never can carry us beyond our own persons, and it is by the imagination only that we can form any conception of what are his sensations. Neither can that faculty help us to this any other way, than by representing to us what would be our own if we were in his case. It is the impressions of our own senses only, not those of his, which our imaginations copy. By the imagination we place ourselves in his situation, we conceive ourselves enduring all the same torments, we enter as it were into his body and become in some measure him, and thence form some idea of his sensations, and even feel something which, though weaker in degree, is not altogether unlike them. His agonies, when they are thus brought home to ourselves, when we have thus adopted and made them our own, begin at last to affect us, and we then tremble and shudder at the thought of what he feels. For as to be in pain or distress of any kind excites the most excessive sorrow, so to conceive or to imagine that we are in it, excites some degree of the same emotion, in proportion to the vivacity or dulness of the conception.

4. From Henry Mackenzie, *The Lounger*, 2nd ed., 3 vols. (London and Edinburgh: Strahan, Cadell, and Creech, 1785). 1:181–88

[Mackenzie (1745–1831) wrote *The Man of Feeling* (1771), arguably the paradigmatic sentimental novel. Over the next fifteen years, however, he developed strong doubts about that genre. He expresses these doubts in this essay, which first appeared in the 18 June 1785 issue of his own periodical *The Lounger*.]

No species of composition is more generally read by one class of readers, or more undervalued by another, than that of the *Novel*. Its favourable reception from the young, and the indolent, to whom the exercise of imagination is delightful, and the labour of thought is irksome, needs not to be wondered at; but the contempt which it meets from the more respectable class of literary men, it may perhaps be intitled to plead that it does not deserve. Considered in the abstract, as containing an interesting relation of events, illustrative of the manners and characters of mankind, it surely merits a higher station in the world of letters than is generally assigned it. If it has not the dignity, it has at least most of the difficulties of the Epic or the Drama. The conduct of its fable, the support of its characters, the contrivance of its incidents, and its development of the passions, require a degree of invention, judgement, taste, and feeling, not much, if at all, inferior to those higher departments of writing, for the composition of which a very uncommon portion of genius is supposed to be requisite. Those difficulties are at the same time heightened by the circumstance, of this species of writing being of all others the most open to the judgement of the people; because it represents domestic scenes and situations in private life, in the execution of which any man may detect errors, and discover blemishes, while the author has neither the pomp of poetry, nor the decoration of the stage, to cover or to conceal them.

To this circumstance, however, may perhaps be imputed the degradation into which it has fallen. As few endowments were necessary to judge, so few have been supposed necessary to compose a Novel; and all whose necessities or vanity prompted them to write, betook themselves to a field, which, as they imagined, it required no extent of information or depth of learning to cultivate, but in which a heated imagination, or an excursive fancy, were alone sufficient to succeed; and men of genius and of knowledge, despising a province in which such competitors were to be met, retired from it in disgust, and left it in the hands of the unworthy.

The effects of this have been felt, not only in the debasement of the Novel in point of literary merit, but in another particular still more material, in its perversion from a moral or instructive purpose to one directly the reverse. Ignorance and dullness are seldom long inoffensive, but generally support their own native insignificance by an alliance with voluptuousness and vice.

Even of those few Novels which superior men have written, it cannot always be said, that they are equally calculated to improve as to delight. Nor is this only to be objected to some who have been professedly less scrupulous in that particular; but I am afraid may be also imputed to those whose works were meant to convey no bad impression, but, on the contrary, were intended to aid the cause of virtue, and to hold out patterns of the most exalted benevolence.

I am not, however, disposed to carry the idea of the dangerous tendency of all Novels so far as some rigid moralists have done. As promoting a certain refinement of mind, they operate like all other works of genius and feeling, and have indeed a more immediate tendency to produce it than most others, from their treating of those very subjects which the reader will find around him in the world, and their containing those very situations in which he himself may not improbably at some time or other be placed.

Those who object to them as inculcating precepts, and holding forth examples, of a refinement which virtue does not require, and which honesty is better without, do not perhaps sufficiently attend to the period of society which produces them. The code of morality must necessarily be enlarged in proportion to that state of manners to which cultivated æras give birth. As the idea of property made a crime of theft, as the invention of oaths made falsehood perjury; so the necessary refinement in manners of highly-polished nations creates a variety of duties and of offences, which men in ruder, and, it may be, (for I enter not into that question), happier periods of society, could never have imagined.

The principal danger of Novels, as forming a mistaken and pernicious system of morality, seems to me to arise from that contrast between one virtue or excellence and another, that war of duties which is to be found in many of them, particularly in that species called the *Sentimental*. These have been chiefly borrowed from our neighbours the French, whose style of manners, and the very powers of whose language, give them a great advantage in the delineation of that nicety, the subtilty [*sic*] of feeling, those entanglements of delicacy, which are so much interwoven with the characters and conduct of the chief personages in many of their most celebrated Novels. In this rivalship of virtues and of duties, those are always likely to be preferred which in truth and reason are subordinate, and those to be degraded which ought to be paramount. The last, being of that great cardinal sort which must be common, because they apply to the great leading relations and circumstances of life, have an appearance less dignified and heroic than the others, which, as they come forth only on extraordinary occasions, are more apt to attract the view and excite the admiration of beholders. The duty to parents is contrasted with the ties of friendship and of love; the virtues of justice, of prudence, of œconomy, are put in competition with the exertions of generosity, of benevolence, and of compassion: And even of these virtues of sentiments there are still more refined divisions, in which the over-strained delicacy of the persons represented, always leads them to act from the motive least obvious, and therefore generally the least reasonable.

In the enthusiasm of sentiment there is much the same danger as in the enthusiasm of religion, of substituting certain impulses and feelings of what may be called a visionary kind, in the place of real practical duties, which in morals, as in theology, we might not improperly denominate *good works*. In morals, as in religion, there are not wanting instances of refined sentimentalists, who are contented with talking of virtues which they never practise, who pay in words what they owe in actions; or perhaps, what is fully as dangerous, who open their minds to *impressions* which never have any effect upon their *conduct*, but are considered as something foreign to and distinct from it. This separation of conscience from feeling is a depravity of the most pernicious sort; it eludes the strongest obligation to rectitude, it blunts the strongest incitement to virtue; when the ties of the first bind the sentiment and not the will, and the rewards of the latter crown not the heart but the imagination.

That creation of refined and subtile feeling, reared by the authors of the works to which I allude, has an ill effect, not only on our ideas of virtue, but also on our estimate of happiness. That sickly sort of refinement creates imaginary evils and distresses, and imaginary blessings and enjoyments, which embitter the common disappointments, and depreciate the common attainments of life. This affects the temper doubly, both with respect to ourselves and others: with respect to ourselves, from what we think ought to be our lot; with regard to others, from what we think ought to be their sentiments. It inspires a certain childish pride of our own superior delicacy, and an unfortunate contempt of the plain worth, the ordinary but useful occupations and ideas of those around us.

The reproach which has been sometimes made to Novels, of exhibiting "such faultless monsters as the world ne'er saw,"[1] may be just on the score of entertainment to their readers, to whom the delineation of uniform virtue, except when it is called into striking situations, will no doubt be insipid. But in point of moral tendency, the opposite character is much more reprehensible; I mean, that character of mingled virtue and vice which is to be found in some of the best of our Novels. Instances will readily occur to every reader, where the hero of the performance has violated, in one page, the most sacred laws of society, to whom, by the mere turning of the leaf, we are to be reconciled, whom we are to be made to love and admire, for the beauty of some humane, or the brilliancy of some heroic action. It is dangerous thus to bring us into the society of Vice, though introduced or

---

1   John Sheffield, Duke of Buckingham (1648–1721), "An Essay upon Poetry" (1682). Buckingham cautions prospective writers against creating perfect characters because "There's no such thing in Nature, and you'l draw/A faultless Monster which the world ne're saw" (*An Essay upon Poetry* [London: Hindmarsh, 1682], 15).

accompanied by Virtue. In the application to ourselves, in which the moral tendency of all imaginary characters must be supposed to consist, this nourishes and supports a very common kind of self-deception, by which men are apt to balance their faults by the consideration of their good qualities; an account which, besides the fallacy of its principle, can scarcely fail to be erroneous, from our natural propensity to state our faults at their lowest, and our good qualities at their highest rate.

I have purposely pointed my observations, not to that common herd of Novels (the wretched offspring of circulating libraries) which are despised for their insignificance, or proscribed for their immorality; but to the errors, as they appear to me, of those admired ones which are frequently put into the hands of youth, for imitation as well as amusement. Of youth it is essential to preserve the imagination sound as well as pure, and not to allow them to forget, amidst the intricacies of Sentiment, or the dreams of Sensibility, the truths of Reason, or the laws of Principle.

5. From Mary Alcock, *Poems* (London: Dilly, 1799) 17–19, 89–93

[Alcock (c.1742–98) was born in England, but spent most of her life in Ireland. She grew up in a family of writers and clergy. Most of her writings were published posthumously in *Poems*, from which this exerpt is taken. The two poems demonstrate a growing ambivalence towards sensibility (and the Gothic novel) in the late eighteenth century. On the one hand, the poet addesses it as if it is a god; on the other, the poet mocks it when it is in excess. Alcock reinforces these ideas in prose essays later in the same volume. The word "receipt" in the second title has the same meaning as "recipe."]

"On Sensibility"

If e'er to Friendship's call you lent an ear,
Or sympathysing dropt the soothing tear,
Oh, Sensibility, receive my prayer!
Attend, and pardon that I seek to know,
If in a world so fraught with various woe,
Thy votaries find thee most their friend or foe.
Thy joys and grief alike let me survey,
Then fairly ask thee if thy joys repay
Those pangs, which soon or late the heart will rend,
Where thou art nourish'd as the gentlest friend,

When rude misfortune, with resistless sway,
Tears from that heart what most it loves away;
Whilst feelingly alive to every pain,
Thro' thee it tastes each sorrow o'er again;
Thus, crush'd beneath Affliction's heaviest blow,
It bears a double weight of human woe:
Ah cruel, thus to steal into the heart,
And cherish'd there to act a traitor's part.

    Come then, Indifference, thou easy guest,
Assume the empire o'er my tortur'd breast;
And by thy trifling, pleasing, giddy sway,
Chace every heart-corroding pang away;
Teach me another's griefs unmov'd to hear,
And guard my eye against the falling tear;
Drive recollection from her inmost seat;
Nor let my heart with agitation beat;
Be thou my champion thro' life's varying round,
And shield my bosom from the slightest wound.

    Yet pause awhile! and let me take a view,
Lest with the pains I lose life's pleasures too.
Say, doth not duty, love, and friendship give,
The greatest pleasures we can here receive;
And can a heart untouch'd by others woe,
The joys of friendship, love, and duty know?

    If such the purchase to be freed from pain,
Oh, Sensibility, to thee again
I turn—do thou my every thought control,
'Tis thine to animate or soothe the soul;
'Tis thine alone those feelings to bestow,
From which the source of every good doth flow;
Since these thy joys, thy griefs I'll patient bear,
And humbly take of each th' allotted share;
To Friendship's shrine the ready tribute bring,
And fly to Sorrow on Compassion's wing,
Enjoy the good, against the worst provide,
By taking Resignation for my guide,
In her safe conduct patiently submit
To every pain, which Providencee thinks fit.

"A Receipt for Writing a Novel"

Would you a fav'rite novel make,
Try hard your reader's heart to break,

For who is pleas'd, if not tormented?
(Novels for that were first invented).
'Gainst nature, reason, sense, combine
To carry on your bold design,
And those ingredients I shall mention,
Compounded with your own invention,
I'm sure will answer my intention.
Of love take first a due proportion—
It serves to keep the heart in motion:
Of jealousy a powerful zest,
Of all tormenting passions best;
Of horror mix a copious share,
And duels you must never spare;
Hysteric fits at least a score,
Or, if you find occasion, more;
But fainting fits you need not measure,
The fair ones have them at their pleasure;
Of sighs and groans take no account,
But throw them in to vast amount;
A frantic fever you may add,
Most authors make their lovers mad;
Rack well your hero's nerves and heart,
And let your heroine take her part;
Her fine blue eyes were made to weep,
Nor should she ever taste of sleep;
Ply her with terrors day or night,
And keep her always in a fright,
But in a carriage when you get her,
Be sure you fairly overset her;
If she will break her bones—why let her:
Again, if e'er she walks abroad,
Of course you bring some wicked lord,
Who with three ruffians snaps his prey,
And to a castle speeds away;
There close confin'd in haunted tower,
You leave your captive in his power,
Till dead with horror and dismay,
She scales the walls and flies away.
    Now you contrive the lovers meeting,
To set your reader's heart a beating.
But ere they've had a moment's leisure,
Be sure to interrupt their pleasure;
Provide yourself with fresh alarms

To tear 'em from each other's arms;
No matter by what fate they're parted,
So that you keep them broken-hearted.
    A cruel father some prepare
To drag her by her flaxen hair;
Some raise a storm, and some a ghost,
Take either, which may please you most.
But this you must with care observe,
That when you've wound up every nerve
With expectation, hope and fear,
Hero and heroine must disappear.
Some fill one book, some two without 'em,
And ne'er concern their heads about 'em,
This greatly rests the writer's brain,
For any story, that gives pain,
You now throw in—no matter what,
However foreign to the plot,
So it but serves to swell the book,
You foist it in with desperate hook—
A masquerade, a murder'd peer,
His throat just cut from ear to ear—
A rake turn'd hermit—a fond maid
Run mad, by some false loon betray'd—
These stores supply the female pen,
Which writes them o'er and o'er again,
And readers likewise may be found
To circulate them round and round.
    Now at your fable's close devise
Some grand event to give surprize—
Suppose your hero knows no mother—
Suppose he proves the heroine's brother—
This at one stroke dissolves each tie,
Far as from east to west they fly:
At length when every woe's expended,
And your last volume's nearly ended,
Clear the mistake, and introduce
Some tatt'ling nurse to cut the noose,
The spell is broke—again they meet
Expiring at each other's feet;
Their friends lie breathless on the floor—
You drop your pen; you can no more—
And ere your reader can recover,
They're married—and your history's over.

The virtue of adversity
is fortitude p 157

Select Bibliography and Works Cited

Adburgham, Alison. *Women in Print: Writing Women and Women's Magazines from the Restoration to the Accession of Victoria.* London: Allen and Unwin, 1972.

Aesop. *Æsop's Fables. With Instructive Morals and Reflections.* London: Osborn, 1740.

Anon. *Adventures of a Valet.* 2 vols. London: Robinson, 1752.

Anon. *The History of Charlotte Summers.* 2 vols. London: Printed for the Author, [1750].

Ballaster, Ros. *Seductive Forms: Women's Amatory Fiction from 1684 to 1740.* Oxford: Clarendon Press, 1992.

Bannet, Eve Tavor. *The Domestic Revolution: Enlightenment Feminisms and the Novel.* Baltimore and London: The Johns Hopkins UP, 2000.

Barker-Benfield, G.J. *The Culture of Sensibility: Sex and Society in Eighteenth-Century Britain.* Chicago and London: U of Chicago P, 1992.

Barnett, George, ed. *Eighteenth-Century British Novelists on the Novel.* New York: Appleton-Century-Crofts, 1968.

Bataille, Robert. *The Writing Life of Hugh Kelly: Politics, Journalism, and Theater in Late-Eighteenth-Century London.* Carbondale: Southern Illinois UP, 2000.

Batchelor, Jennie. *Dress, Distress and Desire: Clothing and the Female Body in Eighteenth-Century Literature.* Houndsmill, Basingstoke: Palgrave Macmillan, 2005.

Brewer, John. *The Pleasures of the Imagination: English Culture in the Eighteenth Century.* New York: Farrar Straus Giroux, 1997.

Carlile, Susan. "Charlotte Lennox's Birth Date and Place." *Notes and Queries* 249.4 (December 2004): 390–92.

Cohen, Michael. "First Sisters in the British Novel: Charlotte Lennox to Susan Ferrier." *The Significance of Sibling Relationships in Literature.* Ed. JoAnna Stephens Mink and Janet Doubler Ward. Bowling Green: Bowling Green U Popular P, 1993. 98–109.

Cooke, William. "Hugh Kelly." *European Magazine* 24 (November 1793): 337–40; 24 (December 1793): 419–22; 25 (January 1794): 42–48.

Fielding, Henry. *Joseph Andrews.* Ed. R.F. Brissenden. Harmondsworth: Penguin, 1977.

——. *The Covent-Garden Journal and A Plan of the Universal Register-Office*. Ed. Bertrand A. Goldgar. Middletown, CT: Wesleyan UP, 1988.

Folkenflik, Robert. "Tobias Smollett, Anthony Walker, and the First Illustrated Serial Novel in English." *Eighteenth-Century Fiction* 14.3–4 (April–July 2002): 507–32.

Gallagher, Catherine. *Nobody's Story. The Vanishing Acts of Women Writers in the Marketplace 1670–1820*. Berkeley and Los Angeles: U of California P, 1994.

Hammelmann, Hanns. *Book Illustrators in Eighteenth-Century England*. New Haven: Paul Mellon Centre for Studies in British Art (London)/Yale UP, 1975.

——. "Eighteenth-Century English Illustrators: Anthony Walker." *The Book Collector* 3.2 (Summer 1954): 87–102.

Hawkins, Sir John. *The Life of Samuel Johnson, LL.D*. London: Buckland et al., 1787.

Hodnett, Edward. *Five Centuries of English Book Illustration*. Aldershot: Scolar Press, 1988.

Isles, Duncan. "The Lennox Collection." *Harvard Library Bulletin* 18.4 (October 1970): 317–44; 19.1 (January 1971): 36–60; 19.2 (April 1971): 165–86; 19.4 (October 1971): 416–35.

Italia, Iona. *The Rise of Literary Journalism in the Eighteenth Century: Anxious Employment*. London and New York: Routledge, 2005.

Johnson, Samuel. *The Rambler*. 3 vols. Ed. W.J. Bate and Albrecht Strauss. New Haven and London: Yale UP, 1969.

Johnson, Samuel. *A Dictionary of the English Language*. 2 vols. London: Knapton et al., 1755.

Jones, Vivien, ed. *Women and Literature in Britain 1700–1800*. Cambridge: Cambridge UP, 2000.

Keymer, Thomas. "Sentimental Fiction: Ethics, Social Critique and Philanthropy." *The Cambridge History of English Literature, 1660–1789*. Ed. John Richetti. Cambridge: Cambridge UP, 2005. 572–601.

——. *Sterne, the Moderns, and the Novel*. Oxford: Oxford UP, 2002.

Langford, Paul. *A Polite and Commercial People: England 1727–1783*. Oxford: Oxford UP, 1989.

Lennox, Charlotte. *The Lady's Museum*. 2 vols. London: Newberry, 1760–61.

Manning, Susan. "Sensibility." *The Cambridge Companion to English Literature 1740–1830*. Ed. Thomas Keymer and Jon

Mee. Cambridge: Cambridge UP, 2004. 80–99.

Mayo, Robert D. *The English Novel in the Magazines 1740–1815*. Evanston: Northwestern UP, 1962.

Michie, Allen. *Richardson and Fielding: The Dynamics of a Critical Rivalry*. Lewisburg: Bucknell UP / London: Associated University Presses, 1999.

Mullan, John. "Sentimental Novels." *The Cambridge Companion to the Eighteenth-Century Novel*. Ed. John Richetti. Cambridge: Cambridge UP, 1996. 236–54.

Olson, Kristin. *Daily Life in Eighteenth-Century England*. Westport, CT: Greenwood Press, 1999.

Pope, Alexander. *The Poems of Alexander Pope*. Ed. John Butt. New Haven: Yale UP, 1963.

Porter, Roy. *English Society in the Eighteenth Century*. 2nd ed. Harmondsworth: Penguin, 1990.

——. *London: A Social History*. Cambridge, MA: Harvard UP, 1994.

Raven, James. *British Fiction, 1750–1770: A Chronological Checklist of Prose Fiction Printed in Britain and Ireland*. Newark: University of Delaware P/London and Toronto: Associated University Presses, 1987.

Raven, James. "The Anonymous Novel in Britain and Ireland, 1750–1830." *The Faces of Anonymity: Anonymous and Pseudonymous Publication from the Sixteenth to the Twentieth Century*. Ed. Robert Griffin. New York: Palgrave Macmillan, 2003. 141–66.

Richardson, Samuel. *Pamela*. Ed. Thomas Keymer and Alice Wakely. Oxford: Oxford UP, 2001.

Richetti, John. *The English Novel in History, 1700–1780*. London and New York: Routledge, 1999.

Rochefoucauld, François de la. *Moral Maxims. A New Translation from the French*. Dublin: Exshaw, 1751.

Schellenberg, Betty. *The Professionalization of Women Writers in Eighteenth-Century Britain*. Cambridge: Cambridge UP, 2005.

Schofield, Mary Anne. *Masking and Unmasking the Female Mind: Disguising Romances in Feminine Fiction, 1713–1799*. Newark: U of Delaware P, 1990.

Schürer, Norbert. *Lennox and Smollett in the Literary Marketplace: Authorship and Readership after Fielding and Richardson*. Ph.D. Diss., Duke University, 2001.

Séjourné, Philippe. *The Mystery of Charlotte Lennox: First Novelist of Colonial America (1727?–1804)*. Aix-en-Provence: Publications des Annales de la Faculté des Lettres, 1967.

Seneca, Lucius Annæus. *Seneca's Morals*. 8th ed. Tr. Roger L'Estrange. London: Bowyer, 1702.

Small, Miriam Rossiter. *Charlotte Ramsay Lennox: An Eighteenth Century Lady of Letters*. New Haven: Yale UP, 1935.

Smollett, Tobias. *The Life and Adventures of Sir Launcelot Greaves*. Ed. Robert Folkenflik and Barbara Laning Fitzpatrick. Athens and London: U of Georgia P, 2002.

Spacks, Patricia Meyer. "Sisters." *Fetter'd or Free? British Women Novelists, 1670–1815*. Ed. Mary Anne Schofield and Cecilia Machewski. Athens, Ohio: Ohio UP, 1986. 136–51.

Spender, Dale. *Mothers of the Novel*. London and New York: Pandora, 1986.

Starr, G.A. "Sentimental Novels of the Later Eighteenth Century." *The Columia History of the British Novel*. Ed. John Richetti. New York: Columbia UP, 1994. 181–98.

Todd, Janet. *Sensibility: An Introduction*. London and New York: Methuen, 1986.

——. *The Sign of Angellica: Women, Writing, and Fiction, 1660–1800*. New York: Columbia UP, 1989.

Vickery, Amanda. *The Gentleman's Daughter: Women's Lives in Georgian England*. New Haven and London: Yale UP, 1998.

Villemert, Pierre Joseph Boudier de. *The Ladies Friend, From the French of Monsieur de Gravines*. London: Nicoll, 1766.

Warner, William. *Licensing Entertainment: The Elevation of Novel Reading in Britain, 1684–1750*. Berkeley: U of California P, 1998.

Williams, Ioan, ed. *Novel and Romance, 1700–1800: A Documentary Record*. New York: Barnes & Noble, 1970.

Young, Edward. *The Complete Works* (1854). 2 vols. Hildesheim: Olms, 1968.